Naughty and Nice

Compiled by Megan Landon, Sigh, and Olivia Lawless
Cover by Tallis Salar

Table of Contents

I was alone for the holidays after yet another miserable breakup when I discovered a strange six-foot-tall Xmas gift addressed to me. It couldn't be what I thought it was, could it?

A young woman attends her boyfriend's office Christmas party out of a sense of obligation but makes new friends who show her a more fulfilling and rewarding possible future ... all helped by some special spices.

Seduced by the sights and scents of the holiday, Carlotta conjures up the man of her dreams. Will her true Christmas wish become a reality?

A Bite of Magic
by Scarlet Lee Winters

Twitter: @lux_indulgences
Medium: @missscarletwinters

Magic could distort magic. Magic affected magic. Seaver paced, his arms folded defensively in front of his chest. He needed something with magic to gain access to victims. He wanted them in greater numbers. He was thirsty, a vampire with few choices, with humans staying indoors more to avoid the graupel, snow and winds that tore at their comforts leaving them exposed.

He had never studied magic. He knew only the few spells that were innately known to vampires. Healing, invisibility and seeing in near darkness. In the endless stark white months upon him, he would have time to learn a few spells and that could prove useful for the following winters. Seaver, however, needed to slake his bloodlust now. He needed to happen upon a lost hiker or meet somebody checking a bump in the night despite the frigid winds.

Seaver stopped at the window. Winter made its presence known once more with a flurry of snow pouring onto the homes in the valley below. He longed for blood. He longed for the dark, erotic sound of his fangs puncturing flesh, then the flood of warm sustenance coating his tongue. Seaver was pulled from his sexual reverie by lights. Lights of different colors blinked in a window visible through the snow. It was winter and the lights that went up then marked the times when magic behaved differently. Saint Nicholas, the immortalized fae creature was what the lights were for and why winter passed at a different rate than other seasons.

Inspiration hit Seaver. Time magic on Christmas day and the bag of infinite space that Saint Nicholas carried were what differentiated him from the other creatures that could use magic. His purpose of giving gifts and visiting all believers in magic in a single night would have proven impossible without the time magic in effect then, but most importantly, Saint Nicholas always had an invitation.

❄ ❄ ❄

Nicholas sat in his easy chair reading through the letters he had received that day. Using his fae magic, he would slow or stop time so he could get through every letter from anybody in the world. Nicholas tore open each new letter and the occasional card offering love and well wishes with gusto and the same level of enthusiasm as the first. The good feelings he inspired and the happiness he could bestow sustained him.

Sipping warm tea and snacking on gingerbread cookies, Nicholas went from the children who wrote about toys and outfits they had their hearts set on to the adults who were in the Christmas spirit enough to send Santa a letter. The adults often asked for things on behalf of others, especially the children in their lives. Many even asked for a piece of their childhood, warm nostalgia felt through a toy that brought joy, even if the memory was a tinted rosy hue.

Nicholas was happy to oblige those on his nice list through magic, those who were good to others, even if their wishes seemed impossible to grant. But that was the point of magic, no? To bring about the impossible. His very purpose was to grant happiness in one of the darkest months of the year when people were isolated and cold. Why would he deny even a strange request an adult made?

Nicholas checked that the sender's name was on his nice list. Since she did, he made a mental note for her since some magic might be required to manifest this Christmas wish. He had a few days of letters left before he had to send off the "naughty" list to Krampus. That meant he had time to put together the incantation in his mind, letting his subconscious work through any strange requirements that might be present, even for a nigh omnipotent magus such as Santa Claus.

❄ ❄ ❄

Seaver waited eagerly for the month to crawl to the twenty-fourth of December. Even if his plan failed, having something to look forward to was a pleasant change of pace. Snow and graupel fell, melted, then fell again. Cold air blew. The sky remained the dreary snowy grey hue despite the joyous celebrations held during the month. He read every book he could find to pass the time, but his unsettling hunger reminded him often that he needed it to become Christmas as soon as possible.

When night fell on the fateful day when the vampire would test his ploy for blood, he trekked down the mountainside through the cold, hard snow. Invisible against the roaring snows, Seaver climbed the nearest brick home and waited for the fae to appear. To his surprise, the red sleigh pulled by flying reindeer—another fae magic with Nicholas—selected this tiny cottage first. The portly man with a dark beard and attractive round face stepped out of the seat and shouldered his magical bag. The reindeer remained still, unbothered by the wind while the saint vanished down the chimney in a burst of magical energy. It was near an eternity of time standing still before Nicholas returned to the roof.

Seaver muttered the spell that would render him invisible from the fae's gaze. His mouth watered as he anticipated feeding throughout the night. Seaver climbed into the back compartment where the magical bag was stowed. After Nicholas called out to each of his familiars to make them fly, Seaver opened the bag and tumbled inside. He was in a sea of presents, all of them nicely wrapped with festive bows, save for the stocking stuffers on top that sat in tidy rows.

It truly was like a second world in the bag of infinite space. It was as if the physics of the universe ceased to exist. The presents were not tossed or flung about while the sleigh was in the air, everything remained neat which gave the vampire a problem with his plan. Seaver did not anticipate the movements of the real world not affecting the contents of the bag, so he was surprised when a mittened hand reached inside. Seaver backed up and dodged Nicholas' grasp. If he were discovered, he'd need to fight the powerful saint fae and Seaver was too weak to fare well.

With Nicholas' magic, the presents floated out of the bag one at a time. The fae never looked inside which was a relief to the stowaway. After the planned presents and stocking stuffers for the residents were all in their intended spots to be found in the morning, Nicholas sat and rested his weary feet in an easy chair. The family left hot cocoa and cookies for the beloved fae and he was eager to partake.

Seaver peeked over the bag. The house was dark, save for the fireplace where the hearth crackled and warmed the room. The house smelled of cinnamon, mint and pine from the decorated tree. He heard quiet snoring, so as quietly and quickly as he could move, the vampire crawled out of the bag. Careful to leave the portly fae asleep with a partly eaten sugar cookie in hand, Seaver made his way to the bedrooms. He was relieved his plan to get inside people's homes worked to get inside people's homes. He had his doubts that piggybacking an invitation might go awry or get him expelled from the present bag as soon as Nicholas' feet crossed the threshold. Seaver's mouth watered when he got a whiff of the sleeping woman in the first bed.

The petite blond woman nestled a pillow on her side beneath a heavy quilt. Seaver brushed her hair away from her throat, then while sugarplums danced in her head, his fangs stabbed her neck and the wound quickly bled. Seaver moaned gratefully as the warm red liquid graced his tastebuds. Seaver sucked and slurped until he felt satiated; he would normally have held back, but he was starved. He savored the taste and the moment as it was his first feeding in weeks since people remained indoors to shield themselves from the elements.

Seaver did not want to press his luck. He was a hungry vampire, but he was smart. Being smart now meant being cautious. He could not risk being left behind if he was to get a season's fill of feedings in a single magical night. He had no idea how long Nicholas would be nodding off in the chair. Utilizing an innate spell, Seaver turned into a bat and returned to the living room. The fae was still napping much to his surprise, but he already decided that one neck was enough per home. He intended to treat himself for as long as he could feed, then fly home before sunlight breached the morning sky. Seaver returned to the bag and waited impatiently inside. He occasionally turned invisible and poked his head out to check in on the fae. A long while passed before Nicholas once more shouldered the bag. He spoke an incantation that twisted the tongue, then in a puff of fae magic they were on the roof once more.

Curious and needing to keep an eye out, Seaver remained invisible with his face exposed to the winter storm pouring down on the valley. Nicholas would call to the reindeer, they'd stop and then he would lift the bag to bring the presents out. Seaver happened to glance upward at the snowy sky, then his eyes went wide. The snow stopped above them as though it were a movie paused. Yet the reindeer breathed and turned their heads as if unaffected by the paused time. The next thing he realized, Nicholas had brought them both down the chimney, safely past the vigorous fire, and set the bag beside the Christmas tree.

Seaver scurried out of the bag, then toward the bedrooms in the home. The pine scent was pungent here, throughout the house. He picked a sleeping victim then drank from their throat before turning invisible and creeping back to Nicholas' location in the home. Seaver stood with his arms folded and remaining unseen to the toiling fae. The curious vampire's eyes toured the room. Decorative holly, mistletoe and pinecones were throughout the home. The ephemeral scent of sugar cookies and warm chocolate could be caught in a breath. His gaze stopped on the Christmas tree, then realization struck. The lights on the decorated pine tree were dim, but the star on top gave off silver light. He traced the cords with his eyes to the wall where they were plugged in and receiving power. Seaver tilted his head, now fascinated by the effects of this fae on the world around him.

Time ceased to pass outside his magical influence. The snow had stopped, the blinking lights were affected as well. A closer look at the fire revealed it to be unmoving, not devouring the wood that was left for it to burn overnight. Seaver watched Nicholas help himself to more cookies and cocoa. The presents were already placed so the task there was already done, save for the short trip up the chimney then back to the sleigh. Seaver returned to the bag and mulled over what he learned about Nicholas the fae.

House after house, their routine remained unchanged. Time would stop, Nicholas would set about giving presents to the residents, then helping himself to the sugary treats that were left as offerings for him. Seaver's nose would be assaulted by the remaining smells of freshly baked cookies, vanilla, chocolate, cinnamon, and ginger. Those aromas clung to the walls and curtains whereas the bracing, icy scent of the pine tree harvested to be the tree and the mixing of smells of any residents. When he could sneak away, Seaver would make a beeline to the bedroom, feed, then return to the bag so he could be carried along to his next meal. This pattern went on for what on a normal night may have taken six or seven hours, but time and even magic itself seemed to behave differently around Nicholas so it felt like the span of a mere five minutes passing.

Seaver considered parting ways with Nicholas after the next house. He procrastinated his departure several times. He decided on his last house when he was fuller than he had ever felt as a vampire. He wanted to make certain that he was as satiated as he could be before his continued forced pseudo hibernation for the season. Once more in the bag he poked his head out, then waited until he could scurry to the bedrooms to feed.

Seaver found a delicious-smelling redhead snuggled beneath several comforters. Beside her was a half-drank glass of water on the end table and tinsel wrapped around the edges of the table. The Christmas lights on the window and around the crown molding gave the room a soft, faint white glow. While licking his lips, he pulled down the blankets to reveal her pale, freckled throat. He pushed her hair back, draping it over her pillow. His eyes took in the poetic sight, a bare, fair throat pleading, made to bite. Made for him and his desperate dagger-like fangs. He savored the view a breath longer. The feelings were intense. Her warm flesh against him. Seaver leaned down and bit her, then drank mouthfuls of her sweet blood. He thought he heard her moan, but Santa's magic would have kept her asleep, frozen in time like a scene in a snow globe. He was hearing things. Perhaps his own voice seemed dissonant from his exhaustion?

Seaver retreated from the woman's neck, then froze. He was pulled down onto the redhead.

"More," Kinsey said firmly.

Seaver's ashen skin turned red. He pulled back from the seeping wound. He had to be hearing things. His imagination was getting away from him. Perhaps a child asked for a talking doll, and he heard its voice? With blood dripping down his lower lip, he scanned the shadows. "W-what?"

"Bite me again. Harder this time," Kinsey whispered. She slid her hands up his lithe back to his shoulders. "Harder. Until I beg you to stop." She held a coy smile while ogling the blond man with red eyes. He looked the way she hoped a handsome vampire visitor would. She bit the inside of her bottom lip, hoping she hadn't spooked the stranger. The biting was arousing, and he was exactly her type.

Seaver gulped down the mouthful of the woman's blood. He processed the situation and what he had just heard. Terrified that he had somehow broken the spell of Christmas magic that Santa had used to circle the world in a night and keep the folks at home asleep so they would be surprised by the deposit of surprises in the morning, he did not want to look closely at the redhead beneath him. Then another explanation occurred to him. His panic was doused. Sleep talking. The woman was dreaming and talking. His imagination filled in the nonsense with conversational words.

"What are you waiting for?" Kinsey asked. When the vampire did not immediately reply to her, she seized his face with her hands. She held his gaze in line with hers. "Hey, vampire."

Seaver was a stunned deer in the headlights. He stuttered incoherently. His nerves were in overdrive. He was mentally preparing himself to become a bat and flee from his victim's home.

"Don't you want to bite me again?" Kinsey asked. She flashed a pouty look briefly. She released the vampire's face, then she turned her head so that the vampire might be tempted by her unpunctured flesh on the opposite side of her throat.

Finally, Seaver could muster words, "You want me to bite you?"

"Yes. I want to be bitten and fucked," Kinsey answered.

Seaver's red face took on a deeper hue. "I ... I ... alright ..." he whispered. His mind was once more empty. All he could think to do was comply and bite the delicious redhead for as long as she would allow it. He nibbled gently at her throat. He saw no reason to drink more of her blood; his sanguine and sexual appetites were repeatedly answered throughout the night with her. Seaver listened to the soft moans. His teeth met her skin several times. The gentle, playful nibbles elicited excited responses from the woman each time. She ran her hands up and down his back, she gently scratched. On a whim, Seaver licked up the woman's throat to her ear. He gave her a gentle bite and she jumped.

Kinsey pulled Seaver closer. "Oooh! More!" she begged. Her fingers snatched at his hair and tugged furiously.

Seaver rolled off the young woman. He pressed his back to the headboard and pulled Kinsey onto his lap. Kinsey tossed her hair to the side and offered her neck to the vampire once more. She felt his cock, hard against her pussy. The vampire leaned forward and nipped at her flesh again. Kinsey moaned and pressed their bodies together. Her voice caught in her throat as the vampire's biting became rougher. She was screaming in pleasure, writhing, and rocking as the combination of pain and pleasure teased her every nerve.

The vampire seemed to hear her thoughts. He stopped biting her then let her toss her nightgown aside. Kinsey wiggled out of her panties. Simultaneously, the vampire threw his clothing aside. Kinsey straddled him, sliding her wet pussy over the head of his cock.

Seaver pulled her into a kiss. It felt odd. He didn't know the woman's name and they were immersed in foreplay. The fervor that sparked between them couldn't be helped. He was a vampire and being with him always meant slight pain during foreplay by design or accidental fang grazing and she enjoyed the pain of his teeth against her bare flesh. Their lips met and parted. Seaver's fingers trailed up Kinsey's spine, a gentle tickling to both be playful and savor the warmth of a person. Their drawn-out kiss ended, and they took a respite from the roiling attraction. The vampire and human panted to catch and steady their breaths.

"I'm called Seaver," he whispered.

After several more gasps of air she replied, "Kinsey."

"Well, Kinsey," Seaver smirked, "you are making my Christmas very worthwhile." The vampire brushed her bangs away from her face, tucking the errant tresses behind her ear. He touched his forehead to hers. His breaths were still fast and uneven from exertion.

Kinsey tittered. "You are the perfect present for me, Seaver." She looked into the vampire's scarlet eyes. "Have you had enough of a break?"

"Hmm?"

"I am desperate for your fangs and cock," Kinsey explained.

Seaver's cheeks took on a light red hue. "I am definitely up for that."

Kinsey rested her hands on Seaver's shoulders. Still straddling him, she eased down onto his cock. She moaned softly at first, while she moved slowly. Seaver fisted a handful of her red hair and had his free hand cradling Kinsey's cheek. He tugged her hair playfully and nibbled at her neck. Used to his size, her rate quickened, then louder and more pronounced cries of delight followed. Kinsey continued to bounce, moving Seaver's shaft in and out of her. Her nails grazed his shoulders as they enjoyed their sensual encounter. Getting to know the other's body was immensely satisfying.

Seaver groaned sporadically. He relinquished control of their pace to Kinsey. She was enthusiastic and enjoyed the experience of being intimate with a vampire. He teased her with his fangs, never puncturing her skin, but instead letting the points scrape gently across her skin. His cock was soaked from her fluids. He had quieted his blood appetite by drinking on many unsuspecting people earlier in the night, so there was no need for him to bite her and drink again. He was entirely in the surprising, passionate moment, attentive to each minute detail. Her scent—cinnamon and vanilla—her taste, the sweetness of her skin, her warmth, the sounds of her breaths—often distorted with moans—how silky her hair felt, all of that was on his mind. His orgasm was long off, but he enjoyed being wanted. Quiet, appreciative moans filled his breaths.

Seaver tugged her hair, nibbled gently and dragged his tongue along her throat between her bouts of energetically riding him. He enjoyed her attention, and he craved the ending of their encounter in which he would pierce her delicate flesh again then lie with her as she writhed in pain and pleasure.

Kinsey met the vampire's gaze. She was getting close to cumming. She quickened her pace and dug her nails into his shoulders. She broke their intense stare and squeezed her eyes shut. "Yes, yes, yes!" her words were almost a blurred scream. Her breath caught in her throat. She tightened her jaw. Kinsey felt the inner contractions. Craving the closeness, she pressed her body against his. She moved her hands to his hair and yanked two handfuls to channel the ecstasy jolting through her. Kinsey sobbed the vampire's name, then every muscle in her body was taut. Her pussy pulsed and she was exhausted from undulating.

Seaver held the woman against him. Her wetness seeped down his shaft. Her breathing was ragged. Her skin had accumulated a layer of sweat. Sensing she needed to rest to recover, he pushed her hair aside again. He gave her a gentle bite that did not puncture her skin. Kinsey moaned in response. Kinsey not moving much, he guessed she was tired, but still aroused. Seaver nudged her backward, rolling them so she was on her back, and he was on top of her. He took her hand, then kissed her knuckles. "Still aroused?" His eyes met hers.

Kinsey nodded and smiled. "Very," she answered between breaths.

"Good," was his reply. He kissed her lips, then he peppered soft brushes of his lips down her chest. Kinsey squirmed beneath him, moaning affirmations, and appreciation for the act. His lips against her sensitive skin left a moist trail, then his hot breaths following made Kinsey shiver. Waves of irresistible, aching need rolled through her. Each muscle and vein felt the tugging ripple of sexual yen. Kinsey was already wet; she was into the vampire man's fangs. To her pleasant surprise the gentleness mixed with controlled pain kept her going. She was antsy waiting for his lips to reach her pussy. He had stopped at her abdomen.

Seaver laid several kisses near her navel. He shifted his weight, bolstering himself with flat palms on either side of her. The vampire flashed a crooked grin, then he dragged his tongue up to Kinsey's chest. She screamed and tore into the bedding, her nails catching seams. Seaver took Kinsey's nipple into his mouth. His tongue caressed and he suckled, eliciting delighted screams from her.

Kinsey moved her hands to Seaver's hair. She arched her back and simultaneously pulled Seaver closer. He moaned. "Suck harder," she instructed. After Seaver complied she screamed happily. "Yes, like that!" Her cheeks were flushed. The raw sexuality boiling in her blood intensified. She wanted more of him. She needed to feel his tongue, his cock, and his body cool against her fevered flesh. "Nibble. A little," she whispered. Seaver gently bit her nipple. "Oooo," was Kinsey's reaction.

"More?" Seaver whispered.

"Yes," Kinsey confirmed.

Seaver switched to pleasuring her other breast. His teeth grazed playfully. He licked and sucked. Her nipple stiffened in his mouth. He moaned, enjoying the warmth of her flesh and the intimacy of the moment. Wanting to take his time still but pleasure the woman one hand trailed down her abdomen. Kinsey whimpered and squirmed. She pulled Seaver's hair and scratched his shoulders. She did anything she could think of to show her appreciation for the building desire and ecstasy he awakened and stoked. His fingers brushed past her pubic hair. He spread her moist pussy lips apart, then she threw her head back. Seaver moved up from kissing and biting her breast to her neck. His lips, tongue and teeth moved up her throat. His fingers glided through her accumulated fluids, teasing with no particular rhythm at first. "You like that?" he breathed the question in her ear.

"I do," Kinsey replied. Her fingers explored the vampire's body while her clitoris was rubbed tenderly. "I'd love for you to keep going."

"I intend to," Seaver said.

Kinsey pulled him into a kiss. His fingers kept moving, massaging her sensitive skin. She slipped tongue into the kiss, and she gently clawed his shoulder blades. When they paused to breathe, she blushed. "I am incredibly turned on," she said with urgency.

Seaver tittered. He flashed a crooked grin. "As am I. But I have all night." His lips gently brushed against hers, barely touching. "And you are delicious," he slid his index and middle fingers inside her.

Kinsey moaned, relieved. Her lust would be addressed, answered. "I want you to fuck me and bite me," she squirmed and shivered.

"And I will." Seaver kissed her again. Kinsey melted. She held onto the vampire's silky blond hair. His gentle fingering brought her close to cumming again. She soon could no longer concentrate. She was close to an orgasm and that was all that mattered to her body. She involuntarily squirmed and recoiled from physical delight. She broke their kiss to breathe and moan. Her eyes rolled back. Her pussy spasmed. Seaver's fingers stopped moving. He let Kinsey enjoy the moment, then he bit Kinsey's bottom lip.

With the taste of her blood on his tongue, he reached for his shaft. "You are perfectly delicious."

Kinsey whimpered. "I like when you bite me."

"And I'll do it more." Touching himself, massaging, rolling his fingers slowly he welcomed another kiss. Seaver leaned into the kiss, moaning. He could still taste her blood. She was invigorating and exciting. Eager to continue their tryst and to feel her flesh break against his fangs, he needed a way to experience both. He stopped masturbating. Seaver ended their kiss. He scooped up the tiny redhead and carried her bridal style to a reading chair in the corner of her bedroom.

Kinsey's feet touched the floor. She turned and looked at Seaver. He settled into the chair, then smirked, patting his lap. She coyly twisted her hair around her fingers. "How do you want me?" Anxious for his reply, she rocked from the balls of her feet to her heels.

"Facing away from me." Seaver looked her up and down with yen, licking his lips. "Trust me, it will slake both of our appetites … what I have planned." He moved his arms, so they rested on the chair. "Unless you don't want me to bite you and fuck you."

With trepidation, Kinsey sat on the edge of the chair between Seaver's legs. He wrapped his arms around her waist, then pulled her against him. With several quick maneuvers, Kinsey's pussy lined up perfectly with his cock. Seaver toyed with her spice-colored hair, fisting a handful. Kinsey held her breath anticipating the pain of being bitten. Seaver's lips teased her throat with tender kisses. He let his hot breath send shivers of excited anticipation through her body. "I-I've never done this position before," Kinsey said. She shivered and blushed.

Seaver kissed her earlobe. "It will prove most pleasant," he whispered in her ear. His hands inched across Kinsey's chest. He planted gentle kisses on her neck and shoulder sporadically. His fingers found her stiff nipples. Eager to savor her body, he forced himself to take his time. His focus was on her soft, perky breasts and touching her silken flesh. Kinsey tilted her head back. As Seaver's hands caressed her, she would let out moans and whimpers.

Much of her body was still unmarred by his fangs. That thought tempted him into hastening his way through this next position so he could bite her everywhere he could reach. Seaver bit his lower lip and braced himself. He braced himself against the temptation of speeding through their encounter. He slid his hands down Kinsey's body to her hips. Gently grasping, he eased inside her. They shared an appreciative moan.

"Bounce," Seaver said.

Kinsey grasped the arms of the chair. She undulated her body, moaning as she adjusted to the new position. His cock felt bigger in the new position. She enjoyed the attention the vampire was giving to her entire body. "Feels good," she whispered.

"It'll get better," he promised. His hands savored her breasts and her belly. Gentle tickles and occasional kisses graced her. Seaver groaned quietly, still fighting off his urge to bite Kinsey everywhere. He had to channel time management. There was plenty of time before the sun came up and he needed to be shielded. Why should he leave their mutual present—their paths crossing at all—early? He wanted to last. He needed it as much as he needed her warm blood coating his tongue. Seaver suppressed a primal moan. It sounded like a lusty growl, which it was in part.

Kinsey reached back and caressed Seaver's cheek. "Getting close," she said between pleasure grunts. "You?"

Seaver shook his head. "I'm good. Savoring you." He bit his lip harder. When he tasted his own blood. he stopped. "Cum as often as you can. I'll cum soon enough."

Kinsey nodded. "Of course." She leaned into the physical rapture. The vampire's cold, gentle touch and his occasional, teasing nibbles had her needing to cum. She was close, just the tiniest bit of stimulation would push her over the edge, so she chased it. She felt it nearing. Her body was flushed. She was sweating. Then Seaver bit her neck. Kinsey's eyes went wide, and a delighted scream followed. Her pussy spasmed. Then her entire body shook while Seaver sipped her blood from the fresh wound.

Seaver pulled Kinsey against him. She was limp, exhausted from exertion. She didn't squirm against his feeding. He stopped himself after a few delicious seconds to fixate on wanting to grant her wish. He was going to cum inside her again. With her blood gracing his tastebuds, he pulled back from the wound, grabbed her hips, and pulled her downward. Seaver thrust into Kinsey each time he brought her down, plunging himself deep inside her. Kinsey moaned. When she could move again, no longer limp from overwhelming delight, she began bouncing once more. Seaver kept his hands on her hips. He continued his precise, perfect thrusts grunting and moaning in anticipated delight. Kinsey's squeaks, cute and a surprised reaction to the forceful pleasure of their positioning stoked his libido further. "I'm there," Seaver growled through bloody, gritted teeth. He seized Kinsey's body, wrapping his arms tightly around her. He pulled her down twice more, then moaned as his seed torrented into her tight pussy.

"You cumming inside me is indescribably hot," Kinsey remarked. She wiggled her ass and shot a coy smile to the vampire.

He whimpered, helpless to react to the physical pleasure of her body and his oversensitive cock. "Agreed," was the only response he could muster. "But I am still raring to go. I could fuck you and bite you 'til dawn."

Kinsey beamed. "That sounds amazing. Even if I'm exhausted and unable to stand, that is absolutely what I want."

Seaver bit her shoulder. He was careful not to break skin with his fangs. She whimpered and shuddered, enjoying the combination of pain and pleasure. She begged for more in quiet, breath-heavy whispers. The vampire obliged, playfully nibbling her shoulder and neck while his engorged cock twitched for attention. He wanted to fuck her and cum again. Humans were rarely open to being preyed upon by vampires, let alone sexually excited by the act. Kinsey was a treasure for him, a Christmas wish he didn't know he had until having her.

Seaver lifted Kinsey, placing her on the bed. He grabbed her hips and positioned himself behind her. Kinsey got onto all fours and looked back at him lustfully. "Take me," she pleaded.

Seaver tightened his grip on her hips. With one hand he guided his cock to her pussy. He felt his fluids, then bit his lip. Kinsey was still tight and warm. Her pussy welcomed him. He eased deeper in at first with slow methodical thrusts. Her breathy moans and the sounds of their fluids excited him more. He listened and leaned forward more. He wanted to penetrate her deeper than was physically possible. He ground his teeth, to brace himself and tame his libido as much as possible. Her blood was still on his tongue and her taste was as intoxicating now as it was when he first bit her. She squirmed and begged, grabbing at the bedding and throwing come hither looks to Seaver. The longer he went, the wetter Kinsey got. His dick was coated in a mix of their fluids. He was nowhere near close to cumming again, yet that was all he wanted. Kinsey screamed and shivered in delight. She came, her pussy pulsing each time.

"Bite me," Kinsey requested.

Seaver stopped thrusting. He rolled Kinsey over and settled on top of her. Seaver kissed her throat, then teased her with gentle licking. Kinsey ran her fingers through his hair and along his muscular arms and shoulders. She kissed his shoulder and whispered another plea to be bitten. "I don't want to do too much," he whispered back. "I've bitten you a lot tonight."

"Not that much," she replied.

Seaver smirked. "I've spaced it out, but it's been frequent tonight. We have to be careful." He kissed her throat again. Hearing her disappointment, he bared his fangs. He bit down, pressing their bodies together. Kinsey was moaning, clawing at his back. She was elated, screaming pleasurable encouragements for Seaver. Seaver drank in her sweet, earthy taste once more. Her blood flooded his mouth and coated his throat.

Kinsey curled her fingers and toes. She wished she could kiss Seaver. She had to settle for moaning her appreciation and caressing his body. He stopped drinking her blood soon after biting her. Her lips were parted. "It feels so good," she whispered.

"I wish I could do it more," Seaver said. He rolled Kinsey over. "But let's avoid the temptation to bleed you dry." He thrust into her again. He moaned and quickened his movements.

Kinsey remained face down in the pillow. Her mind was still flooded with ecstasy. She grabbed at the bedding when Seaver thrust entirely into her. She smiled, enjoying the sensation of his cock sliding in and out of her paired with their fluids seeping from her pussy. She was exhausted, but still enjoying the sensations of his lust for her body. He still felt cool to touch and his growly grunts made her libido tingle. She turned her head to voice her pleasure with breathy whimpers and sentiments of lascivious yen. Her fingers and toes curled and uncurled.

Seaver changed his position, so he was over Kinsey. His abdomen was against her back. He continued thrusting, eager to be close to the woman that was invigorated by his sanguine nature. He stopped abruptly, "I'm not too heavy, am I?" he breathed the question in her ear.

Kinsey shivered and smiled. "It feels nice. I'll scratch you if you feel too heavy."

"Good." He pecked her cheek, then he picked up again.

He moved his hips slowly, with a deliberate tempo that served his physical craving for cumming. With parted lips, closed eyes and barely any thoughts, he fucked her. His cock plunged deep into her, and he took his time, sensing her exhaustion. She had cum several times already and she was too tired to participate, perhaps too weak from him repeatedly drinking from her veins. His cock was throbbing, begging for at least one more orgasm. Wanting to hasten his release along, Seaver caressed her lips with his index and middle finger. Kinsey parted her lips, then she sucked on and licked his fingers while he pounded into her. The excitement was twofold for him. He was on the brink of physical release within minutes. Kinsey sucked and licked so well he lamented their lack of foreplay. He could only imagine what it'd be like for her to service his cock that way to warm him up instead of just him biting her.

"Another time," he murmured.

Kinsey stopped suckling his fingers. "What?" she whispered.

"Thinking aloud," Seaver answered. His eyes rolled back. "You have me ready to burst."

"Good." Kinsey smiled. "Cum inside me again," she pleaded.

Seaver slid his fingers into her mouth once more. Kinsey suckled again, stopping to let out a muffled moan of pleasure. Tears were in her eyes as her pussy pulsed once more. She was sore and exhausted; her mind teased her with sleep.

Seaver pounded her pulsating pussy. He threw his head back and grunted her name as he came. Intense pleasure filled him, then escaped simultaneously. He was agape as his cock spasmed and spurted into the human. When his wits returned to him, he rolled off Kinsey, realizing his dead weight might bring discomfort for her. He stared at the ceiling, agog and pleased with their series of encounters. It took him a moment to regain his hearing. He hadn't even realized everything was muffled after his orgasm. "You are fantastic," he remarked.

Kinsey turned onto her side then smiled. "As are you." She adjusted her pillow then sighed. That night didn't feel real. Even the residual pain from the repeated vampire bites didn't register as a portion of reality for her. She felt weak, her body felt heavy. There was almost a gentle numbness radiating throughout her body.

Seaver rolled over and pressed his body against Kinsey's. He held her tightly against him and tucked one arm beneath her head. With his free hand he toyed with her hair. It Her hair was silky, perfect between his fingers. He smiled, content with satiating all of his needs. His tongue still held remnants of Kinsey's taste. He was naked, warmed only by Kinsey's tiny, curvy body.

Kinsey shivered. No longer moving constantly or feeling the friction during sex, the room's still air carried the reminders of the winter season. Kinsey wiggled away from Seaver. She retrieved a quilt and unfolded it. With Seaver's assistance she covered them both with it, then she sighed and settled on her side. She was content to be held by her sanguine lover. "You were quite the Christmas surprise," she whispered. Her eyes fluttered shut.

Seaver smirked. "I think the same about you." He snuggled closer to her. "I've never met a woman who enjoyed being bitten."

Kinsey tittered. "How many have you bitten while they were awake?" She reached back and tickled the vampire's cheek with her fingertips.

Seaver was silent briefly. He raised an eyebrow while he thought back over his span of existence as a bloodthirsty undead creature. He pursed his lips, then shrugged. "A few. When I was a new blood … I attacked anything that moved. The need for blood outweighed self-preservation."

"I hope you've gotten smarter," Kinsey muttered.

Seaver draped his arm over Kinsey's belly. He slid his arm under Kinsey's pillow. "Tonight I used Nicholas' Christmas magic to piggyback an invitation into homes and feed off people frozen in time." He beamed with pride. "I'd say that shows a lick more intelligence than lunging at humans that crossed my path."

Kinsey nodded slowly. "That's impressive." They were silent briefly. Kinsey then rolled over and faced Seaver. She stroked his hair while their gazes met and lingered.

Seaver's forehead wrinkled in thought. "We were intimate for a while," he said. Kinsey nodded, agreeing. "Nicholas had to have left your home by now."

"Likely," she said.

"When I came to your room, he was still distributing gifts," Seaver said. "So, how were you awake, not frozen in time like the other people I drank from tonight?" His hand traced the curves of her body.

Kinsey shrugged. "I just came back from getting a glass of water," she answered. "That was before I heard somebody walking around." She smiled sheepishly. "I assumed it was Santa."

"Hmm. You weren't fully asleep when his magic took effect, then," Seaver remarked. He was fascinated by the strange events of Christmas magic and its effects on the world and people. His mind meandered.

Kinsey leaned in and kissed Seaver. She quietly moaned into the kiss.

Her tongue caressed his then she pressed their bodies together.

Seaver whimpered. He broke the kiss and rested his index finger against her heart-shaped, tempting, pink lips. "It is getting early," he whispered. "You are delectable, and I would turn to ash when hit by the sun's rays."

"I assumed," Kinsey replied. "But why stop our kissing?" She pouted and averted his innocent blue eyes from his gaze.

"If we keep going, I'll either drain you dry or we'll fuck so long the sun will greet us," Seaver said. He cupped her face, then kissed her forehead. "It is for both of our wellbeing that we lie here, recovering."

Kinsey blushed. She shrank. "S-sorry."

"Don't be. I want you as much as you want me. It is flattering," Seaver said.

Kinsey pecked the vampire's lips. "Stay with me until I fall asleep, then?" she requested.

"Or until the dark before dawn," Seaver said.

Kinsey rolled over and snuggled back against Seaver's body. He hugged her against him and nuzzled her. "Thank you. I'm feeling a little dizzy," she muttered. She pulled the quilt up to her shoulder.

"That's the blood loss. When you wake, eat plenty of meat. Don't do anything too strenuous. Drink plenty of water," Seaver said. His fingers were mindlessly lost in her velvety red tresses. She smelled sweet and salty from a mix of their sweat. Her body was warm and her slow, steady breaths were soothing to him.

"I will," Kinsey promised. Her voice was quieter, heavier. Sleep was beginning to take her. Her breathing slowed more.

Seaver replayed the events of the night in his mind. His magical sponging off Nicholas' bizarre fae magic gave him a successful manner of feeding at least once during the darker months of snow, ice and graupel. He no longer felt the bloodlust tearing at his every waking thought. Most of that was thanks to Kinsey and her intense sexual attraction to vampires. He wanted to know more about that, but he did not want to wake her. She looked adorable, at peace. As much as he wanted to continually touch her fair freckled skin and fiery hair, he knew she needed sleep. She had to recuperate her energy and her blood. He remained rooted in place, wondering about the woman who was turned on by vampires and how their paths had crossed somehow.

Seaver gave it a few moments before he slipped out of bed. He tucked Kinsey in, dressed himself, then wandered around Kinsey's home. He was curious about the layout, and he knew he needed to test his ability to leave without being in Santa's magic bag. Would the invitation extended to him in the present bag let him leave or would he have to hide in a closet until nightfall and ask for Kinsey to invite him in, then accompany him outside? He completed tasks on his mental checklist, then he gingerly reached for the doorknob. He sighed with relief when he wasn't burned, stung, or flung backward. He opened the door, then was met with the still, icy air of Christmas morning. Seaver locked the door, shut it firmly, then he transformed into a bat. His small, winged form, out of place in the wintery mountainous landscape, soared through the night, only inhibited by the occasional frigid zephyr.

❄ ❄ ❄

Kinsey woke at midday. It was a stark contrast to her usual early morning waking to greet the presents left by Santa. She felt weak, as if her limbs were too heavy to move on their own. As her mind adjusted to the situation around her, the stabbing, bruising pain of her wounds and her pussy feeling sore registered with her at the same time. She patted the left side of her neck. Kinsey winced and hissed. The vampire had been real. It was not a sex dream she had gifted herself. Straining, she pushed herself upright. She threw the quilt back and looked at the dried mix of translucent white fluids from their repeated sexual encounters the previous night.

She looked at the end table she had decorated with alternating red and green tinsel. There was a full glass of water, a slice of ham from her previous night's dinner leftovers and a note.

Eat plenty of meat. Stay hydrated. Don't do anything too strenuous. You lost a lot of blood and exerted yourself plenty last night. ~Seaver

Kinsey blushed. She hugged the note and sighed. With the utensils Seaver left with the slice of meat, she enjoyed breakfast in bed then downed the glass of water. Kinsey cleaned up the dishes then she set about opening her presents from Santa. She added the novels to her bookshelves in her to be read section, then she folded the pajamas and other clothes into her wardrobe.

Kinsey did her makeup to hide her crimson night of passion from visiting friends, then she prepared for the normal activities of the season.

❄ ❄ ❄

Nicholas chuckled to himself as he went through the lists from this year. The fae enjoyed keeping track of the presents he had given so as not to repeat them unless that was requested. He had not expected Kinsey's present to come to him so easily, but the stowaway vampire slaking his appetites during the winter weather would grant a wish. He was there to bring magic, presents and happiness, to grant wishes. The vampire didn't send a letter to Santa, but he expected a few blood meals were always on Seaver's wish list. It was a long night of time standing still and granting wishes. He would have time to rest before his mailbox was flooded with present ideas and hopes to answer, but he felt particularly proud of this Christmas' deliveries.

❄ ❄ ❄

Kinsey sat up in bed reading one of the novels Santa had left for her. She asked for books she hadn't yet discovered and clothes to replace her threadbare, loved to death outfits that kept her warm during the lonely months. She had gotten over the mountains of toys and such requests as a child, but she still believed in Christmas magic. That is why she asked for a vampire companion to slake her unusual appetites.

It was a dark, snowy night and she intended to remain inside with a mug of hot cocoa and her stack of books she hadn't read yet. She was still recuperating from her encounter with Seaver, and reading was her idea of taking it easy so she would not overexert herself before she was well again.

Kinsey turned a page, delving deeper into the fictional world she held in her hand. The words consumed her, painting an intricate, evocative world in her mind. She smiled, anticipating the next plot events unfolding between the characters. She was antsy and eager to know if she was right.

A knock startled her. Kinsey fumbled the book and marked the page with her finger. She listened again, uncertain if she had heard correctly. She heard another knock, so she marked her page then grabbed her heavy robe. She ventured to the front door and opened it, flinching from the biting wind and blinding bright snow.

Seaver stood in earmuffs, a fur-lined coat and snow boots. He balanced a serving tray stacked with containers of sugar cookies, a turkey, chocolate liquor and black pudding. They remained silent until another gust of wind made Kinsey shiver. Seaver dropped his gaze. "Do you mind if I come in? It is cold out here and I doubt you're dressed to stand in a blizzard." He gave her a crooked smile and kept his scarlet eyes on her dear, freckled face. He did need the invitation to cross the threshold. He felt the repelling, intense pulse radiating from the doorway.

Kinsey shook herself from her disbelieving stupor. "Please, come in, Seaver," she said. She motioned for him to enter, then she closed the door behind him. She was stunned, not at all expecting to ever see the vampire again. She took the tray of food from him, surprised by its weight at first. She took it to the kitchen while he removed his outer layers, leaving them beside the door. "Not that I'm complaining about your visit, but I did not expect to see you again." Her heart went into overdrive. The handsome vampire with high cheekbones, full lips and a mess of blond tresses followed her into the kitchen. She turned around, then braced herself against the countertop. She noted the vampire's casual manner of dress, grey sweatpants, and a white t-shirt. She wasn't dressed to impress with her flannel robe and green plaid pajamas. It was hardly a sexy reunion for them, given the intense orgasms and her getting to live out a sensual fantasy with her visitor.

Seaver fiddled with his hair. His eyes were on the floor, finding his thick socks and Kinsey's faux fur slippers to suddenly be the most interesting objects in existence. He was flustered, less confident than he was when he intended to drink Kinsey's blood, then leave. His cheeks were the same hue as his eyes as he stammered through his thoughts, "I-I wanted to make certain you were recovering," he said, barely audible.

Kinsey scoffed. "That is why you show up carrying food," she retorted. She caught a glimpse of the vampire's embarrassment. They were on even footing, though he was too distracted to realize it.

Seaver tittered. He lifted his gaze. "I like you," he blurted out his thought. He hadn't been able to stop thinking about her since he left her to recuperate from their meeting. Thoughts of her adoring blue eyes and sweet, freckled skin against his were invasive, intruding on every thought he had. They didn't have much time to bond, but from the glimpse of her personality he gleaned, he liked her. He wanted to know more.

Kinsey's stomach flipped and fluttered. Her heart thundered in her throat. She tucked a strand of errant hair behind her ear. "I like you, too, Seaver," she replied. She enjoyed his sanguine nature, but his intellect and the caring gestures he made deepened her attachment to him. "I'm still bruised though. A bit lightheaded day to day." She moved her hair aside to show him the puncture wounds he left on her swan-like neck.

Seaver nodded. "Blood in the black pudding for that." He cleared his throat, "For me. You, too, if you like it," he said.

"Oh," she turned back toward the food her guest had brought. "And what else?"

"Turkey. Spiced the way I like it. I got the recipe while traveling." Seaver approached Kinsey. "Sugar cookies. They're what you made Nicholas. I assume you like them, too. He rarely eats every offering so ..." he shrugged. He hoped he was right about Kinsey and the guesses he made about her likes.

"I do. They're my favorite. You can add icing, chocolate, have them the way they are ... they're perfect," Kinsey said.

"And chocolate liquor," Seaver said, picking up the bottle. "It makes hot chocolate more fun." He smiled and shrugged.

Kinsey turned toward Seaver. "Mister vampire, are you asking me on a date with this spread?"

Seaver tittered. "I am. A stay- in- date given the weather."

"And the blood in the pudding will be enough?" Kinsey asked.

"It has been before," Seaver replied.

"And what if we wanted things to take a sensual turn?" Kinsey asked. She smirked, letting her imagination wander.

"I can bite without bleeding you dry if that's what you're asking," Seaver answered. He looked down at the petite, fiery-haired woman. She rocked on the balls of her feet to her heels. Seaver leaned down and parted her lips with his.

Kinsey leaned into the kiss. She welcomed the vampire's tongue with hers. The kiss was short, but passionate. Seaver pulled back and sighed. "Delicious?" she guessed. Seaver nodded. Kinsey leapt into Seaver's arms. She wrapped her legs around his waist. She felt Seaver's cock through his sweatpants. He was hard already, and she knew she was excited herself.

"I have missed you," Seaver moaned. He carried Kinsey to the nearest wall. He kissed her fervently while she massaged his cock through his sweats. His tongue worked slowly and fingers quickly to unfasten her pajama pants. He tugged her pants down, breaking their sloppy kiss. Kinsey cooperated, stepping out of her pants. Seaver smiled at her, seeing no panties this time. She dropped to his knees and licked her pussy.

Kinsey threw her head back. She pulled Seaver's hair, melting as Seaver brought her intense pleasure immediately into their sexual encounter. She became lost in the deft movements of the vampire's tongue. "Don't stop, don't stop," she begged. She was close already. His tongue worked her clitoris delicately. He lapped up her fluids and moaned, the gentle vibrations exciting her more. Kinsey melted and her eyes rolled back. She was agape. Her pussy spasmed. Then the oversensitivity to touch followed. She squeaked when Seaver continued licking. She screamed for mercy for him to stop stimulating her.

Seaver complied but eyed the panting woman with yen. A devious smirk crossed his lips. "May I bite you? I won't suck from the wound."

Kinsey nodded. "You may bite me," she said under her breath.

"Thank you." Seaver punctured the skin of Kinsey's thigh. She screamed and pulled his hair. He licked the wound tenderly. He kept his word, not drinking more blood from her.

Kinsey blushed when Seaver stood and met her gaze. "That was amazing."

"Good." He kissed her throat.

Kinsey toyed with the drawstring of his sweatpants. "What about you? You were already hard from the kiss ..."

Seaver shook his head. "I'm a giver. No need to reciprocate ..." he tugged his pants down partway. "Especially not when you let me drink from you so generously."

Kinsey smiled. She crouched down and worked his sweats down to his ankles. On her way back up she pecked the head of his cock, then licked the precum. He whimpered. "Now, where were we?" she said, pressing her back against the wall.

Seaver picked her up again and let Kinsey wrap her legs around him. He loved feeling her heels digging into the small of his back. Her fingers gripping his shoulders and tugging his hair elated him. Kinsey eased down onto him. He whimpered and bit his lip. He had to control his wants. It wasn't impossible, but it was more difficult when he was aroused. He grunted and groaned as he thrust into Kinsey.

Kinsey bounced the best she could in their position. She moaned and grunted. She was still wet from him performing oral on her and his perfect timing and soothing scent aroused her further. She was turned on by his strength and endurance, his ability to hold her up while they fucked, the spontaneity of his visit, their like confessions and everything about that moment combined into the perfect second date for them. She dug her nails into the vampire's back. Writhing and barely able to hang on, she came again.

Seaver thrust faster, pounding into her pulsing pussy. He braced himself against the wall, feeling his inner contractions starting. Kinsey hugged him tightly, peppering his muscular chest with kisses over his shirt. "I'm close," he grunted. He wanted to last longer, but the fervor between them was too much. He would either cum or bite her, and she needed to recuperate from their last time together. He kept reminding himself not to bite her throat, to bite down on the inside of his cheek instead.

Then Kinsey pushed him over the edge. She bit the side of his neck and dug her nails in hard. Seaver moaned her name and his knees buckled. The painful pleasure of being bitten with Kinsey's warm, partly naked body pressed against his, coaxed an orgasm from him. He stood. His mouth felt unable to close as his seed flooded into her pussy.

Kinsey sighed. "You really know how to plan a second date," she whispered.

Seaver set Kinsey's feet flat on the floor. Still panting, he pulled up his sweats. "As do you."

Kinsey retrieved her pajama bottoms and dressed herself again. "Do you want to take some cocoa and cookies into my bedroom and let me keep you warm?" she said coyly.

"That sounds wonderful," Seaver said. "But I haven't planned anything for when the sun comes up. I'll need to check the time often." He frowned, disliking the one unfortunate reality of their relationship.

Kinsey shrugged. "I have lightproof curtains. Perhaps the decorative ones up now could use a wash?"

Seaver smiled in reply. "You want to keep me around?"

Kinsey heated up milk, then made Seaver's cocoa. "I may have asked Santa for you," she coyly admitted.

Seaver quirked an eyebrow curiously. He grabbed the container of sugar cookies and chocolate liquor and followed Kinsey into her bedroom. She insisted he make himself at home while she blocked the window with dark curtains and objects. "You asked Santa for me?" he asked. He browsed the contents of the shelves in Kinsey's bedroom.

"I wanted a vampire boyfriend and I believe in Christmas magic," Kinsey said. She blushed mildly, but she continued working on blocking out the sun.

Seaver chuckled. "That's adorable." He settled in bed with a notebook, a pen, and a cookbook.

Kinsey returned to bed, then picked up her book. "I thought having a vampire in my bed for Christmas would prove more fun than simply reading about it." She brandished the book emphatically.

"Is that what that's about?" Seaver asked.

Kinsey's face became painted with embarrassment. "Maybe."

Seaver turned onto his side. He rested his chin on his palm. "And how am I comparing to the literary vampire boyfriends?"

Kinsey smiled sheepishly. "Better, definitely. They bite like one time, and they're done," she explained.

"For women who crave teeth against their supple flesh?" Seaver asked. "What torture."

Kinsey glanced over at Seaver. Her embarrassment deepened. "It's not like we can spend the entire night fucking, right? We should get to know one another better. Occasionally eat, bathe ..."

Seaver shrugged. "We could try."

Kinsey laughed. "Try which part?"

"Whatever you'd like," Seaver said. He turned, picked up his cocoa and the liquor. He spiked his drink, then passed the bottle to Kinsey. "I have all the time in the world."

Kinsey added alcohol to her drink as well. They toasted, took a sip then sat again with their attention on their reading materials. The house was quiet, save for the hearth. "One of my cookbooks?" she inquired.

"I like cooking," the vampire reasoned. He looked at Kinsey again. The adoring reaction she had to him and the glimpses of his undercurrents, her sweet scent and her being a sweet ginger beauty who invited him to bed again combined in the moment to bring their roiling lust to the surface once more. He pounced on Kinsey, kissing her lovingly and forcefully. Kinsey moaned and writhed in pleasure beneath the vampire's weight. They made out for a long while eventually leading to another night of sex and biting, but without Seaver drinking from the wounds and licking them to help along their healing.

A Bite of Magic

The Spice Merchant and The Glass Smith
by Megan Landon
www.meganlandon.com

Water

Cassia

The last of the flames disappear into the surf, and I pull my wool poncho tight around me against the late autumn chill. I watch a long time, the wind whipping my hair around my face, as the raft sinks beneath the waves, taking Marina to her love.

On the beach, Marina's family and friends—the entire village it seems—bustle around sharing their regrets and remembering her matriarchal antics. My in-laws, Heron's sisters and brothers-in-law, embrace me and thank me for taking care of her in her last days before making their way to her cottage beyond the dunes. When the raft disappears into the waves, I turn my back to the water and look beyond their retreating forms to the mountains.

It will be weeks before Heron learns of his mother's passing. A cold ache nestles against my heart for him. He'd left believing he'd see his aging yet vital mother when he returned by the solstice.

We were to travel to the healer's festival in Mossgrove with him, but when Marina became ill, I stayed with her, insisting he go for the Samhain. Healers' festivals are lucrative for him, and there won't be another Black Moon Samhain for nineteen years. He planned to return by the winter solstice, still four weeks away.

Heron's sister Cordelia slides her arm through mine and tugs me along toward the dunes, where her young ones forgo the path to chase each other through the grasses.

"Thank you, Cassia," she says as she maneuvers us side-by-side along the path, trailing the family headed to Marina's cottage. "My brother was unhappy that you couldn't join him in Mossgrove, but he'll be grateful that you were here for her. Especially since he couldn't be."

"I am grateful to have been a comfort in her final days," I say, "but she was the one who gave me comfort."

"That was Ma. Always caring for everyone else. She loved you something fierce. As much as she loved us, her own children."

I laugh at that. "Hardly." Marina loved everyone. But it's true we'd had a special bond since I'd arrived in Gran Onada, and she'd busily set to the task of matchmaking Heron and me. Though it hadn't been necessary, since I'd noticed him immediately upon waking after he'd found me in the forest half dead from the cold.

❄ ❄ ❄

The cold had penetrated my bones when I'd first woken up in the little seaside cottage a year ago. My travels had never brought me far north before, and my clothes had been inadequate for the wet cold. The snow had come on fast and heavy. Saffron and I had been unfamiliar with the rocky terrain and the trail had been icy. My blond stallion was unsteady on the ice, and when the ground gave way beneath him, his hooves slid downslope, taking my small caravan with it. I was thrown in the air, my world upended to the sound of wood splintering, glass breaking, and wet snow spattering. I'd hit the ground hard to the sound of Saffron screaming in a way I didn't know horses could. And then nothing.

❄ ❄ ❄

"I'm sorry that we left you to care for her," Cordelia says, pulling me back from my memories, as we huddle together against the wind. "Had we realized she was so sick ..." Her voice trails off with some unspoken lament.

"I think she intended for you and your sisters not to worry," I say. "She wanted to ease that burden on you."

"I'm still sorry the burden was left to you."

"It was no burden. It was my pleasure to care for her. And to help ease your load. I don't have family to worry over."

She stops and turns to look at me. "We are your family."

"That night, your mother admitted she had no regrets in life," I tell my sister-in-law, wanting to ease her guilt.

We turn back to the trail, our shoulders pressed together as we walk against the cutting wind.

Heron's sisters had been in the cottage in those last days when it became clear Marina was preparing to cross over. That last night, she bid her children and grandchildren a good night and said she'd see them in the morning. Her voice had been soft but sure.

"Marina was a healer. She had prepared for her end."

My sister-in-law scoffs at that.

"You know what she told me?" I don't wait for Cordelia's response. "She said, 'I'm grateful the road brought you to us. Especially to Heron.'" My voice tightens at the words. But I can't help my laugh as I share Marina's next words. "Then she said, 'Even though I've kept you from traveling with him, I'm quite selfishly enjoying your company.'"

Cordelia's laugh softens the lines in her face. "That's Ma. Impish to the end. She probably planned it."

Marina had taken my hand in her final moments, and with a surety in her eyes that betrayed her dimming light, she'd called me daughter. "Take care of my eldest," she'd said. "He waited for you a long time." Then she closed her eyes, and her soft grip on my hand released. Even in her weakened state, Marina lit the space around her with bright hope until the moment she took her last breath. That night, the surf roared as if the ocean wailed for the loss, climbing onto the land to retrieve a beloved daughter. For a long time after, I held her hands in both of mine.

It's not the same hollow ache I'd felt when my own mother passed, but maybe that's because Marina had been prepared. She had done everything she intended in life. And she was leaving her son and me in each other's care. My mother had left me long before either of us were ready, and she'd left me alone.

Cordelia and I walk in silence, not hurrying despite the cold, until the path through the dune grasses splits into two. When Cordelia turns to take the path toward Marina's, I slide my arm from her protective hold.

She turns to me, the crease in her brow returning, more pronounced than before. "You're not coming in?"

"I want to take in the air a little longer." With all Marina's family and the villagers, the cottage will be stuffed like a sausage.

She takes my hand and squeezes it reassuringly. "Naith has offered to take word to Heron in Mossgrove," she says.

"That's kind," I whisper, recognizing the dragon keeper's generosity.

"He is a good friend to the family and close to Heron. Naith didn't want him to return to the sad news."

"Will he go by dragon?"

"Maybe." And with a hopeful glint, she adds, "And maybe he'll bring Heron back with him."

"Heron planned to train young people in glass-smithing and return for the solstice. If he's made commitments, he won't be able to return sooner."

"For the solstice then." She gives my hand another squeeze before letting go. "Join us when you're rested," she says, knowing me and understanding my need for solitude. "I'll bring you a plate later, if I don't see you."

In the cottage I share with Heron, the silence is welcome, though the faint song of the violin and drums and laughter over the roar of the surf is also a comfort. The kitchen table is covered with bottles of oils and scents we used to prepare Marina's body for her final voyage. We'd rubbed her favorite scented oil into her hands and feet to prepare her to reunite with her love.

I set my own sadness aside as I tidy after the chaos of the past few days. With the grief of his mother's passing, Heron will suffer the guilt of not having been here. He'll be freezing and road sore when he returns.

I scan the labels of my bottles on the window shelves. The infusion of wolfbane, helichrysum, and gotu kola that Marina and I made at the end of summer.

There won't be much I can do to assuage the guilt, but I can ease his physical discomfort. I'll make him a balm to soothe his muscles after his journey home.

Heron

The ball of molten glass glows red on the end of the pipe. I transfer it to the cool rock slab and roll the malleable material into a cylinder shape.

"Keep rolling," I tell Ren, stepping aside so he can take over. "Always keep rolling."

The students are learning a lot, young tradesfolk in the making. This trade is one that folks have to travel to the cities to learn. But if I can bring the trade to the villages, glassware can be sold locally without having to travel to the cities or waiting for merchants to pass through the village. The products can be basic, but the craftier glass blowers can elevate the art. That's how I got started, when a glass-smith came to my family's seaside village to teach his craft.

Once you learn the techniques to build a good furnace as well as creating functional pieces, imagination is the only limitation.

"If we have two furnaces," Ren says, "we could work while one furnace cools and make pieces every day."

"That's a good idea," I say, appreciating the enthusiasm. "If you form a cooperative and share resources and space and the work to maintain the furnaces, you could do that. That's something you can decide later. Right now, you're still learning the basics."

Ren blows into the pipe, and we watch as the air bubble enters the malleable glass sphere. "More heat," I say, and after Ren holds the ball of hot glass in the opening of the furnace for a few moments, we watch as the breath of air expands within the glass ball.

"That's very good," Grace encourages. "You have good control."

The trio works well together. They haven't worked with glass long enough to know what their individual strengths and weaknesses are. As a group, their strength is how well they work together.

Grace takes the wood paddle and shapes the cylinder, helping Ren work it into his desired shape. I step back and watch as Noe helps Ren transfer the piece to a second pipe. After Ren heats the bowl, Grace returns with the paddle to shape the mouth of the container.

This trio mastered the skill, helping each other work the furnace and shape glass. Sharing a workshop is within the realm of possibilities for them.

When Ren is ready to break the piece off the pipe and smooth the base, Noe is prepared with the softened leather pads to hold the bowl and bring it to the shelf at the furnace entrance next to the other pieces we made today.

I work alone, so I rarely get to enjoy collaborating. My teacher, a traveling craftsman, worked with me. He taught me to speak, the importance of giving clear instruction when working with someone. When you work with another gaffer, their hands become extensions of yours. Being able to communicate specific instructions is one of the first skills you learn.

"I can help with annealing," Noe says.

"I can take a shift too," Ren says.

"Noe, you take the first shift while Grace has dinner," I say, attending to the furnace to begin the first stage in the long and arduous process of lowering the temperature to control the gradual cooling of the pieces so they don't crack. It will take a night and a day. It's the reason we only work the furnace a few times a week. "Grace, you take the shift after dinner. I'll take the overnight shift. Ren, you'll come in the morning."

"When will we work with magic?"

I gesture to a lopsided bowl. "Not for a while yet."

They all laugh at that. "It's not just the quality of the pieces. Where would you get the magic from? And what magic would you use? It's a separate craft. Focus on learning this one. The magic comes later."

I'd arrived for the Black Moon Samhain and set up a stall with a furnace to demonstrate my craft. Grace and a few others had shown interest in the trade. That was four weeks ago. There are another four weeks until the solstice.

Ren is the most curious about the materials, showing interest in mixing sand and ash and lime to make strong glass. Noe is the most creative, pushing the limits of what the glass can do. Grace has a sensitivity for the malleability of molten glass and a fearless approach to experimentation. Her father, the town blacksmith, agreed to build a furnace in their yard, near his own workshop.

When Gray enters the yard with a newcomer, it takes me a moment to place the stranger with a familiar face. Naith, a dragon keeper and friend. Here, in Mossgrove? My stomach sinks at the unexpected visit.

"What's amiss?" I ask as they approach. "Is it Cassia?"

"It's your mother, Heron," Naith says, meeting me. "She passed away a few nights past. She was sent to the sea today."

"Nights?" So fast. I look around. He must have ridden a dragon, but I see none. The dragon keepers' ways are mysterious. Part of the strength of our friendship rests on my ability to accept Naith's peculiarities.

"Cassia is well. She took charge of preparing your mother. Your sisters helped her, but they were a little lost with the suddenness of her decline. Cassia took on the task of making decisions."

"I should've been there," I say, more to myself than to Naith, feeling a pang of guilt that my thoughts went straight to Cassia and not my mother who'd been ill when I left.

"She succumbed to her illness. They said it was simply her age. She went peacefully. I came after her burial. They gave her a fisherman's farewell so she could join your father."

I only half hear him, slow to take in his words. Unable to speak, I slap a hand on his upper arm before I turn from my friends and look to the clouds gathering over the mountains. There's rain on the horizon.

I should have stayed when Ma took ill. How sick had she been? How had Cassia managed? Cassia has my sisters, but they have their own households. I should return home, but I hesitate to leave my students. What remains to be taught here? I should never have left Cassia.

Behind me, Gray asks Naith, "Will you take a meal with us?" The two men continue their conversation in low voices, giving me space to think.

Their words join the tumult of thoughts chasing each other through the growing fog in my mind. It's difficult to catch any one idea, so I focus on what needs to be done.

I need to gather wood before it rains. My students need to know how to source and filter sand for material. They need to know how different woods—oak, ash, pine, and cedar—burn and how to control the heat. They need to know the basic techniques so they can practice while I'm gone.

When I first brought Cassia into my home, she'd been trapped. First by her illness. By the cold. By the loss of her horse and caravan. Then by her love for me.

Ma was a force in all our lives, much like Cassia has been since the day she opened her eyes and illuminated my days. It's why she and Cassia took to each other. Cassia is wild, cheeky, inquisitive. Content with herself. They are—were—both fearless, carefree spirits. We'd become her family. The village her home. My mother, her friend. Me, her love.

❆ ❆ ❆

I'd come upon her overturned caravan on the slope below the trail while I was gathering wood in the forest. The early snowfall last year had caught us all by surprise.

The dead stare of the blond stallion first caught my attention, the unsettling quiet in his eyes. He was shivering, but not from the cold. I rested my hand on him, but he had no fight in his body. His legs were twisted grotesquely, the shards of bone poking out through his flesh. I had no blanket to cover him. My chest physically ached to look into his eyes. I don't know how long he'd lain there. I'd turned my gaze from the shocked beast to survey the scene, and that's when I saw her. A woman wrapped in a blanket, face down behind the overturned wagon, mercifully not crushed by her horse or cart. Faint puffs of vapor escaped her nostrils and mouth, but she was cold to the touch.

Moving quickly, I took pity on the beautiful beast and raised my crossbow to ease the creature's suffering. Lack of action would have prolonged the horse's pain.

I turned to tend to the woman. Her hair was tied back in a thick braid, but long black strands had escaped to frame her ashen face. Her lips were blue. I had to get her to warm shelter quickly.

I unfastened my own cart and hoisted the woman onto my mare with me as I mounted. I positioned her across my lap and pulled her against me to share the warmth of my body and then set Sea Mist to a steady canter.

Passing through the village, I arrived at the cluster of cottages that were my family's homes and called to Ma as I rode past her cottage. By the time I was laying the woman in front of the hearth, Ma was already entering the front door of my house.

"Take care of her wet clothes," I said, striding to my bedroom at the back of the cottage to stoke the fire. When it was blazing, I grabbed a blanket and returned to the hearth where my mother had removed the woman's wet clothes and slipped one of my shirts over her.

"There are no broken bones that I can tell. Keep her warm," Ma said, hustling to put water to boil.

I lifted the woman and brought her to my room. I wrapped the blanket around her limp form and sat in front of the fire, pulling her body against mine, rubbing her arms and legs.

"That's a good sign," Ma said when she began to shiver. "Her body is starting to fight for itself."

I tucked her in my bed, and Ma stayed with her while I returned with my brothers-in-law to recover what we could from her cart and tend to her horse's remains.

The contents had been tossed about, but I was able to recover boxes and carefully wrapped bundles containing glass bottles of different colors, ointment pots, small carved boxes, leather bladders, and ceramic jugs. Some items were enhanced by magic. There were powders and roots, oils and salves, and dried herbs and seeds. The exotic creature warming in my home was a traveling spice merchant.

There were larger bottles filled with oil, but most were broken. The smaller bottles, packed in cloth for travel, were well protected.

There weren't many clothes in her small caravan, save for the blankets used to pad her merchandise. She had been wearing two thickly woven wool blankets—one of which had a hole in the middle for her head to poke through—as well as her own clothes layered on her body.

Over the next day, Ma and I took turns caring for her, though she didn't rouse. She went from freezing to feverish without waking. We went from getting heat into her to cooling her burning skin, and Ma brewed willow bark to reduce her fever. We took turns tending to her.

When she finally opened her eyes, they were a blazing amber that brightened the room. And when she smiled, it felt like the sun breaking through fog to warm my skin.

❄ ❄ ❄

Turning away from the mountains, I rally my thoughts. I need to gather wood before it rains.

"Do you want to return home?" Gray asks, coming up behind me.

"I do," I say. Though it's an honest answer, it's impossible. "But I won't abandon the students right now. They're in the beginning of their training."

"You can return in the spring. And bring your wife then."

"They're just getting the feel of the glass," I say, peering into the open door of the workshop to where the furnace is still cooling from yesterday's work, the bottles annealing inside. If I can't make it back, their training will be incomplete. I turn to meet Gray's concerned scrutiny. "Cassia is expecting me for the solstice in four weeks. I'll stay the week and make sure Grace, Ren, and Noe know what they need to practice on their own. If I can finish the first part of their training by the end of the week, when I return, it will be to refine their craft."

I look back to the mountains.

I need to return home, but I can't. Not just yet.

With me gone, with Ma gone, will the road call to Cassia again?

Niggling doubt eats away at my confidence. She lived a lifetime of freedom with the road as her comfort. In the past year, I'd been her comfort, her home.

Cassia is my wild, adventurous spice merchant. Pure excitement. I'm a provincial, taciturn oaf. Unyielding. And I'm not there to be her comfort now.

Air

Cassia

I wake to the murmur of a gentle surf. The ocean calmed in the night as if it cried itself out with the violent crashing of its waves on the shore. The hazy morning sun shines through the windows and the jars filled with dried flowers steeping in amber oils, casting a golden glow in the room.

Someone, likely Cordelia, built up my fire and left a plate of food for me on the table by the hearth this morning.

Eager to make Heron's body balm, I skip my morning meal to gather supplies. Linseed oil infused with herbs to reduce swelling, alleviate pain, and heal sore muscles. Helichrysum grown from seeds I'd planted with Marina in the spring. The dried gotu kola leaves from my eastern travels. Dried clove flower buds I'd traded for in the southern extremadura. I add an infusion of arnica, which grows wild here, though they call it wolf's bane. Dried ginger root, which Marina and I grew in my sunny window nook.

Last spring, Marina made a show of setting up my garden and planting some of the seeds I'd been carrying with my supplies. Heron had built the nook in the cottage where I could grow plants from seeds that needed more sun and heat, and steep oils with weeds, roots, and barks. Marina was sure the plants would survive the northern winter in that sunny little closet. She and Heron did everything they could to make me feel welcome and comfortable. To keep me here. They needn't have. I stayed for Heron.

I strain the oils through a linen cloth into the pitcher with the pour spout Heron made for this purpose and strain the dried leaves, petals, and roots. Once the oil has been strained, I press the cloth in my hands to squeeze out the last drops of infused oil. I set aside the cloth with the dregs and rub the oil into my hands. Then I crumble honeycomb from Cordelia's hives and add it to the oil, set the pitcher in a pot of water, and heat it.

While the oil heats and the wax melts, I tend to the fire, remembering the way firelight dances on the skin of Heron's broad shoulders. So much has changed in the past year, but not my fascination with his powerful body.

❄ ❄ ❄

I awoke in a warm bed, enfolded in thick blankets, to the steady roar of the nearby sea. A man with broad shoulders was building the fire across the small bedroom. When I sat up, he turned and stood, towering in the room and casting a shadow over the bed. Stormy gray eyes met mine. He held my gaze, and I couldn't speak or take note of my surroundings. I shivered at the sheer power and broody tension he exuded, and I smiled at the sensation. I didn't know where I was or who he was, but I felt safe in his presence.

I was released from his spell only when an energetic older woman bustled into the bedroom and threw her hands in the air.

"Quick, get some water," she said to the man. "You must be starving," she said to me, putting a hand on my forehead. Without a word, the big man slipped out of the room. It was weeks before he looked at me like that again.

I learned that Heron had found me under a thin layer of icy snow and brought me straight to his home. He and his mother, a healer, had taken turns caring for me. With what they told me and what I remembered, I was able to piece together what had happened.

Saffron had stumbled and slipped on ice. Unable to regain his footing, he came down hard on a knee and toppled, taking me and my caravan with him. I leapt from the cart, but I don't remember anything after that.

Heron had mercifully put an end to Saffron's suffering. "Two broken legs," he had said, resting a big, calloused hand over mine, a gesture that soothed far more than the touch of a stranger should. But he didn't meet my eyes. "He fell badly and was stunned silent when I found you. There was nothing I could do."

Saffron had been my travel companion since I was fifteen—the year after my mother had died.

He was sorry. Not for putting Saffron down, but for my loss.

"Where did you leave him?"

"We dug a shallow grave and covered him with rocks."

The rush of sadness was too much to share with anyone. "Thank you," I choked out. Unable to say more, I rolled over with my back to him.

Heron rested a hand on my back, big and solid, holding me together with a silent gesture when I might have shattered. We stayed that way a long time until I stopped crying. I don't remember his leaving. When I woke the next morning, he was sitting by the fire. A quiet presence.

"I need to get the goods from my wagon," I said, sitting bolt upright.

He urged me back down with a gentle hand on my shoulder. Looking at the fire, he said, "I brought them here. Most of it was spared. Some bottles broke, but many were intact. The cart can't be repaired. It's only good for firewood."

He left and returned with my cases and sacks. I leaned against the headboard, fascinated by the careful way he laid out my merchandise on a blanket on the bed.

"So you can see what remains intact," he said. "The broken ones are outside."

Heron and a wide-eyed Marina helped me unwrap glass vials and ceramic pots. We spent the afternoon picking through my products and checking my inventory. Marina poked through my stock, captivated by the exotic herbs and spices, all the new scents, and the healing possibilities.

Heron was especially drawn to the containers, interested in the origin of each. The brown bottle that held my vanilla, purchased from a Yujatnun grower from the jungles to the southwest. The small ceramic bowl made of Aksawaya clay preserving mushrooms used to reveal mysteries from dreams.

He was curious about vessels hewn with distant earth magic to protect valuable spices, preserve delicate specimens, or increase the potency of medicinals. He showed me his own bowls and bottles, imbued with the breath of dragons. One of many reasons I'd come this far north.

I watched his big hands handle each bottle with delicate reverence. He offered to replace my containers.

Heron took turns with his mother to bring me food. He'd disappear for long periods. Marina said he was working in his shop, getting wood for the furnaces, or tending the animals.

I eagerly awaited his return whenever he left. Every time his powerful shoulders filled the doorway, my heart jumped. And each time he returned, he'd ask how I was feeling, but he never met my gaze.

Not until the day I finally captured his.

❄ ❄ ❄

Once the wax is melted, I pull the pitcher from the simmering pot and dry it quickly to keep water out of the fragrant mixture. I add a few drops of concentrated winter spearmint oil and the sweetly peppery copaiba balsam I'd traded from a merchant from the plains south of Aluzeo. I pour the warm oil mixture into small wide-mouth glass pots to cool and firm.

This morning, the ocean is at peace. The stillness of the water, its rippling calm, its soothing murmur. Like my husband, a quiet constancy.

I take the breakfast Cordelia left me and go outside. Sitting on the bench, I scan the horizon with my plate in my lap.

The sound of the ocean is soothing, but it's the mountains that call to me. Their winding roads leading to ever-changing landscapes, fresh diversion, and novel challenges. And escape from sadness.

A world of mysteries and scents to discover. Like the wild scent of brine on the air near the ocean. The earthiness of vetiver. The sweet bite of ginger. Heron's scent. The scent of home.

The road calls to me. As does my husband. My greatest adventure.

Before the balm has cooled, my decision is made. I'll take my gift to him.

Heron

In the morning, I hitch my wagon to Sea Mist and set my axe in the bed of the cart.

"Can we help?" Noe and Grace ask.

"Not today," I say, forcing my attention to them. "If you want to help, work with Ren. You'll continue the gradual cooling today."

That's a lot of responsibility so early in their training, but the pieces we made yesterday were functional, mostly to practice making bowls they can sell. The cooling stage is an important step that they'll each have to master if they want to keep their work from cracking. Mistakes at this stage will teach them first-hand the importance of proper annealing. They need to work without my supervision.

Today I need time for myself. I lead my gray mare away from the village square toward the foothills to collect firewood for the furnace.

Walking beneath a canopy of lush evergreen and leafless deciduous trees in the stillness of the forest, my mind waivers between loss and longing.

My sleep last night was restless, and when I finally slept, Cassia and Ma both visited my dreams. Ma was working at the table, kneading bread and chattering happily to Cassia, whose face was turned toward the window, past the jars on the shelves to the mountains beyond. Ma turned to look at me, and with a wink, she said, "I'm going to find your father now." She wiped the flour onto her apron before taking it off and shuffling toward the door with her typical bit of bounce. "Take care of each other," she said and swept through the door as if Pa was outside waiting.

I'm tossed between thoughts of leaving Cassia to care for Ma and feeling guilt at not being there for my mother.

Sorrow trailing behind me, I get to a point on the forest road where Gray and I had marked some aged trees for felling. I leave Sea Mist on the trail and trek into the brush with my axe.

I find a dying ash, and warm from my walk, I raise my axe. The wood grain of the handle matches the calluses on my palms and fingers, and the grip is familiar, comfortable. With the force of my body thrown into each arcing blow, the strikes hit their mark. The scent of green wood fills the air around me as heat radiates through me, fueling the sadness and the guilt. But the memory of Cassia in my dream, her face looking to the mountains, haunts me.

At home, sometimes I see her catch a scent on the air and look to the mountains, longing in her gaze. The only thing that keeps me secure is the same longing I see in her face when she looks at me.

❄ ❄ ❄

In those first days when she'd been recovering, she was dazzling, though I did my best not to look at her. At first, it didn't feel right to ogle an unconscious woman. Later, I dared not lose myself in her spell, knowing she'd move on when she recovered. She was a traveler, her various pots and bottles telling the story of where she'd been.

I'd gone back for her cart and found it full of glass containers of all shapes. Some basic, functional glass bottles, others well-crafted and ornate. Ointment pots with wide mouths, medicinal bottles with narrow openings. Some topped with a cork, some with wax. Some with magic, most without. There were powders and roots, oils and salves, and dried herbs and seeds.

I carefully unpacked the bags to make sure they weren't broken and repacked them to bring her the unbroken wares. The contents of her cart were priceless, as exotic as her fawn-colored skin and shiny black hair. The alluring woman in my bed was a traveling spice merchant. She was from the south, unprepared for traveling in the cold winters of the north.

From the moment she opened her eyes and captured my attention, I resisted meeting her gaze. They were big and bright, inviting but knowing. To get lost in them would be to lose myself.

Cassia often wore a wickedly playful smile on her full, flushed lips. She had a gray streak in her wild mane of hair. Her inquisitive eyes were lined with laughter and had a youthful spark that made it impossible to tell her age. Her lively expression flashed from wide-eyed wonder, to avid interest, to glee, to sadness, to mischief, to fiery disagreement with the slightest change in conversation. The casual way she made demands sound like suggestions. Her ready laugh that filled all the quiet spaces.

I tried to keep myself busy outside the house. Ma was more than capable of caring for her, but I always found myself drifting back inside to check on her.

"Do you think that's too many blankets?" I asked Ma.

"She has a chill, and it's best for her to sweat out the illness."

"Do you think a dunk in the ocean would douse her fever?" I asked.

"Not this fever. Ice baths are for scaring off the heat. This fever comes from a chill. She needs to fight it off at her own pace."

"Does she need a bigger fire?"

When she opened her golden-brown eyes, something inside me stirred. But when she opened her mouth and laughed, her cheer brightened all my empty spaces, like warm scented oils filling a cold, unyielding vessel.

When she was stronger, she'd risen from the bed, and had insisted on helping around the cottage.

"I need to bathe," she said one morning in her husky voice that woke every part of me.

"I'll bring you a basin and heated water," I said, not looking up to meet her beguiling eyes.

"Thank you," she said. The weight of her gaze, disarming in its brazenness, wrapped around me like a furnace fire.

❄ ❄ ❄

Hoisting a sectioned log length onto my shoulder, I make my way back to Sea Mist. I sweat in the cold air. The work is good, the hefty burden a cathartic pull on my body, the exertion drawing my thoughts to a single point.

The longing expression on my wife's face turned to the mountains.

I didn't need a shadow healer to interpret my dream for me. Beneath the grief and missing my wife, I'm scared. Scared she won't be there when I return.

The solitude of the road had been solace for her. The constancy of change, the surprises the world had for her. She'd been on the road since her mother died. Now that Ma's gone, would she take to the road again?

What if I'm not there? Is the promise of my return enough? Am I enough? When I'm with her, I know I am. But with my mother and I both gone, is there anything to hold her back? My own doubt shakes me to my core. The fear that she has nothing to tether her.

My guilt is more chilling than the cold air on the sweat of my heated body. Guilt that my worry over losing Cassia eclipses the sadness of Ma's death. But Ma would understand. Cassia is my future.

My thoughts return to the shadow healer's commission at Samhain. He asked me to make a magically enhanced phallus for his wife, one that would ensure pleasure with each use. He'd also requested a matching plug.

I could create a set for Cassia. To ensure she'd always want to stay with me. If I can satisfy her, keep her intrigued, she won't take to the hills.

I'll complete my work here and make her the phallus. When I see her again, I'll show her I can be as adventurous as the road that calls to her.

Fire

Cassia

Cordelia finds me loading my riding packs onto Midnight, the black mare Heron and I purchased last spring when we married. Concerned I'm not eating enough, she's brought me another plate, laden with honey biscuits and sausage.

"Are you sure?" she asks when I tell her my plan. "The roads may not be passable further north."

"I'm sure. The road is calling to me."

"Without a cart, you can be there in five days. Do you have enough supplies?"

"Yes, and I'm prepared for the weather." I'm bundled in a wool sweater and two pairs of leggings instead of a skirt—an under layer of wool and an outer layer of leather. I'm wearing a comfortable traveling corset and my wool poncho on top. I also have a fur-lined cap gifted by one of my brothers-in-law and a change of clothes in case I get wet. Heron had made sure I knew how to dress to travel in the cold last winter, and the family was always gifting me fur-lined clothes and woolen layers, since I—a southerner—didn't know how to dress properly. It would have been tiresome if it didn't make me feel loved.

"Eat this," she said, thrusting the plate into my hands. "I'll pack food for the journey while you eat."

"I have food," I call after her.

"A little more won't hurt," she calls over her shoulder without looking back. "I'll be quick."

Knowing I won't stop to hunt or fish, Cordelia sends me off with enough bread, cheese, smoked meat, boiled eggs, and dried fruit for a week. "You should make it before the first snow, so long as it as it doesn't come early again this year."

Dappled sunlight dances on the road as I skirt the foothills north toward the Bosq kingdom, and to Heron. Midnight is sure-footed on this terrain, but the weightless, sickening feeling of being thrown lingers in my body.

Midnight's foot stumbles on loose rock. My heart jumps into my throat as my fingers clench on the reins. I flash on the moment my cart flipped, Saffron's terrified whinny rending the sleet-streaked afternoon. Midnight recovers her footing, but it takes several beats of hooves on the road before her rhythmic canter coaxes my body to unclench and my heart to steady.

Time moves so fast. One moment you're reveling in the thrill of majestic trees thriving in an icy frost, and the next you're mourning the loss of a friend. A parent.

An unexpected shudder runs through me. It's not the chill on the air, but the memory of stumbling in snow. I'm accustomed to traveling with my cart. Today's light load feels like flying. I force myself not to ease our pace to a safe but slow trot.

A break in the canopy reveals a blue sky with a white mist hugging the mountain peaks. A dragon flies from the north and disappears in the mist. Sightings are rare, but since the dragon keeper chieftain and the princess of Devantdemar wed last year, they've made themselves more visible.

I'd heard rumors of dragon magic on the trade routes, which is why a year ago I'd meandered this far north. By the time I arrived, there had been a battle with corrupt mages, and the creatures emerged from legend once again to regain their standing in the region.

I feel a kindred connection to the magic beasts. Though I'm earthbound, the freedom of the road satisfies something deep inside me.

The anticipation of the unknown. Hearing foreign languages and learning about different cultures. Facing challenges. Discovering spices and flavors. Staying with families, seeing mothers and fathers with their children. Meeting the occasional bachelor with something to teach and something to learn.

But today something else pulls me. Heron. A grounding force that settles me.

I give Midnight her lead, and we canter at a lope beneath the tall pines.

My mind is a fog like the mists on the mountain peaks. I close my eyes and enjoy the sunlight that shines through the canopy to warm my face. Beneath the trees, I lose track of time.

My thoughts flitter, remembering my mother, with her fearless lust for exploration, and Marina, who savored all the fruit that life had to bear, sweet and sour, joyful and sad, and her unapologetic matchmaking. Saffron, my mischievous joker always vying for carrots and apples. Heron and the sweet way he negotiated his mother's whims, sometimes accommodating her and other times humoring her until she changed her mind.

Midnight picks up her speed to a pleasant gallop for a short stretch until we stop to drink by the river. The days are short, and I dare not ride in the dark, but I take advantage of each minute of daylight. Midnight, sensing my urgency, keeps a steady pace and takes few breaks.

When night comes, I build a fire, and in the long dark night, my thoughts turn to my husband and the heated looks he gives me. Unlike those first days, when he'd avoided my gaze so intently. I had seen how his eyes lingered on me when he thought I didn't notice, and I'd made a game of trying to catch his gaze. But he'd always thwarted me, by keeping busy tending the fire or walking out the door.

His looks do more than heat me. They ground me. Tether me. Bind me to something bigger than me. I'm a child of the whole wide world, and I'd only ever skittered over it. Until I met Heron, and I'd planted my feet, relishing solid ground, feeling earth between my toes. Until I'd grown roots and allowed myself to become entangled.

I remember the moment I knew I had found my home. The day I

seduced him and made him mine. It took some encouragement to lure him. He had kept a respectful distance, but I saw it for what it was—caution. His eyes told me all I needed to know. If his averted gaze revealed a poem, his searing glances sang a song. He wanted me too.

Heron wore silence like a comfortable blanket. I'd been weakened, as much from heartsickness over losing Saffron as from my illness. Heron took care of me. He kept the cottage stocked with wood he chopped with his own hands. He fed me soups prepared by his mother and siblings. He cooled my skin by washing me with damp cloths on my face, my neck, my arms. For all that Marina healed my body, Heron healed my spirit. With his calm and comforting presence, he settled me.

Too cold to travel in the winter after I'd recovered, Heron and his family—especially Marina—did everything they could to make me feel comfortable and welcome in Gran Onada. They convinced me to stay in their village until spring, when it would be safe to travel, and they promised to help me find a horse when the time came to leave.

When Heron spoke, his deep baritone was a caress that reached deep inside me, a rich resonance that strummed somewhere low in my core. He didn't look at me, but the room always heated with the strain of him looking away. I always sensed when he was near, felt it in my whole body—a solid, comforting feeling, grounding. Steady.

One day as I watched firelight flicker over the severe lines of his stubbled face, I said, "I need a bath."

The jaw on his strong profile tightened, and his back stiffened.

The sun had set by then, the days in the north so short when the solstice was almost upon us. He warmed water for me and filled a high-backed tub in the kitchen.

"I'll give you privacy," he said, making to leave the cottage.

"Keep me company?" I asked in a casual tone, as I prepared to get in the bath.

His hand clenched and unclenched once before he sat in a chair facing the fire, his back to me.

"Heron," I said. "Can you wash my hair?"

That's when I finally caught his gaze. He turned to face me, his eyes locking on mine with a flash of warning. I had been pushing him. Walking around the cottage in his shirt. Letting him spoon-feed me soup, though my hands worked just fine. His eyes told me I could only push so far.

I hadn't been wrong. The heat that radiated between us pulsed like a threat.

I slipped off the shirt that fell to my thighs and held his gaze, inviting him to look. He no longer avoided looking at me. His eyes roamed my body.

I slowly stepped into the tub with little concern for modesty and lowered myself into the steaming water.

I watched deliberation play out on his stoic face, until, without a word, he came to kneel next to the tub. I said nothing, unwilling to snap the spell that kept his eyes on mine. When he did move, it was to fill a pitcher with water from the bath. His thumb, rough and calloused, traced a line along my jaw. I tilted my head back for him and shivered in the hot water as he poured it over my hair.

He was gentle, lathering lavender-scented soap in my hair, then pouring more water over my head to rinse.

When he finished, he moved to leave. I turned to face him again. There was heat in his eyes, but also a plea. For mercy? I would give him none. He wanted me as much as I wanted him. As hard as he'd been working to ignore the charge that ran between us, I needed him to look at me, to know that I felt it too. Maybe I wasn't being fair, breaking down his reserve.

Despite the warm water, my breasts tingled and puckered, sending delightful tendrils of awareness through my body and between my legs.

He leaned toward my ear and in a gravelly voice said, "Be careful, spice merchant, I may not let you go when the weather warms."

His words didn't fill me with fear, but with a deep sense of belonging. Would I mind being tied to this place where the wind blew relentlessly and the ocean roared, reminding the residents who was true king here? Where mountains cast shadows and dragons danced in the clouds? With this man, whose voice settled something deep inside me?

No.

Facing him, I pushed myself onto my knees, the water sluicing down my body, my hair dripping. I'd take my chances.

"I'm not afraid," I told him, smiling. It wasn't a challenge. It was the truth.

He pulled my wet body tight against his, and with the hunger I'd sensed during our shortening days and lengthening nights together, he took my mouth.

His kiss was unrestrained. He kissed my lips and my cheeks and my eyes before returning to my mouth. I opened for him, and he plunged inside, exploring my mouth as I explored his, our tongues desperately seeking to know each other. He turned his head to fit us together, and I melted against him, wet breasts pressed against his now-wet shirt. His hot chest was hard against my tight nipples, his arms gripping me as I clutched at his hair.

I didn't feel trapped. In his arms, I felt free.

Standing awkwardly, he pulled me up with him, water pouring off my wet body and soaking his shirt and pants.

"You're shaking," he whispered against my mouth as he carried me to the bed.

I tried to argue that I wasn't cold, but his mouth came down on mine as he walked, trapping my words between us. I wrapped my legs around his hips and clung to him as he lowered me to the bed. I didn't loosen my grip but pulled him down on top of me. He nestled his rigid cock between my legs, and I rocked my hips against him.

The blaze in the small fireplace in the bedroom crackled loudly, but it was his body setting me on fire. He pulled the blankets tight on either side of me, cocooning me.

Then he rose to his knees and pulled his wet linen tunic over his head. Instead of lying back down on top of me, he eased down to kiss my neck, then my collar bone. A hand settled on my breast, fingers spread wide, clutching hungrily, possessively. Then, slowly, he tented his fingers, and dragged his fingernails across my skin, tracing my breasts until he pinched my taut nipple. The gentleness of his hands conflicted with the need in his eyes. Then he lowered his mouth to my breast and painted a smoldering line across my nipple that shot a bolt of electricity straight to my already pulsing clit.

His movements were tempered and infuriating, working my body and molding my need. Tentative yet confident. Never lost to our heat, though I was melting in it.

He lapped one nipple. After pinching the other, he moved to lap at that one. I moaned and spread my legs wider, trying to rub myself against him, making him grin around the nipple in his mouth.

"You do have a sense of humor," I whimpered.

With a smile, he slid further down my body and lowered his face between my spread legs. "I've been wanting to taste you for days now," he rumbled as he spread my folds open and dipped his tongue to lick at me.

I dropped my head back, enjoying how swollen and slippery I was at his touch.

"If I take you, I won't be able to let you go," he said, and the sheer possessiveness of his words burned through me like a physical caress in a way I wouldn't have believed if I hadn't felt it. It didn't scare me, the idea of being bound to something. Instead, I felt an expansion in my chest. I didn't feel trapped. In his arms, I took flight.

"You are exquisite," he said between noisy, wet lapping.

I wasn't a young woman, though age wasn't something I feared. I'd embraced the changes in my body. My belly had softened with the years. My face had lines from laughing too loud. My skin bore spots from traveling in the sun with no hat. My thighs were strong from riding, but my ass had widened.

"I love this especially." He gripped my ass tight.

He dragged his tongue through my folds and around my clit before dipping into my channel.

"Do you like this?" he asked sweetly.

I could only moan my response.

He drove two fingers inside me, watching my face. His rough hands were calloused and scarred from years of chopping wood and working with fire. Gracelessly panting with need, I tilted my hips up to him as he stoked my lust.

His mouth was soft and hard. Dirty and possessive, belying his stoic demeanor. He pushed my thighs wide, and I rested my heels on his back, the lewd sounds of lapping filling the room as he tickled my clit with the tip of his tongue. I writhed beneath him and pulled at his hair.

"I'm going to cum," I said, trying to pull him up my body by his hair. "I want your cock."

He didn't budge but rather pumped his fingers inside me, so wet and slick, his thrusts deep and unhesitating. I watched his strong shoulder as his arm pumped sure and hard, his fingers fucking me and his tongue working my clit.

So close. The tension in my body reached its peak.

"Cum on my face," he said, and his words released me from the tight grip that had been building.

I collapsed against the bed as the pleasure ripped through me, his fingers and mouth relentless, coaxing every drop out of me, every shudder through me. My inner walls gripped his fingers as my body shook. He didn't stop lapping at me until I was lying limp beneath him.

Then he dragged me to the end of the bed and released his cock from his pants. I watched hungrily as he stroked himself before pushing my legs up and out by the backs of my thighs. He slid inside me in one long stroke with no warning.

He pumped in long, languorous thrusts, my muscles clenching around his cock as he fucked me through my orgasm.

"Fuck me," I shouted, not caring that I was louder than the ocean.

On my command he thrust his hips, deep and hard, and I was poised to explode again around his thick heat filling me.

He watched me beneath him. "Cum, spice girl. Cum for me again."

His thrusts were hard and steady, driving me to the edge again. I relaxed into the bed and dropped my head back. A big hand cradled my nape, lifting me so I was forced to meet his eyes as he powered into me. He watched my face as his thrusting became faster, harder. I gave myself over to him, and the rush of pleasure swept me away again.

When I clamped around his cock, Heron sucked in a breath between clenched teeth, and his thrusts became more urgent. Harder. Faster. Uncontrolled. Until he was bucking into me, lost in sensation, grunting as he came inside me.

❄ ❄ ❄

The lulling rhythm of Midnight's hoofbeats gives way to another rough step. We stumble, but she recovers quickly. I barely have time to tighten my grip before we're steady again.

After four days on the road, I've traveled further north than ever before. Each day I grow closer to Heron, my soul settles and my body awakens.

I spur Midnight into a gallop for a little while to cut the distance. It hasn't snowed yet, and I send a thought to the sky gods to hold off for one more day until we get to Mossgrove.

Heron

The hotter the furnace, the smoother and more flawless the product. I also use the higher temperatures for dragon magic, which is what I'm working with now.

I prepare my workspace, while tactfully encouraging Grace, Noe, and Ren to leave. This project is exclusively for my wife, and I need to work alone. But they linger.

"I'm sorry about your mother, Master Heron," Noe says, pulling me from my thoughts.

"Thank you. I appreciate that," I say. "Help me get this fire as hot as possible, then I want the three of you to rest."

"Can we help you with these commissions?" Grace asks.

"Not these," I tell them, giving them my full attention. "The three of you did a great job annealing yesterday's projects. You didn't lose a single piece. You're getting the hang of the furnace. Tomorrow you'll gather wood while I anneal these pieces." Wood needs to be seasoned for a year prior to using it in the furnace. When we take from Gray's well-seasoned woodpile, we add green wood to the shed to be seasoned for next year.

"Then we'll be working very long days with the last of your lessons before I leave." In three days.

They shower me with a flurry of questions.

"Will we be able to learn everything we need to by then?" from Ren.

"You're coming back, aren't you?" Noe.

"Are you bringing your wife when you come back?" Grace.

"Yes, yes, and yes. Before I leave, you will have all the skills you need to practice simple glassware pieces."

"Will we be able to sell them?"

"When your glassware looks like … this." I set a glass bowl on the cool stone counter. The rim is even all the way around, and the wall of the bowl is smooth and balanced.

"So, no?" Ren says.

"Not yet." I laugh for the first time since I left home, an eagerness to return rising in me. "But keep practicing, and you will soon."

In addition to Cassia's gift, I have a few finer commissions for magically infused pieces that I need to make. While the trio are building muscles and stocking wood tomorrow, I'll anneal the pieces. Then we'll work for two more days before I leave.

"Do the pieces you're working on now have dragon magic?"

"They do."

"Will you show us?"

I study their faces for a long time. "Okay," I say. I had planned to demonstrate working with magic before I revised my plan. But I could still show them something. "I'm making a special bowl for your mother, to thank her for her hospitality. I'll do that one first."

I set to work making the piece as the novices look on. Once I've gathered the molten glass on the blow pipe and mixed it with broken shards of cobalt glass for the color, I blow into the pipe to create the glass sphere. The three are familiar with this process.

But then, I blow the angelica powder into the pipe and into the glass bubble. They study the malleable glass ball at the end of the pipe. "The challenge of infusing glass with dragon magic is not in blowing the glass," I tell them as I continue rotating the pipe and allowing the bubble to expand, making the sphere bigger. "It's in befriending a dragon who trusts you enough to share their magic with you."

That surprises the three. "I never thought about where the magic comes from," Grace says.

Before they launch into a round of questions too big to answer today, I heat the glass ball again and begin the process of shaping the bowl by sucking on the pipe. The sphere begins to collapse and, with some shaping of the wooden paddle, becomes a concave double-walled shell. Once complete, I set the bowl on a shelf at the second opening of the furnace.

"Is that all?" Ren asks.

"Yes."

"That's just a regular suck bowl," Noe says.

"But this bowl can increase the potency of its medicinal contents," I say, understanding their disappointment. They were expecting colorful sparks and fire in the shape of dragons.

Ren and Noe don't look impressed, but Grace, whose mother is a healer, asks, "What's the powder made of?"

"Dried angelica."

"Do different powders have different effects?"

"That's a great question," I say. "I will have to ask my friends to find out. Now it's time for you all to rest. Tomorrow will be a hard day."

The boys go home, but before Grace goes in to eat, she asks, "Can I bring you a plate of dinner?"

"Thanks, Grace, I appreciate that. I'll come in for it later if you don't mind setting one aside for me. I want to finish these pieces before I stop for the night."

"Okay," she says, and runs off with more enthusiasm than the boys, probably to tell her mother about the bowl.

When the young gaffers are all gone, I set to work on Cassia's piece.

This fire is as hot as any I've ever worked. I insert a pipe into the crucible to gather a ball of molten clear glass. Cassia's gifts will be solid, so I don't need the blow pipe for her pieces.

I roll the pipe on the cool stone surface of the marver in front of the furnace where I've sprinkled glass colored with cobalt, the same color I used for the bowl. I return the glowing ball to the furnace to melt the colored pieces, and then bring the malleable glass ball back to the marver, rolling it smooth and lengthening it. I reheat and reroll it, working the color through and creating a length of glass for the core.

The pieces a shadow healer commissioned for his wife a few weeks ago were my first time making such specialized pieces. For that one, the inner core and outer coat had been uniform in shape with a gently rounded tip.

The inner core of Cassia's piece will be sculpted into an undulating wave, and the clear outer layer will be textured. Once I'm satisfied with the shape, I sprinkle angelica powder onto the marver.

The magically infused angelica powder won't stick to molten glass, so it needs to be locked between two layers. For the outer layer, I gather more clear glass and pour it over the core shaft, rotating the pipe on the cold stone slab until it's covered completely.

With the angelica powder caught between the cobalt core and the clear outer layer, I repeat the process of heating and shaping, rolling, lengthening, and clipping until I find the ideal length and girth Cassia will appreciate.

The toy is a little larger than myself. I want to pleasure her, not terrify her. I have multiple uses in mind for the toy. Thoughts of all the ways we can use it come to mind.

I imagine spreading her out on the bed, removing each piece of clothing slowly, revealing her like a gift.

I'll slide the tip over her bottom lip and have her lick it, slide it in and out of her mouth and watch as she wets it with her tongue. I'll trace it over her chin and her neck to circle a nipple, which will pucker at the cold, hard surface. I'll slide it over her stomach and between her legs.

She'll be slick and shiny, and I'll use the gift to spread her slippery folds. It won't take long for the cold glass to warm against her hot skin.

I'll dip it inside her, no more than an inch, teasing her the way she likes, and make her watch as the phallus slides in her juices.

Then I'll hold it in a shallow length when I present her with the plug. Again I'll tease her, licking and nuzzling her sweet cunt before I flip her over and tease her ass with the plug.

❄ ❄ ❄

As I fantasize, I continue spinning the still-malleable shaft to the light. The fine magic powder glistens between the layers of glass. For the finishing touch, I drizzle molten clear glass threads over the staff as I rotate the pipe. Then I roll it out on the marver, smoothing and flattening it, heating and cooling it, until it's covered in a subtle texture that's reminiscent of the pulsing veins of my own cock. I rub the surface of the molten shaft with waxed leather to a smooth polish.

I reheat the tip one last time, to round it out and smooth it. And, finally, I tap the punty to release the piece. I apply more heat to the end to create a smooth, blunt base.

Glassware containers infused with Rowena's powder preserve their contents as they imbue medicinals with potent healing energy. This magically infused toy will ensure pleasure and heightened ecstasy.

Then I set it to rest while I work on the matching anal plug.

Earth

Cassia

When I arrive in Mossgrove, it's afternoon. It takes one quick question of the first Mossgrovian I meet to learn that the visiting glass-smith is staying at the home of Gray the blacksmith and Saramina the healer. I ride to their home nestled against the forested foothills at the edge of the village, where an exuberant woman tending to three equally exuberant children greets me.

"What a wonderful surprise! He's out back." The woman, Saramina, dries her hands on her apron before leading me out to the yard. "Heron says you're a spice merchant. Did you bring any spices with you?" she asks by way of conversation.

"A few, but not many, since I packed light," I say, losing my train of thought when I see my husband chopping wood with a group of youngsters, each wielding their own axe.

A smile breaks over his stubbled and angular face when he sees me. He strides to me in a few Heron-length steps and reels me into his arms with little concern for the audience in the yard.

"I missed you," he says, his voice thick and grumbly against my ear. He kisses the hollow at the base of my neck.

Everything falls away. The sounds of receding footsteps, a babbling creek nearby, the clucking hens, and the chattering children all become the distant roar of a faraway sea.

"I'm sorry about Marina," I say, resting my cheek against his chest, still hot from swinging his axe.

"Me too." His low voice rumbles against my cheek, the words coming from somewhere deep in his chest. "But I'm sorry I left you alone to care for her."

"I wasn't alone. I had your family."

"Our family," he corrects. "She was so strong. I never imagined she'd pass."

"She behaved younger than her years. She was content in her final days. Happy with her life. She passed quietly on her own terms. I think now that you were comfortable, her last child to marry, she was ready to leave this realm."

He shakes in my arms, and I hold him for a long time.

"I missed you," he croaks out again.

I turn my face up to his. He closes his eyes, but not before I see the shine in them. And I kiss his lips.

"I missed your mouth." He sucks on my lower lip. "Your sweet lips."

I wrap my arms around his neck. My normally quiet husband has so much to say today. "I guess you're glad I came?"

"Aye. I can't believe you're here," he growls against my mouth. "I was getting ready to leave." He grips me tightly to him. "I don't know what I'd have done if I'd missed you on the road."

"We'd have met on the road," I say, unconcerned. "I've found the rarest spices in the world. I could find you easily enough."

He holds me tight, as though ensuring I'm really here. As if I'd disappear if he let go.

"You're not angry I came by myself?" I ask.

"Yes, I am, but I'm more glad you're here. You can take care of yourself. I just wish I had thought to come get you."

"I'm here now. You don't have to leave."

"No. I don't," he says with another kiss.

There's giggling from behind one of the small sheds in the large yard.

"I missed your smell," he says, pressing his face into my neck and against my hair, inhaling deeply, ignoring the giggles. "I can't believe you came alone. Never do that again."

"I had to. It felt good to be on the road."

He tightens his grip. "I was worried you'd leave and take to the road again."

"I did."

He pulls back with a puzzled expression, looking at my face, his big fingers anchoring my hips through my layered leggings.

"I did," I say again. "It brought me to you."

Another round of giggles erupts from behind a shed with steam escaping through the windows. Then Saramina's voice calls the children inside, and they scurry out from their hiding space to run inside, complaining like they'd been betrayed.

Instead of pulling me back into his arms in front of our audience, he leads me after the children to introduce me to our hosts, their children, and his students, who are all sitting around the table with cups of hot tea.

Before dinner, I gift Saramina a face oil made with wild rosehip and a small jar of the same balm I made for Heron. "I'm sure you can use this."

Before Saramina can answer, Gray cheerfully accepts the gift. "Yes, she can. Thank you."

"It's for me, you freebooter," she says, holding her hand out.

"She said it's for sore muscles," Gray says, reluctantly handing it to his wife.

"I'll give you sore muscles," Saramina scolds her laughing husband as she pries out the cork and sniffs the contents. "Hmm. Smells potent."

Over dinner, Heron watches me as I answer the children's questions, his eyes never leaving my face, except when he takes the occasional bite of food.

"You came alone?" the blacksmith's daughter Grace asks.

Heron proudly says, "She's a great traveler. As a spice merchant, she's probably seen the five oceans." My husband gives me a look that prompts me to tell one of my stories.

"Really?" Grace's eyes are wide, as are her siblings' as they push at each other around the table, trying to carve out elbow room.

"I got caught in riots in Sorrenc Pensul, where locals were being held under siege by forces who were progressively squeezing them closer to the ocean. I had unwittingly wandered into a war looking for linichoc, a rare beetle used to create a deep red dye, grown on the sandy peninsula. I was forced to stay with the family of a grower until it looked like I'd never leave. The family arranged for me to be smuggled out by boat."

"If you could leave by boat, why couldn't the people?" Nena, the youngest daughter, asks.

"They knew no other home and would not abandon their ancestral lands."

Heron rubs the back of my hand with his thumb, eating his soup with one hand. He rests his spoon to dip bread in his soup before taking a bite from it, never letting go of my hand.

"Do you ever stay put?"

"It depends." I never had before arriving at Gran Onada. And I only left to be with Heron.

He squeezes my hand in my lap. "When Cassia gets restless, we'll travel."

"With a blacksmith father and a healer mother, how is it you want to work with glass and not iron or herbs?" I ask Grace.

The girl is thoughtful in her answer. "It's like glass lets me work both crafts. I get to use my hands to form useful objects from earth. But those objects are finer for working with herbs. And I'm also a natural healer, so I feel like I know what each herb needs to do its best work. Glass-smithing allows me to use all my talents. Otherwise, I'm not sure that I'd have been able to choose."

The girl's parents both look at their daughter with slack-jawed amazement as Heron takes a sip of ale, pleased with his student's view of his trade. "Grace promises to be an exceptional gaffer. She has a genuine interest in the material, its malleability, and its potential." He squeezes my hand under the table as if he's making a point. But I think he just likes squeezing my hand. I squeeze back.

Gray muses aloud, "We have so much company these days, I wonder if we should build a small guest house and convert the back room into a workroom for you, Saramina."

"Heron built a windowed nook in our kitchen for me to grow my warm-climate plants and steep my own spice oils," I tell them. "A windowed space like that could be useful for a healer."

"Maybe we can talk about windowpanes before you return home," Gray says to Heron.

Saramina interjects. "Now that Cassia is here too, you don't have to leave so soon, do you, Heron?"

"I'll talk about it with my wife, but no. I'm no longer in a hurry to leave."

I squeeze Heron's hand. Just to squeeze him.

"We'll let you make your plans when you've rested," Saramina agrees, "but we hope you stay for the solstice. Especially since you missed the Samhain festival, Cassia. We're sorry you couldn't be here. And for the circumstances that kept you away."

"I was where I needed to be. I was happy to spend Marina's last days with her."

Heron's lips form a tight line, and I see the guilt in his eyes.

When the children launch into another round of questions, Saramina says, "Okay, let Heron and Cassia catch up."

Turning to me, she adds, "Cassia, we have a bathhouse in back. You probably want to bathe after your long journey and get rest."

"I do. Thank you."

"I'll light some candles out there and bring out fresh linens."

Outside, in the privacy of the dark yard, under a canopy of sparkling stars, I pull Heron close. "Your mother wanted you to go. I think, as her oldest baby boy, you've taken care of her. She wanted you to be free of that last responsibility. She loved you very much."

His jaw clenches against my forehead. He says nothing and kisses the top of my head.

❄ ❄ ❄

The bathhouse is a stone structure next to a hot spring, one of many in these foothills. Water from the spring is piped to a stone pool in the shed, which then drains out to one of many creeks.

"Did you bring primrose oil?" Heron asks.

I meet his eyes and a slight shiver runs through my body, guessing at what he intends to do with that oil.

"I did," I say, giving him a little smile. "I also brought you this." I hold out the little ceramic pot of ointment. "I made it to soothe your muscles after your journey home. I can use it on you later if you're sore from chopping wood."

"Or I could use it on you after your long journey."

"I'd like that," I say, inspecting the bathhouse. "I wouldn't mind something like this at home."

"Let's talk to the family. I think we can build something like this. We'd have to heat our own water, but we're close to the river, so we can do something between our cottages."

He peels off my layers and has me step into the shallow, steaming pool. When I'm seated, the water comes to my shoulders. My sore muscles relax after the long ride, and my body begins to re-energize as I watch Heron undress.

Once in the water, he soaps up a cloth to wash the road from my body. He rubs the cloth over my neck and shoulders in small circles as he tells me about his students and building the permanent furnace on the property with Gray.

When he scrubs my chest, I lean back and let my arms fall to my sides, my legs spreading out under the water as I wantonly succumb to his clever attentions. He moves onto my arms, raising each one out of the water. I giggle when he washes my armpits.

He pulls me against him, and I laugh as he reaches around me to scrub my back. Until I moan at how good it feels. I slide onto his lap, straddling him, my chest pressed against his and my head resting on his shoulder. He scrubs gentle circles on my hips as he tells me about the types of wood in this region and how quick his students are to learn.

He doesn't push me away from him to wash my legs, opting to wash each while wrapped around him as he tells me about the festival and how successful he'd been. He reaches behind himself to scrub my feet with both hands.

When he's ready to wash my front, he peels my languorous body off him and leans me back. Rubbing little circles on my stomach, he shares the high points and curious events of the festival. The villagers found the bodies of two healers burned to charcoal in their tent as they slept. A mystery that was never solved.

As he scrubs one breast, he tells me about the characters in this not-so-sleepy village. My body tingles and my pussy throbs when he slides the cloth to my other breast and circles the nipple with the same loving attention as the other. He tells me how much he missed me.

He stops talking when he lets go of the cloth and rubs his hands together to build a lather, then slides one soapy hand between my legs to wash me. In silence, he watches my face as he slips his fingers into my folds, gently stroking me until I'm panting.

Then he stops.

He slides me off his lap before standing and reaching for a linen to dry himself, leaving me needy and throbbing in the hot water.

The disbelieving look I give him must be funny. He chuckles and says, "Patience."

He spreads a dry linen on the stone slab next to the bath and extends his hand to me. Once I'm out of the water, he uses a fresh linen to dry my body with the same deliberate attention he used to wash me.

"What hurts?" he asks, pulling me down to the dry linen on the ground.

"Everything," I say with a little smirk. I lie down and spread my legs for him to use me any way he likes. Too tired to speak, I trust him to read the language of my body.

He chuckles. "Roll over onto your belly."

I comply, eager to see what he has planned.

"You're sore from riding."

"I am," I say, realizing it's true.

The front of my body is cooled by the stone slab beneath me while my back is hot from the steamy bath. I close my eyes as he rubs balm onto my ass, working it in with strong fingers. I feel a penetrating tingle as he massages the thick salve into my sore muscles.

"Don't use too much," I scold playfully. "I made it for you."

"I'm enjoying it. Thank you." He spreads my thighs and massages the emollient into my inner thighs and along the backs of my legs. "I made something for you too," he says.

"For me?" I say, happily surprised and a little groggy. He already makes me all the bottles and bowls I can ask for. What could he have made for me?

Heron

She rolls her hips and spreads her legs, exposing her swollen pink folds to me. My hands spread wide over the backs of her legs as I stroke the crease of her inner thighs, spreading her pussy lips. She's wet, but I don't touch her.

Maybe I am punishing her a little for traveling the roads by herself. What if she'd had another accident? The thought of her lying unconscious on the side of the road sends a jolt of fear through my chest. I swallow hard and distract myself by leaning forward to breathe in her scent.

As much as I want to delay her pleasure and toy with her, I'm unable to resist her rich, earthy scent. I lick her and nuzzle her ass.

Her body toasty warm from the steam in the bathhouse, I pull myself away from worshiping the abundant globes of her ass and slide my hands to work the balm into the muscles of her back. She moans as I draw out the tension from her ride, the stress of caring for my dying mother, and the ache of burying her. I take my time to give Cassia what she needs before I descend on her like a starving wolf.

When she's pliant and supple, I stand to admire the rosy golden glow of her skin, a goddess of the elements—she steals the air from my lungs, stokes the fire in my heart, inhabits the ether in my soul.

I wrap her in a warm, dry towel and cover her with her poncho before carrying her to our room at the back of the house. There's no one in the yard, not that I'd notice with my wife in my arms.

Gray had stoked the fire in the hearth, and Saramina had lit candles in our room. The house is warm and quiet, the family having long since gone to bed. In our room, I set her on the bed and lock both doors. The room is toasty, so I feel no remorse when I remove her poncho and unwrap the towel from her body. She lets me.

She watches, naked, nipples puckered and cheeks rosy, as I remove a bundle from my bag, carefully hiding it from her curious gaze.

"Primrose oil?" I ask.

She gestures to her bag on the table by the door. "My present?" she asks.

"Soon," I whisper. "You'll see." Or feel. "Turn over."

She obeys, sighing heavily against the sheets when I position her ass in the air with her head down on the bed.

I pour a stream of oil into her ass crack and begin to rim her hole. She moans and tilts her hips up to me, widening her legs. I kiss one cheek as I slide a finger in her tight hole, and she presses against my hand. I work the oil in, holding her hips steady and not letting her control the movement.

I drizzle the primrose oil over the plug, letting the extra liquid drip onto her ass, and press the cool, tapered end to her puckered hole.

She gasps. "It's cold." But she tilts her ass up anyway, widening her legs further, exposing herself to me.

"Take it, spice girl."

Her legs tremble. As I apply slow pressure, the plug spreads the tight ring of her asshole. I hold my breath as the tip disappears inside her. She's warm and oily from my earlier penetration, but now the plug spreads her wider, until it reaches the widest part, and she moans throatily. I pull back a little and glide it back and forth, fucking her with it, before I slide it in fully and watch the puckered skin of her hole grip the neck of the plug.

"It's hot. And there's a hum, a tickle."

An unexpected benefit of the magic. The magic makes the pieces responsive to the touch of flesh, making it vibrate softly.

"Good?"

"Yes," she says on a throaty breath.

"You like this?" I ask, my thumbs rubbing the oil into the sensitive flesh on either side of the plug and down to her folds.

"Hmm," she moans.

"Kneel up, and turn over," I tell her, enjoying the glow of her flushed skin. Her kiss-swollen lips. "That's one present. I have another. Close your eyes." She leans back against the pillows, legs spread to display the large ornate bead sticking out of her ass, her pussy slick.

The temptation of her swollen pussy is too great. The dildo will have to wait. I lower my mouth to her cunt and take possession of her pleasure, tonguing her. She pulls her knees up, opening herself to me completely, and I sink two fingers into her pussy. I pump and lap at her like a starving man, trusting the magic of the dragon plug to drive her body to the brink and over.

She groans loudly, and I reach up with my other hand to sink two fingers into her mouth. She sucks on them greedily, moaning around them as I finger fuck her, adding a third finger and flicking deliriously at her lusciously ripe clit with my tongue.

Until she cums with a spray all over my hand and face, her gasping shudder spreads to my own body, and I shake against her.

Cassia

He slides his fingers out of my core and laps at my juices, groaning against my pussy. He sucks and drinks, cleaning me with his tongue and riding out my orgasm, which is intensified by my muscles clenching around the plug in my ass.

I'm a hot, sloppy puddle beneath him.

He sits up on his knees and looks down at me, erratic hands roaming my body with a casual curiosity, gliding over my legs, thumbing my clit, plucking at my nipple. I peer at him through half-lidded eyes, drunk on ecstasy.

"Close your eyes," he orders, and I comply, again, wanting whatever he has to give me.

Something cold and hard presses against my lower lip.

"Lick it," he whispers. I slide my tongue out to feel something blunt and round, hard and smooth. Glass.

"Open your mouth," he says, and I part my lips for him.

He slides the solid glass object between my lips. I moisten it with my tongue before he slides it in and out a few times.

It's a phallus. A glass phallus. A little larger than his cock at its hardest. I swirl my tongue around it and feel the smooth, raised ridges. The gasp that escapes me opens my mouth wider, so he presses it in a little deeper before pulling it out.

"Open your eyes," he orders.

When I do, my eyes land on a breathtaking blue-and-clear glass cock, ornately sculpted. It's a work of art. My pussy clenches at air while the plug, which is likely as beautiful as the phallus in my hands, thrums gently in my ass.

I moan softly and say, "You really have been thinking of me."

He holds it out for me, and I take it with both hands. There's an energy buzzing through it. I become slicker between my legs and reach out to take his hand, guiding him down to stroke my pussy, which is pulsing and dripping again.

"Can you feel how much I love my present?"

He slides two fingers inside as I inspect the work of art in my hands.

Breathless, I ask, "You made it with the dragon-dried angelica?"

"Aye, I did," he says, sliding his fingers out. "It also promises to bring you over every time."

"Hmmm. I like the sound of that."

"On your hands and knees," he says.

Without hesitation, I turn sideways across the bed, head down, ass up, ready and vibrating with excitement. He rests a large, gentle hand on my lower back and touches the tip of the phallus to my ready pussy.

The cool feel of glass against my hot flesh sends another shiver through my body. He feathers a thumb over one ass cheek as he presses the hard toy inside my pussy slowly, the cold shaft a striking contrast to the hot plug in my ass. But the dildo warms as he slides it in and out slowly, and soon both the dildo and the plug are humming.

He fucks me slowly with it.

"If you have this phallus satisfying me," I ask around my panting, "how will I satisfy you?"

He reaches around with his free hand and strokes my bottom lip with his thumb. "I have one idea."

He repositions himself to lean against the pillows, with me still on my hands and knees next to him, his cock below my mouth.

He holds it for me, and I lick the tip the way I did the dildo. I swirl my tongue around the head, noting the striking differences between the velvet heat of him and the smooth glass of the phallus.

He slides the glass dick into my pussy, the plug in my ass making my channel tighter, and they stretch me full. I hiss at the tight sensation. He slides it in and out, and soon my body responds on its own, pushing back on it, riding it, as I suck his cock. I swallow his length hungrily, gagging on him, but wanting him deep.

Fucked completely and deliciously.

I'm unable to maintain the back-and-forth rhythm of my hips with the up-and-down rhythm of my head, so he helps me by fucking me with the dildo while I bob sloppily on his dick.

I fuck him hard with my mouth as I arch my back, urging him to fuck me hard too. Wet slapping sounds fill the room, and the hum that vibrates through my entire pussy and ass drives me back to the edge. I double my efforts to make him cum hard with me, pumping on him fast.

His hips buck up, and I prepare to choke on his cum at the same time the orgasm rips through my body.

I collapse with my head against his belly, still sucking on his cock. When he releases into my mouth, I drink him down as my pussy grips the unyielding shaft inside me. I lap lazily at the cum and spit on his dick as he slowly fucks me, my muscles clenching and my own cum dripping down my thighs.

With care, he slides the phallus out of me and then the plug, resting them on a cloth on the side table. He shifts and lays me on my side. My eyes are closed, but I'm aware of him as he moves around the room. Water splashes before his weight depresses the bed again. A warm, wet cloth wipes between my legs, along my thighs, and over my ass, wiping away the sticky, oily mess.

He settles us in bed with the blankets over us. I let him, greedily enjoying his care.

"I love my present," I whisper groggily.

He blows out the light and pulls me tight into his body.

Heron

"Were you really worried I'd leave?" Her voice is sleepy and soft.

"The thought crossed my mind," I murmur behind her, my face pressed into her hair. "You love the road. I thought that without me there to hold you back, you might return to it."

"You don't hold me back, my love. You ground me. Give me purchase to grow roots, a home to settle my heart." Softer still as she slips into an exhausted sleep, she says, "You are my home."

With those words, all the fear and guilt and sadness flood out of me. I hold my spice merchant in the dark, the tears I hadn't yet shed finally releasing from my body.

Ether

Heron

The longest night is festive in Mossgrove. In front of each house, candles flicker in small lanterns made by children. Bonfires burn along the central road through the village, and, in the square, an older woman tells the children stories of the gods of the elements and the shortest day. Musicians play as villagers dance, and food cooked on outdoor fires fills the air with the rich scents of hearth and home.

In the tradition of the solstice, plans are made for the coming year. Cassia plans to join her two passions—travel and me. I'm intrigued by the many ways to incorporate magic into my craft, and Cassia decides she'll take me to visit a shaman in the far south who works with magical gifts from the sea. Saramina and I discuss the best placement of windows for the workroom Gray will build in the spring, after Cassia and I return home. My students demonstrate the skills they've learned, and we discuss Grace traveling south to Gran Onada with us to continue her training when Cassia and I leave for home. Ren and Noe, who also show innovative talent for the craft, may join her.

Other than the time we spend working during the festivities—Cassia meeting locals, talking herbs and spices, and me working with my students—I never leave Cassia's side.

On the shortest day, when the village is still sleeping after the celebrations of the longest night, we pack a picnic and ride out into the foothills. The backroom of Saramina's house is cozy, but with constant banging around upstairs and the sound of children's laughter, we can't make the noise we'd like to. I want Cassia to experience the full potential of my gifts.

I take her to a small clearing in the woods with a large flat stump, remains from a previous expedition. The clearing is surrounded by tall evergreens, creating a sense of intimacy. Despite the midday sun, it's overcast, so the sky is low, casting a gray haze beyond the trees.

I layer a bed of thick blankets on the ground and cover the stump with a folded blanket for later. Cassia lays out a feast for us while I build a fire with dry wood we brought from the shed. Once our camp is set, I sit back against the stump and set my gaze on my wife.

"Take your clothes off," I order in the low commanding voice she likes.

Cassia

Happily, I slip off my riding leggings. Then my outer tunic. Naked before him, I shiver. But it's not from the cold—I'm warm standing near his blazing fire. It's from his eyes on me.

He unwraps a cloth bundle and lays out my new toys with the bottle of primrose oil.

"Come here," my quiet husband says, his baritone vibrating through my whole body, making my skin tingle with anticipation.

I kneel beside him, and he watches my face as he drizzles oil onto the plug, turning it so the oil coats the smooth glass surface. I get wetter watching his preparations for me.

He positions me so I'm on my hands and knees, my belly across his lap. Then he drizzles oil into my ass, so it drips between my ass cheeks. It trickles past my ass and over the outer folds of my pussy, tickling me enticingly.

"Spread your legs," he says coolly. Then he presses the tip of the plug against my ass.

It's cold and slippery as he rims my hole, and I clench.

"Relax," he purrs.

He glides the plug through the slippery oil and presses it to my ass, breaching my hole. I arch my back to flare my hips and open to him completely. He slides the tapered end inside then pulls out, sliding the tip back and forth, fucking my ass in shallow pulses before pressing deeper. I stretch around it as the neck of the plug strokes the nerves at my entrance. So full, I moan at the sensual pleasure, my nerves hot and tingling and vibrantly aware. He twirls the plug inside me, the smooth ridges massaging my inner walls. I shudder at the charged thrill that shoots through my whole body.

"I love to watch you," he says.

He cups my ass and gives me a little spanking. I moan, pushing back against his hand.

"I've got more for you."

With that, he slides the glass phallus inside my pussy, the motion slow and deliberate. He's giving me a taste of the fucking he'll give me, the penetration blissfully intense.

"What do you want?"

"Your cock," I answer, reveling in the sensations swirling through my core. The hum and heat of the plug, the pulsing I feel inside, and my growing wetness.

"Show me how much."

He unfastens his pants and leans back, allowing me to take him in my hand. I fall on him wildly, unable to tease or play. I just want his cock. I swirl my tongue around his tip in some attempt at slow seduction, but I quickly give that up and suck him into my mouth, filling myself with him the way he's filling my ass and pussy. But I need more. His strokes are too gentle.

I release his length with a pop, and my words come out in a desperate rush. "Please. Fuck me."

With no more prompting, he drives the glass shaft inside me, his hand wrapped around the base to keep it from bottoming out. He pumps fast, the ridged phallus stroking my inner walls, pushing me to the edge, my whole body humming.

He grunts, and I realize I'm gripping his cock, my mouth pressed against him, enjoying the feel of his shaft against my lips, licking but not fucking, lost to the sensations gripping my body.

He slides the phallus out and sets it down on the blanket and shifts us to bend me over the folded blanket on the wide stump. He kneels behind me and pushes his cock inside my slick heat. His hot and hard cock, velvety and giving, is a stark contrast to the unrelenting, hard surface of the phallus.

He resumes his fucking with his own cock, gripping my hips and slamming his body against mine. The friction is different as he bottoms out inside me, spanking my ass with his hips. An energy flows through us, a desperation I didn't feel in the glass phallus. His heat is organic and potent.

I gasp and shout out as I careen over the edge, and then I'm floating on a cloud of ecstasy as I cum around his cock.

He doesn't fuck me through my orgasm but pulls out abruptly. When my muscles contract, they clench around nothing.

Then he flips me so I'm lying on my back on the stump. My head rests on the blanket, but my ass hangs over the edge.

"I'm going to fuck your ass," he grunts as he pulls the plug out with a gentle tug.

Heron

I replace my cock with the dildo, bracing it with my hand around its base so it doesn't slide out. Then I press my cock against her back hole, slick and prepared by the plug. I watch as my head sinks inside, swallowed by the puckered pink skin.

Her body tenses, even after the explosive orgasm that left her loose and relaxed. She watches me as she holds her legs up, taking in every subtle sensation as I penetrate her again.

With the dildo in her pussy, her ass is impossibly tight.

"So good," I say, moaning as I slide in deeper in a slow, controlled thrust.

Once I'm seated inside her, I hold steady, the two of us reveling in the tight feel of each other. Me fitted inside her, her wrapped around me.

"It's humming," I say, feeling the power of the magic through the thin wall that separates her ass from her pussy. "You're so warm. I'll have to make a looking glass so you can see what I see. Truly and completely fucked."

She shudders at that, and I smile down at her dazed expression. She's already poised for her second release in minutes.

I slide my hand up her body, caressing her belly, stopping to squeeze a breast, lingering to tease a nipple and squeeze it lovingly, before bringing my hand along her jaw and sliding two fingers inside her mouth.

"Suck," I order. "I like it when you're completely full."

When she sucks on my fingers, I slide out of her ass. Well-lubricated, I sink back inside and begin to power into her, no longer able to restrain myself. Fucking her hard, my hips slap her ass, and I muster what little control I have left to hold back until she cums again. The humming of the dildo becomes more insistent as I fuck her harder. My balls tighten and I feel the pull in my whole body as I watch her climbing toward her peak.

"Cum," I order through clenched teeth.

She finally lets go with a guttural cry, and I release, shooting my cum into her tight ass in short bursts. When I'm spent, I collapse onto her, kissing her hard.

It takes a while for our bodies to stop shaking, but we ride out the ecstatic waves together as we cling to each other.

At length, I slide out of her slowly and pull the phallus out. Then I fall backward onto the blanket, pulling her over on top of me.

❉ ❉ ❉

Bundled in blankets together and thoroughly replete from our lovemaking, we dine on our feast. We linger a long time, enjoying the hazy afternoon before the sun begins to set and it's time to dress and make our way back to the village.

After a long moment listening to the sounds of the winter forest, she says, "You know, I'd always felt untethered, ungrounded, like a dandelion seed on the wind. Until I met you. You give me solid ground for my roots to grow."

"Hmm." I chuckle. "That's funny."

"Why so funny?" she asks.

I kiss the top of her head. "Because I've always felt settled. Content, but firmly planted. You give me wings. You make me feel free."

❊ The End ❊

Acknowledgements. Thank you to my editor Lindsey Hinkel for her thoughtful insights and infinite patience, to my beta readers Sigh and Ian Smith their helpful comments, and to my Erotica Consortium collaborators for their talent, humor, and enthusiasm.

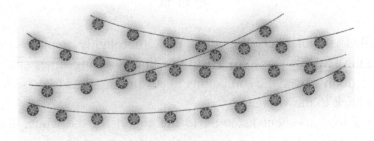

A Taste of Cinnamon
by Saddletramp1956
Twitter: @Saddletramp1951

I sat on the cold stone bench facing my wife's recently dug grave. It was the Friday before Christmas, which came on a Monday this year. The office was closed until January 2, so I had a week to rest and … brood.

I read and re-read the newly erected headstone: "Ginger Hampton. Loving wife, sister, and daughter, taken far too soon. 1985–2023." I wiped the tears from my face before the frigid, gusty wind turned them to ice.

We had only been married for ten years when she was taken from me by a drunk driver who ran a red light and broadsided her car, and as far as I was concerned, they were the best ten years of my life.

Ginger was the best wife a man could ever want. She was the perfect combination of brains and beauty, wrapped in a package of perfect feminine grace.

From the moment I met Ginger, something about her tweaked all my buttons, and all my nerve endings came to life. It's no exaggeration to say she made my heart smile. Her insightful wit and her ability to see beneath the surface of everyone she met touched me deeply.

The devious little smirk she gave when she was feeling frisky and those sinfully plump lips that always distracted me gave me a giddy warmth inside. In short, she was my perfect soulmate—my other half.

Killed the day after Thanksgiving while Christmas shopping. Instantly. I never even got to say goodbye. Just a surreal trip to the morgue to identify the body. The other driver lived.

I don't care if his wife left him for a richer guy that morning. Five years in state prison for vehicular manslaughter seemed woefully inadequate for me having to live without the love of my life. If I had been up to me, he would have been the first human being launched into space without a spacesuit.

We had always wanted children, but she was unable to conceive, thanks to something called Turner Syndrome. It was something she was born with, and it was a sore spot for her. I never let it bother me, but I knew it made her feel less than a complete woman.

We talked about adopting a child or two. Still, the bureaucracy seemed endless and overwhelming, and private adoption was hideously expensive. So now the house was oppressively quiet and terribly empty of anything but memories.

I heard the soft crunch of footsteps in the light snow covering the ground and saw one of the groundskeepers, Amos Farley, walking toward me. I had gotten to know him pretty well since Ginger was laid to rest here a week after Thanksgiving. It was hard to believe that was just three weeks ago. I had only missed one day since then, and Amos had always been nearby.

"Hey, Mark," Amos said as he sat beside me on the bench. "How are you holdin' up?"

"I'm getting by. Thanks for asking," I said. He nodded in response, but I don't think he believed me. Ginger always said I was a terrible liar.

"It does get better, Mark," he said in a firm, fatherly tone as he placed a reassuring hand on my shoulder. I couldn't help but notice the callouses on his dark chapped hand. This was the hand of a working man, and I respected that. "Believe me. I've been there."

"Thanks, Amos," I told him. "I miss her. So much," I added as more tears threatened to escape my eyes. I thought I had cried myself out, but I hadn't. Making things worse was that Christmas–Ginger's favorite holiday—was coming up in just a few days. When I had come to my senses after the funeral, I canceled all my Christmas orders for Ginger. Having them start showing up for the holiday might have driven me over the edge.

"My Cori's been gone darn near ten years now, and I still miss her," Amos said quietly. "At least working here, I can stop by and say hello daily. That helps a lot. You got plans for Christmas?"

"I plan to spend it with Ginger's family," I replied. "What about you?"

"Kids and grandkids coming by," Amos said proudly. "Gonna be a full house."

"Sounds like it," I said. Not having any close family, I had planned on trundling over to Ginger's mother's house Christmas morning and helping her with Christmas dinner, like Ginger and I had always done. When Ginger's sister, Sage, and her family came over for dinner and presents, I would have a little taste of a normal life. But then I would have to drag myself back to my own very empty house later. I was definitely not looking forward to that.

"Anyway, we're getting ready to close for the day. Sunrise to sunset, you know. You're welcome to come by tomorrow if you want," Amos assured me.

"I may do that," I replied. I had only missed one day so far, and that was because I slept the whole day after a binge of self-pity and alcohol. Afterward, I threw all the bottles out and apologized to Ginger on my next visit.

"And we'll keep you in our prayers. I have a feeling things are gonna start looking up for you sooner than you think."

"Thanks, Amos, I appreciate that more than you know," I replied sincerely. We stood and shook hands for a moment.

"Merry Christmas, Mark," he said with a smile.

I swung by my parents' and brother's plots on the way down the low hill. They had all died in a fire years ago. Ginger had held me and comforted me through that terrible grief. Now my nearest relative was a crazy uncle living off the grid in a log cabin two hundred miles north of the Arctic Circle in Alaska where he claimed "they" couldn't get to his DNA. In a very real sense, Ginger's family was all the family I had now.

I trudged back to my car, got in, and realized I needed to pick up a few things at the store. I was getting dangerously low on coffee and a few other staples. Ginger used to handle all this stuff, and I was still learning my way around the kitchen. Another widower at work had advised me to get an Instant Pot, whatever that was.

I grabbed a few things–coffee, creamer, and some other odds and ends to tide me over for a few days. I was only in the store for a half-hour, if that, but the temperature outside had dropped by at least 15 degrees, and the snow was coming down even harder than before.

When I got to my car, I saw a woman sitting on the curb next to my front tire with her head buried in her arms. From the way she was shaking, I could tell she was crying. What upset me was how people were just walking by without even glancing at her.

I put my things in the back seat, then looked back at the woman. She looked to be young, perhaps in her mid-20s. I knew, however, that could be misleading. Ginger was 38 when she was killed but could easily pass for someone ten years younger. I couldn't explain it, but I felt compelled to do something. After all, it wouldn't be right to just drive off and leave her there without doing anything. Compassion shoved my normally cautious self aside.

"Excuse me, miss," I ventured. "Are you okay?"

The face that looked up at me was the most forlorn and angelic I had seen since … I put that out of my mind and focused on this young woman. Rivers of tears coursed down her cheeks as she visibly shivered.

"I … I'm so cold. And hungry," the woman stammered. "Please, mister. Could you help me?"

My heart instantly broke. And there was something about her I couldn't quite grasp. I couldn't explain it, but something inside me said I needed to help her–almost as if my eternal soul depended on it. I took in her shoulder-length auburn hair and doe-like green eyes and melted inside for this woman.

"Of course," I said, now feeling the sudden drop in temperature. "Let's get you out of this weather. Why don't you come sit in my car?" Her face lit up as she broke out into a wide smile.

"Thank you," she gasped gratefully, taking my hand. I helped her and looked to see if she had a purse or a backpack. I saw nothing, which I found to be very strange. I took in her clothing, which looked clean but thin and worn. It's certainly not appropriate for the season.

Opening the passenger door of my car, I helped her get inside and closed the door when she was seated, then went around the car and hopped in the driver's seat. I started the car, turned the heater on, and then looked at her to ensure she was belted.

She looked back at me expectantly.

"You might want to put your seat belt on," I prompted, adding, "It's the law–if the engine is running, the belt must be buckled."

She looked at me funny for a few moments, then turned and grabbed her seat belt and looked at it as though it was a foreign object. I watched her struggle with it and then helped her connect it.

"Do you have everything?" I asked. "What about a purse or a backpack?"

"I … have everything," she stammered.

"What about a phone?" I persisted. "Is there someone we can call?"

"No. No one," the woman said quietly, shaking her head and sending her hair swaying like tinsel on a tree.

"Any wallet or ID?" I prompted.

She patted down her pockets, even turning some of them inside out. She gave me a tragic, lost look and shook her head again.

"Is there someplace you'd like to go?"

"Can we go to your house? Please?" the woman begged.

That startled me. I instantly thought about refusing but realized I had no idea where else to take her. I had no idea where the city's shelter was. The morning news said it was overfilled anyway. I briefly considered dropping her off at the nearest police station, but dismissed that idea, not wanting to see her in such a depressing environment. And I couldn't very well toss her back into the weather after barely giving her a chance to stop shivering.

My mother-in-law's house was a considerable distance from here, and while my parish priest might know a family who would put her up, getting hold of him just a few days before Christmas would be darn near impossible.

I felt a little 'thump' in my head like someone had given me a mental nudge with an invisible elbow. "All right," I replied slowly after a few moments. "Do you have a name?"

"Cinnamon," she answered quietly.

"That's a very pretty name," I said, hoping I didn't come off like a creep. "I'm ..."

"Mark," Cinnamon said, interrupting me.

I was taken aback and said nothing momentarily as I gathered my thoughts. The hairs on the back of my neck stood up, and I briefly felt like I was in an old Twilight Zone re-run. "How did you know that?" I asked sharply.

"I don't know," she said, almost bewildered. "It just ... came to me."

"Are you working with someone?" I demanded suddenly, wondering if I was being entrapped in some elaborate hoax.

Cinnamon looked at me as though I had just struck her. "No," she pleaded, shaking her head as fresh tears fell down her pretty face. "Your name just popped into my head. I can't explain it."

I didn't believe her but had no evidence to support my suspicions. I couldn't kick her out of the car into the worsening storm. My car was now caked in a white shell. After a moment, I tamped my emotions and nodded.

"All right. Let's go to my place." My cautious self muttered that any competent defense attorney would have some choice words for me if this turned out badly, but I shoved that aside again. What would Ginger want me to do? Help, I was confident. "I've got some leftover meatloaf from yesterday if that's okay," I said.

"That would be wonderful," Cinnamon replied earnestly.

I put the car in gear and headed for my house. The snow had begun to pick up considerably, and the roads were already covered. Not wanting to cause an accident, I kept quiet and focused on the worsening street conditions. I pulled into my garage about 25 minutes later, grabbed my groceries, and escorted Cinnamon into the house.

She looked around the place while I put my stuff away. When she wasn't looking, I put my phone on RECORD and laid it casually on the kitchen table. If this was an elaborate scam, I wanted evidence for my defense. I desperately needed a cup of coffee.

"Would you like a cup of coffee?" I asked as I poured a mug.

"Coffee?" Cinnamon replied as if she had never heard of the stuff.

"Yeah. You know, hot black liquid. Perfect on a cold day like today," I said, surprised. I wondered briefly if she had amnesia or a mini-stroke or something. I glanced at her hands. No ring or ring marks on her hands.

"Uh, yeah, sure. That sounds good," she said hesitantly.

"Would you like cream and sugar?" I asked, a bit more kindly.

"However you like it is fine with me," Cinnamon replied absently.

When it was finished, I poured a cup of coffee and then added some of the French vanilla creamer I purchased to each cup.

"Careful, this is hot," I said as I handed a cup to Cinnamon. She blew on the liquid before taking a tentative sip.

"This is quite good," she said gratefully. "And warming. Thank you."

"You're welcome. Are you ready for some warmed-up meatloaf?"

"Yes, please. That sounds wonderful," Cinnamon replied with that angelic smile I had to look away from.

Shrugging, I wondered how badly off she must've been to consider warmed-up meatloaf "wonderful." To each his or her own, I decided. I removed the metal meatloaf pan from the fridge, warmed up the oven, and put the pan inside before returning to Cinnamon.

"If you want, you can hang your jacket on the back of the chair, or I can put it in the closet," I said, hoping to make her feel comfortable. I wanted to get to know her and see if I could find out her situation, but I wanted her to feel at home before I delved too deep into things.

"Thank you," she said, taking the thin jacket off. As I watched, she hung it on the back of her chair. She wore a short T-shirt underneath that exposed her midriff. No wonder she was so cold. I asked myself, who goes out in this season dressed like that? I was determined to find an answer.

Living and working in the city the way I did, I had seen—and smelled—a lot of street people. But there was nothing about Cinnamon that suggested she was one of them. Her skin, what I saw of it, was flawless and looked to have been scrubbed clean. There were no tattoos or body piercings, and she smelled fresh as if she had just taken a hot bath. This puzzle was getting stranger by the minute.

She was relatively small up top, much like Ginger was when she was younger. I estimated Cinnamon was probably a B-cup, and I noticed her nipples threatening to poke through her thin top, so she was bra-less. Like many women her age, her jeans were tastefully ripped, showing hints of nicely formed legs. I shook myself and looked away again. The down-and-out young woman didn't need me leering at her.

"Would you like some green beans with your meatloaf?" I asked on the way back to the kitchen.

"That sounds good. Yes, please," she said.

"One can of green beans coming up," I replied, grabbing a can from the pantry. I opened it and dumped the contents into a small pan, which I placed on a low heat. As everything warmed up, I pulled some dishes from the cabinet and set the table as Cinnamon watched with rapt attention.

"Tea or soda?" I asked.

"What?" Cinnamon responded. I could see the confusion on her face.

"To drink. Do you want iced tea or soda?" I asked, puzzled but trying to be patient. Maybe she had some hearing issues? That would explain some of it.

"Uh, I guess I'll have iced tea, please," she said with a hint of uncertainty.

"Wise choice," I told her as I filled our glasses with ice from the refrigerator door. I set the glasses on the table and pulled out two cold tea bottles. She watched me open the bottle and pour the liquid into my glass. When I finished, she mimicked my movements slowly and precisely. Interesting, I thought.

The food was warmed sufficiently by then, so I took it to the table and dished out a healthy slab of meatloaf and a good helping of green beans. Cinnamon watched me handle my fork before taking a bite of her food. Strange. It was almost as if she had never used silverware.

"Dig in," I told her. "There's more if you're still hungry."

She took a bite of her food before saying anything. "This is very good. Do you eat like this all the time?"

"Not all the time," I admitted somewhat sheepishly. "Sometimes, I just warm up a TV dinner."

"TV dinner?" she asked, a frown on her face. "What is that?"

I couldn't believe she just asked me that. "Basically a pre-frozen pile of chemicals made to look like food," I joked.

Cinnamon looked at me funny before replying."Why would you eat something like that?"

That was a good question. Ginger would often say the boxes were healthier than what was inside them. I chuckled at the memory.

"Save time, I guess," I said.

"So, are you going to visit Ginger tomorrow?" Cinnamon asked between bites.

I froze in place when she asked that. How could she possibly know about Ginger? I never mentioned her name. I glanced around. Other than some pictures of me with Ginger, there was nothing readily available with her name on it. Cinnamon set her fork down and looked at me, her eyebrows raised.

"Well? Are you?" she asked, completely innocently.

"How do you know that name? What do you know about Ginger?" I asked, trying to maintain my calm and barely succeeding.

"I … don't know exactly," Cinnamon said defensively. "It just … came to me."

"That's what you said in the car," I told her. "Who are you? Really? What do you know about me and how do you know it?" I could hear my voice getting sharper and louder, but I couldn't help myself. I was getting more than a little creeped out.

"I do not mean to upset you," Cinnamon said as tears began to form in her eyes. "I'm sorry. I don't know how I know your name or Ginger's. They just came to me."

I studied Cinnamon closely, trying to figure out what was happening. As I looked at her, I realized I could see a slight resemblance to my now-deceased wife. Was Cinnamon one of Ginger's cousins I never knew about? Was she here looking to capitalize on my wife's death? I had a tough time believing her, but there was something so vulnerable about her. I took a deep breath and forced myself to be calm. If she was a con artist, she was also a superb actress.

"What happened to you?" I asked, changing the subject. "How did you come to be by my car in that parking lot?"

"I was … someplace else. Someplace warm and … happy. Surrounded by love. Then I was there next to your car. It was cold, and I felt sad. So sad. And alone. I can't explain it," she said, sounding as confused as I felt.

"Where was this place? How did you get to that parking lot? Did someone drop you off?" I asked, the questions tumbling out.

"I don't KNOW," Cinnamon cried, her face red, plainly overloaded and frustrated.

"All right. Settle down. It's okay. We'll just take it slow," I said, hoping to calm her down. Indeed, she knew where she was before I found her. But something didn't feel right about all of this. Not WRONG, but definitely not right. I had the distinct feeling that there was a … presence … behind me with its arms crossed, tapping its foot, and glaring at me in exasperation. I shook my head.

"I can tell I make you uncomfortable," she told me sadly. "You can take me back if you want."

"No. I could never do that. It's far too cold out there. You'd die of exposure. You have no place else to go, so you can stay here tonight. I have a spare room you can stay in. We'll figure something out tomorrow," I said.

"You never answered me. Are you going to see her tomorrow?"

"Yes, I am," I answered automatically.

"Can I go with you?" Cinnamon asked. "Please?"

"I … suppose so," I said. My 'reality' meter was now pegged out on 'surreal.' "If you want."

"I would like that very much," Cinnamon said. "I can tell you loved her a great deal. What happened?"

"I still love her," I said in a hollow voice. "And I always will. She was hit by a drunk driver. Died instantly, I was told."

"I'm so sorry," Cinnamon said as a tear slid down her pretty face. I thought I saw Ginger's face transposed over hers for a moment, and a chill ran down my spine. Was I hallucinating? What the hell was going on? Ginger's face dissolved and was quickly replaced by Cinnamon's sad visage.

"Uh, that's all right," I said, trying to control my emotions. My mind was playing dangerous tricks on me. "It wasn't your fault."

We finished our meal in silence, and I collected the dishes, rinsing them in the sink before placing them in the dishwasher. Ginger would be so proud of me for doing that, I thought. She had chided me for years about rinsing my dishes before putting them in the machine. I had grumbled about the silliness of washing the dishes before putting them into the dish-WASHER but had eventually caved. Cinnamon sat at the table, intently watching me clean up from dinner.

"Would you like to watch some television before going to bed?" I asked as I dried my hands on a dishtowel.

"Television?" she asked, confusion blossoming on her face.

"Yeah. You know. The boob tube. The idiot box," I said. There was that prickly, strange feeling again. Surely, she knew what television was.

"Uh, yeah. Sure. If you want to," Cinnamon said.

"Bring your tea if you want," I said, motioning toward the front room. She followed me in, then sat on the couch as I took my usual place in my recliner. "Anything in particular you'd like to watch?" I asked.

"Uh, no," Cinnamon replied.

I went through the channel listings, seeing nothing that grabbed my attention. I noticed an older version of the old Dickens classic, "A Christmas Carol," was just starting, so I selected that. It was one of Ginger's favorite movies, and we often watched it together.

"What is this?" Cinnamon asked.

"It's an old classic," I said. "A Christmas Carol. Is this okay?"

"Sure," she said quietly. The movie was about halfway finished when Cinnamon piped up. "I'm sorry, Mark, but it doesn't work that way." I looked at her, surprised.

"You realize this is only a movie, right? None of this is real," I explained.

"It's not?" Cinnamon asked, astonished.

"No, none of this is real. They're just acting. It's from an old story. Fiction," I told her.

"Oh," she said as relief swept over her face. "I'm glad to hear that."

"You didn't think this was real, did you?" I asked.

"I … didn't know what to think," Cinnamon admitted.

At that moment, I didn't know what to think either. Nothing about this woman seemed to add up. She appeared out of nowhere. She can't say where she had been or how she got to my car. Apparently didn't know how to use silverware but knows my name and knows about my dead wife. And to top that off, she doesn't seem to understand that movies aren't real life. Her body suggested she was in her mid-twenties, but her demeanor was much younger. Had she escaped from a supervised group home?

Something was wrong with this picture, but I couldn't figure it out. As we finished watching the movie, I let that thought rattle in my head. When it was over, I looked at Cinnamon and saw she had fallen asleep. I was tired as well and decided to call it a night.

I turned the television off, then gently shook Cinnamon. She woke up with a start, then looked at me, confused.

"You fell asleep," I told her. "C'mon, let's go upstairs." I casually picked up my phone and put it in my pocket.

"Okay," Cinnamon mumbled as she stretched. I helped her up, guided her to the stairs, and showed her the guest room.

"You can use the bathroom across the hall if you need to," I said. "Let me see if there's something here you can sleep in."

"Thank you," Cinnamon said as she entered the guest room.

Friends had suggested I donate Ginger's things as quickly as possible to avoid triggering too many melancholy thoughts. Still, there were too many items I wasn't ready to part with just yet. I went through one of Ginger's dresser drawers and found a long nightshirt resembling something Cinnamon could wear. I walked into the guest room without thinking, since the door was wide open, and saw that she had already undressed and was completely naked.

"I'm sorry," I blurted out, shutting my eyes. "I didn't mean to barge in on you like this. I just wanted to give you something to sleep in if you need it," I said, holding the nightshirt out toward her defensively, wondering if she would scream.

"You don't need to apologize. This is the way I was made. I'm not embarrassed," Cinnamon said calmly and casually as she stood before me totally naked. "You look funny with your eyes all shut up tight like that," she added, amused.

I had seen Ginger naked thousands of times and was perfectly in control. I chanted to myself and forced my eyes open again. Walking around with them shut would get me a tumble down the steps or a run-in with a door.

She was such a vision of loveliness, and I couldn't help but take in her curves. She reminded me a lot of Ginger in many ways. She even had the same tuft of auburn pubic hair Ginger had when we first got married. "This was hers, wasn't it?" Cinnamon asked as she took it from me and held the garment to her face.

"Yes, it was one of her favorites. I thought you might like to have something to sleep in," I replied, trying not to stare.

"Thank you, Mark. It's beautiful. I normally don't wear anything when I sleep, but I'll wear it if I get up in the night," Cinnamon said. She walked to me, not trying to hide her nudity, and planted a chaste kiss on my cheek. "Sweet dreams, Mark," she whispered in a surprisingly sultry voice.

"Thank you. Sweet dreams yourself," I mumbled before practically fleeing the room. I needed to get out of there before she saw the effect her body had on mine. I may be widowed, but I'm not dead. Sweet dreams were a given unless I forced myself to think of something else.

I reached the master bedroom, closed and locked the door, and turned off my phone. I got ready for bed, climbed under the covers, and thought back to the day I proposed to Ginger. I had taken her out for a romantic dinner at Luigi's, a popular–and expensive–Italian restaurant. After a beautiful meal, I took her dancing at a club next door and then to my apartment.

When we were inside, we kissed and made out as we always did, and then I pulled the box out of my pocket and got down on one knee. She looked down at me, wondering what I was doing. I opened the box and showed her the ring.

"Ginger, I've never been so much in love with anyone in my life. Will you do me the honor of marrying me?" I asked. Her reaction startled me.

She sat down on the couch and began sobbing. I asked myself what was wrong with this picture. Was it my breath? Did I say something wrong?

"What's the matter, sweetheart?" I asked.

"I'm sorry," she said in between sobs. "You deserve … someone … better than me."

"What? What are you talking about? How could anyone BE better than you?" I asked.

"I can't. Oh, God, this is so hard. I … can't … give you any children. I want to. I love you so much. But I'm not a complete woman. I can't ever have kids, and I know you want children," she cried.

I instantly took her in my arms and held her tight as she sobbed. "But why?" I asked.

"I was born with something that keeps me from conceiving," Ginger said as she wiped the torrent of tears from her face.

"Whatever it is, I'm sure the doctors can find a cure," I said, hoping to encourage her.

She shook her head vigorously. "No. There's no cure for this. It's called Turner Syndrome."

"I've never heard of that," I told her.

"I was born with it. It's the result of a partial X chromosome. It's not as pronounced in me as other women who have it, but the effect is the same. I can't have children. I'm sorry. You deserve someone better. Someone … whole."

"That's nonsense," I said. "I fell in love with you! Not your ovaries or your chromosomes. I'm not complete without YOU, Ginger. I love you, and I want to spend the rest of my life with you!"

"All the doctors say my life expectancy could be shorter, and I may develop heart issues or other problems. I can't put all of that on you. It wouldn't be fair," she protested.

"Then we'll get through it together. You and me. As one," I countered.

"Do you really mean that?" Ginger asked as tears fell down her face.

"With all my heart," I told her earnestly.

"Oh Mark, I love you so much," Ginger exclaimed as she threw her arms around my neck. "Yes, I'll marry you. And I promise I'll be the best wife you could ever want."

I put the engagement ring on her finger and carried her to my bed, where we made love for the first time. I admit it wasn't always easy being married to Ginger and dealing with the issues that went with her condition. But we managed it.

Fortunately, her doctors and parents recognized the symptoms early on. They gave her various treatments to help her growth and physical development. Her mother, Rosemary, told me puberty was tough on Ginger, and they relied on hormone therapy to help get her through that.

As Ginger got older, she received extra help to get her through school. As I understood it, women with Turner Syndrome can experience learning disabilities despite their intelligence levels. Ginger was an exceptionally brilliant woman, capable of grasping even complex concepts, but sometimes had difficulty reading or understanding simple directions.

As for the physical side of our relationship, we relied on hormones, creams, and other therapies to make it work. I learned early on that a great deal of foreplay was needed to get her ready for penetration. I never complained, however, as I loved exploring her soft, supple body. And Ginger kept her promise the whole time we were together. She was the best wife and the best lover a man could want.

Yes, our marriage could be challenging, but I loved every minute. Ginger was worth it all to me, and I felt blessed to be part of her life. The deep, deep ache was still there, but the bleeding had stopped, and some kind of numb scab seemed to be forming in my spirit. With a quiet sigh and an unshed tear, I held her pillow close to my chest and drifted off to sleep.

I awoke when I felt a change in the bed. Looking to my left, I was stunned to see … Ginger. She was more beautiful than ever, and I nearly gasped out loud. And she was radiant, glowing in the dark room like a sky full of stars.

"Ginger? Is that really you?" I whispered hoarsely, afraid to move in case it chased this marvelous dream away.

"Shhh," she said, putting a finger to her lips. "Yes, sweetheart, it's really me. I don't have much time, but I was allowed to come and see you for a few minutes." Then she smiled, and my heart grew three sizes. "It is almost Christmas, after all, and the world fills with miracles."

"Oh, Ginger, I've missed you so much," I cried, taking her in my arms. It was HER! I felt her warmth against mine.

"And I've missed you, too. But this visit isn't about me. It's about you. It's really sweet that you come to see me so often, but you need to move on with your life."

"But you were my life," I protested.

"I know. And you were mine. But you need to find a new love." Ginger looked toward the guest room where Cinnamon slept, then back at me.

"She's never experienced life or love, at least not the way I have. You can make that happen for her. And I want you to."

"No," I countered. "I can't do that. It would be like cheating."

"Yes, you can. And you must. It wouldn't be cheating. You have fulfilled our vows before God, after all. Consider it my final present to you. Love her as you loved me. And in return, she will give you everything I never could. Promise me," she said as she leaned in to kiss me. It felt so good, and I wanted her to stay there forever. As her mouth covered mine, I tasted cinnamon.

"But," I began before she cut me off with a finger pressed firmly against my lips.

"Promise me," she stated firmly in that trademark way wives have.

"All right," I finally said. "I promise."

"Thank you, Mark. And know that I will always love you and I'll always be watching over you."

"If I hug you really hard, can I keep you from leaving?" I gasped desperately, no matter how silly I knew it sounded.

She shook her head, and I thought I saw tears, like diamond dust, powdering her cheeks, but she smiled angelically. "We will hold each other again at the proper time. When you are where I am now, you will know that love doesn't end but becomes eternal."

"I love you so much," I replied, but she disappeared before I could finish my sentence.

I sat in bed and looked where Ginger had been just a few moments earlier. The bedspread was disturbed, and the mattress rose slowly as if a weight had just been lifted. I ran my hand across the bed and thought I caught a fading hint of warmth. Had it been real? Or was I dreaming? I licked my lips and detected the cinnamon flavor I tasted when she kissed me. What the hell is going on here? The hammering of my heart slowed, and I took a deep breath.

I got out of bed and went to the bathroom, relieved myself, and washed my hands and face. Looking in the mirror, I heard Ginger's voice in my mind, whispering, "Promise me." Perhaps it was all in my head, I thought. Maybe I wanted to see her so badly that I did.

Chuckling awkwardly to myself, I recalled the line from the movie where the Scrooge character thought the ghostly image of Marlowe was the result of an underdone potato. Perhaps this dream was my mind telling me I needed to forge ahead with my life.

I thought about Cinnamon lying in the spare room, naked. She certainly was a delightful sight for sore eyes. And any thoughts or concerns I might have of betraying my wonderful wife had been clearly laid to rest. Assuming, of course, that it really was Ginger who visited me and not a fragment of a dream or my spirit craving comfort. Shaking my head, I went back to bed and fell deeply asleep.

Although I had washed my hands and face, I woke up tasting cinnamon on my lips the following morning. I still had many questions, but I felt better than I had since Ginger's untimely death. I did my morning business, dressed, and went downstairs to make coffee and breakfast.

"Good morning, Mark," Cinnamon said when I entered the kitchen. She was dressed in the same jeans and T-shirt she wore the previous day. She sat on one of the chairs and watched the snowflakes swirl outside the window with a rapt, childlike wonder. "I hope you slept well."

"I did, thank you. You?"

"I slept well also. Thank you for asking."

"Are you up for some breakfast?" I asked.

"That sounds wonderful," Cinnamon replied, beaming.

I rustled up some fried eggs, bacon, and toast, then poured each a cup of coffee. We sat at the table and ate our breakfast, then discussed the plan for the day.

"Before we go to see Ginger, I think we need to get you some more appropriate clothing," I said. "It's pretty cold out there, and I don't want you getting sick."

"Okay," Cinnamon said.

"Maybe after that, we can go see Ginger's mother, if that's okay," I suggested. Maybe Cinnamon could stay with Rosemary, I thought. She could use the company. However, the thought of returning to an empty house again wasn't all that thrilling.

"Sure," Cinnamon agreed, but something in her expression concerned me.

"Are you sure it's okay?" I asked.

"Yes, it's fine," she said.

I wasn't convinced but decided not to pursue it–for now.

"Let's go, then. Walmart is waiting for us," I joked.

"Who is Walmart?" Cinnamon asked, her brows furrowed.

"It's the name of a store," I told her. Surely she's heard of Walmart, I thought. This just keeps getting stranger by the minute.

The snow had let up some overnight but was still coming down. At least three inches of the stuff had to be on the road. I took my time and found a parking space near the store.

We spent at least an hour as Cinnamon tried on several pairs of jeans and warmer clothing, including a couple of nice sweaters. I insisted she also get a new coat, socks, and underwear. Much to my relief, one of the store workers helped her pick out a few things.

After putting out about three hundred dollars, we walked out with several bags of vital necessities. I also bought her a new toothbrush and offered to get her some makeup, but she declined. Honestly, she didn't need it, at least in my opinion.

I suggested she go into the ladies' room and put some of her new clothes on as it was getting colder outside, reminding her to take the tags off of the new clothes. She emerged from the room wearing a new sweater and jeans and replaced her old jacket with the fresh coat I had just bought.

"You look wonderful," I told her.

"Thank you," Cinnamon said with a wide smile.

From there, we drove to the cemetery and walked to Ginger's grave.

"Hello, Ginger," I said. "I brought a friend with me. Her name is Cinnamon," I added after making small talk.

Cinnamon knelt by the headstone and placed her bare hand on the ground by the marker. She closed her eyes briefly and smiled as she looked up at me.

"What?" I asked.

"She wants me to remind you to keep your promise to her," Cinnamon said, causing a chill to run up and down my spine like a shock wave. I looked around, almost expecting to see Rod Serling in a dark suit smoking a cigarette by a tree as he watched me. I heard footsteps and looked to see Amos making his way toward us.

"Hey, Mark. How're you doing?" Amos asked.

"Doing well, Amos. Thanks. How are you?" I asked as we shook hands.

"Hangin' in there. Who's your friend?"

"Amos, this is Cinnamon," I said. "Cinnamon, this is Amos."

"Good to meet you," Amos said as they shook hands. "That's a pretty name."

"Thank you. It's a pleasure to finally meet you face-to-face," she said. Amos and I were both shocked by her statement. What did she mean by that?

"Have we met before?" Amos asked, stunned.

"Not directly, no," Cinnamon replied.

"The only other Cinnamon I know of is buried right over there," Amos said, pointing toward other headstones. "C'mon. I'll show you."

We followed Amos to a small headstone marking the grave of a very young child. I read the marker: "Cinnamon Thompson. February - August 1988."

Cinnamon's face went dark as she looked at the marker and the tiny grave. I could tell it bothered her–a lot. But I couldn't figure out why.

What bothered me was the last name–Thompson. That was Ginger's maiden name. Granted, Thompson is a reasonably common surname, so it could have been a coincidence. On top of that, Ginger never mentioned a younger sister. Neither did her parents or her older sister, Sage. But the grave clearly upset Cinnamon for some reason.

"Can we leave now? Please?" Cinnamon asked tersely.

"Sure," I said. "Amos, we're gonna call it a day, I think. Thanks for showing this to us."

"You're welcome," he said. We shook hands and left the cemetery. Cinnamon was upset by what she saw there, but I couldn't understand why. I didn't say anything until we were going to Rosemary's house.

"What happened to you back there in the cemetery?" I asked gently. "Did you actually talk to Ginger?"

"A little," Cinnamon replied quietly. "I told her I met you, and you were kind to me. I mostly just listened, though."

"Oh?" I asked with a bit of skepticism. "And what did she tell you?"

"That she loves you with all her heart. And she sincerely hopes you keep your promise to her."

"Wait a minute," I said, astonished. "Did she tell you what I had promised?"

"No, but I already know," Cinnamon said so matter-of-factly that I almost doubted my ears.

"You do? How?"

"I can't explain it," she replied quietly. "Besides, I don't think you'd believe me."

"Maybe. Maybe not," I said. After an awkward silence, I ventured, "What happened at that child's grave?"

She hesitated. "I got very ... uncomfortable. It's hard to explain."

"I can imagine that—seeing your name on that small marker must've been a bit of a shock," I probed.

"Yes," Cinnamon said. "It was." I glanced at her face when there was no traffic around us. I was surprised at the wide-ranging emotions that seemingly chased each other across her open, innocent face.

By then, we were at Rosemary's house. It was the same house she had shared with her late husband, Frank, for years. The mortgage was paid after he died in a freak accident at a construction site three years ago, crushed to death when a pallet of bricks fell on him.

The investigators could never determine how the pallet, supposedly lashed down, was pushed off its platform ten stories above Frank. No one was on the platform when it happened, and no high wind or anything else could explain the incident.

As a result, Rosemary received a million-dollar insurance payout, and the company Frank worked for paid a large settlement to keep from getting sued. I pulled into the driveway and stopped the car.

Cinnamon looked at the house, and I saw that familiar gamut of emotions cross her face. I couldn't tell if she was afraid or angry.

"Are you okay?" I asked, concerned for her. I had slipped into a protector, provider role without even being aware of it.

"I'll be fine," she assured me quietly.

We got out of the car and walked to the front door. I rang the bell, and Ginger's older sister, Sage, answered a few moments later. We hugged, and I introduced her to Cinnamon.

"Cinnamon," Sage said quietly, staring intently at my companion's unsettled expression. "Interesting name. Where did you two meet?"

"I met her yesterday at the store. She needed some help, so I took her home and fed her. It's Christmas, after all, and I couldn't just leave her out there in the cold," I said, suddenly defensive.

"I see," Sage said slowly. "Please, come inside. We were just getting ready to have some lunch."

We stepped inside, removed our coats, and hung them on the coat rack next to the door.

"You know, I used to have a sister named Cinnamon a long time ago," Sage said cautiously.

"Sage! You know we don't talk about that," I heard Rose shout as she entered the front room.

"Rose, this is Cinnamon," I said. "Cinnamon, Rose." The older woman's face turned slightly pale as she looked at Cinnamon, and she was unable to move or speak for a few moments.

"It's a pleasure meeting you," Cinnamon finally said, breaking the ice. Her expression was now intent as if looking for something and not quite finding it … yet.

"Likewise," Rose said, looking away hurriedly. "Please have a seat." I was astonished to see her trembling slightly.

As the women sat on the couch, I couldn't help but notice the familial semblance between them. If I didn't know better, I would have laid odds that they were all related. After a few moments of awkward quiet, Rose stood and looked at me.

"Mark, could you please give me a hand with something?" she asked.

"Sure," I said. I followed Rose into her bedroom and watched her pull an old manilla envelope from her chest of drawers.

"Where did you meet this woman?" Rose asked quietly but firmly.

I explained the last day's events, from the grocery store to showing up on her doorstep. I left out Ginger's appearance, or my dream, from the night before. I watched the blood run out of Rose's face.

"What's going on, Rose?" I asked, now more concerned than ever.

"I had a third daughter in 1988," Rose said brusquely. "She died in

August of that year when she was six months old. Ginger had just turned three when it happened. The doctors all said it was Sudden Infant Death Syndrome. Her name was Cinnamon, and she had the most beautiful green eyes, like her father and her sisters.

"But there's more. My daughter had a birthmark on the inside of her left wrist. Depending on how you looked at it, it could either resemble a Christmas tree or an arrowhead. That … woman out there has the exact same birthmark," Rose said tensely.

"Is it possible that maybe they both have the same birthmark? That it's just a coincidence?" I asked, unnerved by the supernatural seeming to flood my mundane existence.

"I guess it's possible, but I've never heard of it," Rose conceded doubtfully.

"There's more to this, isn't there?" I asked. Rose looked at the floor, and I could tell she was embarrassed.

"Yes. Frank wasn't very happy when he learned I was pregnant for the third time. You remember how he could get after he'd been drinking."

"Yeah, I remember," I told her. Frank was usually a great guy to be around, except when he got drunk. Then, he would get angry and unpredictable, and anything could set him off. "Did Frank do something to your daughter?" I asked.

"Yes," I heard from the bedroom door. Turning, I saw Cinnamon and Sage standing there, looking at Rose. "He shook me when I cried. More than once. Very hard," Cinnamon said through gritted teeth, her face a mask of tragic pain.

"Is that true, Rose?" I asked, shocked at the revelation and even more shocked to hear it from Cinnamon.

"I caught him once and made it quite clear that if I caught him doing it again, it would be the last thing he ever did," Rose hissed.

"But that's not all, is it?" Cinnamon asked, her face now a mask of anger.

"No, it isn't," Rose admitted.

"What's going on, Mother?" Sage asked, her eyes darting between Cinnamon and Rose.

Rose said nothing momentarily, and then tears began pouring down her face.

"Rose?" I asked. She held her hand up, then slumped down on her bed.

"I … I cheated on your father. It only happened once, a very long time ago," she told Sage.

"Oh my God," Sage gasped. "What happened?"

"You and Ginger were very young. We got in over our heads. Your father started taking jobs out of town so we could pay our bills off. I agreed to stay home to watch over you girls while he worked.

"Jake Wilson, your father's boss and friend at the time, would come by occasionally to check on us and ensure everything was okay. One night, he suggested I get a babysitter, and he would take me out for dinner. It sounded like a good idea, so I agreed.

"You must remember that Jake was your father's friend, so I trusted him. He ended up getting me drunk, and then he took advantage of me. I never felt so ashamed in my life.

"A few days later, I learned I was pregnant with you, Cinnamon. Your father came home for the weekend, and I was going to tell him about you. But everything blew up. Jake couldn't wait to brag about what he had done.

"Your father got drunk and heard all about it. He beat Jake to a pulp, putting him in the hospital. Then he confronted me. I never saw him so angry in my life."

"And Jake never reported Frank to the police?" I asked.

"No. I went to Jake and told him that if he ever filed a complaint against Frank, I would file one against him for rape," Rose said. "So he never fingered Frank."

She paused for a moment to collect her thoughts. "Things got worse when your father learned I was pregnant. I tried to tell him I was pregnant before I … screwed up with Jake. But he didn't believe me. Things were pretty bad around here for a long time.

"I thought for sure your father would divorce me, but he was told that a divorce would break him financially, with alimony and child support. Plus, he would still have to cover any medical expenses involving my pregnancy. So he held off.

"After you were born, Cinnamon, I could tell right off that you were

Frank's child. Hell, anyone could. Everyone, even the doctor told him you were his." She stared at the wall sadly. "But he wouldn't listen. It was before easy DNA testing."

"And that's why he was so hard on me?" Cinnamon asked, her voice hollow.

"Yes," Rose admitted quietly, nodding in the affirmative. "And then, that day in August, I walked into your room and found you in your crib— dead." She made a small agonized noise deep in her chest.

"I thought my life was over. Maybe God was punishing me for what I had done with Jake."

Rose broke down, sobbing uncontrollably. After a few moments, she looked at Cinnamon.

"I'm so sorry. Please, God. Forgive me! Please," she cried as tears flowed freely down her face.

Cinnamon's face softened as she briefly looked up, then back at her mother. She walked to Rose's bed and sat next to the older woman.

"There's nothing left to forgive ... Mother," Cinnamon said softly as she touched Rose's shoulder.

Startled, Rose looked at Cinnamon briefly, then began sobbing again. This time, her sobs of anguish became tears of joy as Cinnamon held her tight. The room seemed to brighten slightly as the demons of guilt and shame that had tormented Rose for over thirty years fled the premises.

Rose put her hand to her mouth. "Oh, Sweetheart, how are you back? I, I ... I buried you! You were six months old! I thought my heart would stay shriveled forever."

Cinnamon flashed another angelic smile. Only this one was teary. "Sometimes the cosmic scales get ... rebalanced, you know. And things work a bit ... differently ... where I was. Two lives were tragically cut short, but one gets a second chance. Basically, one life was exchanged for another. I don't know how long I have, but I intend to live every minute of it."

"My baby," Rose cried as she held Cinnamon tight. "My beautiful baby girl is back." Sage joined them on the bed, and they held each other tight as they cried joyful tears of reunion.

I couldn't help myself. I felt tears escaping as I witnessed the emotional avalanche before me.

"Is this why you're here?" Rose asked after the girls broke their hug.

"It's one of the reasons," Cinnamon said before looking at me. She stood, walked to me, and put her hands on my face.

"When I was cold, sad, and lonely, you comforted me while others walked away," she said quietly. "I was hungry, and you fed me. I was thirsty, and you gave me drink. I was homeless, and you gave me shelter from the storm and a safe place to sleep."

"I only did what any decent person would've done," I said.

"No, Mark," Cinnamon said with a slight smile. "You went beyond what anyone would have done. What anyone actually did. You saw someone in need, and you took action. You did all of that without asking or expecting anything in return. Ginger was right. You are a rare find–a good, kind man with a soft heart.

"But your heart aches, and there is a gaping hole in your soul. I would like to heal your heart if you'll let me," she said.

"That could take a long time," I told her.

"I'm okay with that, Mark, if you are," Cinnamon replied. As I gazed into her face, I saw Ginger momentarily nodding in approval. I felt a blanket of love surround me, and for a moment, Cinnamon's face glowed with pure joy, unlike anything I had ever seen.

"I … love you," I whispered. "I don't know how, but I do."

Cinnamon smiled sweetly, then kissed me on the lips. "I love you too," she replied. "And I always will."

"Well, this has been quite a day," Sage said, snapping us out of our reverie. "If you don't mind, I'll wipe my face and return home. I have to get dinner ready for Mike and the kids. I hope we'll see you on Christmas morning."

"Of course," I said. "We'll be here, won't we?" I asked Cinnamon.

"I wouldn't miss it for anything," she replied. "Are you going to be okay?" she asked Rose.

"I'm going to be better than okay," my mother-in-law said as they hugged. "Thanks to you."

"Not just me, but I understand," Cinnamon said.

Rose wrapped me in her arms and held me tight.

"Thank you for looking after Cinnamon," she said. "And for bringing her over. Take care of my baby girl, please."

"I will Rose," I promised, bringing a smile to her face. Perhaps it was my imagination, but she looked happier than I had ever seen her. And she seemed a few years younger than when we first arrived.

"We'll see you two on Christmas?" Rose asked. Christmas Day was on Monday this year.

"I promise we'll be here Monday morning," I said. We left Rose's house and headed for home. Cinnamon looked at me funny before saying anything.

"I can tell you have questions," she said quietly.

"Yes, I do. A couple of them at least. First off, do you know what happened to your father?" I asked Cinnamon as I drove.

"Yes," she said quietly. I had a feeling it was a touchy subject for her. "After what happened to me, he changed. He had a tendency to make bargains with creatures who know nothing of mercy or forbearance."

"You mean, like the mob?" I asked.

"Hardly. These things make the mob look like children. He finally owed much more than he could afford to pay with money. So they took ... him. Or to be more precise, his soul," Cinnamon said sadly.

"I'm sorry to hear that," I said. Part of me was horrified at the thought, and another part of me was okay with that fate for someone who could hurt their own innocent child.

"It was his choice to make," Cinnamon said with an undertone of deep pain. "He chose ... poorly."

I let that hang in the air briefly before asking what I wanted to know.

"When we first met, I had the impression you didn't remember very much," I said. "What happened?"

"You're right. I didn't remember very much. It didn't come to me until I was forced to face my own fate. It all came back to me when I saw my grave," she said quietly with more than a hint of sadness.

"That had to have been quite a shock," I said.

"It was. More than you can know. Profound," Cinnamon agreed. "But at that moment, I knew exactly why I was back, and what I needed to do."

"Thank you for your honesty," I told her.

"You're welcome. I will always be honest with you, Mark. I know what dishonesty does to a relationship and I know how much you value the truth," she said.

I turned onto my street and realized for the first time this season that my house was the only one without any decorations. I had boxes of lights I always put up every Christmas, but with Ginger's passing, they meant nothing to me. I hadn't even put up the tree this year.

Sitting next to brilliantly lit houses, my dark place looked sad and lonely. I originally wasn't planning to do anything, but I changed my mind.

"What do you say we put some decorations up tomorrow?" I asked.

"Decorations?" Cinnamon asked.

"Yeah. Some lights. Maybe a Christmas tree," I said.

She looked at the other houses before her eyes settled on my place, then nodded. "Sure. Why not? Christmas is supposed to be a time of joy, is it not?"

"Yes, it most definitely is," I replied. We pulled into the garage and went inside. I carried the bags of Cinnamon's clothing upstairs and was about to put them in the spare room when she called me.

"Would it be all right if I stayed in your room? With you?" she asked.

This was moving at a dizzying speed, but I was all right. "Are you sure?" I responded.

"Yes, I am sure," Cinnamon said.

"Okay," I told her. "I'll put your things in … our room," I added. It felt strange saying that to Cinnamon since only one woman had ever been in that room since we bought the place.

"Thank you," Cinnamon replied sweetly before entering the hall bathroom.

We finished the meatloaf that night and watched some television before going upstairs. I felt a little nervous undressing in front of Cinnamon until I saw that she was utterly and unabashedly naked.

I couldn't help but notice that her pubic hair was gone. She was the most stunningly beautiful woman I had ever seen, and I felt myself start to respond.

"Do you approve?" Cinnamon asked, spreading her feet shoulder-width. "Ginger said you liked it this way."

"I most certainly do approve," I said. Ginger always kept herself shaved and smooth, knowing how much I liked to taste her womanhood.

"Aren't you a little overdressed? Or do you plan to sleep in your clothes?" Cinnamon asked coyly.

I quickly shed my clothes and climbed into the bed as naked as her. By now, I was completely erect.

"I've never done this before, but Ginger told me all about it," Cinnamon murmured huskily as she wrapped her small hands around my erect cock. I thought I would explode from her touch. We kissed deeply, and then I started working my way down her body.

"Oh my," she moaned as I kissed and savored her soft skin. Her panting increased as I kissed my way along her toned legs until I reached her smooth slit.

"That's it. Taste her," I heard Ginger's voice say in my mind.

My mind was completely overloaded. My deceased wife was mentally cheering me on as I made love to her re-born sister. Was I making love to Cinnamon, Ginger, or both? My body didn't care; my heart was whole again, and one never questions a miracle.

"Did Ginger tell you about this?" I asked before licking her lower lips, which had opened like a spring flower. I just got my first taste of Cinnamon, which was delightful!

"She ... mentioned ... something ... Oh! Keep doing that! I love it!" Cinnamon exclaimed as I found her clit. Her pants increased and grew louder as I licked and sucked on her soaking wet sensitive parts.

"Oh yes. Don't stop," Ginger's quivering voice encouraged me inside my head. It almost sounded as if her spirit was close to orgasm.

"It's happening! Keep going! Ahhhh," Cinnamon moaned as I tongued her sweet pussy. Her first orgasm hit, and I found myself soaked in her juices, which I didn't mind at all.

I laid on my back, and Cinnamon smothered my face with kisses as she climbed on top of me, mashing her wet pussy into my extremely hard cock.

"I. Love. You!" she exclaimed as she kissed me with closed eyes.

"I love you too," I said. And it was the truth. I loved this girl as much as I loved anyone, even Ginger. I knew this was happening fast, like shooting over the edge of a waterfall in a canoe, but I couldn't help myself. Somehow, I didn't think Ginger would mind.

Cinnamon opened her eyes and gave me the sultriest look I had ever seen on a woman. Was 'heavenly lust' an oxymoron? I was finding out. It was almost scary. "I am going to fuck your brains out and make you mine," she declared as she grabbed my rock-hard cock.

"Oh, yes," Ginger's voice whispered in my head. "Let her fuck your brains out, baby. I wanna see this."

"Such language," I jokingly thought. Ginger could be explicit at times, but she was never like this. And I never suspected she would want to watch me with her younger sister. Some vague part of my whirling mind wondered if Ginger was cheering Cinnamon on, too.

I wondered what I had just signed on to. Still, I had to admit I thoroughly enjoyed what Cinnamon did to me physically and emotionally. I smiled as I looked into her lust-driven face.

"Go for it, girl," I replied. "I'm all yours."

"You got that right, lover," Cinnamon said as she impaled herself on my cock.

I gasped out loud when I felt her warm, velvety depths envelop my cock. There was some resistance, but not much. Cinnamon was technically a virgin, after all. She rode me like a mad woman, and it was all I could do to keep up from exploding immediately.

Cinnamon threw the bedspread aside and sat up so I could see her riding me. Watching my cock disappear inside her over and over got me even more excited, and I could feel her vaginal muscles repeatedly grip and release my manhood, milking me to orgasm. I felt the urge coming and warned her. She was either a natural lover or halfway possessed by Ginger. Either way, my body was on fire.

"I'm getting ready …"

"Yes … Do it," Cinnamon moaned. "Cum inside me. Please."

I saw stars when I exploded inside her. I felt like it would never end. Her orgasm hit at the same time, and we frantically grabbed each other as we slowly returned to reality.

"That was … fantastic," I gasped in between breaths.

"Yes, it was," Cinnamon agreed impishly. "Did I do it right?"

I chuckled at that, then held her face and kissed her.

"Oh yes, you were wonderful," I told her, causing her to smile.

"I wanted it to be good for you."

"It was. The absolute best," I reassured her. "And I wanted it to be good for you."

"I'm glad and it was," Cinnamon whispered before laying her head on my chest. She felt so light and warm. I wrapped my arms around her and held her close to me. She belonged right where she was, and I didn't want her to move.

"I really do love you," Cinnamon said quietly.

"And I really love you," I replied. I felt her snuggle closer to me if such a thing was possible. We stayed like that for some time, basking in each other's warmth. Eventually, Cinnamon rolled off of me, and we spooned tightly until we fell asleep.

I found myself walking cautiously through a thick white blanket of fog. Cautiously, because the fog was so thick, I wasn't sure if whatever I was walking on would suddenly disappear. I knew this was a dream but wasn't taking any chances. I stepped through a particularly thick cloud and found myself in a small open space.

On the other side of the void was another figure dressed in what looked like a soft, white hooded robe. The fog swirled around us but came no closer. The figure reached up, pulled the hood back, looked at me, and smiled–it was Ginger, just as beautiful as she was the day we married. No, more beautiful; she was flawless and speckled with stardust.

"I see you survived your first encounter with my sister," she said with an indulgent smile.

"Yes," I agreed. "I never knew you were such a voyeur at heart. Were you there the whole time?"

"I was," Ginger replied without the slightest trace of embarrassment. "And to be honest, I never knew that I would enjoy seeing you with another woman. If I were still alive, I probably would have rubbed myself silly—then ripped your balls off."

"No doubt," I told her, my guts twisting. I wanted to leap the few feet between us and hug her, but somehow, I knew that was not … permitted.

"But now?"

"It's different now. We kept our vows to each other, forsaking all others, until the very end. You were released from those vows when I passed."

"Still, there's a part of me that felt like I was cheating," I admitted, reaching deep down and admitting to the dark little cloud that was slinking around in the back of my mind.

"No, my love. You're incapable of that. I told you to love her as you loved me, and you did. I was in her mind, too. You did a wonderful job … I was experiencing as well as coaching. She is now bound to you, body and soul. Promise me you'll make her as happy a woman as you made me," Ginger suddenly pleaded quite earnestly. "She is my sister, and I love her, too."

"I will," I promised. "Are you going to be there every time we … you know …"

Ginger chuckled before answering. "Maybe not every time. For a while perhaps. And I might pop in now and again when permitted. I've given Cinnamon a few more tips. If you don't mind, that is."

"I can handle that," I said. "Did you know about your parents?"

"I suspected, but I didn't know the whole story until I came here," Ginger said. "Of course, I knew I had a younger sister, but I was too young to remember her, and no one spoke of her while I was growing up."

"Did you know why she was sent back?" I asked.

"I knew. We talked about it before she left. There were some things she had to face first."

"I understand, I think. What about your father? Is he … with you?"

"No," Ginger replied sadly. I knew what she meant, and the implications made my skin crawl. If there is a Heaven, there must be … the thought trailed off.

"I'm sorry to hear that. I love you, Ginger," I said.

"I know," she said. "I love you too. And I always will."

"I wish," I began, but Ginger interrupted me. I wanted to say that I wish she could come back.

"That can never happen, darling. My life was exchanged for hers. It's all part of the plan. Do you love her?"

"Yes," I said after a few silent moments. "She's like you in so many ways but completely different if that makes any sense."

"It does. Trust me, that's good," Ginger replied with another angelic smile. "Because I know she loves you as well. I will … try to guide her as much as possible when I can, while I can. She hasn't experienced life like we have, so many things will be new to her. I know you will be patient with her and look after her well.

"There is one thing you should know about my sister, though."

"What's that?" I asked.

"She has a bit of an exhibitionist streak in her," Ginger said. "It's normally not an issue here …"

"So, she's an exhibitionist, and you've become a voyeur. This should prove interesting," I said.

"At least you can never say your life is dull or boring," Ginger joked.

I laughed, then looked at her intensely before speaking. "Is … this … going to be a regular thing?" I asked, looking around at the dense fog.

"The idea is to help you move forward with your life. You can't do that if we keep … this … up, now, can you?" she sighed.

"I suppose not," I admitted sadly.

She looked like she wanted to dart forward and claim a hug but was also restrained. "I can't feel anything physical anymore. But I can remember all of my memories and emotions perfectly. And Cinnamon is my sister; we are very close blood kin, so I can 'pick up' what she feels if I am close enough. That was a good sensation, which I will cherish forever." She looked at me with such love that I ached. "So move forward. Daily visits are no longer necessary. But …"

"Yes?"

"I would deeply appreciate three visits a year; red roses on our anniversary, yellow roses on my birthday, and white roses on the anniversary of my passing. And when the time is right, bring the kids and tell wonderful stories about me." The ghost of a tear of molten silver sparkled down the perfect curve of her cheek.

"Four," I croaked. "Red roses at Christmas. In memory of the wonderful, selfless gift you have given me, us, on your favorite holiday."

I could see how much and how deeply my words touched her.

"Christmas is when everyone receives the most precious, generous gift of all time. It's a time when miracles can, and do, happen," she said in a dreamy, teary voice that echoed in the fog around us.

"I won't visit every day, but I will remember you every day, and your initials are carved on my heart." My love was so keen it was plain. She smiled indulgently.

"And I forgive you for missing that one day. I could see your pain."

"Thank you. I felt guilty. And it stopped me from dulling my pain with alcohol."

"We'll see each other again soon enough, in comparison to eternity. We may talk now and then. You'll probably feel my presence from time to time. I've been given a lot of leeway under the circumstances, but there are limits," Ginger said.

"I understand," I told her. Not really, but it seemed right.

"I must go now," Ginger said as two gigantic beings made of pure light and with the shapes of magnificent wings folded against their backs stepped into the open space on either side of her. "I love you, Mark. And I always will. Farewell, my love."

"Farewell. I love you!" I cried as the three of them turned and stepped into the fog bank, vanishing. The fog closed in on me, and I woke up in bed to see Cinnamon staring at me.

"You saw her, didn't you?" she asked breathlessly.

"Yes," I said. I shivered, but it was a warm shiver. "We spoke for a few minutes."

"Are you okay?" Cinnamon asked, concerned and tracing the side of my face with her fingertips.

"I am now," I told her. "Very. And very, very thankful."

"Good. Let's get some sleep, okay?"

"Sure," I said.

"Sweet dreams, my love," Cinnamon said, punctuating her statement with a kiss.

"Sweet dreams to you as well," I told her, kissing her back before closing my eyes.

The next thing I knew, it was Sunday morning–Christmas Eve. Cinnamon was already out of bed, so I went to the bathroom to do my morning routine. After dressing, I went downstairs to start breakfast and heard noises in the kitchen.

"Good morning," a smiling Cinnamon said when I entered the kitchen.

"Good morning. What are you doing?"

"I was hoping to surprise you with breakfast, but I realized I don't know how to cook anything," Cinnamon replied with a sheepish smile.

"That's okay," I said. "Why don't you let me show you?"

"That would be nice. Thank you."

I showed her where everything was in the kitchen, started the coffee, and grabbed a skillet and some eggs and bacon from the fridge. Cinnamon watched as I cooked the food, asking questions along the way. I grabbed some slices of bread and popped them into the toaster. A few minutes later, we walked to the table with our food.

"Wow. I didn't know there was so much to do," Cinnamon said as we sat down. "I don't know if I'll ever get all of that right."

"That's okay," I said. "We'll manage." We ate our breakfast in silence, and then it hit me–I hadn't gotten Cinnamon anything for Christmas. I already had gifts wrapped for Rose, Sage and her family, and felt terrible that I hadn't bought anything for Cinnamon. I knew the local Walmart would be open, and I also planned to put up decorations today.

"If you don't mind, I need to run to the store real quick before we put the decorations up. Would you be okay here by yourself for a little bit?" I asked.

"Yeah, I think so. Can I watch your television while you're gone?" Cinnamon asked.

"Of course," I said. "As far as I'm concerned, this is your house as well, so you don't need to ask permission."

"Thank you," she said in response, beaming.

After rinsing the dishes, I headed to Walmart while considering what to get for Cinnamon. There were so many things she needed, and I wanted to get her something she could use and something she would like. I decided to get her a new phone and a charm bracelet.

It didn't take me very long to find what I wanted. The card was a bit of a challenge since most of them were already gone, but I found one that was nice–a little romantic and a bit humorous. I hoped she would like it and moved on to get the rest of my purchases.

I bought the latest Android smartphone with a plan sufficient for her, a lovely bracelet, a Christmas tree charm to mark the holiday, and an angel charm for obvious reasons. After standing in line for a half hour, the gifts were wrapped in colorful paper.

Feeling better, I carried my purchases to the car and drove home. After I pulled into the garage, I eyed the boxes of Christmas decorations. I signed the card and then put the gifts in the car's trunk, where I knew they would be safe until the following day.

Cinnamon was watching some talking head program when I walked into the house. She set the remote down and looked at me as I entered the living room.

"Did you get what you needed?" she asked.

"Yeah, I did. What are you watching?"

"I don't know. A bunch of people talking about stuff."

"It's Sunday, so that's pretty much all that's on right now," I told her. "Do you wanna help me decorate the place?"

"Yes, that would be fun," Cinnamon exclaimed as her face lit up.

"Grab your coat, and let's get to it," I said.

We spent much of the day putting lights and decorations on the house and trimming the artificial tree that had sat in its box in the garage since last Christmas. Ginger usually let me handle this alone, but Cinnamon was by my side the whole time, suggesting ways to decorate the place.

Cinnamon didn't understand the mechanics behind putting the decorations up, but she certainly had an eye for design. Her suggestions were just what the doctor ordered, and the place soon looked better than it had in Christmases gone by.

"Hey, neighbor," I heard from behind me as we finished with the outdoor lights and decorations. I turned to see Alan Williams walking toward us from his house.

"Hey, Alan. How's everything?" I asked.

"Doing good. I was beginning to wonder if you were gonna do anything this year. The place looks wonderful!"

"Thanks," I said. "You can chalk that up to Cinnamon."

"Cinnamon?" Alan asked, confused.

"Yeah. Alan, meet Cinnamon. Cinnamon, this is my neighbor, Alan Williams," I said.

"It's a pleasure meeting you, Cinnamon," Alan said. "You look a lot like Mark's wife."

"I'm her sister," Cinnamon told him.

"Oh! Are you staying here with Mark?" Alan asked.

"As a matter of fact, she is," I said, realizing our relationship might lead to some awkwardness with the neighbors.

"Welcome to the neighborhood, Cinnamon," Alan said. "Maybe you guys can come over for some egg nog or something this week. Pepper made up a huge batch of it."

"Pepper?" Cinnamon asked.

"Yeah. That's my wife," Alan proudly declared. "She always makes enough for the whole neighborhood."

"We may just take you up on that, Alan," I said. "Thanks!"

"My pleasure. By the way, it's good to see you back in the land of the living. Quite a few of us were getting a little worried about you. We all figured you were still mourning, so we didn't want to intrude. We were gonna give you until Christmas before we did an intervention," Alan said.

"Well, I'm doing much better now. Thanks," I said.

"You're welcome. You two have a merry Christmas, you hear?" Alan asked.

"You do the same," I said as we shook hands. We watched him walk back to his house before going inside.

"I don't know about you, but I'm hungry," I said. We had both worked hard that day, putting up the lights and decorations and trimming the tree. We only broke once for a light lunch at noon.

"I'm hungry as well, but I really don't feel like eating a television dinner," Cinnamon said, prompting laughter from me. "What's so funny?" she asked.

"Television dinner?" I asked. "You mean, TV dinner, right?"

"I thought that's what TV meant," Cinnamon said.

"It is," I told her. "How about some pizza?"

"Okay," Cinnamon replied.

I called three places before I found one that was still open and delivered, so I ordered a large combination pizza. When the driver arrived half an hour later, I gave him an extra-large tip–it was Christmas Eve.

After watching me for a moment, Cinnamon took a bite of her pizza, and her face lit up.

"This is good," she said, her mouth full of food.

"Yes, it is," I agreed. We ate our pizza and then settled in front of the television.

"What did you talk about with Ginger?" Cinnamon asked, genuinely curious.

I marveled at how there seemed to be no jealousy whatsoever between the sisters who now, kind of, shared a husband. The fact that Ginger was giving pretty explicit 'pointers' to Cinnamon about our intimate love life was mind-boggling. Still, it proved to me how much she loved us both. That and picking up echoes of orgasms. I smiled at the thought of still making love to her soul in a second-hand kind of way.

"How much we miss each other. How much she loves both of us. How happy she is that we are together." Cinnamon beamed. If anyone could capture that smile on a Christmas ornament, they'd make a billion dollars. "And she was tutoring you in the art of love and would hang out with us for as long as possible." If anything, the smile got brighter. I explained about moving forward, not visiting the cemetery so often, and the four days to bring roses.

"Oh, shoot!" I exclaimed.

"What?"

"Tomorrow's Christmas! I promised we'd bring red roses on Christmas!" I dove for my phone and looked up every flower store in the city. Twenty minutes of frantic phone calls found the one store still open. They would deliver a dozen red roses to our porch on Christmas morning for a not-quite-outrageous charge to my credit card. I breathed a sigh of relief.

"Listen, I don't know about you, but I could use a shower after all that work we did today. Care to join me?"

"You mean, get naked with you?" Cinnamon asked eagerly.

"That's the general idea," I said, chuckling at her response.

"Of course. I love to be naked with you," Cinnamon squealed.

We raced up the stairs, flinging our clothes off as we went. I started the shower and stepped in when the temperature was right, then held out a hand for Cinnamon as I ogled her nude form.

"You really like looking at me naked, don't you?" she asked as she stood before me.

"I love looking at you naked," I said. "You're perfect in every way."

We spent some time washing each other's bodies, then rinsed off. Cinnamon took my hardening cock in her hands and stroked it a few times, a wicked grin on her face.

"Ginger showed me something last night," she said. "She promised me that you would absolutely love it."

"Oh? What's that?" I asked.

"This," Cinnamon whispered as she knelt before me. She kissed the length of my cock, then opened her mouth and took my manhood inside, running her tongue along the underside of my member.

"Oh my God," I gasped, grabbing the sides of the shower as Cinnamon proceeded to give me the best blowjob I could ever remember.

"Does that feel good?" I heard Ginger ask in my mind.

"You know it does," I thought, surprised that I could have any coherent thought.

"Good. I taught her everything I could. I've got ten years of experience, after all. It'd be a shame to let that go to waste. Do you like the way she sucks your cock, baby?" she cooed.

"You know I do," I responded in my mind.

"Look. She's taking all of you inside her mouth. I always had a hard time with that. She wants to swallow your cum."

I looked down and saw that Cinnamon had taken my entire erect cock into her mouth with no trouble whatsoever. If I didn't know any better, I would say she had had a lot of practice.

"You're enjoying this, aren't you, sweetheart?" Ginger's voice asked in my mind. "I know I am. Look. She's fingering herself while she sucks you off. She's so hot, isn't she?"

I looked down and saw Cinnamon rubbing herself furiously with her left hand while bobbing her head on my cock.

"Yes, so … hot," I gasped, fireworks filling my mind and fire filling my belly as I built toward …

"You're about ready to cum, aren't you, baby?" Ginger teased in my head. "Do it. Cum in her mouth. She wants it so bad. And I know you want it, too."

"Ahhh," I gasped as I erupted inside Cinnamon's mouth. She greedily took as much as she could, but some escaped from around her lips. Cinnamon opened her mouth, looked up at me, licked her lips, and gulped as she swallowed. She opened her mouth to show me it was all gone.

"I taught her to do that," Ginger's voice echoed in my head. "Isn't she so sexy?"

"Yes. So sexy," I answered in my mind.

"Well? Did you enjoy that?" Cinnamon asked after wiping her face.

"You have no idea how much I enjoyed that," I told her as I caught my breath. "Now it's my turn to return the favor."

"Your turn?" Cinnamon asked.

"Yes," I replied, carefully kneeling before the beautiful creature. I kissed her softly before burying my head between her legs.

Cinnamon pulled my head into her as I took in her intoxicating taste and aroma. I was like a man who hadn't eaten a meal in days as I lapped and kissed her most intimate parts. Soon, her orgasm swept over her, and my face was covered with her juices.

I kissed my way back up her body, paying particular attention to her small breasts and hard, erect nipples. She melted into my arms, and we kissed intensely as we looked deep into each other's eyes.

"Let's go to bed," she finally whispered.

"Let's dry off first," I suggested.

"Okay," Cinnamon replied.

I helped her out of the shower, then dried off as fast as I could as she did the same. I hung our towels over the shower bar, and we climbed into the bed, hugging each other as we snuggled under the bedspread.

"Make love to me," Cinnamon pleaded as she took me in her arms.

Who was I to argue? I kissed her deeply, then made passionate love to her until we both screamed from our orgasms. After we settled down, I realized something was missing–Ginger's encouragement. I realized that, at some point, I would have to get used to not hearing her voice in my head. No time like the present to make that happen, I thought.

Cinnamon didn't say anything when we kissed each other goodnight, but I'm sure she also felt Ginger's absence. I slept like a baby that night, waking up at 7:30 the following day to the smell of bacon and coffee.

I did my business, dressed, and went downstairs to find Cinnamon in the kitchen. Surprisingly, she had made eggs, bacon, and coffee without destroying the kitchen.

"Good morning," she chirped, bringing a plate of eggs and bacon to the table.

"Good morning to you," I said. "Merry Christmas."

"Merry Christmas," she replied, giving me a kiss. "I hope you like breakfast."

"If it tastes as good as it smells, I'm sure I will," I said.

Cinnamon brought her plate and another plate with toast to the table and then sat down.

"You went all out," I complimented her. "Delicious," I said after taking a bite of my eggs. "Thank you."

"You're welcome," she said.

"You picked that up pretty quick," I added.

"I'm a quick learner," Cinnamon quipped.

"Apparently so!"

We finished our breakfast and then gathered our things to take to Rose's house, where I knew Sage, Mike, and the kids would be waiting for us. I looked in the front room and saw an arrangement of red roses in a simple vase.

"They came by about a half-hour before you got up," Cinnamon said. "Are we going to stop by the cemetery first?"

"Yes, I think that would be best," I said. "Are you okay with that?"

"Sure," Cinnamon replied. We packed everything up and locked the house before leaving for the cemetery.

When we arrived, we walked to Ginger's grave and placed the roses next to her headstone. Cinnamon knelt next to me and held my arm for emotional support.

"Merry Christmas, Ginger," I said. "I ... we ... both miss you."

"And I miss you," I heard Ginger's voice. "But there's something else you need to see."

"What?" I asked.

"Cinnamon knows," Ginger said.

I looked at Cinnamon and saw her face turn toward where we saw her marker. She stood and took my hand.

"Come," Cinnamon said.

I followed her to the tiny marker and, to my surprise, saw that Cinnamon's name was no longer on it. Instead, it read, "Poppy Henson. Feb–August 1988." Next to it was a larger marker engraved, "William and Anise Henson. 1965–1988." This was obviously a family plot.

"What the heck?" I asked. "Who are these people? How did this happen?"

"It means I've been given a complete second chance; a whole new life," Cinnamon said quietly.

"I don't understand," I replied.

"We don't have to understand. It's Christmas. A time for miracles. Wouldn't you agree?" Cinnamon rhetorically asked, looking at me inquisitively.

"Yeah. I suppose so," I said quietly, feeling a chill chasing itself up and down my spine.

"Come, my love. It's time to go," Cinnamon said, offering her hand. I took it, then walked with her to the car.

I looked toward Ginger's grave and saw a hooded figure standing alone in a small cloud of mist that glowed in the weak winter sunlight. I knew inside it was Ginger and waved. She waved back before disappearing into the mist.

Yes, I thought as I held my new love's hand tight. Christmas is a time of love, joy, and miracles.

Saddletramp1956

The Key in the Wood
by Clea Salar and Tallis Salar
Twitter. @CleaSalar
www.salarstories.com

Soft, light flurries of snow drifted down as Oscar stomped through the ever-darkening forest, axe in hand. The power at the house was out (again). Utilities said it would be fixed by tomorrow—an old tree had fallen and taken out the line, no one's fault, but they weren't fixing it fast enough. Grumbling slightly, Oscar wished he had a cherry picker; he'd fix the line himself. Or rather that's what he was joking to himself, trying to keep his spirits up. Regardless of who could fix it faster, he was low on firewood, and with snow coming, he didn't want to risk running out in the middle of the night. If the house got too cold, the pipes would freeze, and he didn't need to lose both electricity and water.

Thankfully, the woods behind his house were not regularly cleared, so there was a fair bit of deadfall. The large canvas bag he carried—specifically designed to carry split logs for the fireplace—was already half full. He could see another bit of split tree up ahead. He set down the bag, sized up the log, and flexed his fingers to get blood pumping into them, then took a hold of the axe once more and started to go to work on the split. Oscar had always been a big guy, but he'd been nearly living out of the gym the last few months, and his additional bulk was certainly coming in handy now. There was something very satisfying about the feel of the axe as it came down, the reverb up his arms as the head met the wood. It was different from lifting weights. While his job as a lineman was also plenty physical, it was different from that, too. Chopping wood had a rhythm to it, and Oscar relaxed into the motions. In no time at all, his canvas was full.

Perhaps living out here wouldn't be so bad, Oscar thought as he tucked the last of the wood into the canvas and cinched it tight. As he stacked the last of the split log, he noticed something. A glint in the mixed dirt and snow beneath the wood. Pausing, he kneeled and fumbled around with whatever was on the ground. His heavy gloves mostly just moved the dirt and snow around. Eventually he peeled the glove off and picked up … a key. Delicately wrought, golden and untarnished. It didn't look beaten up enough to have been sitting out here for long, but this was Black Forest. No one would have been on his land passing through. His neighbors were mostly retirees who had moved here in the 70s. It wasn't a small key either; it didn't look like a charm that had come off the necklace of a passerby (and again, who would be passing by up here?). It looked like it fit a door.

Oscar took a look around to see if there was anyone nearby. Black Forest was dark even during the day, but at night in the snow, it was nearly impossible to see anything past his immediate area.

"Hello," he called out, "anyone drop something? Bit cold out to be walking around." Silence. Pocketing the key, he pulled his glove back on and hefted the canvas bag up onto his shoulder.

The walk back to the house was uneventful, and as lonely as the walk out had been. The one-bedroom A-frame sat quiet and dark, the only light a flickering candle in the main room that shone softly through the large window. Grandpa had left the house in Black Forest to Oscar with a note about how he would "know how to take care of it." Oscar's sister had inherited their grandmother's china and a couple pieces of jewelry, and while she rolled her eyes at the disparity, it hadn't impacted their relationship. It was just as well: Maggie was married with five kids; all she could have done with the house was clean it up and sell it. And as Oscar was learning, that would have probably taken more money than he or his sister had ready.

Despite being old and dated (and immediately needing a new roof), it was a nice house. Not having to pay rent for his former expensive studio apartment was already making a difference, despite his extended commute. And the A-frame was at least three times as big. All in all, it wasn't so bad.

Stepping inside, Oscar stomped off the snow and carefully removed his coat and boots, not wanting to scatter snow into the house. The main floor consisted of the living room, kitchen, and bathroom. His bed was in the loft. The garden level was the remains of his grandfather's workshop, the mudroom, and a small sauna (which worked) next to a small hot tub (which did not).

It didn't take long to get a good fire going. The fireplace was in the dead center of the main room, glassed in on all sides and providing a nice, central warmth. As Oscar straightened up to enjoy his hard work, the phone he'd left on the counter pinged. Brushing off his hands, he picked up the phone.

"Y'ello, Oscar here."

"Ozzy!" An impatient, feminine voice greeted him. "I have been texting you for an hour! I've been sitting here debating driving out tonight instead of tomorrow morning, afraid you were dead out in the wilderness!"

"Hey, Mimsy," he said with a chuckle. "I'm alive. Sorry, I just got in. Power went out, and I had to get firewood, so I don't know if you want to head out tonight."

"I hate it when you call me that," Mimsy—or more accurately, Naomi—muttered. Oscar knew that she didn't really hate it, but it had been her childhood nickname. "Do you need me to bring candles or batteries or flashlights? I can be there tonight with supplies if you need anything!"

"Sounds like you're looking for excuses," he commented. "I'm good here, got the fire going, will probably make sure the sauna is still functioning. But if you want to brave the back roads and drive up tonight, I can't tell you no."

Looking out the window, he sighed and shook his head. "Honestly, I hate to say it, but it might not be a bad idea. It's snowing light right now, but who knows if it'll get worse. Not a lot of road plowing out here. You have snow tires, right?"

"Oz, it's a rental, I have no idea if it has snow tires. It'll be fine. I looked up your address; you still have an actual road outside your driveway." Naomi's voice was getting lighter as she talked, the concern giving way to excitement. "I can't believe I'm finally going to get to see you! It's been what, two years?"

"Yeah, sounds about right. Ever since you abandoned me for Germany," he said jokingly. Naomi was the younger sister of Oscar's best friend, Ezra. They'd known each other since high school and sometime after that became close friends. Oscar had seen Ezra far more recently.

"The company offered me so much money, it was impossible for me to say no." Naomi sounded a little weary, like she'd had to explain this many times. "But they also paid to move me back to Denver. See you in a couple hours. Maybe less, depending on the highway."

"All right, drive safe. Call me if you get stuck or something. I've got the duty truck, and I'd get there a lot faster than a tow service," he said. "See you in a few, Nomi."

"See you soon, Ozzy."

Well, if Naomi was going to be there this evening, Oscar maybe needed to work on setting up somewhere for her to sleep. The house didn't have a guest room, though there was a storage room downstairs that Oscar intended to turn into one. Eventually. For tonight, Naomi was on the couch. Or … maybe upstairs in the bed with him. That might be smarter, if the power didn't kick back on before morning. They'd stay warmer. He could wear a t-shirt and boxers for once.

Oscar had fancied Naomi when they were younger, but she'd always been so solidly in the "forbidden" camp, what with her older brother being his best friend and all. Time went on, they had their own relationships, she moved to Germany, and he didn't even think about it anymore. Or that's what he'd told himself. The idea of sharing a bed with her was more exciting than it should have been. They were in their 30s now, both single, and she'd just moved back. Maybe it was a subject worth revisiting. Or not. Regardless, he was glad he wouldn't be spending Christmas alone.

A little after 6 PM, headlights coming down the dark driveway caught Oscar's attention. It looked like Naomi had gotten an SUV from the rental company. Oscar had already put his boots back on and had been cleaning up the workshop a little. She pulled up in front of the house and climbed out. Her hair was longer. That was the first thing Oscar noticed, the cape of dark hair that fell down her back, illuminated briefly by the interior lights of the car. She must not have cut it the whole time she was in Germany.

Donning his jacket, he stepped outside and smiled at Naomi. "Hey there, Nomi," he said, walking toward the car. Good chance she had some luggage, and he was there to help.

"Ozzy!" Naomi excitedly turned around, backlit by the hatch of the car which did, in fact, appear to be full of stuff—and practically launched herself at him. His arms were very quickly full of excited friend. Holding her was surprisingly easy, and he gave her a squeeze.

"It's so good to see you," she said, giving him a squeeze back. She then looked up at him. "You're, uh, you're more ... solid than you used to be."

"Yeah, been working out a lot recently," he grinned, seeing no reason to set her down immediately. "Good seeing you too."

"And you're just holding me in the air," Naomi said, her eyes a little wide as she looked at him. Her hands were on his shoulders now, and she felt along his shoulders and arms. "Damn, Oscar, what have you been up to?"

Naomi, by contrast, actually felt a little softer than Oscar remembered. He'd never say it, because he cared about his friend and didn't have a death wish, but he was pretty sure she'd put on some weight in Germany. Mostly in the hips from what he could tell.

He set her back down and started pulling out the larger pieces of luggage. "Told you, I've been to the gym a lot. Every single article ever written about dealing with depression says to work out. So I did."

"Yeah, you did," Naomi muttered, seeming a bit dazed, then she snapped out of it. "Okay, so, unfortunately we have to bring those three bags in, because I don't remember where I packed what. I've been using an overnight bag at Mom's. She says 'hi', by the way. She's sorry you missed Hanukkah, but Ezra told us you were working the poles."

Oscar elected to ignore the pole joke—she'd made it before. "Yeah, I feel kinda bad about it, haven't seen your folks since Passover."

Her grin flashed as she handed another suitcase off to Oscar, then grabbed the laptop bag, duffel, and weekender case, leaving the other bags still in the car. "I promise I am not moving in."

"Good thing, because this place only has one bedroom, and I'm already trying to find a place to put ya."

"So you're on the couch and I get the bed, right?" Naomi asked with another grin, her smile making it clear that she didn't actually expect that.

"I don't fit on the couch," he grumbled back. "So you gotta figure yourself out." He did leave it hanging as to where that place would be.

Making sure every bag was cleared out and in hand, he escorted her into the house. After all, it was still very dark, and he wanted to ensure she didn't trip on the half-steps in the mudroom or on something he might have forgotten in the shop. "Up the stairs; living room is pretty bright as I have the fire going."

They headed inside and up the stairs. The fire was doing its job—not so much when you left the main room, but once there it was warm enough to take off coats. He looked her over as he set her bags down near the stairs. The better light showed that, overall, Naomi had adopted a more fashionable aesthetic than Oscar remembered. Under the wool coat was a snug sweater over pointelle pants that accentuated the newfound roundness of her backside. Also more jewelry than Oscar ever remembered her wearing.

"Well, this is … dated," Naomi said teasingly. "But it's nice!"

"Yeah, it's not too bad. But it's mine, so I can fix it up, change it up. Grandpa didn't have any stipulations that I knew of." He shrugged and smiled.

"Well, and your grandfather left it to you," Naomi pointed out. "The dead should focus on rest, as Mom would say, and leave us to our lives."

"Fair, but I like to honor wishes too, if I can." Oscar shrugged. "Hungry?"

"Oh, yes, absolutely." Naomi put her duffel bag on the couch and started going through it. "What have you got that we can eat without power? Or do we hop back in my car? We're only, what, 20 minutes from Old North Gate Road? There's restaurants there that should be open."

"Water and gas still work, so I can cook us something. But if you don't want to bother, I'm game for whatever you want to do. You're my guest, after all," he said, smiling. Naomi briefly hustled past him and shoved a bunch of containers she'd brought into the fridge before closing it again, quickly.

"Dude, I love your cooking; I am happy to sit right here and watch you make magic." Naomi considered for a moment, then pushed herself up onto the counter to sit. "Or, you know, I could try to help, but if it's not ramen or matzo balls, I will need a lot of direction."

"I've been practicing. And, since I knew you were coming, I got some steaks. So, how about I butter baste some steaks, steam some broccoli, and heat up some bread? Basic, but it'll only take a couple of minutes as opposed to the Christmas dinner I've got planned," he said, now braving the fridge to pull out the ingredients for the described meal. "You can just sit on the counter and look cute."

Naomi looked surprised for just a second, but it passed quickly. "I'm in. Though, how cute? Like, natural cute, or Hallmark movie cute? Not sure I can manage the second one; I really don't own anything festive. Y'know, it's not actually my holiday, all those things."

"I hadn't thought that far ahead—you decide. I have steaks to season and water to boil," Oscar said, giving her a wink. It had just slipped out.

The dinner prep was a quick affair, seeing as none of it took longer than about twenty minutes. He had a custom seasoning mix by this point that had salt, pepper, garlic, onion, smoked paprika, and some crystalized lime juice that went well with beef. He'd also gotten used to the kitchen by now and knew where everything was.

"So how are your parents?" Naomi asked as she watched him bustle about. There was a soft little smile on her face, like she was just so happy she couldn't keep it in. "They're on a cruise right now, right?"

"They're doing just fine," he said with a chuckle, tossing the broccoli into the steamer basket and putting the lid on. "They're enjoying their retirement. Third cruise this year, in fact. Barely ever home. They said they felt guilty leaving this time of year, but not sure I buy it."

Glancing up at her, he gave another half-smile. Setting the steaks in the hot pan, he started the sear before moving on to the butter basting.

"You said that you guys did something in early December, so it's not like they forgot." Naomi spoke with a careful tone.

"Yeah, that's why I don't think they meant it when they said they felt guilty. I mean, it was all planned, we had the holidays around the twelfth, then everyone went back home," Oscar was in fine spirits and even reached over to squeeze her thigh in reassurance.

"I'm glad they're enjoying themselves. I talked to your sister last week, which was kind of a shock. I think she called me because she knew I was coming out to see you. She's pregnant again?"

Laughing, he nodded and flipped the steaks before continuing to baste them. "Yup. It's like her life's dream or something. I think she wants to man a whole football team by herself. Well, her and Jerry."

Naomi made a face. "I cannot even imagine. It's a vagina, not a clown car. Well, if she's happy, I guess that's what matters. Also, that smells amazing."

Oscar just gave her a shrug and continued cooking. Bread was in the oven warming, and the broccoli was currently soaking up some seasoned melted butter.

Sliding off the counter, Naomi looked around. "Here, I'll find your table and put candles on it. So we can eat like civilized cavemen sitting in the dark."

"Okay, there should be a couple on the counter over there. Silverware in that drawer," he pointed out. The dishes were already sitting next to him, waiting for the food to be plated. By the time the candles were lit, Oscar was presenting dinner on the table with the bread sliced and in a basket with a tea towel over it.

Candles lit, table set, Naomi sat down and waited patiently for Oscar to set down plates. Like it or not, the meal had a decidedly romantic feel to it between the candlelight and the fireplace, and Naomi across from him looking like she was on a date.

"This smells so good," she said, smiling. "I've missed your cooking."

"Good thing, 'cause you're going to be subjected to it for the next few days," he smirked, cutting into the steak. "So, did you come from a holiday party or something? You look nice and gussied up."

"Hm?" Naomi looked up at him, then down at herself. She had just popped a piece of steak in her mouth, so Oscar had to wait.

"This is … just how I dress now," Naomi said at last, a little self-conscious. "I used to spend weekends in Paris. It's only 5 hours by train. People in Europe think that's an ungodly amount of time, but it's nothing for us, right? I just … I don't know, started caring a little more about looking put together." She wrinkled her nose and ran a hand through her hair. "Ezra said something similar when I saw him the first time, though he was more of a shit about it."

"No, you look great," Oscar said, making sure he wasn't coming off like Ezra had. "Just a change. Now I feel horribly underdressed." Laughing he looked himself over. Currently he was just in a flannel shirt and dirty workman jeans. It had been a busy day, after all. "That would explain all the proposals you got in Germany, though," he teased.

"Oh, god, what makes it worse is that there was more than one." She rolled her eyes. "The proposals started before the wardrobe changes. If you want to start up a family, though, head to Germany. It's a hot market if you're interested in having babies." Oscar already knew from their correspondence that Naomi was not in the market for babies, but her tone hammered it home.

"Nah, I'm good," he said, taking a bite of steak. "I think I'd make a good uncle. Maybe."

Naomi took a bite and looked back up at Oscar. "You look fine. You look … well, like you, and that's pretty awesome in my opinion."

Raising a brow, he looked himself over and chuffed. "I'm sure you would not want me within ten feet of you looking as you do, with me looking as I do, in a public setting."

Naomi furrowed her brow. "Why? It's not a contest. I mean, I would expect you not to go to a nightclub or the theater like that, but why would I be bothered being seen in public with you?"

"Oh, no, sorry, didn't mean it like that," he said, slumping a little. "Just, you do look really good, all nice and made up, and I'm just a big, messy dude."

"Do I need to go change into sweats? Is that what needs to happen here? I brought some." Naomi smirked at him and ate another bite.

"No, no," Oscar replied, straightening back up. "You eat that steak and then you can get just as comfortable as you please. I said 'public'."

"We'll discuss this later," Naomi said with fake menace, waving her fork at Oscar, then happily went back to eating.

As they finished dinner and collected plates, the lights flickered back on and they heard the old heater roar into wakefulness.

"Oh thank goodness," Oscar said with relief as he started to fill the sink basin with hot water. "I was worried I'd have to take the food out and hang it in a bag from a tree overnight. Guess we won't need the furs tonight either."

"I'm kinda disappointed I missed out on furs, not gonna lie." Naomi grinned again and grabbed a rag to wipe the table.

"I mean, I suppose I could turn the heat off if you really want," he said, starting to wash dishes. Naomi just snickered.

Returning with the rag, she paused at the counter and picked up the golden key laying on it. "What's this?"

Turning around, he looked at the thing in her hand. "Oh, yeah, totally forgot. Found that out while I was gathering wood. Strangest thing. Not tarnished, not buried. Like someone dropped it, but I didn't see any footprints or hear anyone."

Her head tipped to the side as she turned the key over in her hand. In the brighter light, it was easy to see just how finely detailed it was. "It looks old," she murmured. "Not the sort of thing you see anymore. And this was just in the woods?"

"Yup, not too far out, either. No idea what it goes with. Not like there's any mysteriously locked door in the house that I've found," Oscar added, finishing up with the dishes and leaning against the counter.

Looking up, Naomi grinned again. "A fun little mystery for you. Maybe there's something in the woods nearby? Like a chest with the greatest treasure known to man!"

"We're in Black Forest," he chuffed again, drying his hands, "If someone buried a 'treasure' here, it's probably some shotgun shells and a Bible."

She set the key back down on the counter and turned to Oscar. "All right, wanna give me the tour and start arguing over where I'm sleeping?"

Chuckling, he gestured toward the stairs up to the loft. "Sure, we'll just go top to bottom then. Up there, we have the bedroom, as it were," he started as they moved through the house, and he flicked on a few lights to push away the darkness of the season.

Naomi followed him up to the loft and laughed a little at how his bed filled almost the entire thing. It made sense; he was a big guy and needed room to spread out. She giggled about the lime green shag carpeting in the loft and on the stairs. They'd already seen most of the main floor, but he made sure she knew where the bathroom was and how to turn on the shower (its age made it a little tricky). They walked through the lower level, poked about the workshop, and Naomi chastised him a little for not having the hot tub working yet (though she also mentioned she didn't have a swimsuit, so he wasn't sure what she might have been implying there). Overall Naomi declared it to be a nice little house, and she looked forward to seeing what Oscar did with it.

They ended up on the couch together watching Die Hard. Naomi changed into her sweats—which were also nicely fitted—and pulled out some fancy popcorn mix she'd brought with her. It looked like Naomi had just kind of grabbed everything they still had at Target that looked vaguely Christmassy, including a little tree that came with its own bulbs, which she put on the mantle next to the fireplace.

"Can you believe some people do not consider this a Christmas movie," he said incredulously as the terrorist quietly slipped out of the elevator in the middle of the office Holiday party. "Including Bruce Willis."

"Artists never understand the impact of their own work," Naomi said, grabbing another handful of popcorn. "We can watch Violent Night tomorrow, maybe. Or some of those weird old stop-motion videos. I've only ever seen the Rudolph one, but I guess they made a bunch of them, and near as I can tell they're entirely secular."

"Haven't seen Violent Night yet," Oscar said, stretching out. It had been a relatively long day, power outage aside, as he had tried to get the house ready for Naomi's visit. "Whatever you're game for; I'm just happy having you as company for the holiday. Buuuut, I think I'd rather watch the action movie," he answered with a wink.

"Fair. My parents did a surprisingly good job of avoiding Christmas media when we were growing up, so I'm just fascinated by everything." Naomi smiled at him, then shifted, wiggling in close and leaning her head on his shoulder. With her movement, he chuckled and gently put his arm around her. After all, the setting was perfect for a cuddle: snow outside, fire crackling, classic movie on TV.

"I'd just rather watch silly action, but if you want to dive into the world of twisted claymation, I'm alright with it."

"We can do silly action first. We'll move to twisted claymation if we're still awake."

She smelled nice. Woodsy but also sharp, with a hint of spice. That was also new. This wasn't their first cuddle, but Oscar didn't remember Naomi having a fragrance. Unless it was after Taco Bell, but that was different. He could feel the day catching up to him. Having someone warm and delicious smelling snuggled up against him didn't help. It was right around the time the roof of the Nakatomi building exploded that Oscar was drifting off. He'd sunk into the couch more, held Naomi a little closer, but was a touch gone. He hadn't been this comfortable in a while, both physically and emotionally.

He'd suffered a bad breakup a few months ago. His ex, Angela, had stormed out in a huff about one thing or another. False accusations, dislike for his work, not enough gifts. He couldn't really remember anymore, and it didn't matter. She was gone and it was for the best, but the sense of loss and that he'd failed at another relationship had spiraled into depression. At that moment, however, he wasn't feeling it.

Settled, warm, full, and comfortable, Oscar slept. He passed through comforting, enveloping darkness back into the woods behind his house. He realized pretty quickly that he was dreaming, but he didn't seem to have much control. As he floated through the wood he heard a tinkling, like delicate wind chimes. He felt drawn to it. He wanted to follow the noise, and the dream let him. He felt himself almost reaching out for it, plodding forward with a touch more than wonder.

He recognized where in the dream he was. It wasn't far from where it had been gathering firewood earlier that night. Just past the fallen log where he had found the key, there was a tight copse of trees. He floated in a circle around it, but then saw something just past the roots of one of the trees. Something glinting and gold. He drifted toward it and saw an escutcheon, an ornamental plate with a keyhole just large enough for the delicate gold key on his counter right now.

The chiming had grown louder, and in the musical sound he thought he heard a voice. "Find us …"

The chiming continued its crescendo, and then he realized it wasn't chimes. It was his phone. Someone was calling.

Awakening with a bit of a start, Oscar took just a moment to get his bearings. He was still on the couch, still holding Naomi, his feet dangling off over the arm. They had shifted, and she was laying almost on top of him, the blanket that had been wrapped around her now draped over both of them. It wasn't too late, the fire was just dying, and the TV was cycling through trailers from the streaming service. He was rather surprised he'd shifted so much, and groggily patted Naomi to wake her up so he could reach his phone. He didn't mean to pat her butt—that's just where his hand had landed.

"Mmf, whossat," he grumbled, trying to shift and reach over to grab his phone. He didn't get called all that much, and only a handful of people knew his personal phone number, so it must have been important.

Naomi murmured in her sleep and shifted against Oscar. No, not shifted—rubbed against him, murmuring a little as she did. She nuzzled his chest, rubbed her thigh against his crotch. That was unexpected, and Oscar wasn't entirely sure his brain was firing correctly. She then yawned and picked up her head, blinking.

"Huh?" she said intelligently as the phone kept ringing.

Hand on the small of her back to hold her in place, he rolled over just enough to finally reach his phone, then slumped back into the length of the couch. Yawning, he answered it. "Y'ello, Oscar here," he said, realizing as he spoke that he hadn't bothered to look at who was calling.

"Hey!" Ezra's mildly annoyed voice sounded through the phone. "I'm glad one of you finally picked up! What have you been doing? Y'know what, I don't wanna know. Did the twerp make it? It's snowing like mad up here and Mom's worried."

"Oh, hey man," Oscar said, another yawn and he laughed. "Yeah, Mimsy made it. Sorry, we were watching Die Hard, and the day caught up to me. Passed right out. She did too. But we're safe, power's on, plenty of firewood."

Naomi grumbled something about her stupid brother and dropped her head against Oscar's chest again, snuggling back into him and rubbing her leg against his crotch once more. That was…distracting.

"Oh, okay, cool." Ezra's tone relaxed. "Yeah, it was a long day; we went and visited some friends, and then I know she ran to the store to get stuff for visiting you. She said she knew you wouldn't have anything. I— Hang on." Oscar could hear Ezra pull the phone away, but it wasn't far enough to miss what he was saying. "Yeah, Mom, they're fine. Watched a movie and fell asleep. No—no, Mom, she—No, Mom, I was making a joke, they're just friends—"

Sighing, Ezra put the phone back to his ear. "Thanks for answering. I'll let you guys head to bed. Have a nice holiday, man."

Oscar rolled his eyes a little at Libi's, Ezra's mom, suspected comment. "Yup, all good," he said, yawning once more and stretching a little underneath Naomi. "Tell your mom I'm sorry I missed Hanukkah, especially her latkes. I'll see ya on New Year's. Night."

Hanging up the phone, he set it down on the coffee table and then took a moment. He was trying to remember the dream; it seemed important, and he had to hold on to it because his sleep was broken. Naomi murmured and shifted against him again. He could remember the dream, though. Maybe … maybe they'd go for a little walk tomorrow. Naomi would be down for it. She'd probably be even more encouraging if he told her a dream had told him where to go. She liked those kinds of weird adventures.

As nice as this was, though, Naomi needed to move. Aside from the fact that her thigh kept rubbing against his cock through his pants, his feet were already falling asleep from hanging off the couch.

"Oookay," Oscar said, patting Naomi a little more soundly. "Time to get up, Nomi. Legs are going numb."

Yawning, Naomi picked her head up again. "What ... oh. Right. I'm at your place, and we're on the couch."

"Yup, and still need to figure out where you're sleeping," he said, chuckling again. She carefully wiggled her way back and to the other side of his leg, so he could swing his legs around and get up. After hefting himself up and a little dancing around, the pins and needles started to go away and the immediate threat of him falling over dissipated.

"Couch, as has been displayed, is very comfy," he said, presenting it as if she hadn't already been on it for the past couple of hours. "On the threat of the power going out, however, the bed is also an option to ensure neither of us freeze to death."

"Mmmmhmmm." Naomi stretched out on the couch again, barely hearing him. "Comfy couch." She pulled the throw pillow under her head and nestled in.

"Problem solved," Oscar said gently. Rummaging around, he found one of the furs that might be needed and rolled it up at her feet in case the power kicked out in the middle of the night. Taking his phone, he went upstairs and wrote a note to himself about the dream. He had to get as many details as he could remember, because he knew he wouldn't remember by morning. Stripping down to his skivvies, Oscar crawled into bed and sprawled out. It wasn't long before sleep overtook him once more. That was the joy of a long day; it was easy to end it.

There were more dreams. One of them involved Naomi, the couch, and things going places they hadn't. But halfway through pounding Naomi into the cushions of a couch that seemed to keep getting bigger, the dream shifted, and he was drifting alone in the woods again. It was just like before: the trees, the chimes, and a voice asking to be found. The voice wasn't frightened or mournful—it seemed to be happy. Cheerful, even.

The sound of movement downstairs woke Oscar. He wasn't used to noises in the house. The sun was up, but the encompassing trees kept it from being too bright. Sitting up, Oscar blinked his eyes a few times and realized he was going to need a pair of pants and some careful tucking before he went downstairs. As he sat up, he could see it had snowed enough to be aesthetically pleasing, but not enough that he would need to shovel his way outside.

Sighing, he ran a hand over his face. He hadn't thought about Naomi that way in years, not since she'd gone off to grad school. They had started talking regularly and visiting, and in a lot of ways their friendship was deeper than his friendship with Ezra. More current, at least. And that was also a problem—they had such a friendly history, he certainly didn't want to misread her signals. And big as he was, he tried hard not to put people into positions where he felt he was intimidating them. All this was something to ponder later. He had a guest to tend to.

Finding a heavy pair of canvas workmans pants, he got himself situated, then found his shirt from last night and was buttoning it up as he plodded down the stairs. Naomi was up, the couch straightened, and the fire had a fresh log on it and was starting to build up again. Her hair was pinned up, and she wore a short tank top with her sweatpants—it was easy to guess that activity had made her warm enough to take off her sweatshirt. She was in the kitchen by the stove, pouring some oil in a pan, and it looked suspiciously that she was about to make latkes. As she moved around, her breasts swayed and bounced in a manner that made it very clear she wasn't wearing a bra.

Oscar stifled a groan of frustration and cleared his throat. "Sleep, okay?"

"Hey!" Naomi looked up and smiled brightly. "Yeah, slept pretty good. I see you managed to leave me on the couch after all."

"Well, you stated how comfy it was," he chuckled, moving to tend to the fire a little. "Didn't want to upset the comfy. Comfy is a sacred thing." Standing back up, he walked over to the kitchen and leaned against the wall. "So, got a plan for today?"

"Not really." Naomi set the bottle of oil down and pushed a lock of hair out of her face. "Just spend time with you, do whatever holiday things you want to do. We can play in the snow if ya want."

"Oh, do you need to be tossed in a snowbank? It's been a while," Oscar said, grinning widely and stepping toward her with grabby hands.

Naomi glared at him. "I did not miss the snowbanks. And I am aware that you're still perfectly capable of throwing me over your shoulder."

"You're the one who suggested playing in the snow," Oscar humphed. "But yes, throwing you around would probably be significantly easier than it was fifteen years ago."

Naomi started placing preformed latkes into the oil. Libi had probably sent them. The kitchen filled with the sound of sizzling. "I mean, I dunno, have you seen the size of my ass lately?" She pouted and sort of wiggled her butt in his direction. It jiggled with the motion through the soft, snug pants. "I may not be as easy to lift."

"I see it," he said with a smirk, raising his eyebrows as he looked back at her eyes. "What I'm not seeing is a challenge."

Did she blush? Just a little? Naomi wrinkled her nose at him and turned back to the latkes in the pan, scooting them around and adding a few more, but from where Oscar was standing her cheeks definitely looked pinker than they had a minute ago. Oscar's smirk softened into a smile, a hopeful one. Maybe they'd have a conversation before she left.

Something dawned on him, and he straightened up. "Wait, snow, that's right," he started. "Okay, you're not going to believe this, but I had a dream last night where I might know where that key goes."

"I'm down for an adventure; I brought my hiking books," she said, not looking up as she flipped latkes. "We can eat and then try to find your treasure. Sound good?"

Finding a seat, he watched Naomi bounce around his kitchen. "Sounds good. I just commented to your brother last night about how I missed your mom's latkes."

"They are the best. Have you got coffee?"

"Uh, yeah. Mom gave me one of those pod coffee things," he said, walking back into the kitchen and finding the device in question in one of the cabinets. "Also got me a sampler, if you want something fancy. Might have some French roast, Ms. Paris."

"If you've got anything that says 'medium roast,' I'll take it," Naomi said, "French roast is fine, but it doesn't have as much caffeine. Medium roasts are the most caffcinated."

By the time Oscar got the coffee maker set up, Naomi had the second batch of latkes in, the first draining on a paper towel. Sour cream and applesauce sat on the counter next to them, everything in order and ready for consumption. He set the coffee on the table and then moved back to stand next to Naomi.

"How many more batches we got to go, Nomi?" he asked.

"This is the last one," she said, flipping the latkes. "Mom sent enough to feed a family, but I'm only making half. We can freeze the rest for New Year's. If you want some out of the first batch, go for it! These'll be done in a minute."

"Aww, wouldn't want to eat without you," Oscar said while already pulling several of the hot potato cakes onto a plate and moving toward the table.

"You can find me some milk and sugar for that coffee, and then I'll be right there." Naomi smiled at him again before turning back to the pan.

In minutes they were both seated at the table with a pile of latkes between them that was probably more than either of them would eat. Well, more than Naomi would eat. Oscar had found that working out had given him an increased appetite.

"So, winter adventure, then back here for the sauna?" Naomi asked, smearing sour cream on her latkes and then topping them each with a little bit of applesauce.

"Sounds like a winner to me," Oscar responded, taking a drink of his coffee. "I don't think it's terribly far. Impossible to say, dreams and all that, but it felt like it was just out a bit past where I was hunting for wood."

"It'll be absolutely wild if we actually find something," Naomi said with a laugh, "but even if we don't, it'll be a nice hike in the snow."

They wrapped up breakfast, Naomi managing to get through two cups of coffee in the time it took Oscar to finish one. She was almost bouncing as they bundled up and got ready to head out. Remembering the key, Oscar tucked it into his pants pocket to make sure it didn't get lost. Pulling on his boots and his heavy winter coat, he got his gloves with pads in the fingertips so he could still use his phone. Naomi looked like a ski bunny with her puffer jacket and fur-trimmed hood. He opened the door for her.

"All right, it's a little walk, not much. Just over this way," he said, pointing in the direction he had taken to fetch wood.

Fresh snow muffled their movements. Outside was quiet and still. Oscar was far enough off the main road that there was no traffic noise—only people who lived on his street would be braving it after a fresh snowfall, and they were probably all happily inside.

"Wow," Naomi murmured as they walked through the snowy woods. No one had lawns in Oscar's area of Black Forest, and most of the houses were old enough that whatever trees had been cut away to build them had grown back. "I feel like a city girl in a Hallmark movie walking through a forest for the first time. This is incredible. It's … magical."

"I always liked coming up here in the winter," Oscar said with a nod, looking at her then scanning the area around. "We only had Christmas a couple of times in the cabin, since there's not a lot of room for hosting." Smiling, he glanced over at her again. "But you're back now, so you can come visit every winter if you like."

It didn't take long to get back to the fallen log. In the clear morning light, Oscar saw the splinters from where he'd split the log, and the rotting stump it had once fallen from. As he looked around, he saw the copse of trees from his dream. A tingle ran up the back of his neck. This much, at least, was real.

"Okay, yeah, this is starting to get kinda freaky," Oscar said, his delighted voice a contrast to his words. He pointed to the trees and started walking toward them. "This was the place. Or at least, it looks just like it."

Stepping up next to him, Naomi looked at the trees with interest. "Okay, so, voice of reason: you might have seen these last night. This might be subconscious influences or something. But definitely promising. Now what do you remember?"

"Okay, look around the roots," he said as they approached the thicket.

"If my dream wasn't just a crazy sleep-driven imagining, we might find a keyhole around here somewhere."

They circled counterclockwise around the copse together, brushing away snow as they did. They made a complete circle and found nothing but tried a second time just to make sure the snow had been properly clear. It was on the second trip that Oscar saw it, and he felt that rush beneath his skin again. A golden lock, embedded into stone between overlapping roots. It was just like his dream.

"Oh, shit," Oscar exclaimed, "I found it! I'm getting goosebumps. Look at this!" He waved Naomi over and presented the plate to her proudly.

"God of my fathers," Naomi murmured, her eyes wide.

"Should we?" he added, producing the key from his pocket.

She nodded slowly. "I mean, we came this far …"

Nodding, Oscar placed the key into the lock and turned it. There were no handles, no knobs, nothing to open. The key turned mostly smoothly, like maybe there was a little ice or snow in there, but the motion was far easier than one might expect of a lock sitting out in the woods. There was a click and a whirr. Something told Oscar to take the key out. The whirring got louder, and the stone that the keyplate was set in began to move, sliding out of the way then collapsing and shuffling upon itself. Naomi gripped Oscar's arm so tight he could feel the pressure of her nails through her gloves and his coat. Reaching over, Oscar gently put his hand over Naomi's and held it, trying to be reassuring. It was just incredible, something like this hiding out in the middle of the woods, near his grandpa's place. He had so many questions. In minutes the stone had neatly moved itself out of the way, revealing a stairway down to another door.

"I am going to pray tonight for forgiveness for every time I told my bubbe she was crazy for her superstitious nonsense," Naomi said, her voice surprisingly even for all that she still had Oscar's arm in a vice. "And I really wish I'd bothered to study the Kabbalah."

"I'm not sure what it would say about this," he commented, "but, as you said, we've come this far." Giving her hand a squeeze, he started to slowly descend the stairs.

The stairway wasn't wide enough for them to walk down next to each other, so Naomi let go of his arm somewhat reluctantly and followed him down. They were at least a floor down—the flight of stairs was just a little longer than the stairs from his main floor to the garden level, with a wide landing in front of the door. The door itself was heavy wood, inlaid with metal accents in swirls that made Oscar think of the wind. It had another gold lock and latch, decorated similarly to the key in his hand.

"I'm guessing this goes here as well," he said, gesturing with the key. "Ready?"

Naomi took a deep breath and let it out shakily. "Yeah. Yeah, okay. Let's do this."

Gently, he eased the key in and turned it, removing the key and tucking it away before slowly opening the door. After the strange stone entrance, the door was refreshingly simple. Oscar pressed the latch and pushed open the door. Inside was unreal opulence, like they had stepped from the Colorado Front Range into Baroque Germany. Like stepping into a fairy tale. The room had overlapping carpets upon which rested gold and velvet furniture, delicately wrought furnishings, and walls covered in shelves that contained ornate books, ornamented boxes, statues, and other trinkets. In the center of the room was a tree, its leaves silver and gold. The wind that came down the stairs behind them made the tree shudder, the leaves tinkling like delicate wind chimes.

"What the actual fuck," he heard Naomi murmur behind him in shock.

"Are we still asleep?" he asked, stepping it. A part of him was thinking that maybe they should close the door and not let the winter in. "Like, did we take acid to make Die Hard funnier and forget all about it? Did I slip on some ice and knock myself out and I'm just in a coma?"

"It's also possible that the power's still off, the pilot light went out, and we're slowly dying from exposure to natural gas," Naomi said as she followed him into the room. "Though this seems ... very solid for a hallucination. Like, I've taken acid before—it's not like this."

"Oh, have you now?" he said with a raised brow, the offhand confession strangely centering.

Before Naomi could answer, Oscar became aware of the sound of movement. It was faint, but there was something in the back of the room, on the other side of the strange golden tree.

"Hey, sounds like there's something here," Oscar whispered, crouching slightly. He was a big guy, stealth wasn't exactly in his wheelhouse, but he'd seen it done. He was trying.

There was a distant, faint giggle as Oscar crouched. "I think they already know we're here, big guy," Naomi said dryly.

Sighing, he dropped his hands in defeat before standing back up. "Well, they're giggling. Doesn't sound maniacal, that's a good sign."

"Yet," Naomi said in the same tone. "Doesn't sound maniacal yet."

They made their cautious way around the tree and saw two figures, one a bit taller than the other, very obviously hiding behind the tapestries hung on the far wall.

"They can hear you," the smaller one said in a harsh whisper that traveled well in the quiet room despite the lush drapings.

Another small giggle. "Aren't they supposed to?" the other voice whispered back. "Isn't that the new Guardian? He has the key!"

Oscar looked at Naomi and raised a brow. "Guardian?" he whispered to her. He realized he didn't have a reason to keep stretching this out. "Yes, I have the key," he said, no longer whispering and even adding a little depth to his voice. "So, show yourself and we can all stop hiding and being silly."

The larger figure moved first, a hand coming out from behind the tapestry and waving a little awkwardly, followed by a … hoof? As the figure emerged it looked much like a woman from the waist up, wearing a white blouse with elbow sleeves, a wide embroidered belt of sorts, and an apron. From the waist down, however, she looked like a centaur with only two legs. She also had long ears peeking up through her gray and blond hair that reminded Oscar of a donkey. Despite the gray, she didn't seem old, and the donkey ears were the same gray color, growing darker at the tips. She also had a very generous figure, her breasts causing what must be an enormous strain on the neckline of her blouse.

"Guten tag! Hi!" The woman looked shy but friendly, and overall very pleasant.

"We are definitely hallucinating as we die of gas fumes," Naomi said flatly.

"I, uh …. huh," was Oscar's well-thought-out response. "I smelled a lot of fresh air from the walk. You sure it's a gas leak? And is that a, um, satyr?"

The woman giggled. "No, I'm not a satyr. I'm a biereselin!"

Naomi looked down and her brow furrowed in thought. "Bier is beer, but esel … eselin … donkey? A beer donkey?"

The woman laughed happily and clapped her hands as if Naomi had done something clever. "Yes! Exactly! My name is Elke. I'm so happy there is finally a new guardian!"

"A beer what?" Oscar started to say, trying not to stare both in general and at the strange woman's chest in particular.

Naomi started to say something else, then stopped, her gaze moving to the other tapestry, where it did not look like anything still stood. "Where did the other one go?"

"You're slow, human," a smug, feminine voice said from behind them. "And your manner of dress is most strange, but you do not smell dishonest or foul."

"Well, that's not very nice," Oscar said, scowling as they turned.

Behind them was a … cat. A lovely, midsized, shorthair, black cat. The cat looked at them for a moment with wide yellow-green eyes, then in a blink was replaced by a woman with a lithe figure in a beaded short vest, cropped just under her breasts, and nothing else. A black tail swished behind her, and furry black ears rose up from her head amidst thick, shaggy black hair.

"Humans are slow! It is how they are; it was not mean," the woman said, looking them both over. "And your manner of dress is very strange. Tell me, human, what year is it?"

"Oookay, so a beer donkey and a cat," he said, making sure he was, in fact, seeing this. "Um, it's 2023. How long have you been down here?"

"Ah, biereselin, if you don't mind," Elke said, chiming in. "Beer donkey is the literal translation, but … well, there's a lot lost in translation. And, oh my, we've been with the vault since before it was moved here. How long has it been, Ada?"

"A very long time," the cat girl—Ada, apparently—said as she circled back around the two of them again, her expression thoughtful and critical. "Though we have not had a visitor since ... 1926, I believe." She leaned in toward the both of them and sniffed. "You are not of their line. It is for the best. They did not understand the vault. And," Ada continued, drawing herself up. "I am not simply a cat. I am a katerpolter. You would do well to stay in my good graces, human."

"Sorry, I'm sorry," Oscar said, not liking being surrounded, even if he didn't really get any negative feelings from the two. "Just having a hard time believing this is real. So, Elke and Ada, yes? It's nice to meet you. You keep calling us Guardians?"

"You're ... house spirits," Naomi said, brow furrowed. "Like faeries, or ... I didn't read enough of those stories. But you take care of things, right? If humans are kind to you, you care for them."

Smiling, Oscar looked at Naomi. "And you know who they are?"

"Know is a very strong word in this context," Naomi said, holding her hands up almost defensively. "I am trying to piece together things I heard or saw in Germany."

"And we have called you, specifically, Guardian," Ada said, tapping Oscar lightly on the chest. "You hold the key. Your friend is very lovely, but only one line can be Guardian, and you two are not bound. Yet, anyway."

"Me? A line? Do you mean family line?" he asked, now trying to think how long grandpa had had the cabin, or even the land.

Elke stepped lightly forward, moving with a surprising delicateness. "Ah, I sense this will take a little explaining. Come, sit down! I don't have much to serve you, but I can find something!"

"Um, all right," he nodded to Elke and gently took Naomi's hand before moving to the seats. If anything, he at least knew she was real.

Naomi squeezed his hand back, and Elke led them to a table with two golden chairs that were lined with a plush velvet. The table was inlaid with different metals and dotted with gemstones. The amount of wealth on display in the room was absurd.

"So," Ada said, sitting on the table next to Oscar. Her legs were crossed, but it was a lot harder to ignore her relative nudity this close. "Yes, I meant family line. I'm guessing you just found the key? It wasn't given to you?"

Oscar's eyes strayed but he was good enough to snap them back to Ada's when she spoke. It was just … sudden. All of it, not just the nakedness. With the amount of opulence, it was no wonder they had called it the vault.

"Yeah, yesterday. I'm guessing one of you, or both, was the one calling to me in the dream," he said.

"Not precisely," Elke said, smiling, as she set down crystal goblets made of deep-blue sapphire with diamond-like stems. "Ah, just water for the moment. The vault doesn't know you yet. It takes time in the beginning. But we didn't call to you; the vault did."

Naomi was giving Ada a small amount of side eye. "What do you mean, 'doesn't know him'? And how does a structure call to someone?"

"Magic," Ada said, smug again.

SIghing, Elke glared at Ada. "Being the Guardian isn't one-sided. There are benefits. One of them is comfort. The stores of the vault will fill as we come to know you."

"Magic. Sure, why not," Oscar said with a shrug.

"You know, you're saying that flippantly, but … what else could this be, right?" Naomi looked from Ada to Elke. "This just keeps going and we haven't woken up yet, so maybe … maybe why not magic?"

"Well, I don't think my imagination could have created all of this," Oscar said, things starting to sink in a bit, but it was too much to completely settle. "So … maybe? All right, but what does it mean to be a Guardian? What do I need to do? What's the catch, as it were. I mean, you two seem pretty nice, and this place is, well, magical. Sooo," he drew the word out, "what's the cost?"

"The Guardian does just that. Guards." Ada said, though not rudely this time. "There was a time when that meant fighting off thieves. But … even with our last Guardians, each generation remembers less and less of the old stories. Thieves or hunters don't come for us anymore. So now, you guard the land."

Elke nodded. "You make sure the vault can continue, that the land is safe. And you make sure the vault itself continues. The vault is many things. You'll come to understand in time. You guard the vault, and the vault will make sure your every comfort is seen to."

"Your every comfort," Ada said with a grin. Elke blushed. Naomi seethed.

Oscar looked at Naomi and mouthed, "What?" though she just shook her head a little in response. "This is my land now, so protecting that comes with that. And, yeah, I have never heard anything about magic vaults, Beer-esel-ins, or catterpolers anywhere near this area, so that secret's safe. As for comforts … I'm trying to think of something that could prove I'm not just going crazy or delusional."

"I mean, your friend here would be going crazy in the exact same manner. The fact that you're not alone and she's having the same experience you are should count for something," Ada pointed out, pragmatically.

"I've known N—her for years," Oscar said, correcting himself; he remembered rules about names and fairy tales. And then remembered the animal girls had both given their names and felt silly. "So I could just imagine her reacting the way she's reacting." Ada rolled her eyes.

"But is that it?" Naomi asked, focused, her brows still creased. "He just makes sure no one buys the land from him or develops it or something? That can't be it."

Elke clasped her hands in front of her. "Well, there are rules. The vault does not exist to be plundered. That was the problem with the last Guardian."

"And what happens if you break the rules?" Naomi persisted.

Ada slid off the table and turned to look at Naomi. "You will lose the key and become very unlucky. You will never know comfort or fortune again."

"That tracks with what little I know of fairy tales," Naomi muttered.

"The vault can be moved, though," Oscar said, thinking. "So, how is the vault moved? Is it just tied to the lock, and we can set it somewhere else?"

"It's a little more complicated than that, but yes," Ada said, quirking an eyebrow. "And nothing living can be in the vault while it is moved. Including us. Why?"

"Well, if it's not that hard to move, and I'm the new guardian," he started, looking at Naomi again, who was along for this ride, "then wouldn't it make sense to move it close to the house. Or in the house?"

Naomi blinked. "I suppose that makes sense, yes. It would certainly make it harder for someone to stumble across it accidentally." She looked a bit like she didn't love the idea.

"That was my thought," he nodded, becoming more accepting of all this. But he was still trying to figure out why Naomi looked like she was getting ... angry? It was subtle, though.

"Oh, we haven't been a part of a house in ages!" Elke danced in place a little bit, a quick clopping of her hooves. "If you set the plate in your house, we can see to the care of it as well! Though, um ... do you have beer?" She looked shyly and adorably hopeful.

"I think we have a beer or two. Are you particular to a certain kind?" Oscar asked. Some people were such beer snobs. He was one of them, truth be told.

"Oh, well, you know, I'm not too picky ..." Elke demurred, still looking very excited.

"She doesn't like light beer," Ada said, her smile fond rather than smug as she looked at her fellow keeper. "Well, if you're serious about this, you will have to break the stone that the escutcheon is set into. Don't worry, you can't break the lock. Then you'll need to mount it somewhere in your home. I recommend your bedroom." Ada grinned saucily at Oscar.

"You can stop now," Naomi said, her tone ice cold.

Ada looked blandly and innocently at Naomi. "Stop what?"

Oscar paused for a moment, looking between Ada and Naomi. Was she ... jealous? Or just protective? He'd be pretty happy either way, but much more understanding if she were jealous.

"I was actually thinking somewhere in the basement," he said slowly.

Ada pouted and Naomi smirked at the cat girl, satisfied with that answer. She still didn't look happy, though. Just briefly mollified.

"Can … can we do this now?" Elke looked too happy to care about whatever was taking place between Ada and Naomi. "You'll need tools to break the stone. We can get ready while you go fetch them. I mean … you … you have tools, don't you?"

"I definitely have tools," he said, standing up. "Nomi, you okay with this?" He valued her opinion, even if it was just altering his own house. And gaining two new roommates, both of whom were female, and one having a very strong interest in things aside from tending house.

"It's your home, Oz," Naomi said, getting up as well. "Though I hope they know your house doesn't have rooms for them both."

"Oh, we'll still live in the vault," Elke said cheerfully, which did seem to relax Naomi a little bit. "It's our duty to keep it. We can just also help in the house!"

"With anything you need," Ada added, and Naomi's shoulders grew tight again.

"Well, it's a fixer-upper at this point, so the help would be appreciated," Oscar responded, purposefully ignoring Ada. "All right, let's do it. Ada, you have some clothes you might want to put on? It's cold outside."

"Hmph. Clothes." Ada tossed her head, and then in a blink was a sleek black cat again. "This will be fine."

"We'll be ready when you return," Elke said, looking so happy she might burst. She turned and started scampering about. Naomi nodded and made her way to the door.

"It's a plan," Oscar said and escorted Naomi out of the vault and up the stairs back into the snowy woods. It was just like Colorado to dump snow on the during the night, then be relatively warm and sunny during the day.

"Hey, you all right?" he asked, putting a hand on Naomi's shoulder.

"Sure," Naomi said, as they walked, though the smile she flashed was too tight. He'd seen her do that before; he knew that meant she was full of shit. "I mean, it's a whole lot of weird, and I'm still not completely convinced it's real, though I'm getting there. I might still be passed out on the couch. Or, y'know, we died from gas inhalation."

"Right," Oscar chuckled a bit, trying to lighten her mood, but didn't press further. "It is a ton of weird in a half-ton trailer, but the few things I do remember about fairy tales was to always be nice to them, because they can seriously fuck up your life. And right now, life is going pretty good. Wouldn't want to ruin that." Smiling gently, he gave Naomi's shoulder a squeeze and guided her back to the house.

"Yeah," Naomi murmured, glancing up at Oscar with a strange, unreadable expression. She was quiet as they continued their way to the house and headed up to the main level to check messages while Oscar dug through the workshop for a large hammer and the heftiest chisel he had. He briefly considered the pneumatic hammer, but figured hauling the compressor into the woods was a bit much and was probably overkill besides. With a large chisel and his grandpa's old blacksmith hammer tucked in the tool pocket and loop of his pants, he headed upstairs to check on Naomi once more.

"All right, Mimsy, you ready to move a magical vault into my basement and hopefully befriend a pair of—what'd you call them—house sprites?"

"No, but fuck it," Naomi said with a wry smile as she zipped her coat back up. "If this is real, let's pray we don't regret this."

Naomi headed back out before he could question her, leaving Oscar to follow her. He was about to ask her to be honest. He wanted her opinion, tell her it mattered to him. But she'd left and he wasn't going to drive it home. When the crazy had calmed down, they needed to talk. Maybe she was just upset because impossible things were happening, but that also didn't seem right. Maybe she was jealous. And if she was jealous, that meant they should talk about it even more, right? They should probably go out to dinner that night, just the two of them, have a talk away from spirits that would likely be very nosy about the goings-on in the house.

He caught up back at the entrance to the vault, where Elke was handing Ada off to Naomi, who took her with a bit of a grimace. Elke then bounded back down the stairs, coming back in a thick fur coat that was long enough to mostly cover her very-not-human legs.

"Okay!" Elke said cheerfully. "Guardian—Oz, right? May we call you Oz? Anyway, you need to relock the entrance before you attempt to move the lock plate."

"It's Oscar, but whatever works I guess," he said with a shrug and knelt by the plate.

Naomi flinched. "I call him Oz," she said, looking a little upset. "You should call him Oscar."

"Of course!" Elke said, smiling at Naomi. "That's special to you—I wouldn't intrude! Thank you for telling me!"

Naomi looked surprised, then smiled at Elke. It was a genuine smile. Oscar suspected it was impossible to be upset with Elke. She was a cinnamon roll (with the most impressive rack Oscar had ever seen, but still a cinnamon roll). The name thing made sense; he should have been more thoughtful about that, but Elke was diplomatic and wanted everyone happy. Even better, he was almost positive at this point that Naomi was jealous. Ada just purred in Naomi's arms, content to be held and not made to step in the snow.

Taking out the key, he locked the entrance as Elke had recommended, then produced the chisel and hammer. "Okay. Just crack the rock and take the plate, right?"

"Oh! Yes!" Elke stepped to the side, aware that she was blocking the way. "You don't have to break the whole stone, just break where it's sealed to the escutcheon. Once the seal is no longer true, you should be able to pick it up."

"Easy enough," he said, setting the chisel next to the edge of the plate where it met the stone. With a straight-forward angle, set mostly to crack the stone, he gave it a heavy swing and smashed into the rock. It took several whacks. Stone started to chip away, but Oscar wasn't certain if he was doing it right. Then, on the fourth hit, he felt more than heard something from the stone, and reeled back slightly. The lock shifted to the side, and when he picked it up it was like it was nothing—just a pretty ornamentation waiting to be added to a door.

"Very good," Ada said, yawning. "Can we go? It is cold out here."

"I told you to put on clothes," Oscar said, standing and pocketing the lock plate.

"She really doesn't have any," Elke said with another giggle. Ada didn't comment.

He motioned toward the house. "Shall we? You ladies will soon see the quaint mess you've decided to inherit."

As the house came into view, Elke gasped. "It's so strange looking! I mean, not entirely, it is a house, but so much has changed!"

Naomi's brow furrowed. "It can't be that different from the 20s."

"We didn't leave the vault then," Ada said, shifting a little in Naomi's arms. "We only leave the vault when it is moved or joined to the Guardian's home, and neither event has happened in a very long time."

"I think grandpa originally built this place in the 40s," Oscar said as they walked up to the front door, and he opened it for everyone to step in. "While not the most advanced, there's going to be a lot of new stuff to discover."

He paused at Ada's words and looked at the two of them. "Can you leave the vault, or the house attached to it? I don't mean while it's being moved, I mean, just for fun?"

"No," Elke said, shaking her head and smiling a little sadly. "But we knew that when the tree was planted, and the threshold built. We were not bound unwillingly; we chose this."

"But that is why it is exciting to be brought into a home again," Ada continued, leaping out of Naomi's arms and prowling into the house.

Everyone headed inside, and the two spirits gazed around, fascinated by how everything was different, before hurrying farther in to investigate. Naomi smiled, seeming to be amused in spite of herself. "So where are you going to put the vault?" she asked as she undid her coat.

"Where do you think would be good?" he asked, looking around the basement. "I was thinking near the sauna because it wouldn't be a place people would snoop? They'd just see a sauna and not much more."

"But people will still be near the sauna. They'll see it and be curious, unless you hide it behind something." Naomi looked thoughtful. "Maybe the workshop? No one visiting you is going to go in there and mess with your tools or anything."

"Ah, so that kind of well-hidden. Yeah, why not. Curious how it'll open once it's set." He nodded and moved into the workshop to find a good spot.

"Is it close to Weihnachten?" Elke asked, coming down the stairs. "I saw your little tree. It's so tiny!"

Naomi looked embarrassed. "Ah, yes. I … I brought it. I wanted to keep him company, and my family doesn't celebrate Chri—ah, Weihnachten because we're Jewish, but Oscar does and I thought, you know …"

Elke smiled again. "What a loving friend you are! It is a lovely little tree."

Chuckling at Elke's response, he walked up to Naomi and pulled her close by the hip, nuzzling her head. "She is a perfect, loving woman who is too good to me," he said, intentionally leaving out anything about them just being friends, to test her reaction.

Naomi blushed and leaned into Oscar, appreciating the show of affection. She did not clarify their relationship either and seemed happy to let him hold on to her as long as he wanted. Elke just beamed at them.

"Oh, I should tell you how to set the lock," Elke said. "It's easy. You just hold it against the wall or floor or wherever you want it and tap it with the key. Make sure you're happy with where it is, though, because you'll have to break the surface to get it back."

He took a moment to consider as he let Elke finish the directions and look around the room a little more. Once he thought of a good spot, he gave Naomi a squeeze and let her go to place the lock plate.

"What about here?" he asked Elke as he tapped the door that went into the small mechanical room. "It looks like any other lock, and there'd be no reason to keep my mech room locked, so it would just sit there until I locked it and unlocked the vault? Forgive me, I'm not sure how magic works, but it was a good idea in my head."

"That will be perfect," Elke said, clapping her hands. "Hidden in plain sight. Very clever."

"Great," he said, nodding. He placed the lock plate right below the handle to the door. With a tap, he sealed the magic and moved the vault, or so he assumed.

"I agree, clever idea," Ada chimed in. She was back in her human form, still wearing nothing but the vest. "I got the fire going again, by the way."

"We have a heater as well," Oscar offered, "so we won't always need a fire, especially at night when we head to bed. But we have plenty of time to go over all of that, I suppose."

"I suppose you should unlock the vault and make sure it worked," Naomi said, a bit uncertain.

"Oh, my, yes." Elke nodded. "And I would like to put my coat away."

"Here goes," Oscar said, closing the door and turning the key inside the lock.

As the key clicked, the door began to change, shifting from the simple hollow-core, yellowed white slab to a heavy door elaborately carved and ornamented. When Oscar turned the doorknob and opened it, what once was a closet was now a stairway heading down to the same landing and doorway from before.

"Oh, wow," Naomi breathed.

"Excellent," Elke said, stepping past Oscar and, as she did so, pressing against him, possibly unintentionally given she wasn't that delicately built.

As the reality was starting to settle and the adrenaline and excitement and confusion was starting to wane, Oscar couldn't help but notice how soft Elke was, all over, and filed that away for later. "I'll put this away and be right back!"

"I … am going upstairs," Naomi said, running a hand through her hair. She looked toward the windows. "Ah. And it's snowing again."

"I'll join you after getting rid of my coat and boots. I'm getting hungry again, and I know one of my new guests is going to want to go through my porter collection. Or what's left of it," Oscar added and moved to the mud room to doff his heavier clothes.

As he headed up the stairs, he almost bumped into Naomi, who was still sitting at the top of the stairs, just staring at the room. It was clean. Not that it had been a mess before, but now it was clean. The breakfast dishes were sparkling in the dish rack, and the old hardwood floors looked refreshed in a way Oscar hadn't thought possible.

"They … they were only up here for a minute," Naomi said, flabbergasted.

Oscar pressed against Naomi as he leaned over her to get a good look at the room. While not as lush as Elke, Naomi also felt very warm and soft. "I … Wow, yeah," he started, then snickered and leaned in close to her ear, whispering. "I thought a glass or cup would be knocked off a shelf and broken, what with Ada having the most time alone."

"I'm sure we'll find something," she said, grinning. It took a moment, but she finally walked forward into the room and out of the way.

Oscar moved to the fridge to start rummaging. "Okay, so I know Elke wants beer. Ada, what's your favorite thing?"

"I enjoy many things," Ada said, coming up the stairs behind them. "Though I would enjoy trying one of your beers. It has been a long time. The vault provides all we need to live, but not necessarily all we would enjoy. Particularly when there is no Guardian."

Naomi tipped her head to the side. "Why is that?"

"Because of the enchantment on the vault," Ada said, as if it were obvious. "The stores fill with what we need to survive, and what would please the Guardian. It's tied to their wants."

"Well, I happen to enjoy beer too, so hopefully that'll start stocking in due time," Oscar said.

Naomi quietly pondered that for a moment, and Elke came up the stairs. "What is that large bathtub contraption next to the sauna?"

Now Oscar really had to fix that thing. "It's a spa. Usually has hot water in it with little jets to push it around to ease muscle soreness and bubbles for, I dunno, texture? It's broken right now, though. I haven't gotten around to fixing it."

"That sounds fun!" Elke was enthusiastic about everything.

Naomi sat down at the table. "We should maybe eat lunch if you're contemplating having a beer with your new roommates."

Stepping up behind Naomi, Elke gently rubbed the other woman's back and began to gently play with Naomi's hair. Naomi looked shocked, but she also shifted to make it easier.

"Would you like us to cook for you?" Elke asked.

"No, that's all right. I think what you're doing right now is far more important. Whatever Naomi wants, make her happy," he said as he started to go through the fridge and thought about lunch. "Ada, I'm sure I know your answer, but Elke, do you have any issue with eating meat?" he asked, pulling out three dark porters, popping the tops, and setting them on the counter. "Also, beer."

"I prefer not to," Elke said, fluffing Naomi's hair and stepping away, "though I can if I need to. I can eat anything. But I prefer vegetables, bread, pastries, those sorts of things."

Contemplating the bottles, Ada picked hers up gingerly. Elke picked hers up almost reverently. Naomi seemed distracted, scrolling through her phone like she was looking for something. Elke took a long draught from the bottle and then let out a blissful, almost orgasmic sound.

"Oh, it's been so long!" Elke took another drink and made the same ecstatic sound. "And it's a good beer, too!"

"You won't have to worry about light beer here," Oscar chuckled. With Elke's preference in mind, he decided to pull out the makings for a salad, and he had some leftover chicken he'd grilled when he was meal-prepping earlier in the week.

For those that did eat meat, it was diced chicken on a bed of greens, blue cheese, some dried cranberries, and some segments of clementines that he'd halved, topped with some sunflower seeds, because he always had a ton of those laying around, and a raspberry vinaigrette. For Elke, the same save the diced chicken. He presented the ladies their bowls with forks and another beer for Elke and finally retrieved his own.

Like everything else, Elke set in enthusiastically, eating happily and complimenting Oscar on the flavors. Naomi ate more slowly, her appetite a little off from the strangeness of everything, but she didn't look like she'd be leaving anything in the bowl. Ada picked out all the chicken, some of the cheese, had a couple bites of greens, then gave the rest to Elke.

The snow was coming down heavier. Hopefully the vault would do whatever replenishing the girls had talked about, because the chances of Oscar getting out for groceries was starting to diminish. As they finished eating, Ada stood and gathered up all the dishes, walking them over to the sink. Elke was gleefully finishing Ada's beer, seeming very happy with life as a whole.

"So will you all just be here in the house every day?" Naomi asked, curious and with a small amount of trepidation.

Ada gestured dismissively. "No, most days you won't even know we're here. Unless you want us to be more present."

"But that takes time," Elke said, getting up to help Ada. "Some Guardians we only saw once a year. Some we saw very frequently. You'll see evidence of our being here more than you'll actually see us."

"I could certainly get used to that. But not too much—might make me lazy," Oscar said with a grin. Leaning back in the chair, he looked out the window. "It's really coming down. Haven't seen it snow like this since Halloween."

Naomi laughed a little. "It always snows on Halloween."

Well, his original plan for escaping with Naomi seemed to be gone with the blanket of snow. His truck could get out, as could her rental SUV, but getting back after might be a different story. "You ladies feel free to keep looking around and doing your thing," he said as he stood up, then offered Naomi a hand. "Join me upstairs for a quick chat?"

Naomi looked a little surprised but got up and took the offered hand. Elke waved cheerfully and Ada smirked suggestively as Oscar led Naomi upstairs.

Once they were in the loft, he moved as far into it as he could to limit possible snooping. "All right, Nomi, I want your full, honest opinion about this weird magic stuff going on. You've mostly been quiet or just agreeing with me, minus the issues you have with Ada. So … lay it on me."

"It's … it's hard to have a full opinion," Naomi said, sitting down on Oscar's bed and rubbing her eyes. "It's hard to do a lot more than just go with the flow. I … I still feel like it can't be real? I keep waiting to wake up or something. But if it is real, it seems … fine? Like, I can't see a downside. Other than …" she trailed off and shook her head, looking grumpy again.

Oscar crouched down in front of her, hands on her knees, and looked up with a gentle smile through his short beard. "Other than? You can be completely honest with me, Nomi. You should know that."

Naomi scowled at him, though she didn't look mad, just uncomfortable and maybe a little embarrassed. "Other than Ada regularly throwing herself at you."

Giving her leg a squeeze, he sighed and laughed softly. "Okay, I want to ask you something, but I want some reassurance that you won't be mad or disgusted with me if I do. Like, wrong question, forget-it-was-ever-asked type thing."

Naomi looked at him suspiciously but nodded. "Okay. What've you got?"

"Are you upset at Ada because you're being protective ... or because you're jealous? Because I wouldn't mind if you were. You'd have way better chances anyway," Oscar said with a fun, reassuring grin.

"I am not—" Naomi began, defensively, then stopped as the rest of what Oscar had said filtered in. "What ... are you implying, exactly?" She didn't look upset. If anything, she looked hopeful.

"I'm implying that if you hadn't been Ezra's little sister, I would have tried dating you a long time ago. But here we are, in our 30s and great friends, and I don't think you being Ezra's little sister matters that much anymore," he said, just letting it out.

For a long moment, Naomi just stared at him. Then, suddenly, she was in his arms, almost knocking him back on his butt, and kissing him hard. Oscar was only surprised for a moment—he hadn't expected such an encompassing response. Naomi was certainly a passionate person, and free with hugs, but Oscar had never seen her with someone. He'd never seen this part of her. The kiss deepened and her hands were in his hair, and she was soft and warm and wanting against him. Wrapping his arms around her, he scooped her up and held her close to him. He'd wanted that kiss for well over a decade.

They parted finally, and Naomi stared into his eyes, panting. "Do ... do you remember, when you and Ezra came to get me from college?" She stroked his cheek, and leaned in to kiss him again, then started to kiss across his jaw. Running his hands along her back, he slipped them under

A Key in the Wood

her shirt to touch her soft skin, to draw his fingers along her spine and just feel her. She'd been teasing him subtly since she arrived, things he could brush off, but he couldn't anymore. Oscar also didn't need to hide her effect on him either.

"We had to sit in the back while Ezra drove, because that damn cello took up the front seat," she said softly into his ear between kisses. "And we just talked for hours, and when I started to get tired you held me so I could stretch out and sleep. I knew then, I knew that I loved you, and I would always love you. And that it didn't matter, because I was Ezra's little sister."

"Of course I remember," he said gently, leaning in to kiss along her neck. "I started seeing you differently my senior year, but I just pushed it away." Reaching up, he took a handful of her hair, and she moaned as he moved her head to the side to get more at her neck and lay soft nibbling kisses. "But then you came back from college that first summer in that sundress, the red one that fit you like it was made for you, and … fuck, you looked amazing."

One of her hands slid over his chest until it found the buttons on his shirt and started to undo them. There was a voice in the back of Oscar's head trying to remind him that they weren't alone in the house, and that the loft has no doors or walls to block sound, but that voice was not half as loud as the sound of Naomi's breath catching as his fingertips explored her skin.

"When we fell asleep on the couch last night," Naomi said, her voice breathy, "and you woke me up, I could feel you beneath me. How hard you were. I wanted to follow you to bed. To just climb on top of you and tell you everything as I rode you. But I was … I was so convinced you wouldn't want me …"

"Took everything I had not to take you with me," he moaned gently, then leaned up to bite her earlobe, "and I dreamt of pounding you into the couch. I've always wanted you."

Naomi let go of him long enough to pull her sweater off, throwing it aside. Oscar was pretty sure it sailed down into the living room, but who cared? It was a good opportunity to get out of his own shirt. She wore a vividly red bra, all the brighter against her creamy skin, with touches of gold and silver embroidery. Something else she must've bought for the holiday. His hands returned to her body, moving lower now to grab her ass and press her against him more. Rolling forward a little, he hoisted her back up onto the edge of the bed but didn't let go.

Naomi let out a soft laugh and ran her hands over Oscar's chest. "My God, you have been spending a lot of time at the gym. I remember the last time we went to the reservoir. You did not look like this." She leaned in and kissed at his collar bone, tongued at his shoulder, then bit down.

Hissing at her bite, Oscar suddenly lifted her and tossed her back onto the bed, climbing above her. "It was a good way to fight depression. Now I'll need another reason to go," he said, leaning in again to go at her neck.

"I've thought of this so many times," she said, her hands sliding down his chest and stomach until she found his belt, fingers deftly undoing the buckle. "You feel better than anything I could have imagined."

"We're not dreaming anymore," he panted.

She bit him again, where his neck met his shoulder, a little harder this time. Her teeth sent electricity through his body in a way he'd never known before, and he loved it. She then loosened her bite and sucked at his skin. It would definitely leave a mark.

"Good god, that's awesome," he muttered as he grabbed her and rolled onto his back, letting her perch atop him so he could work on removing the lovely bra.

"Really?" A smile curled Naomi's lips and she leaned in and kissed him again, roughly, biting his lower lip as she pulled away. "I like to bite. And scratch. Normally I have to dial it back a little, but if you like it …"

"Naomi, I'm a big guy, I can take it. You can't hurt me," he growled, tossing her bra the way of her sweater and cupping her breasts, his hands barely containing the soft flesh he had spied earlier when she was just wearing a tank top, moving freely with her every step.

She gasped and leaned forward, eyes closing. "God, that feels good. We're still wearing too much clothing."

She pulled reluctantly away from his hands, undoing her pants and wiggling out of them. "We are going to spend the entire time you have off talking, making out, and having madly enthusiastic sex all over your house, and then have serious discussions about whether or not I'm just moving in, but for right now—" she climbed back off of him, tossing her pants away and undoing his, "I have wanted this cock for ten years, and I'd like to get it. Immediately."

"Goddamn, you are gorgeous," he said, taking a breath to soak in her figure lit by the midday sun. He then came back to himself and assisted in getting the hell out of the rest of his clothes. The pants and boxers got kicked away, and if there was one thing someone could say about him, it was every part of him was big and thick. Every part.

"I honestly don't know why you're not riding it right fucking now," he smirked.

"Oh," Naomi's eyes grew wide. "Okay, yeah, challenge accepted."

She slid her hands up his legs and crawled back up on top of him. "You are so fucking hot," she said as she reached down and took hold of his cock. She stroked him with her hand just for a moment, just to feel the length of him, then held him in place as she carefully lowered herself onto him.

"Oh, God," she moaned as she worked herself down. She was impossibly wet and more than a little tight. Reaching out, Oscar's hands slid over her as she moved over him, sliding over her shoulders and breasts, then moving to her hips. To his credit, he didn't pull her down, letting her slide on at her pace. Soon, though, her pelvis was flush with his hips, and she shuddered as she got used to the size of him. Once she'd sunk down completely upon him, he let out a long groan and rolled his head back.

"Good god, you feel amazing," Oscar groaned, very slowly starting to move her, lifting her and setting her back down all the way. "I think your plan is perfect, because I will never get enough of you."

Naomi leaned in again for another hot, devouring kiss as Oscar's cock stretched her.

"Das ist erstaunlich," Ada said, a touch of awe in her voice. "I can't entirely believe she took it."

"It's beautiful," Elke said with heartfelt sincerity.

Oscar barely registered that other people were talking. Naomi was occupying his full attention and his entire world. Kissing back, his tongue danced with hers, years of restrained passion pouring into them. Grasping her hips, he started to move his own, thrusting into her firmly but at a steady pace, wanting every bit of her for as long as he could have it. She sucked his tongue, let him move her hips, and wrapped an arm around his shoulder. When the kiss broke, she gasped for air and set her forehead against his.

"They're—ahhh!—watching us." She didn't push away or tell him to stop, and her hips were starting to match his rhythm, adding a bounce to his thrust.

His hands moved from her hips to her ass, sinking into the plush curves as he pulled her down onto him with each thrust, sheathing himself completely in her warm vice of a pussy. Oscar could already feel himself starting to swell, the intensity of it sudden and needed.

"They can watch," he started panting, kissing her back, moving down to attack her neck once more, "or whatever. I have you."

Naomi smiled at him, and he couldn't think of anything more gorgeous in that moment. "Yes, you do." Then they were kissing once more and ignoring Elke's sounds of delighted encouragement.

As the kiss broke Naomi pushed herself back up to ride him properly, the shift in weight making his thrusts deeper, and she clawed at his chest while she cried out.

Hands back to her hips, back arched, Oscar started to bounce her on his cock. It was too much; her tightness, how beautiful she was, how amazing it was they could finally be together, the noises she made, the scratches on his chest. The oncoming orgasm was inevitable.

"I'm coming, Nomi," he grunted, not slowing in the slightest. "You ready?"

"Fuck yes," she moaned. "Come in me, Oz. Please." The please was a desperate whimper.

"Oh fuck," he groaned, wanting her so much. Grasping her hips, he pulled her down as completely as he could, thrusting up to bury his shaft completely inside her as he came. It felt like he was pouring a decade's worth of want, desire, and love into Naomi as he roared out in ecstasy. She was everything he wante,d and she was in his hands, laying atop him, riding him.

As Oscar started to slow, Naomi let herself fall forward again, kissing his face, his neck, leaving sharp little bites. "You're amazing," she breathed. "You are everything I dreamed you would be. You're more than I dreamed you would be."

"I love you, Nomi," he said, kissing her back and grasping her hair, rubbing her ass and lower back. "Have for so long."

"You two are so beautiful together," Elke said quietly, a lot closer than she was the last time. Like, edge of the bed closer.

Turning his head, Oscar saw both Elke and Ada kneeling on the far side, looking like they enjoyed the show. He laughed a little, which transferred into bouncing Naomi and made him twitch inside her.

"Oh, hello. Have fun?" he said, more amused than anything else. Not like he could blame them—it's not like they could ignore the relatively noisy sex with no buffer or walls.

"It's a start," Ada said, her voice a little heavy, and Oscar realized she was touching herself. He couldn't see what her right hand was doing as it was below the bed, but her left was very obviously massaging one of her breasts; the vest she'd worn all day was gone.

Elke was still dressed but squirming in place. "Will you … will you do it again? And maybe … maybe will you let us help?"

Turning to look back up at Naomi, he raised a brow at her. They were magical spirits. Did they count for …? Well, he had no idea. "Um, what's your thought?"

"We're definitely doing it again," Naomi murmured and licked Oscar's neck. "You two can do whatever you like so long as you don't get in the way of what I want."

"Remember you said that," Ada said with a grin, then in a blink she was next to them on the bed, gently lifting Naomi's hips until Oscar slid out of her. Ada pushed Naomi forward, then started to lick up the cum dripping from Naomi's pussy.

"Oh," Naomi said, looking at Oscar with wide eyes.

"Delicious," Ada said, purring. "Elke, come on, he's too big for me."

"Well ... okay," Elke said, before climbing up on the bed and easily wrapping her mouth around Oscar's cock.

"Oh shit," he muttered as Elke sucked his sensitive and still quite hard cock. Running a hand through Naomi's hair, he pulled her down and kissed her deep, tongue teasing and daring hers to respond in kind. Whimpering, Naomi held tighter to Oscar. Her kisses were so hungry, and she felt so warm in his arms.

Ideas and plans started to formulate in his head as to how the two animal girls could assist with his intention to thoroughly ravish Naomi. That could wait, though, as for now he had a second round to start. He could just barely hear Ada's purrs over the sounds coming from Naomi. Elke was doing an amazing job teasing him. There was a reasonable chance this was the best blowjob he'd ever received. Naomi's whimpers got more fervent, and she started to tense in Oscar's arms. She was going to come.

"Elke, that's perfect," he moaned. Reaching down, he held Naomi's legs apart with a firm grip, so she stayed spread. "Keep it up, Ada. Make her scream."

"Ah!" Naomi looked up at Oscar, eyes glazed, as he held her legs open. He could feel her tensing, straining against his grip, but if he wanted to keep her in place, she couldn't stop him. Her nails dug into his shoulder, and she dropped her head next to his, filling his senses with a plaintive cry as she spasmed through her climax.

"Girls, move," he said, maybe a little more forcefully than he had intended, but he had a position to fill. Ada and Elke got out of the way quickly, giggling and pleased with themselves as they did. Still holding firmly to Naomi's legs, he rolled her over once more, this time beneath him. Hooking her legs in his arms, ankles braced against his shoulders, he lined himself up and pressed his girth deep into her.

"Fuck, you're incredible," he rumbled as he started to saw his shaft in and out of her. A combination of her own wetness, Ada's saliva, and whatever was left of his cum made for a slick medium for his cock to plunge into her again and again with little resistance. Naomi exhaled sharply, as if he had knocked the air out of her, then moaned happily.

"Yesss." Naomi caressed his arms then scored them with her nails. She was leaving marks all over him, as if trying to show the world that he was taken, that he was hers. Every scratch, every red mark on his flesh just drove him more. Oscar even surprised himself with how much it turned him on, but the firing of his nerves made him want more.

It was time to make another dream come true, and he had every intention of pounding her into the mattress until she couldn't come any more, or the bed broke. It wasn't a feverish fucking, he wasn't in it for speed; he was making sure she felt completely and utterly rutted. Firm, deep strokes of his cock came with the rise and fall of his hips, and his hands and body held her firmly in place.

"Oh, God, Oz!" Naomi stared up at him, her skin flushed, her lips red. "Fuck, I'm … I'm still so sensitive, if you … if you keep that up …"

"Do it," he growled, not missing a stroke. "Come for me. Come hard and loud. Scream it out for me." God, this is how he'd wanted her. For so long, right here, the two of them feverish for each other. It was happening, no trepidation, no awkward dodging around feelings. Nothing felt more perfect.

"Yes," she whimpered, her voice growing louder. "Yes!" Her nails dug into his arms again and her eyes rolled back as she came. She squeezed tight around his cock. Her body tensed, and he could feel her legs pushing against him for a minute, and then she went soft beneath him, gasping, her arms falling to the side as she moaned through her afterglow.

Smiling, he gently laid her legs down, shifting to hold her hips while he continued to thrust into her, slowing but not stopping. She moaned and shifted beneath him, slowly coming back to herself, whimpering as his cock continued to slowly fuck her. He let go of her hips so he could lean in. He kissed her softly now, tenderly. Moving down, he couldn't get enough of her, his lips grazing over her neck and down her chest before teasingly kissing over the soft mounds, gracing her nipples with his lips and tongue.

"You're so beautiful," he murmured.

Naomi gasped. "You are … there aren't enough words. Handsome.

Breathtaking. I'm … I'm still afraid this isn't real, because it's perfect. You're so perfect."

Elke gently cleared her throat and set glasses of water down on the nightstand. "You were both so delightful to watch. Thank you for letting us join you. Would you like a snack, perhaps?"

"Maybe in a bit," he grinned, sitting back on his heels and pulling Naomi up so that he stayed buried in her, even as he reached over for a glass of water. "I'm definitely not done. But I need to work up my appetite a little more."

Naomi laughed a little, pushing her hair out of her face as Oscar drank his water. "Are you always like this? I'm not complaining. I'm … God, I'm still aching for you to fuck me." She turned pink at that, shy to admit that she was still hungry for more, even as her pussy tensed around him.

"Didn't used to be. I've got a lot more stamina now and, well, I really, really wanted this. You're a hell of a motivator," Oscar said, setting the glass back down and leaning in to kiss her. With a groan he finally pulled out of Naomi, still rock hard for her but figuring she could also use a drink. He helped her sit up, and Elke handed over the other glass of water.

"Is there anything else I or Ada can help with?" Elke asked, her smile playful.

"I can think of a dozen things, but I just want Naomi happy. Have you ever, well, serviced a guardian and their lover like this before?" he asked, and felt a little weird phrasing it like that, but his brain was otherwise occupied.

"Yes! Though it has been a very long time, and not very many of them." Elke sat down on the other side of Naomi and began to play with her hair again. "Despite what Ada implied earlier, this is not a service that the Guardian can demand of us. We have … played with previous Guardians that we felt we would enjoy. Ones that seemed like worthwhile people."

Biting her lip, Naomi looked up at Oscar. "I kind of want to hear what these dozen things are."

"Well, you had Ada eat you out, and Elke did a wonderful job cleaning me up. Elke could taste you while Ada finally put her mouth where her hints were," Oscar started. "Perhaps the lovely spirits could show us how they've spent their time in the vault. Or maybe we could pick one you and I could double team. Or maybe one of them would like to help me get another few orgasms out of you." Yes, every combination and position was floating through his mind at the moment, there was so much to choose from. But he'd known nothing about Naomi's desires or predilections before now; it'd rarely come up.

"Oh, I would love to taste you," Elke said, earnestly. "Ada and I have played many games in our time, though not as many as you might think."

"We hibernate when the vault is dormant for long periods," Ada chimed in from the stairs. "We woke back up when the key found a new Guardian. Perhaps that explains some of our eagerness. Though you are both very fetching. And surprisingly naughty for how wholesome you first appeared."

Naomi blushed again and looked away. It was fascinating seeing her get shy. That really wasn't what she was like. She finished her water and held the glass a touch awkwardly. Elke got up and took the glass, setting it on the nightstand, and then turned back to Naomi with that same earnest longing.

"Please? May I?"

"How …" Naomi looked from Elke to Oscar. "How should we do this?"

"I have a thought," Oscar said, sliding off the bed and standing to stretch. He really was a mountain of a man at this point, with the sheen of sweat that coated him making him glisten slightly in the afternoon sunlight. "Come here."

Brows arched in surprise, Naomi stood up and went to Oscar. She leaned into him, licked his chest and bit him again, moaning softly as she did. It sent another thrill through him. He was covered in her marks, and just knowing that made him throb. He grabbed her hips and turned her around so her back was to him. Sliding his hands up her body, he spent a moment cupping and squeezing her breasts, enjoying the weight of them in his hands. Then he took her arms and guided her so that she had them arched back, hands behind his head.

"Hold on," he said quietly, kissing her neck. As he reached down, he effortlessly scooped her up by the back of her thighs, holding her up and spreading her open before the two spirits, her back pressed against him. She gave a surprised gasp, and her hands grasped the back of his neck.

"Oh God, what are you doing?" She let out a little laugh, her breath coming a little faster. "You're so strong. And ... and it makes me wet." He could just see her cheeks turning pink again.

"That's what I'm hoping for," Oscar growled gently and nipped on her neck. Turning to face the two house spirits, he cleared his throat.

"Elke, come guide my cock into Nomi's wonderfully soft pussy. After that, you can taste both of us as much as you want," he started with his instruction. "Ada, pay particular attention to Naomi's breasts. Explore. Let me know what parts of her really make her moan."

With a happy trill, Elke tripped lightly forward and considered their angles for a moment, then sat down on the edge of the bed and motioned for Oscar to step closer. Once he was in position, Elke grasped his cock and gave it a few strokes before swirling her tongue around the head and briefly sucking at it. She then leaned in and gave Naomi's pussy a few licks before sucking at her clit, causing Naomi to cry out and twitch in Oscar's arms. Satisfied that they were both excited enough, Elke did as she was bid and eased Oscar back into Naomi's wet sex.

"Yeah, I'm never going to get tired of this," Oscar commented, feeling the warmth of Naomi wrap back around him. Bouncing her slightly in his arms, Oscar adjusted his grip to make sure Naomi was comfortable and saddled snuggly. "How's this?" he whispered in her ear.

"So good," Naomi whimpered back. "Though I— Ah!"

Whatever Naomi was going to say was lost as Elke began to eagerly lick the two of them, starting from the base of Oscar's cock and up to Naomi's clit, which was pushed forward and on display in their current position. Ada climbed up on the bed and considered the two of them for a moment, then stepped forward and cupped Naomi's breasts in her hands.

"I don't love being ordered about," Ada said with her trademark disdain. She then licked her lips. "Though you are very lovely, and you tasted so good earlier ..." Ada licked at one of Naomi's nipples, getting another whimper.

Oscar let them explore Naomi for a minute, enjoying the way she whimpered and tensed around him, then started to move, just enough so Naomi would feel his shaft sink into her, then slide almost all the way out, only to sink back in again. He didn't want to move too fast, as that would interrupt both Elke and Ada's attentions upon Naomi. He didn't have a plan beyond this at the moment, aside from making Naomi come as much as her body could handle. This position also helped him to last, as he had to focus on the movements and the subtle strain of keeping her lifted. Naomi moaned, her grip on him tightening. Ada figured out quickly that Naomi liked more intense attention rather than light teases—she squeezed Naomi's breasts as if massaging them and sucked hard at her nipples. Elke moaned as she licked and teased the both of them, seeming to love every moment.

It didn't take long before Naomi drew in a sharp breath, clenched her teeth, and dug her nails into Oscar again as she came, her pussy squeezing tight around his cock.

"That's one," Oscar growled.

He kept it slow as long as he could, with the two spirits relentlessly pleasuring the woman he held. She came a second time, then a third, and that was all he could take at that moment. With all the sensations, he'd been riding the edge, but hearing her cry out and the sting of her nails tipped him over. Grasping her thighs, he pulled her down as far as he could, burying his shaft to the hilt before erupting inside her. To stifle his own noise, he bit down on her shoulder, and she cried out as she shivered in his arms.

When he finally subsided, he softly walked them to an unoccupied edge of the bed and flopped down on it. Elke and Ada got out of the way, then eagerly knelt in front of the two of them to kiss thighs and lick at the sweat and cum. Arms around Naomi, Oscar held her in his lap, still joined with her as completely as their bodies would allow. "So good," he moaned, kissing her shoulder where he'd bit her.

Reaching one hand down, he ran his fingers over both Elke and Ada's heads, playing with their hair and ears in thanks for their participation and post-coital clean up. Having them around sure made this a more interesting experience. They also triggered a conversation that might not have happened, and he couldn't thank them enough for that. He would have to tell them so.

Finally, Elke pulled back, and pulled Ada with her. "Perhaps we should see about dinner."

Ada pouted but sighed and nodded. "We should. All right, fine."

"We'll go take care of everything," Elke said, beaming at the two of them. "And we promise not to come back up. We'll see you downstairs when you're ready." Naomi let go of Oscar long enough to wave to the two but was still gasping and twitching around him. It was rather distracting.

"Mmhmm, sounds good," Oscar responded, giving them a wave as well. After the two spirits went downstairs, Oscar continued to kiss along her shoulder and neck, loving the feel of her body against him, wrapped around him, and in his arms. "I love you so much, Nomi," he muttered. "I'm so glad this happened."

She moaned quietly and shifted her hips back against him. "Love you too, Oz. And I'm glad too." She laughed a little. "I'd probably have a more-emotional response, but you're still … fuck, you feel so good."

"I know," he grunted slightly, "you keep squeezing down on me. Want to keep going?" Grinning slightly, he gave her neck a little nip to accentuate the point.

She clenched again. "Oh, fuck, yes," Naomi moaned. "I can't believe you're still so hard, and it's so fucking hot. Though we … we really should talk a little, soon. About what's next."

"I'm amazed too," he said, rolling over slowly to place Naomi on her stomach on the bed and scooting her up so she was fully on it. "I blame you, how gorgeous you are, and how long I've wanted you."

"You make me feel like a tiny doll," she said with a giggle. "You just move me like it's nothing. And I'm the heaviest I've ever been!" She had a tattoo. A Hand of Miriam, in the infamous tramp stamp area. It was very pretty and well inked, but more than a little surprising.

"I think you mean the curviest you've ever been," he said, caressing the small of her back. "Fancy tattoo you have here, Mimzy."

Shifting his weight, he reached up and got a pillow, then lifted her hips with one hand, tucking the pillow underneath her. "There, now we can fuck and talk," he mused, grabbing her ass and slowly sinking back into her pussy as she lay prone. "Fuck, you feel so good." The moan as he sank back in was loud, and Oscar could just barely hear Ada whine something, but Elke sharply cut her off. Probably asking to go back upstairs.

"Oh, God, you … mmmm … you can't tell anyone about the tattoo." She moaned again as Oscar started to move. "I've … oh, yes … I've had it since college. Only three Jewish girls in the dorm, so we all got one together. Mom would kill me, so Ezra never saw it, so you never saw it."

"Saw what?" he asked and gave her a particularly hard shove before resuming his gentle, constant pumping. "You're so tight."

Naomi panted and grabbed at the bedspread. "So hard to think when you're doing that. Um, okay, when are we telling everyone?"

"Maybe, um, maybe New Year's," he said; this slow pace was deliciously agonizing. "Or whenever we decide to leave the cabin."

"Y-yeah," she gasped, eyes closing. "We need to … to get more of this out of our system before we have to deal with Mom. Okay. Um. Should I just move in?"

"That depends," he said, arching his back to get just a little deeper. "Do you, mmm, want to also deal with my two roommates? Live in a house that's—fuuu—a house that's being worked on. More importantly, God, wake up in my bed every morning and sleep with me every night?"

"I really, really want that last part!" Naomi whimpered and writhed beneath him. "Oh, fuck, Oz I can't … Just grab my hair and fuck me!"

"Yeah, talk later," he agreed and grabbed her firmly by the waist. Lifting her up a touch more, he rested himself soundly on his knees and reached forward to grab her hair. Making sure he had a hold of her roots, he guided her up, arching her back like a bow.

Set into position, he started to thrust much harder. This time he had no one to worry about being in the way, no reason to be steady or paced, just a savage pounding into Naomi's pussy from behind, giving her what she wanted and what sent surges of pleasure through him. Naomi's cries filled the loft—filled the whole fucking house—as Oscar railed her. The bounce of her ass was almost mesmerizing as he pounded into her, making a wet slapping sound with each thrust into her cum-filled pussy.

"Yes!" Naomi clawed at the bedspread. "Fuck, yes! Don't stop!"

One thing Oscar had in spades these days was stamina, and stopping was not an option at this point. A solid grip on her hair and a stalwart hold of her hips guaranteed all she could do was take the crashing of his hips just as she had asked. God, she was amazing. She took what he had and screamed for more.

He was in a groove at this point, persistent thrusts of his hips slammed his cock deep into her, making that delicious ass of hers ripple. He knew, though, the moment she was done, when she'd cried out her last, he would be done as well. It had still been a workout, and certainly more cardio than his routine had put in, but worth every drop of sweat.

They were both drenched by the time Oscar felt his final climax racing upon him. He let go of her hair to grab her hips, and she fell forward, still crying out for him though she could hardly move. He came with a roar, slamming into her one more time. Then, panting, he fell down beside her. It was a long moment as they both caught their breath, then Naomi slowly rolled toward him, and he pulled her in to hold her as they both calmed.

It was a perfect moment, both of them sated for now, spent and content. It would have been easy enough to doze off in each other's arms, but then Ada yelled, "Elke says I'm still not allowed up the stairs, but it sounds like you're done, and dinner is almost ready!"

Naomi laughed softly. "I suppose we should be grateful that Ada at least listens to Elke."

"Despite her protest, I think she might have to listen to me," Oscar chuckled in return. Wrapping an arm around her head, he playfully pulled her in and covered her ear as he rolled away from her. "Be down in a second," he shouted back.

Releasing Naomi, he chuckled and kissed her forehead. "Um, I think both your sweater and bra are downstairs somewhere. Unless one of the girls brought them up and neatly folded them," he said, looking around. He'd need more water, too. There was a sigh from down the stairs, and then Naomi's sweater and bra appeared at the top of the stairs, neatly folded. Naomi kissed Oscar one more time, then fetched her scattered clothes and proceeded to get back into them.

"I'm gonna be sore tomorrow," she said with another laugh. "That does not mean you need to hold back or anything. It's like leg day at the gym: sure you're sore the next day, but you have to keep fucking. I think I just ruined that metaphor, but you get it."

"Good thing that was our plan anyway," he said with a chuckle, gathering up his own clothes. He found a hand towel that he used to wipe off, then handed it to her. "Here. We're taking a shower after dinner either way."

Grinning at her, he got dressed, then waited for her to join him in going downstairs to see what the house spirits had done. Naomi got herself together, and they headed down. The main level was quite a bit more festive than it had been. Boughs of greenery had been assembled and hung, and a larger tree was now in the corner of the room adorned with ribbons and trinkets that must have come from the vault. The table was set, complete with tablecloth and place settings that also looked like the decorations from the vault. It was only set for two, Oscar noted.

Elke was composed once more, in a fresh blouse, her hair pulled back and up. Ada was back in cat form, calmly cleaning herself on the edge of the counter.

"This is amazing," Oscar said, looking around.

"Have a seat," Elke said with her usual cheerfulness. "Dinner is ready."

Looking at the table, he turned back to Elke. "Aren't you two going to join us?"

"See, that's why I asked," Ada said grumpily, "but apparently you two have 'had a big day' and 'need time to talk,' and we already 'upset your romantic holiday plans' or some other nonsense." Elke glared at Ada and made a shushing noise.

Naomi smiled wryly. "Elke, I appreciate your thoughtfulness. Thank you."

Elke looked quite happy with herself, and Ada looked grumpy again. Naomi looked like she was trying not to laugh, but just sat down.

"Okay, well, let me set a few records straight," Oscar said, taking a seat at the table. "Firstly, yes, we had a big day and need to talk, that is true. Second, we didn't originally have romantic holiday plans. In fact, it was you two that got us to finally talk about things and make it romantic, and for that I'm not sure how I'll pay you back because," Oscar paused and looked at Naomi, a smile crossing his face, "damn."

Elke seemed very pleased, but Ada appeared slightly confused. "So what does that mean exactly?" Ada asked Elke quietly.

"It means we didn't interrupt anything, but we're still leaving," Elke responded with surprising firmness. "And we can discuss the rest later."

Elke and Ada quickly set covered trays of food down on the table—something else that must have come from the vault, though Oscar recognized his grandmother's soup tureen and briefly wondered how they got it out of the storage room. It was a full Christmas Eve dinner, which was not too surprising, as the ingredients had already been purchased and in the fridge: the chicken that Naomi had brought, dressing, gravy, cranberry sauce, the potatoes and asparagus Oscar had grabbed, and a basket of rolls. The soup seemed to have been put together from things in the fridge, and it smelled divine. Still on the counter was the torte Naomi had brought, and ... fudge? That looked like fudge. Oscar didn't know he had the ingredients to make fudge. Maybe he didn't.

"We'll see you in the morning for breakfast," Elke said as they started down the stairs to the lower level.

"But not too early," Ada chimed in, and then the two disappeared.

Sighing, Naomi looked back at Oscar. "Well. This is quite a bit more than I was planning. It's very nice."

"Obviously," Oscar laughed. "Our original plan was watching movies, eating food, and hanging out, while unwittingly teasing each other the whole time." He placed his napkin in his lap and considered what to eat first. "All right, Nomi, what would you like to talk about first? Revising when we tell people? Seemed like moving in was settled."

It was quiet for a moment as Naomi gathered her thoughts and served herself a bit of everything. Oscar followed suit, filling up his plate. Lunch had been a light affair, and he'd been doing a lot of physical work in the past few hours. The man was hungry. It was a good thing he had planned for leftovers to be eaten over a couple of days.

"I think waiting until New Year's may still be good for telling people," she said finally. "And I don't think we need a hard and fast plan; it doesn't have to be on the day, but we probably need a few days of just each other." She took a bite, still thinking, and nodded to herself. "I might still need to get an apartment in Denver. But I am open to just getting a studio somewhere, setting up a bed and an office, and making this my actual home if … if you think there's room for me. You haven't really said how you feel about it."

"Well, yes, the commute sucks, but," he said, scooping up some potatoes and piercing a piece of chicken, "look, Naomi, I wasn't kidding. I've wanted you for years. Maybe moving in is a fast first step, but I'd love to have you here. You'd really make this place feel more like a home."

Naomi blushed again and pushed her hair back. "I mean, it seems dumb to take it slow. We've known each other for, what, twenty years almost? I know living together will be an adjustment, but I already know you don't snore or keep the thermostat at indecent temperatures."

"If you're sure then I'm sure," he said with a nod. "I mean, the past couple of hours kinda changed my life in countless ways. I'm digging all of it."

"Well, moving in together is basically parametric testing a relationship, so this will go brilliantly, or someone will set the house on fire," she said dryly, reaching for one of the wine glasses and taking a cautious sip. "Oh, that's the sparkling cider I brought. Good."

"Those are two very different reactions," he said, pouring gravy on his dressing. "I figure there was more of a gray area in there, but with you, I guess that tracks."

"Anyway," Naomi said, taking another sip before leaning forward with a playful grin, "how long before I'm allowed to propose?"

His pouring kept going when she asked that question, but he was able to recover himself before he'd flooded his plate. "Um, well, I suppose that should be a bit too. Let's give it a couple of months first, hm?"

Giggling, Naomi pushed her plate over. "Here, you can pour some off on mine. And I'm teasing. Obviously you have to propose. It doesn't have to be a diamond, but it needs to be large enough that Mom can show her friends and make them jealous or something."

With a sigh, Oscar carefully poured his excess gravy onto her plate and wiped up the drips. "Depending, that might be taken care of. I mean, they said the vault isn't for pilfering, but surely a really nice ring isn't too much to ask, right?"

"Seems reasonable." Taking a breath, Naomi looked up again. "I love you, Oz. It's been a mad couple of days. I still have a gift for you tomorrow morning, but I think I already gave you the best gift I could."

Smiling, he reached over to caress her hand. "I love you, too. Yes, you still have a present as well. Eight of them, in fact, because I was paying attention, but you don't have to wait a day between opening them," he grinned. "Though you're right, you are clearly the best present I could have gotten. I mean, I did get a magical vault with two beautiful house spirits that are willing to please, but you're still better."

"Awww, for all eight nights!" Naomi smiled brighter and giggled a little again. "If I had to get in a relationship with a gentile, you're probably the most acceptable one I could have picked. Dad won't care. Dad hasn't cared since the 70s. Mom will, but it will be okay, because it's you."

"I'm almost sure your mom is hoping. She'd said something to Ezra while he was on the phone, and he insisted that we're 'just friends.' Which, you know, was true until a few hours ago," Oscar chuckled.

"You're right, she'll probably just be thrilled I finally picked someone." Naomi tipped her head to the side. "So what do you say? We finish dinner, curl up on the couch, and watch Violent Night?"

"That sounds like a plan. I think I need a little break anyway. Not used to that much activity; I think I need to moisturize."

Snickering, Naomi nodded. "Fine. I'm also a little tender." She picked up her glass again and held it up for a toast. "To the best holiday I've ever had. Merry Christmas, Oz."

"With many more to come," he said, clinking her glass. "Happy Hanukkah, Mimzy."

They both drank, and smiled at each other, and got back to dinner. They could just barely hear from downstairs Elke squee with delight, and Ada   scoff.

My Holiday Superhero
by Sigh
Bluesky: @sighonsocial.bsky.social

Chapter One

A microwave. It wasn't exactly the ideal companion on Christmas Eve, but it was better than nothing.

"Round and round she goes," I sang as my plate of festive leftovers lazily spun around inside the microwave. "Where she'll stop, nobody knows!"

The microwave dinged. I opened the door, cradled the scorching hot plate with a dishcloth and carried it to the kitchen island.

I jabbed at the turkey leg with a fork. "Well, my fowl feathered friend, it would appear that your goose is cooked."

I sighed. Even a lame joke like that would have gotten at least a light chuckle out of my brother if not a mild groan.

I poked at the food. It looked delicious. The cranberries glistened, the mashed potatoes were fluffy and the gravy thick and chunky.

… and yet I had no appetite.

"Merry Christmas, Lois," I said softly and pushed the plate aside.

I looked around and soaked in my surroundings. I was sitting in my brother's spacious kitchen, alone. He, his wife and their two wonderful children were currently on route to a warm destination to enjoy Christmas together on a tropical beach. I'd been invited but had politely declined.

I think I mumbled something about wanting to catch up on some light reading which was complete BS. I just … I just couldn't do it. Not now, not after yet another messy breakup. I was sapped, running on fumes and I didn't want to ruin their vacation by spending it being mopey at the swim up pool.

He'd then offered to let me crash at his luxurious family home and I'd accepted. Besides, it was a huge upgrade from my tiny apartment.

There were a few conditions.

I reached over and checked the list he'd left me. It was short: water the plants every few days and feed their beloved cat Daisy.

Wait … they had a cat?

I stood up, followed the instructions and checked its bowl. It was still full. But where was the damn thing? I swear I hadn't seen it since I'd arrived. It hadn't gotten out, had it?

As if timed, I heard a crash from the basement. Had I accidentally locked it down there?

I set down the list of instructions and left the kitchen.

… how to describe my brother's house.

Think of your favorite warm-hearted comedy from the 80's. Now, do you remember that ridiculously large house they all lived in? Picture that but with the holiday charm cranked up to eleven.

There were Christmas decorations everywhere. I'd stopped walking around the house barefoot because I was constantly pulling tinsel out from between my toes. And don't get me started on the wreaths. If everything wasn't so sickeningly jolly, you'd think you'd stumbled into a funeral parlor.

The crown jewel was the Christmas tree in the lobby. It was enormous. I wouldn't have been surprised if a tree house fell out if I shook it. I'd never seen so many Christmas ornaments concentrated in one space before, nor did I ever want to again. It was actually a bit unnerving, like staring into the infinite universe, seeing a billion stars staring back and feeling pathetically small.

I walked through the lobby to the basement door, opened it and descended the stairs. The finished basement served as a movie den as well as a refuge for my brother's abandoned gym equipment.

"Here ..." What was the cat's name again?

There was another loud bang from behind a closed door. What if it wasn't the cat? I thought as I crept up to it. What if a gang of raccoons had laid low till the coast was clear and were planning to ransack the place? Then what?

Well, it's too late to go grab a pair of oven mitts and a garbage bag, I thought as I opened the door and peered inside.

A shadow hung in the air like a velvet fog. Steel shelves lined the walls stocked with cardboard boxes and plastic bins. One had fallen, spilling its contents across the concrete floor. The family cat lay in the center, chewing on an old plush cat toy.

"Caught you red handed." Smiling, I reached down and scooped her up. She purred loudly as she continued to gnaw on the plush cat toy.

"Keep it," I said as I scratched behind her ears. "If it'll keep you out of trouble, it's all yours."

I was about to turn and leave when something caught my eye. It was the colors. There was something there, the combination of the cherry red and honey lemon that resonated with me, scratching the surface of an old memory.

I set the cat down, reached into the pile of clutter and pulled out ...

"No way ..." I whispered. "He's still got it."

There is a long list of toys from our collective childhood that are most likely now buried in a landfill. Had we kept them safe, hidden from our neat freak of a mother, we probably could have made a tidy profit selling them on the internet. Sadly, it was not to be, and I had assumed none had survived.

One apparently had and I was now holding it. It was a bit weathered; the paint was chipped, and the limbs were loose but there was no mistaking it.

"Well hello, Chuck POW'er," I said as I held up the plastic action figure. "How's your turbo action kung-fu fist? Still got its supersonic spring?"

I pulled his arm back and it snapped forward. "Well, they certainly don't make them like they used to, do they?"

I turned him over in my hand. He was exactly as I remembered him, a ridiculous amount of muscles all painted red with bright yellow undies. I think he'd originally come with a cloth cape, but my brother had lost it during one of his many adventures.

Chuck POW'er had been a staple when I was growing up, back when cartoons served only one purpose: to sell toys. I still remembered how the Chuck POW'er phenomenon swept through our school, his toothy grin slapped onto backpacks, lunchboxes and just about every other product you could think of.

Hell, there was even a cereal! I'd never tried it but could still vividly remember the commercials. Those puffs of golden wheat and brightly colored marshmallows looked delicious!

There was an entire lore built around him, including his allies, enemies, and array of combat vehicles, all carefully posed in the holiday catalogs.

There was only one problem …

Chuck POW'er and the extended POW'er man universe were boy's toys. No girls allowed.

It had annoyed me to no end, and I'd expressly asked Santa for one. Whether the letter was lost, or ignored, I'll never know. I mean … it's a long way to the north pole, a lot can happen along the way.

I still remember that Christmas morning. I woke up at the crack of dawn, rushed down the stairs and feverishly tore through the wrapping paper, only to discover a Susie needs your constant attention doll while my brother not only got a full battalion of Chuck POW'er's closest allies, but he also got his arch nemesis Doctor Torment and his remote volcano command base!

"So stupid," I whispered, the pain of the memory still lingering.

I set the Chuck POW'er doll down and picked up the cat. "That's enough time spent wandering down memory lane. How does some leftover turkey sound?"

The cat meowed approvingly. I carried her upstairs and prepared her a small plate of turkey. She devoured it, flopped down on the kitchen floor and licked her paws clean.

"Will that tide you over for a while? Cause I plan to sleep in, ideally till the new year."

The cat ignored me as I turned off the lights. "Merry Christmas, furrball," I said and walked out of the kitchen. I crossed the lobby, past the giant Christmas tree and headed up the winding staircase.

… a winding staircase. The pleasant pine needle scent and festive garland was a nice departure from the smell of microwaved fish soaked into the concrete of the stairwell I climbed whenever my apartment's ancient elevator broke down.

I prepared for bed, grabbed hold of a pillow, sunk below the bed's thick blankets and drifted off to sleep, my only wish, that this nightmare of a holiday would soon be over.

As I sank into the murky depths of my subconscious, I dreamed.

Chapter Two

In the vanity's pale fluorescent light my makeup was flawless. I'd done it myself, having discovered that no one on the remote volcanic island had any clue how to apply makeup. Seriously, were there no henchwomen amongst them?

My hair was done up in an elaborate bun, held together with a jeweled tiara. I wore a sparkling diamond necklace around my neck. My shoulders were bare, the top of my long, elegant snow white wedding gown just barely holding up my ample breasts. It was a bit on the slutty side, but I was after all … a bad girl.

I reached down and tugged the gown up. The cups kept slipping, my girls eager to escape. Would I make it through the ceremony without popping out? Perhaps.

There was a knock at the door.

"Your elegance?" a voice whimpered through the door.

"What is it?" I growled.

The henchman gently opened the door and peered inside. "The preparations have all been made. We're ready when you are …"

I grabbed a plastic hairbrush from the vanity and hurled it over my shoulder. It hit the door with a loud bang. "I'll be ready when I say so," I hissed.

"Sorry, your excellence, my apologies your …"

I reached for a small oval mirror. They slunk away and closed the door.

Fools, I thought. The lot of them.

My temper had a short wick. It wasn't the first time I'd berated a henchman, and I doubted it would be the last. I blamed it on the volcanic island. From the sky it was a glittering gem, exotic and exciting. But on the beach, after you cut through the thick thorny under bush, you discovered it was infested with mosquitoes and stank like a rotten egg.

Weeks stuck on it had eroded my last nerve. I was about ready to strap myself to the lairs' secret hidden rocket if it meant I could escape this wretched place.

… after the wedding.

I stood up, crossed the room and opened the door. "Still here?"

The henchman cowered on his knees.

"Yes, your excellence. In case I could be of assistance."

… your excellence. They'd been calling me that ever since I'd arrived. I hadn't bothered to correct them.

"Well, don't just stand there," I barked. "Lead the way."

"Yes, your excellence, of course, your excellence," he said, stood up and scurried off down the hallway. I followed him, holding up my wedding gown's long train.

We wove through a concrete maze, turning right, left … and right again?

"Wait, this isn't the way to the magma observatory."

"There's been a … change of venue," the henchman squeaked.

"Has there now," I growled.

"Doctor Torment insisted on it."

"Take me to him, now" I barked.

"Yes, your excellence," the henchman said, cowered before me and continued on.

We dove down further into the twisting maze. Through the thick concrete walls, I could hear the low hum of the generators and smell the thick fumes of gasoline it choked on. I swear if the heat melted any of my makeup there would be hell to pay!

We arrived at a thick metal hatch. The henchman cranked the wheel, opened it and I stepped inside.

"Seriously," I growled as I looked around. "The underwater loading bay?"

Several henchmen were busy climbing ladders, securing thin bands of tropical flowers to the concrete walls. Doctor Torment, my fiancé, was standing on a metal bridge crossing the narrow gap between the open channel of water.

"You've arrived! At last!" he said as he looked up at me, and then shooed away several henchmen that were surrounding him.

I stomped across the thick concrete floor, my pearl white heels firing like revolvers, my anger simmering below a boil.

"Is this meant to be a joke, Brad?" I growled as I pierced his orbit. "You promised me the Magma Observatory, not this stinking submarine bay."

"It's Doctor Torment around the henchmen," he hissed as he looked around. "Remember? We discussed it."

I raised my hand, waving the thin engagement ring he'd given me in front of his face. "Seven years … seven long years. That's how long I had to wait for you to finally stop dragging your feet and propose. I grinned and beared it, and do you know why?"

I didn't wait for him to answer. It wasn't an invitation. "Because you promised me a magical wedding. This …" I said pointing at the drab soot-stained concrete walls. "Is not magical."

He flashed me his signature villainous grin. "And you will, my love, you will. I would never have dreamed of changing the venue had it not been for a very, very good reason."

"Bullshit," I growled.

He walked over to me and touched my hand. He was wearing the same stupid outfit he wore every single day of the week. It was too much purple. It wouldn't have bothered me so much if I didn't know he only owned three identical matching sets.

"I hate to ruin the surprise, but I got you something special as a wedding gift."

"More bullshit," I grunted. "There's nothing you could possibly get me that would …"

"In fact," he said, interrupting me. "It's arriving as we speak."

There was a heavy mechanical whine as the thick double doors of the submarine bay opened. The henchmen frantically ran around as commands were issued over the loudspeakers. Light poured in and … and …

"What is that … a whale?" I asked in horror.

It was gray, bloated and for some odd reason wrapped in a big fluffy red bow.

"Better. Much better," Doctor Torment said as he walked to the edge of the railing. "It's a thermal nuclear submarine, complete with a full payload of ballistic continental missiles."

I stared at him stunned. "Your perfect wedding gift is a … submarine?"

He peered back over his shoulder at me, grinning like a ghoul. "Isn't it incredible! We've been tracking it for weeks waiting for just the right time to swoop in and grab it."

As he spoke, the nuclear submarine pulled up below us and docked. The crew were led off at gunpoint by the henchmen.

"A nuclear submarine … as a wedding gift," I whispered, stunned.

"Why are you still standing there," he said, his voice giddy with excitement. "Do you want to have a look?"

I followed him like a zombie down the metal walkway to the small gangplank leading to the …

"A submarine …" I murmured again. "A nuclear submarine … seven long years and all I have to show for it is a nuclear submarine."

I stepped up onto the slippery surface of the submarine. The entrance was a small circular hatch. Doctor Torment climbed down it with ease.

Had I known I'd be crawling into a cramped submersible I wouldn't have worn heels, I thought bitterly as I navigated the treacherous ladder down into the murky depths below.

I reached the bottom and looked around. It was like I'd crawled inside an old appliance. There was a maze of pipes and gauges. Everything was a cold steel color. It felt cramped, like the walls were squeezing me like a fist. It smelled like an old shoe. It was also uncomfortably hot. I clenched the train of my wedding gown, afraid it might fall into a pool of grease.

"Shall we take her for a spin?" Doctor Torment asked me,

gleefully.

I was about to object, but the words failed me. I'd expected him to throw a wrench into the wedding, find some stupid excuse to stall yet again. But this … this was beyond anything I had imagined.

"Why aren't we moving!" he barked. "I want to hear propellers turn, rotors spin, nuclear engines do … whatever it is they do!"

As I stood there, he went to the periscope and peered through. His crew of henchmen scurried to the available positions and began to frantically push buttons. The submarine lurched to life and jerked forward.

"Backward you clumsy fools. We're about to hit the wall!" he growled as he swiveled the periscope around.

The sub groaned, bells rang and the rotors stopped and reversed. The sub slowed down then began to ease backwards.

Seven years, I thought. Seven long years. I still had the picture in my mind of where I had expected to be. I wasn't even shooting for the stars. A house? Sure, if we could afford it. If not at least an apartment with a decent view of the city. I wasn't against the idea of kids, but a few fur babies would suffice. Maybe I'd finally manage to secure a better job. Beyond that, some sense of stability, a working partnership, maybe a few vacations … at no point did I think I'd be standing in a nuclear sub.

"Find me something to blow up!" Doctor Torment shouted.

The crew of henchmen darted back and forth between stations, ignoring me. He pried his eyes off the periscope and walked over to me, grinning. "So, what do you think? Pretty fucking cool right?"

"Brad …" I said in a calm voice, the one I used right before I was about to explode.

"Doctor Torment," he said, correcting me.

"Doctor Torment …" I said through clenched teeth. "Look, I believe I've been reasonable. When you said you wanted to change careers and pursue world domination. I went along with it. When you held a city hostage, and your only demand was for a canceled sitcom to reunite and perform your finale script I didn't say a word. And when you emptied my account and bought crypto ... did I get mad? No. All I asked was for one day ... one day Brad ... Brad?"

He stared at me with a blank expression. I recognized it. None of what I had just said had registered.

"Babe, as soon as I defeat Chuck POW'er and seize control of all the world's governments I promise you I'll ..."

"Don't babe me, Brad," I hissed. "Ever since you became a super villain you've been obsessed with Chuck Pow'er. Did you know that you talk about him in your sleep? You do. It's creepy. Whenever you two battle, I feel like a third wheel."

"That's Doctor ..."

"A cruise ship on our port ... bow?" one of the henchmen shouted.

Doctor Torment spun around. "Perfect, an easy target. Ready the torpedoes!"

"Torpedoes loaded ... I think." One of the henchmen replied.

Doctor Torment dashed to the periscope, pulled it down and searched for his target. "Where are you ... where ... are you. There you are!" he said gleefully. "Now I have you right where I want you. Fire on my mark. Wait for it ... wait for it."

I stood there, defeated. When would it get better? If not now, when? One voice told me to run, or rather swim in the opposite direction of whatever this was. The other told me to stick with it. I'd already invested seven years. What were a few more? Things would eventually change. I'd eventually wear him down, mold him into a caring and attentive husband who would ...

"Fire, fire now! Blow them all to hell. Destroy, destroy, destroy!" Doctor Torment screeched as he hopped with glee.

"Firing torpedoes," one of the henchmen shouted.

Doctor Torment pulled away from the periscope. "Wait ... you remembered to open the torpedo bay doors first, righ …"

There was a blinding white light. I was torn out of the dream and sent tumbling over the side of the bed. I landed on my ass with a loud thump.

"The fuck …" I grunted as I looked around confused. I was on the floor. I'd pulled the sheets off the bed with me and was tangled in them. My ass stung like I'd been paddled, which, without going into too much detail about my sex life, I have.

I checked the time. 3 am.

"Ho ho hilarious," I groaned as I pulled myself off the floor. I was about to wrap myself tightly in my blankets and go back to sleep when I caught the faint smell of …

… gingerbread?

Most of the house stank of the wretched spice but it smelled fresh and somehow … familiar. I stood up. Had I accidentally left gingerbread cookies baking in the oven? I tended to be absent minded when I was mopey. Maybe I'd tuned out and gone on a rogue binge baking spree.

I tossed the blanket on the bed and walked out of the room. With the house to myself I didn't bother changing out of my loose t-shirt which just barely covered my panties … just barely.

I crept down the hallway … wait, why was I creeping? It was Christmas Eve and I was a grown ass adult. I could do whatever I wanted.

I walked down the stairs, carefully navigating the steps in the dark. There were still a few Christmas lights to guide my way, casting long colorful beams across the walls. I reached the lobby, turned and saw …

I saw …

I …

The brain is a fragile thing. I think it's an organ but I'm probably wrong. Whatever it is, mine has suffered its fair share of abuse. I'm lucky to have made it to the end of my twenties without pickling it … anyway, battle scars aside, as I stared at the six-foot-tall present wrapped with a giant red fluffy bow in front of me I started to wonder if it was time for a trade in.

… I would have noticed a giant present in the living room before I'd gone to sleep right? I feel like that's something that's hard to miss.

I caught the faint hint of gingerbread again. It seemed to be dancing in the air. Then it changed. Was that candy Cane? … No, wait, I smelled eggnog then …

I stepped closer towards the festively wrapped monolith. I was lost under its spell, drawn to it. There was a tag taped to it. Of course there was a tag. I reached out, turned it over and read it aloud.

"To Lois. From … Santa," I whispered.

I looked up at the present. Should I open it? I could wait till the morning or …

If it was a prank, better to get it over with now. Let everyone have their laugh then crawl back into bed and wait for this miserable year to end.

I reached up, dug my fingers into the wrapping paper and tore it open. The bow unwound and fell to the floor. Underneath was …

"No way," I said in awe. "It can't be."

It was. A giant Chuck POW'er, mint in box. The cardboard was brightly colored full of painted explosions and word bubbles describing all his action-packed features.

I peered through the clear plastic. There he was, life size, standing with his fists resting on his waist, head raised, smiling defiantly. It was a perfect replica, every muscle carefully sculpted and painted with a bright coat of cherry red.

… and he even had his signature yellow cape!

My eyes strayed down, following the lines of his perfectly sculpted body. Was everything proportional?

"It's rude to stare."

I leapt into the air, fell back and slammed into the floor, landing on my ass again.

"Fuck," I groaned as I rubbed it.

"Language!"

I looked up. Chuck POW'er was staring back at me. He'd ... he'd spoken?

If this was a prank, I'd already handed them a perfect viral moment. All that needed to happen now was for my brother to come rushing out from behind the tree and gloat.

... none of which happened.

"I hate to be a bother, but could you do me a huge favor?" Chuck POW'er asked me.

I stared up at him, wide eyed. "Ah ... sure."

"Thanks. See those plastic ties around my arms and legs? Could you please cut them? A pair of regular scissors should suffice."

"Cut the plastic ties," I said as I pried myself off the floor. "Sure ... I ah ... I can do that."

"Thanks," he said and smiled. "I really appreciate it."

"I'll ah ... I'll be right back," I said, turned and stumbled into the kitchen.

... scissors, scissors, I thought as I opened the kitchen drawers and rummaged through them.

Seriously, what the fuck was going on? Who was this guy? A paid actor? If he was, they'd done an amazing job casting him. The likeness was uncanny.

I found a pair of scissors and returned to the living room. "Should I just ..." I asked as I touched the thin plastic film window.

"From where I'm standing it looks like there are just a few glue spots holding it in place. Your best bet is probably to just push it in."

"Right," I said, set the scissors down, placed both hands on the plastic and pushed. There was a ripping sound as it tore loose. I grabbed hold of the edge, pulled it free and set it down on the floor.

I reached down, picked up the scissors and turned back to face him. There were five plastic bands pinning him to the back of the cardboard box.

"So just … cut the plastic ties?" I asked.

"Yes please."

"Couldn't you just … you know, use your super strength and tear through them?" I asked.

"You would think so, but no. Thin plastic ties are one of my greatest weaknesses."

"I … see," I said as I stepped into the large cardboard box. I looked up at him. He was poured into his costume, the thick material of his super suit stretched against his bulging muscles. I don't think I'd ever seen a finer specimen of raw masculinity.

As I stood there, stretching up on my toes, I felt the hem of my cotton T-shirt rise, dipping just below my belly. Fuck, could he see my panties? I looked, expecting to see his eyes dart away, but they remained fixed ahead as he patiently waited.

I reached over, slid the scissors under the band on his left arm, snipped it and did the same with his other arm. I reached down to the plastic tie around his chest.

"So, there's a perfectly rational explanation why a life size Chuck POW'er doll … man, is trapped in a cardboard box in my brother's living room, right?" I asked as I fought with the plastic tie.

"This is your brother's house?" he asked.

"Yea. I'm a … house sitting for the week."

"I see. It's quite nice. Very spacious."

"Very," I said as I cut the plastic tie. "You still haven't answered my question."

"Oh that," he said and looked down at me. "I have no idea but if I were to guess, I'd say it was all part of one of my arch-nemesis's master plans to destroy me. It happens quite often."

"I see," I said as I looked down. The last two ties were wrapped around his thighs. There was no easy way to reach them, I'd have to go down on my knees.

… my knees. I'd just met this guy and I was already willing to go down onto my knees? How easy was I?

I'm just going to cut him loose, escort him to the front door then go back to sleep, I thought. When I wake up, if there's still a giant cardboard box in the living room, I'll … I'll. Well, I had no idea what I'd do. I'd cross that burning bridge when I got to it.

I slowly sank down to my knees and tried to avoid staring directly into his nether region It was extremely difficult. He was wearing a bright pair of lemon yellow undies. It was like there was a target painted on his junk, not to mention its size. Good lord, super indeed.

I worked quickly, cut both ties, rose and tugged on the hem of my T-shirt. Apparently, whatever strange BDSM kink this was, I was into it because it was pushing all the right buttons. Seriously, was I actually wet?

"Well, there you go. All done," I said, my eyes searching for a safe harbor or perhaps a bucket of cold water I could douse myself with.

He stepped out of the large cardboard box and stretched. "Thank you. You've done a great service for me and for the forces of truth and justice."

"Right, gotcha … so anyway it's rather late and I …"

"… and I believe every good deed should be rewarded."

"Ah, that's alright, you don't have …"

I gasped as he rose into the air. Wires? my brain suggested, trying desperately to find a rational explanation for what I was seeing.

As he hovered above me, he held out his hand. "It's still early. Let me show you one of the great unknown wonders of the world. I promise I'll have you back before the morning. It's the least I can do."

I stared at his open hand, mesmerized. If this was a prank, what was the point? We were well past the "gotcha moment." What did I have to lose?

I reached up and took his hand. He pulled me up off the floor and I joined him in the air.

"How?" I gasped as I watched my feet dangle below me.

He pulled me closer. "The next part's going to be a bit bumpy, so I suggest holding on tightly."

"I ..." Before I could finish my sentence, we rocketed up, smashing through the ceiling. I screamed, pressed my head against his chest, then peered down. We were moving at an incredible speed, the ground below us a distant memory.

How am I ever going to explain a gaping hole in my brother's fancy house? I thought in horror.

"Sorry, I didn't mean to scare you," Mr. Action Man shouted over the roar of the air as it whipped past us. "Don't worry, at this height and speed it'll be a short trip."

We shot up into the atmosphere, cutting through the coal black night sky. I dug my fingers into him, buried my head against his chest and closed my eyes. Pressed against the thick fabric of his super suit I heard the slow rhythm of his mighty heart, beating like a hammer. I focused on it, emptying my mind until it consumed my world. Everything was still, quiet, peaceful.

"Aren't they pretty?" he asked as we slowed down and coasted.

I pried my eyes open. "What?" I asked.

"The stars. They're a lot clearer up here above all the light pollution."

I looked up. Through the thin veil of ozone separating us from the eternal void of space, I saw the cosmos, intimate and naked, the stars, the size of softballs, sparkling like diamonds.

"It's ... stunning," I whispered. "And it's so ... quiet."

"It is. Every now and again a satellite will cruise by beeping loudly, but otherwise it's really quite peaceful. Whenever I get super stressed after an epic battle I like to come up here to relax. I wish I could just float up here all day. Sadly, gravity has other plans."

As he said this we slowly started to drift back down, building momentum. "Hold on tight," he shouted. "The next part's a lot like the down slope of a roller coaster."

I buried my head in his chest again and closed my eyes. The wind built into a mad frenzy, howling like a feral animal as we plummeted back down towards the ground. I think he spoke, but his voice was drowned out by the thunderous noise.

I prepared for the end. There was no way we could possibly survive the descent. I may not have paid much attention in high school, but I had a general understanding of what happens when you drop something heavy from a very high height. I believe the scientific term is "splat".

The life flashing before my eyes was half-hearted. My bucket list was a blank scrap of paper. Had I not had enough time? Had I had too much time and just wasted it?

"So … what do you think?" he asked me.

I opened my eyes. "Am I … dead?" I asked.

"Not that I'm aware of."

I was still clinging to his chest. I looked around. We were hovering above a sheet of ice at the bottom of a vast crater. In the center was a …

"Are those … domes?" I asked.

"Ice domes," he replied. "It's the former residence of the notorious evil genius Baron Von Frigid. After his last mad escapade, the governments of the world decided they'd had just about enough and were going to nuke him off the face of the globe."

As he spoke, we floated across the ice field towards the domes. I looked down at my bare legs dangling above the frozen glacier. How was I not cold? Was that another one of his super powers?

"… luckily I intervened, popped up here and grabbed him. He's cooling off in a cell as we speak. I doubt we'll be hearing from him anytime soon."

We approached a large frozen archway. Its sealed door was like a slab of granite. "You brought me up to the North Pole to see a super villain's lair?" I asked, confused.

"Not quite," he said as we gently landed. My feet touched the snowy plane … there was no chill, no cold. Nothing.

He stepped over to the door and it slid open. "Not much use for home security when you're tens of thousands of miles away from civilization."

"I suppose not," I said as I followed him inside the dome and saw…

"Wow," I whispered in awe.

"Right!" he said as he stood back and let me absorb it all.

The interior was like the inside of a snowglobe. Flakes of snow drifted lazily in the air. Two spiraling staircases rose in the center up to a second floor.

"It's … it's incredible," I said, softly. "And everything is made of ice?"

He walked down the steps to the atrium. "Yea. He cut it out of a glacier. It's prehistoric. I always meant to ask him if he designed everything, or he brought someone in to do it. If it was him, he missed his true calling. He would have been a fantastic designer."

"What's up there?" I asked, looking up at the spiraling staircase.

He peered back over his shoulder and smiled. "That's what I brought you here to see."

"Oh," I said nervously.

We ascended the stairs. Surprisingly, the thick slabs of ice weren't cold, nor was there a chill in the air. Was it the adrenaline from the trip?

We reached the second floor. A frosted dome of ice hung above us. In the center of the room was a circular bed. Its sheets were glacial blue with snow white pillows.

… a bed, seriously? I thought.

"The button should be …" he said as he walked over to the wall and searched. "Here!'

He poked the wall. The dome split into two halves and opened. I looked up. The sky was a velvet canvas, the stars like white flecks of paint.

"I know what you're thinking. It's very impressive and all but that's not why I brought you all the way up to the North Pole."

"It's not?" I asked. "Then why?"

"To see …" He took a deep breath. "This," he said and exhaled. His breath, like a strong gale wind shook the sky revealing a shimmering veil that sparkled like a sea of sequins. The colors were vibrant. I saw lime green, honey yellow and a hint of ruby red.

"Are those the …"

"The Northern lights?" he replied. "Yes. It's more commonly known as an aurora. I won't bore you with the science … most of which I don't really understand myself."

I stepped forward. The glittering light slowly drifted down, blanketing us. I raised my hand. It passed through it. "It's … it's beautiful."

"It is, isn't it? With all the chaos and uncertainty, it's easy to forget that there's still some beauty left in the world."

I ran my hands through the bands of light watching as it passed through them like a spectre. I laughed. I actually laughed. I was enjoying myself, I really was, and what surprised me was I couldn't remember the last time I had. Seriously, when was the last time I'd had a "good day?" I'd been on autopilot for days, months, years, locked in a perpetual loop, terminally online, endlessly doom scrolling. I needed a change, something to get me out of this funk, to jumpstart my life. I needed …

194

Sigh

I looked over at Chuck POW'er. The light danced across his perfect physique. He was a mountain of raw masculinity, every muscle working in unison like a finely tuned engine. And that ass ... don't get me started on that ass.

He turned and looked at me with a raised eyebrow. "Are you ... OK?" he asked.

I knew what I wanted but how was I going to do this? I was terrible at flirting, rarely if ever did I make the first move. 99% of the time I just kept them at bay till I finally gave them the green light, then just lay back and did my best to guide them in ... quite literally.

Seriously, with the endless wealth of free information on the internet you'd think a few of them would have watched a brief tutorial.

"Lois?" he asked, snapping me back into reality.

"What? ... oh, sorry. Yea, I'm fine, I mean ... ah."

How do you hit on a superhero? I thought. Underneath all that tight fabric and a heavy cape, they're really not that much different from any regular guy, right? Well, what works on them?

"You know ..." I said as I slowly crossed the room towards him. "That super suit really suits you. You look good in it."

"I do?" he said and looked down, surprised. "I honestly hadn't put much thought into it. I just needed something to conceal my true secret identity. Now that you mention it ... I do like the colors."

I stopped in front of him. He towered above me. I raised a hand and touched his chest. "Cotton?" I asked.

"No," he replied as he looked down at my hand. "It's a synthetic polymer designed to withstand extreme conditions. Fun fact, it was created by ..."

I leaned in closer and traced the lines of his abs descending from one side to another. "And is it easy to get into ... and out of?"

"Well it's ... ah ..."

I reached up onto my toes, closed my eyes and kissed him.

His lips … were like … were like.

The lump of my brain responsible for creative vocabulary shut down, wiped out by the raw sensation of his lips.

He reached down, wrapped his arms around my waist and pulled me in tightly. I let out a soft gasp, smiled and kissed him again, savoring his delicious lips.

Who was this strange man … and was he even a man? What was his origin story again? He'd escaped a doomed planet, crossed through the cosmos and crash landed on our planet. Was that it? Or was I thinking of someone else?

I'd only ever known him as a toy. Was he even anatomically correct?

… there was one way to find out.

As our tongues intertwined, my hand slipped further down, past his abs and graced the bulge of his hard cock.

… promising I thought.

I gently stroked it, gauging its size. Super indeed.

I then reached up, tracing the lines of his suit, searching for a way inside.

"I'll save you the trouble," he said, as he took my hand and guided me through the complicated maze of his suit and let me wrap my hand around his hard cock.

"How do you know I'm not just trying to seduce you to lower your defenses, then strike when you least expect it," I teased.

"You? A super villain? I never would have suspected you'd pursue a life of mayhem and destruction."

I gently stroked his hard cock, running my hand from the base to the tip, looked up at him and smiled devilishly. "I can be bad."

He let out a light chuckle. "I find that hard to believe."

"I can be!" I pouted then smiled again. "Because I know what bad girls do."

"Do you, now? And what's that?" he asked.

"This," I said, slid down to my knees and pulled his cock free. It was a feast for my famished eyes, thick like a tree trunk and rock hard.

I looked up and kept my eyes glued to him, savoring the power I had over him. He could smash mountains with his fists and yet he was powerless to stop me. I wet my lips, leaned forward and swirled my tongue around the tip of his hard cock, then plunged forward, greedily devouring every inch.

He let out a soft moan and gently rocked his hips, thrusting his cock forward, deep into my eager mouth. I tightened my grip and worked his shaft, rising and falling in a steady wave, never breaking my hypnotic gaze.

Would I let him cum? Eventually, but not yet. First he would have to satisfy my primal aching hunger.

… primal aching hunger. Seriously? Where had that come from? In fact, where had any of this urgency come from? My sex drive had all but puttered out ages ago. I treated sex like a chore, something to mark anniversaries and if they were lucky, birthdays … maybe.

When had I turned into such a wet blanket? I used to be exciting, spontaneous. Was it the dry monotony of my job? It seemed to suck all the life out of the day, leaving me with nothing left to enjoy the evening.

No more, I thought as I pulled his cock from my mouth and started to stroke it. I knew what I wanted, and I wasn't afraid to ask for it.

"Fuck me, hero," I said, looking up at him. "Show me your true super powers."

He looked down at me, surprised.

I let go of his massive cock, rose to my feet, brought my hands down, grabbed the edge of my t-shirt and pulled it up and over my head.

I wasn't exactly well endowed, but there was some bounce when my breasts sprang free. By his corkscrew smile, he approved.

Without breaking his gaze, I leaned down, slipped out of my panties, then spun around and slowly swung my hips from side to side as I walked to the bed. I swear I could feel his laser heat vision warming my ass. I sat down on the edge of the bed, my legs open wide, inviting.

He rose, floated across the room, landed in front of me, reached up and in one fluid motion tore off his suit.

"It's a good thing you have a stockpile of those," I teased.

"It comes in handy when the villains start throwing wrecked cars at you," he laughed.

"Sounds rough."

"It can be."

I leaned back on my elbows and smiled devilishly. "Good … because I like it rough."

He smiled wickedly. "Now that you have me right where you want me aren't, you going to reveal your master plan?"

I raised a finger, licked it, then brought it down and slipped it into my wet pussy. I let out a soft moan, then looked up at him. "Isn't it obvious, or do I need to spell it out to you?"

"No ma'am," he said, then fell upon me, pressing me into the silk sheets. I gasped as he slid inside me. My body shuddered as the pleasure crashed against my fragile shores. I closed my eyes, bit my lip as he thrust his hard cock into me, then reached up and dug my fingers into his shoulder. I pulled him forward as he took me.

"Fuck me," I moaned. "Fuck me hard."

He obliged, throwing his weight into every thrust.

"Faster," I moaned. "Faster!"

His pace quickened, slamming into me with a force that shattered the last of my inhibition. I opened my eyes, wailed, my screams of ecstasy a siren's song. I then looked up at him, wrapped my arms around his neck and whispered in his ears, every word spoken between a gasp.

"Let me ride you," I moaned. "I want to ride your hard cock."

He obeyed and fell to one side. I sat up, crawled up, over the mountain of his perfect physique and mounted him.

… fuck, I couldn't think of a time when anyone had ever made me this wet. The sex had always been … fine. I'd just had to squash my expectations, expect some discomfort, rely on a hearty amount of lube, and when I'd finally reached my threshold, dazzle them with my acting chops as I faked an orgasm.

But this … this was … otherworldly.

Seriously, what was his origin story? Was I fucking a human endowed with super powers or an alien from a distant galaxy?

If it meant I got to ride his hard cock, I didn't care which.

As I rode him, I reached up, grabbed my breasts and squeezed. The sensation was like every happy memory wrapped up with a neat bow.

"Gentle," he said as he grabbed hold of my hips, trying to reign me in. "I'm not made of titanium."

I fell forward and pinned his hands to the bed. "Looks like you've met your match, hero."

"You're resourceful, I'll give you that, but never …" he said, then at lighting speed flipped me over onto all fours. "Assume the fight is over till it's over."

I peeked back over my shoulder. "No fair," I brooded.

"Now to teach you a lesson you won't soon forget," he said, then launched forward and speared me with his hard cock. I shut my eyes, clenched the silk sheets and moaned, the steady thrust of his cock hammering me as he used me like a toy, building to an epic climax and then …

He let out a triumphant cry then collapsed, falling onto the bed beside me. As the waves of pleasure rippled through my body, I crawled up beside him and rested my head on his chest.

I listened as his heart wound down, his chest rising and falling as his body relaxed.

"That was ..." he said, then trailed off.

I closed my eyes and savored the exquisite calm. With all my nagging thoughts subdued I thought of nothing, just coasted, riding the physical high. In a few minutes, it would subside, then they'd come swarming back like a swarm of angry bees ... wait, why could I actually hear them?

I lifted my head off his chest and listened. There was a low buzzing sound like a ...

I looked up. Through the shimmering veil of the aurora, I saw tiny coal gray trails appear as they zigzagged through the sky.

"Are those ..." I asked but was cut off as he bolted upright.

"Take cover!" he shouted, grabbed me and shielded me as the strange objects came screaming down upon us.

There was an explosion and a piercing white light. The ground collapsed below us, and we fell through, spinning as we tumbled through the air.

"Hold on," he shouted as he held me close.

We hit the ground as the dome reigned down around us. Remarkably, when it stopped, we were unscathed.

"Are you ok?" he asked.

"What the hell happened?"

"I ..."

"POW'er, show yourself, you sniveling coward!" a crackling voice shouted out over a loudspeaker.

That voice, I thought. Why did it sound familiar?

"Stay hidden," he whispered as he lifted a chunk of fallen debris and stood up. "I'll deal with this."

I nodded, hid behind a large chunk of smashed glacier then peaked above it. He hovered above the ground as an ominous shape appeared through the ice dust.

It sounded like a mechanical monster, every step landing with a heavy thud as pistons and gears whined.

"After years spent shifting through the data, I've finally discovered the location of your hidden secret lair," a voice cackled as they drew nearer.

"Now, I finally have you right where I wan ... good lord man, why are you naked?"

The mysterious figure appeared. He was wearing a purple mechanical armored suit, his only visible feature, his face.

"Brad!" I shouted as I bolted up right from behind the glacial debris.

"That's Doctor Torment. Wait ... Lois? What the hell are you doing here?"

Chuck POW'er looked between us. "You two ... know each other?"

Doctor Torment looked at Chuck POW'er, then at me ... then back at Chuck POW'er. He went beet red and shook like a boiling kettle.

"You wretched fool. First you foil all my plans for world domination, then you steal my girl?" He growled as his mechanical suit began to power up.

"Hold up, I had no idea that ..."

The glowing sphere in the center of Doctor Torment's chest erupted, firing a white hot beam of raw energy. It hit Chuck POW'er, sent him sailing through the air and slammed him into a wall of glacial ice.

"For fuck's sake, Brad. Get it through your thick skull, we're broken up ..."

"That's Doctor ... it's not important. Really? With my arch-nemesis. How could you?"

"Everyone is your arch-nemesis, Brad. You once swore the

delivery driver was your arch-nemesis because he forgot the garlic bread."

"Well, they refused to refund it, even after I called customer support …"

"Not to intrude," Chuck POW'er said as he appeared from the smoking hole cut in the far wall. "But I believe this is the part where I give you a good walloping."

Doctor Torment looked back at Chuck POW'er then raised his hands, shielding his eyes. "Good lord man, at least put on a pair of pants."

Chuck POW'er flew across the room at hypersonic speed, both hands raised like a mighty hammer just as Doctor Torment threw up a neon blue force field. There was a tremendous explosion as the two collided, both exerting the full measure of their super strengths.

"I'll never let you steal my girl," Doctor Torment growled above the static hiss of his power suit.

"She's mine now, fair and square! We're a thing now," Chuck POW'er yelled back.

"Enough!" I said and stepped around from the chunk of glacier debris. "I said … enough!" I shouted.

The two, stunned by my outburst, fell back. Doctor Torment looked over at me with wounded eyes. "Of all the people you had to rebound with, why did it have to be … him?" he grumbled.

"My love life is none of your goddamn business, Brad. Now go home, or wherever you slithered out from."

Chuck POW'er hovered across the room, picked up a sheet of torn silk bedding and brought it to me. "You tell him babe, I …"

"And you," I growled and refused the sheet. "I'm not 'your girl'."

"Well I just assumed that because … you know, we had … well, you know." He raised his hand to cover his mouth and whispered. "Sex, that we're a couple now."

"You really are from another world, aren't you?" I grumbled.

"Look, the sex was great, and I had a fantastic time tonight but … I'm just not ready for another relationship yet. I just need … I just need some time to myself, to get a sense that my feet are still planted on the ground."

"I … I see," Chuck POW'er said, then looked back at Doctor Torment. "Do you want me to launch him into the atmosphere?" he asked as he offered me the silk sheet again.

I laughed and took it from him. "No, no that's alright. Let him go. He's an idiot but he's a harmless idiot."

I turned to look at Doctor Torment. "Brad, seriously, enough with the quests for global conquest. Get some therapy."

Wounded, Brad looked between us and grumbled. "I'd look that good naked too if I tried."

He turned and stormed out through the hole cut into the dome.

Chuck POW'er turned to look at me. "Well, that was quite an unexpected adventure."

"It was," I said as I wrapped the silk sheet around my body. "I'm sorry if I sounded a bit cruel there, it's just …"

"No need to apologize. I tend to do everything at supersonic speed. I should learn to ease up a bit."

"Maybe we could try again sometime, see where it leads. Just … just take it one step at a time."

"Of course," he said and smiled. "I'd like that."

"Till then …" he said and at a speed that I only registered as a blur, darted away and returned dressed in a new super suit holding my discarded t-shirt and panties.

"I think we've both had enough excitement for one evening. Wouldn't you agree?"

I nodded, took the clothing from him and quickly changed as he turned his back.

"All set?" he asked over his shoulder.

"I am, I replied. "And thanks … for everything."

He turned around, walked over to me and offered me his hand. I took it. He pulled me closer, and we blasted off, throttling up back into the stars before coasting back down towards my brother's house. We slowed down and passed through the gaping hole in my brother's house's ceiling.

"I still don't know how I'm going to explain that to him," I said with a nervous laugh.

"I'm sure it will make for a fascinating tale," he said as he gently set me down on the floor.

I stepped back as he hovered above me. "So, I'll call you?" I asked.

"You need only whisper my name and I'll be here in a flash," he said smiling.

"Ok," I said as I toyed with the hem of my t-shirt. "Good night … Chuck POW'er."

"Good night, Lois," he said and then with the speed of a rocket blasted up and away.

I stood there, staring up through the hole in the ceiling, watching as a few stray snowflakes drifted down through the opening. I closed my eyes, stepped forward, tilted my head back and let them land on my skin as I breathed in the cold winter air.

As I stood there, I started to drift, falling into a deep sense of calm, empty of thought or sensation.

Time stood still.

… Then, the world slowly started to reemerge. It was the warm rays of sunlight which I saw first, peeking through the window blinds. I sat up and took in my surroundings. I was in my brother's guest bedroom, in bed. So it had been a dream … or had I simply stumbled upstairs in a daze?

I crawled out of bed, my feet hitting the cold floor. There was one way to be sure, I thought as I crept across the floor, opened the door, walked down the hallway and peered up at the ceiling.

... No gaping hole. So it had been a dream and yet it had been so vivid, so real.

As I stood there, I caught the faint hint of ... was that gingerbread?

I walked down the stairs, crossed the lobby and walked into the kitchen. There on the kitchen counter was the small Chuck POW'er toy, and a plate of cookies.

The cookies were piping hot, a ribbon of steam rising from them. I hadn't accidentally baked cookies in my sleep, had I? And the toy, I swear I left it down in the basement.

I walked over to the kitchen island to investigate. I picked up one of the gingerbread cookies. It was still warm. I took a bite. It was delicious, the fresh ingredients reminding me of all the cookies I'd savored in my youth.

"Meow?"

I looked down. My brother's cat was circling my ankles.

"Merry Christmas, furrball," I said, reached down and picked her up. "Would you like a bowl of festive milk?"

She purred approvingly. I set her down, walked to the cupboards, grabbed a saucer, filled it from a jug of milk from the fridge and set it down for her.

As I stood up, I noticed something tucked under the plate of cookies. I lifted the plate and looked underneath. There was a note. Had I written myself a note?

I turned it over and read it.

I had a wonderful time last night, it said. Hope to hear from you soon. You know how to reach me.

... It was signed.

Chuck POW'er.

Super indeed, I thought, smiled and took another bite of the gingerbread cookie.

My Holiday Superhero

❄ The End ❄

Sugar and Spice
by Ian D Smith
Twitter: @ians2005
Facebook: @dr.ian.d.smith

"Should be a great party," Greg said. "The gang from the office are all going to be there."

Susie turned away and pulled a face at the taxi window. "How about their partners and girlfriends?"

Greg shrugged. "Probably. It was an open invitation. The senior management like us to have supportive partners, and this is one way for them to say thanks. You know, for all the late nights and short-notice business trips."

The little details you didn't mention until you'd started the job. "Likely to be many I've met before?" She'd met some of his colleagues at other social events earlier in the year, and hoped she could avoid spending too much time with them. They'd behaved like overgrown schoolboys at every event she'd gone along to, and Greg had eagerly followed their example. But at least she'd found other temporarily-abandoned women to chat with. Greg's behaviour seemed pretty typical, something she was unwilling to tolerate for much longer.

"Can't say." He tapped away at his phone. "You'll be fine, you never find it hard to start a conversation."

She felt her temper flare and forced herself to relax. "So I guess you'll be with your chums most of the evening?"

"Great chance to circulate, network, make a good impression on the management team."

She guessed he'd be hobnobbing with his awful boss Craig, along with some of the other pushy tossers from his company. Assuming he didn't get into some silly drinking game with his fellow team members. She had no doubt he'd try to chat up some girl if he thought he could get away with it. They'd had a couple of angry exchanges over that in the last few months. What he claimed was simply being friendly looked very much like an attempt to score as far as Susie was concerned.

"One of the managers is thinking about offering services to smaller companies," Greg said. "Probably much the same as your firm. I'll introduce you. He'd probably love someone with your track record on the team. And all the clients would be pretty local, not all over the country."

Susie managed not to sigh. "I get the impression your place has a rather masculine culture," she said. "Not sure I'd feel comfortable there."

"Not all our women are in admin and support roles." Greg grinned at something he'd seen on his phone screen. "They seem to fit in okay."

"Will any of them be there tonight?" See what they say.

Greg shrugged. "No idea, none in my team. I think most of them only come into the office now and again."

And what does that tell me about the workplace atmosphere? Susie thought. She enjoyed the freedom to work from home when she wanted, but Greg insisted he had to go into the office, even though his company obviously accepted remote working. Mind you, I couldn't cope if he wanted to work from home with me.

She thought back to the conversation she'd had with her director the day before, about a short-notice six-month secondment to a team based in Bristol who were getting more business than they could handle. The arrangement could be made permanent if all went well and she wanted that. She knew she'd have to spend some time there, getting to know the area, her colleagues and their clients, but she could work remotely from home as well. Tempting to get a break and a chance to think.

The taxi driver's sat nav announced that they'd reached their destination, and the driver slowed to check house numbers and names. He pulled up by a pair of gates for a large house set back from the road. "This is the place, but the drive's already packed out with cars, so I'll have to drop you off here," he said. "I'll be here at two, like we agreed."

Greg handed him a few bank notes. "Cheers." He climbed out, slammed the door and set off along the drive.

The driver, a middle-aged man with kind eyes, watched Greg, shook his head, then turned to Susie, holding the cash out to her. "He's already paid on-line."

"Consider it a bonus," Susie said. She'd enjoyed chatting with him on the way from her home to pick up Greg. "His loss."

He grinned and held out a business card. "Give me a call if you decide to leave earlier, love. Busy night, of course, but I'll be here as soon as I can, even if it's only for you."

She took the card. "Thanks."

He raised an eyebrow. "And if you decide you want to drop him off then go back to your own place, just send me a text."

She smiled her thanks then set off after Greg.

There were a few other people hovering around in the patch of light spilling from the wide-open front door. When she joined Greg, he put a hand on the small of her back and propelled her forward.

Craig, tall, overweight and balding, was in full-on jovial host mode, in high spirits and greeting everyone loudly. "Greg, my man. Brought your little lady with you?" He nearly crushed Susie's hand with his, then leaned down to kiss both her cheeks. His breath suggested he'd already had a few vodkas.

Susie immediately wondered about his exuberant bonhomie. She was pretty sure Greg had taken some cocaine before they set off, and he'd hinted that it had been circulating at a team-building event a few weeks before. "I'm Susie, thank you for inviting me."

"Lovely to meet you at last." Craig gave her a quick once-over, lingering for a second on her chest. "So, where are you from in Yorkshire?"

Susie wanted to slap the man but felt her face smile politely. "Cheshire, actually. Just south of Manchester."

"Never can get my head around all those North Country dialects." He looked around. "Trouble at t'mill and all that, eh?" he boomed in a caricature northern accent.

A middle-aged woman in a wine-red Stella McCartney shift dress appeared alongside Craig and glared at him briefly, then looked at Susie and was all smiles. "Pamela, Craig's wife." She made a lightning-fast assessment of Susie's outfit and appearance, then offered a perfectly manicured hand. "You must excuse him," she murmured. "He's dreadful if there's an audience to play up to."

"Oh, it's fine," Susie lied.

Pamela leaned a little closer. "He's one of those jerks who think London's the centre of the universe," she said quietly. "The sort convinced that the rest of the country are all hopeless yokels. When we first met, he teased me about coming from Somerset, making awful jokes about apples and cider."

Greg appeared at Susie's side. "I see you've met Susie, Mrs. Stevens."

Pamela looked at him sharply, but almost immediately smoothed her expression into a cool smile. "Ah Greg, lovely to see you again. You'll find the bar and nibbles in the dining room, and we've set aside the conservatory for dancing." She looked at Susie. "Been seeing each other for long?"

"Nearly two years," Susie said.

Pamela's expression hardened for a fraction of a second before smiling genuinely. She patted Susie's arm. "You can leave your coat in the first room on the left. We put up some signs to show the way to the bathrooms. I do hope you enjoy the party."

Once she'd hung her coat up, Susie let Greg take her arm and lead the way into the house. "Didn't know you'd been here before," she said, hoping she sounded conversational.

"Team celebration after we closed a huge deal. Told you at the time."

When they parted at a door so Greg could walk ahead, Susie glared at his back. Oh no you didn't. What am I missing? What was Pamela's reaction all about?

The next room was large, with tables and sideboards pushed against the walls. It was crowded with people in smart-casual clothing, all talking loudly, sipping drinks and eating finger-food from small plates. The women had all made an effort to dress nicely, but the men were almost in uniform, wearing casual shirts and trousers by Hugo, Pierre Cardin or Ralph Lauren, and expensive brown Oxford brogues.

Greg offered to get her some wine and food and slipped away into the crowd. While she waited, Susie looked around the room. Although she felt confident, wearing a short dress which fit her perfectly, sheer pearlescent thigh-high stockings and gorgeous new shoes which coordinated with her handbag, she felt out of place. She already knew she clearly couldn't assume Greg would be keeping her company all evening, and the few people she recognised as his colleagues were those, she considered arse-lickers. She ignored an obvious appraising look from a middle-aged man with thinning hair and a generous waistline. *And the lechers are out in force.*

Greg was quickly back with a glass of wine and a small plate, then he was gone again. The selection was predictable party food: a couple of chicken wings, some breaded prawns, a small slice of quiche and a few filled vol au vents.

She walked in the direction Greg had vanished and spotted him through the crowd near the bar. He was standing close to a well-built and rather pretty girl with a neat blonde bob, who had her hand on his chest in a very familiar way. He leaned down and she said something in his ear, then gave him a distinctly dirty grin. His expression changed from a smile to a lecherous smirk, then he ran his hand over the curve of her hip and down her backside. The girl appeared to be nuzzling his ear.

Susie's view was blocked by partygoers. Cold anger surged. *You're bloody cheating on me, you fuckwaffle badgertwat.* She put her wine glass and plate down on a nearby table, then wove through the milling people, intent on making a scene and maybe kicking him in the testicles. But by the time she got to the bar, there was no sign of Greg or the blonde.

She sighed and her anger drained away, leaving her feeling insecure and a little foolish at her flush of temper. She walked back and sipped the wine in her glass. Faced with obvious evidence of his infidelity, she'd already decided to dump Greg before the night was over, but how much longer would she stay here? She couldn't really slip out with the hosts still greeting people at the door; that would be too rude, and it wasn't their fault. She had the taxi driver's number, but this was a Saturday in mid-December, peak time for work-related Christmas parties, and he'd already said he'd be having a busy night. Restless, she glanced into the conservatory, already full of dancers. Perhaps she could burn off some of her frustration there? It was probably crowded enough for her not to stand out as an unattached woman.

She watched a clearly tipsy middle-aged man in slightly baggy designer jeans and a shirt which was a little too tight trying to hip-bump a much younger brunette, who was elegantly keeping just out of his reach.

Or maybe not, if they've already started trying to grope the girls.

She sipped her wine, deciding she had to pace her drinking. She didn't want to get hammered here, just find people to talk to for a few hours and avoid Greg until she could kill him without witnesses.

The crowd parted briefly, and she spotted a tall, slender and rather pretty young woman with long, straight blonde hair. The girl was leaning against the wall, her arms crossed and a drink in one hand. Her classic little black dress fitted perfectly, accentuating the elegant curve from her waist to her hips. The girl caught her gaze and raised her eyebrows in a clear "what am I doing here" gesture. Susie immediately brightened at that simple friendly act, sure the girl was enjoying the party about as much as she was herself.

As Susie worked her way through the milling guests, she saw the girl walk in her direction. When they met, the girl gave her a warm smile.

"Hi, I'm Susie." She offered the blonde her hand. "I came with my boyfriend. He works for Craig Stevens."

The young woman shook her hand. "Emily, Craig's younger daughter."

Susie was struck by Emily's eyes. She usually associated pale blue eyes with cold, emotionless stares, but Emily's expression was warm and full of fun. "If you don't mind me saying so," Susie said. "You don't appear to be enjoying the party that much."

Emily grimaced. "I'm waiting for my best friend to arrive. She's been held up." She waved a hand around and leaned closer. "Hate all this, it feels like my home's been over-run. There's hardly anyone I know, everyone's older than me, and I don't feel I've anything in common with anyone." She leaned closer. "And I'm really fed up with all these old guys leering at me."

"I know that feeling," Susie said. "At least you're not the only blonde. I feel pretty self-conscious."

Emily indicated Susie's pale gold hair, styled into a side-swiped chignon. "Don't strawberry-blondes have more fun?"

"Not when people make jokes about red-heads and short tempers." She took in Emily's perfect peaches-and-cream complexion. "I think we're probably the two youngest people here."

Emily nodded. "Guess so. I'll be twenty-two next month. Stuck at home for Christmas, but most of the time I'd rather be back at university."

"Twenty-six," Susie said. "Is that close enough?"

Emily made a so-so gesture with her hand, then grinned. "Same as my sister Sally, so, yeah, you're not all that old. Not really."

"Let's get another drink," Susie said. "Then we can compare notes on awful parties."

"Dry white wine?" Emily asked.

Susie nodded.

Emily led the way back to the bar, crouched down to reach back under the table, then stood with a bottle in her hand. "A small secret stash. Much nicer than the stuff in those wine boxes." She filled two glasses, then hid the bottle again.

"What do you do?" Emily asked.

"Just a boring old accountant."

"For Dad's company?"

Susie shook her head. "No, my firm provides local small businesses with advice and help with book-keeping, cash flows and taxes."

"Wouldn't you earn more in a big company?"

Susie felt a flash of anger, which she suppressed as quickly as she could. "Almost certainly. Greg, my boyfriend, is always on at me to move to a big company, but I like my work. We're helping businesses stay afloat, not just providing an ever-bigger return to shareholders. What with the COVID lock-downs changing shopping habits and all the complications from Brexit, a lot of smaller companies are struggling and need advice and support."

Emily nodded. "Dad's said the same thing, but his interest is more in helping his clients buy up smaller companies as an easy way to expand. Is your guy one of his junior flunkies?"

Susie grinned. "He's convinced he's on a fast track to the board room after playing a major role in some big deal. He got a significant promotion, but flunky sounds about right. What are you studying?"

"An MA in fine art. My first degree was in art and art history." She suddenly looked away, grinned and waved at someone on the other side of the room. "My best friend's just arrived. She's great fun, you'll absolutely adore her. She's staying over, so we'll drop her bags off in my room, then I'll be back to introduce the two of you. Don't move, we'll be as quick as we can."

A couple of minutes later, a beaming Emily was back, towing an attractive, petite girl with long, jet-black hair, lovely brown skin and large, dark eyes. Susie guessed her family were originally from either India or Pakistan.

"This is Pritti," Emily said. "We collaborate a lot on our art, sit for each other and stuff like that."

Susie thought she was perfectly named. Pritti wore an asymmetric royal blue wrap-around top over a black silk camisole, with black leggings and leather ankle-boots. Around her neck, a silver chain supported a colourful pendant. Her eyes were artfully accentuated with make-up, and her lips shone with a soft gloss, but otherwise she seemed to be fresh-faced.

"I'm Susie." She held out her hand.

Pritti shook it and gave Susie a wide, friendly smile. "Emily was really eager for me to meet you," she said, in a soft Scottish accent. "Said she'd found someone nice to talk with."

Susie felt anyone as striking as Pritti would get plenty of people keen to talk to her, especially guys.

"Look, I don't want to be cheeky, but is there any chance you could give us some basic advice about tax and stuff?" Emily asked. "We're selling some of our work, but don't want to end up in trouble."

"Of course," Susie said. "I'll give you my number. Just call and we'll fix a time to meet as soon as you like."

"Oh." Pritti suddenly looked concerned. "We're visiting my folks for Hogmanay, and we're back at uni soon after."

"I'm not doing much between Christmas and New Year," Susie said. "Greg will sulk if I don't let him play golf for a day or two." She realised she was on autopilot, talking as if they'd still be together then, which she was pretty sure they wouldn't be.

"Not visiting family?" Emily asked.

Susie swallowed down a flash of anger at the last-minute change Greg had forced on their plans. "No. I had hoped to, but …"

Emily took her hand and squeezed it gently. It surprised Susie, but she liked the soft warm fingers against hers. "A row?"

Susie nodded. "We visited his family last Christmas, so I'd expected we'd spend it with mine this year. My brother, sister and her boyfriend are staying with my parents this year. But he's just got around to telling me he's playing in a charity golf tournament on Boxing Day. That totally buggers up any travel plans. And if I went home on my own at short notice, I'd get 'are things alright between you two' non-stop, not a lot of fun." Especially as they were anything but alright even before tonight.

Pritti gave her a sympathetic look. "I wouldn't want that either. We're all Sikh. Well, nominally. Me, I'm not religious at all, and my parents aren't that into it either. We do a sort of token Christmas, but Hogmanay's a real hoot."

"Let's make an afternoon of it before Christmas and have a good girlie chat after the tax stuff," Emily said. "Good chance to bitch about awful boyfriends, too."

Susie noticed Pritti was studying her closely.

Pritti grinned at being caught out. "Sorry, must have seemed a bit weird. I was just wondering if I could persuade you to sit for some portrait photos. You've got a great complexion, lovely cheekbones, beautiful eyes, and your hair's a fantastic colour. Please say yes."

Susie blushed at the flattery, unsure how to react. "That's your thing? Photography?"

"I draw, paint and sculpt too, but I really love photography. Especially people. It feels so personal and instant, and it captures something unique."

"She's bloody awesome," Emily said, with obvious enthusiasm. "Got some of her photos of me upstairs."

Susie felt intrigued. "Well, I normally hate photos of myself, but I'd be interested to see your work. I did art at school and college but wasn't keen enough to do it for a degree."

"When you see them, you'll want her to photograph you, believe me," Emily said. She glanced at Pritti, then back at Susie. "Look, why don't we grab my secret supply of wine and get out of this crowd for a while? We can hardly hear each other talk anyway. We can chill, have a nice chat, and you can have a look at the photos."

❄ ❄ ❄

"My sister Sally's really pissed with me," Emily said. "This is her favourite room, but I came home first and claimed it. Mum and Dad only bought this place a couple of years ago, while I was at uni." She lit a few candles and turned the lights off. The music from downstairs was muted to a regular bass thump.

"Do you and your sister squabble a lot?" Susie glanced around the room, which felt more like a nicely-decorated guest bedroom than a personal one, but with some personal items here and there.

"Non-stop," Pritti murmured. "You'd know they're sisters when you saw them together, even though Emily's slim and Sally's a big lass, but they're chalk and cheese in terms of personality."

"Mummy always says she was a proper spoiled madam when I arrived," Emily grinned. "Probably still hasn't forgiven me for spoiling her fun and getting the attention she felt was her due."

"Must be awful," Susie said. "I get on really well with my sister."

"I guess she didn't try to steal your boyfriends?"

Susie shook her head. No, but I slept with one of hers after she ditched him.

"She's probably lining something up, what with all those guys downstairs," Emily said. "She was in a grouchy mood all day, then transformed into an overconfident, pushy cow just before the party. Probably snorted something."

Susie remembered her suspicion that Greg had done the same thing and was probably doing his best to score downstairs right at that moment.

Pritti sat on the king-sized bed and patted the mattress, inviting Susie to join her. Emily opened one of the bottles of wine and poured generous helpings into three glass tumblers. She held hers up in a toast. "To meeting new friends and escaping from awful parties."

They all sipped some wine, then Pritti cocked her head to one side. "Someone just walked past, and I heard a door closing. Sounded like they were trying to be quiet."

Emily shrugged. "Probably Sally sneaking some bloke into her room."

"What? This soon?" Pritti looked surprised. "I guess it's someone she already knows."

"I think she wants to shag every available guy before I even get to meet them," Emily said. "She dropped a half-empty packet of condoms between the bed and one of the bedside cabinets after her last visit, I found it when I was unpacking." She turned to Susie. "She lives quite close, loves parties, and probably tagged along with one of Dad's company piss-ups and shagged someone. Sally's never short of a queue of guys keen to get her knickers off and she's honest about not putting up even a token fight if she likes them."

"Not someone I'd want as a friend, let alone a sister," Susie said.

"Well, if you're my friend, she won't want to know you."

"Her loss, not yours, believe me," Pritti muttered. Then she grinned. "Anyone want a super-special samosa?"

Emily stuck a hand up in the air. "Yay, gimme, gimme."

"What's special about them?" Susie asked, watching Pritti root about in a large overnight bag.

"Pritti makes really nice vegetable samosas, but she makes the odd batch with a few, er, unusual ingredients," Emily said, in a conspiratorial whisper. "Gives them a lovely extra something."

"Officially, it's a mix of a couple of traditional herbal medicines," Pritti whispered. "I put sugar and extra spices in to make them taste a bit less medicinal. With alcohol, the effect is a bit like dope, a sort of legal high. You'll probably feel relaxed, chatty and less inhibited for a couple of hours, the effect doesn't last all that long."

Susie knew the taxi wouldn't be back for hours, and it wouldn't hurt her to relax for a while. She'd had a few "herbal" cookies in the past and enjoyed the relaxed mood they'd caused. "Why not?"

The rich spicy, starchy filling was sweeter than she'd expected, and it had a slightly aromatic and bitter herbal flavour not quite masked by the other ingredients. As they sipped their wine and chatted, Susie relaxed and enjoyed this reminder of friendship. She knew she'd probably get a bit drunk before long, and wasn't familiar with whatever the herbs would do, but she enjoyed feeling a growing closeness between the three of them. Emily and Pritti were obviously close friends but seemed keen to make sure Susie felt included in their conversation. She felt a pang of regret for all the former friendships she'd let fade, and annoyance about the more recent friendships she'd not kept up, thanks to Greg's increasing unfriendliness and unreliability. He'd been a bit of a lad when they first met, but charming, impulsive, generous and fun. His recent promotion meant a significant pay rise and more responsibility, but he'd turned into a selfish, bossy snot as well.

Emily picked up an iPad from a bedside cabinet, fiddled with it for a few seconds, then flopped on the bed near Pritti as she held it out to Susie. "Some of Pritti's photos, see what you think."

Susie put the iPad on her lap and flicked through the collection of portraits. Emily was one of about two dozen subjects, all photographed in a selection of formal and informal portraits. All the photos were crisp and clear. Some were in colour, others monochrome or toned, some mixing areas in full colour with others in monochrome. "These are amazing," she said. "Everyone looks so relaxed, like they're really enjoying themselves."

"They're mostly mates," Pritti said. "We always spend a while just chatting before I start. I take loads of pictures and stop from time to time so we can look at them together. I ask for feedback and use that as I carry on. I used some of these for my degree project and I'm doing more now for my MA."

"Most of these were taken over several sittings, too," Emily added. She shuffled over and sat next to Susie, then leaned towards the iPad on Susie's lap to open a new folder of images. As she did, her arm brushed against Susie's, and she was a bit surprised how she enjoyed the brief contact. Must be the herbs.

"Pritti calls these 'art nude', but I think they're almost sculptural," Emily said. "See if you can guess which ones I posed for. We all wore masks to hide our faces."

Susie pointed to one of a slim, naked man with a fairly long flaccid penis. "I might be wrong, but I don't think that's you." Then she started giggling. His cock's almost as big as Greg's is when he's hard.

"Well, having seen Emily in the nude, I can confirm she definitely lacks that sort of dangly bit," Pritti said, then she started giggling too.

"Fuck, Pritti, how much did you put in those samosas?" Emily asked.

"A bit more than usual. Probably find the drink helps the hit."

Susie carefully looked at all the images. Again a mix of colour, monochrome and toned pictures, some evenly lit, others far moodier with dark shadows. She was intrigued how Pritti had artfully used the shadows, sometimes to hide breasts and genitals, other times using light and shade to reveal or even highlight them. There were probably three men and she guessed five or six different women. "These are great. I see what you mean about them being sculptural, some of the poses remind me of classical statues." It's rather sexy, all these people feeling so comfortable about being naked in front of a camera. She tried not to stare too obviously at the women's bodies, and wondered how her own might look in comparison. She glanced at Emily. "How did it feel, posing for these?"

Emily grinned and leaned her head on Susie's shoulder. "Wonderful," she murmured. "I felt free, nothing to hide. It helped that I've known Pritti well for years." She moved her face closer to Susie's. "Maybe you'd enjoy posing like that? You've got a lovely figure, after all, and bigger boobs than either of us."

Susie felt a flutter of excitement and her heart beat a little faster. She suddenly realised she found the idea very arousing. "Certainly for some portraits, maybe more once I felt really comfortable with the idea."

"I've a few more selections," Pritti said quietly. "But they're more, um, intimate."

"You mean sexy?"

Emily made a dismissive gesture with her hand. "We prefer to say they're sensual rather than erotic or sexy. The idea is to make the viewer feel a little bit aroused but think more about tenderness and love-making rather than just sex."

Susie nodded. Pritti slid closer to her and opened another folder of images.

Susie was fascinated by the pictures as she slowly flicked through them. Close-ups of hips, shoulders, backs, arms, legs, breasts, bottoms, flaccid or semi-erect penises, women with varying styles of pubic hair. Some models had tattoos, others body piercings, and one had both. She stopped and stared at one image, a moody monochrome of Emily, blindfolded, her lips pouted as if for a kiss, and what she guessed from the shape and skin tone was probably Pritti's breast, with a very pert nipple just a few millimetres from Emily's lips.

"Gorgeous, isn't it?" Emily murmured. She flicked to the next picture, in which she'd gripped Pritti's nipple with her lips and pulled it out a little. "These always make me feel hot and bothered." The next image showed Emily, clearly smiling as her tongue lapped the nipple.

Susie's face warmed as she blushed, which she hoped the dim lighting would hide. She flicked through the three images a few times, aware that her own nipples were every bit as pert as the one in the photo. These are so bloody sexy. And I'm straight.

"Technically challenging to do with a self-timer or remote release," Pritti said. "Really need someone else to help in the future, so we don't have to stop and move between shots. Tricky getting the same positions. But it'd have to be someone we both felt really comfortable being with while we posed."

"Stopping to mess around with the camera spoils the mood, too," Emily said. She flicked to the next picture. "This set were hard to get right, too." A monochrome close-up of a dark-skinned woman's breast cupped by a white woman's hand. The next showed the dark nipple being tweaked between two pale fingers.

Warmth blossomed deep inside Susie at the thought of being touched like that or touching another woman's breast in that way. She swallowed. "Surely only one person needed to move?"

Emily leaned her head on Susie's shoulder again and put an arm around her back. "Yeah, but would you want to move at all if it felt nice? Suppose it was your boob? Or your hand?"

"Good point." She stared at the image for a couple more seconds, knowing she'd be in no hurry to move herself. "You're clearly very interested in your art. And trust each other an awful lot."

"That evening, our relationship changed a fair bit." Pritti leaned closer and flicked to the next image. This one showed two dark-skinned hands cupping two light-skinned breasts. "We've sold this to a lingerie company. They wanted women to get the idea that a particular range of bras would be like having warm, soft hands holding their breasts."

Susie was suddenly more aware of her own breasts and felt a little embarrassed at wondering what it had been like to pose for that photo. She nudged Emily. "Hope her hands were warm."

Emily reached across and flicked to the next image. "Of course. Who'd want a cold hand there?"

Susie guessed it was Pritti's hand covering Emily's pubic hair and clearly cupping her pussy. Susie felt a tingle between her legs, wishing Greg was still that tender, gentle and teasing when they made love. He'd been amazing at the start of their sex life, and was now far more matter-of-fact about it all, almost as if he'd lost interest in her. The next image showed, she suspected, Emily's hand and Pritti's body. "I'd squeal like mad," she murmured.

Are these two lesbians?

As if reading her mind, Pritti took Susie's hand in hers. "We're not an item, just very close friends who took things a bit further to see how it felt. We both see guys from time to time, but neither of us wants to settle down."

"So you're bi?"

Susie felt Emily shrug. "Labels are for museum exhibits. We're just us. This is still pretty new for both of us, too."

"Shocked?" Pritti asked quietly.

More turned on than anything. "More surprised you're so open about it."

"Here's my latest project," Pritti said, closing that album of images and opening a new one.

Susie slowly flicked through. There were a dozen or so sets of photos of young women, probably art students from their age, hair, make-up and clothing. Each set was three head and shoulder photos, which seemed to have been taken just before, during and just after the women climaxed. In the first image, they all had a tense expectant expression. The second varied from tightly screwed up faces to totally lost in the moment. The third all showed them smiling and looking relaxed and happy, but quite a few looked a little sheepish too.

Susie wondered how she looked as she came, and if a lover would find it exciting to watch her face. "Was it tricky to persuade people to sit?"

"Not as hard as I thought," Pritti said. "Bit of booze, a herbal cookie, some gentle flattery, and the loan of a vibrator if they wanted one."

"Didn't you feel excited too? I mean, I know you'd want to stand back as the artist, but this is so personal."

"Fuck, yeah," Pritti murmured. "Had to sort myself out afterwards every time. My vibrator was plugged in to recharge a lot more than usual."

They all exchanged glances at a new rhythmic sound. "Sounds like bloody Sally's shagging someone. Her bed's bumping against the wall."

"At least he's taking it fairly steadily," Pritti murmured.

"Let's hope he doesn't last long," Emily muttered. "Sally's pretty noisy when she's excited. Or maybe when she's only pretending she is."

Susie remembered the intimate way Greg and the well-built blonde woman had touched each other downstairs. She'd not seen her clearly, but was that Emily's sister? She remembered Pamela's brief unguarded reaction on seeing Greg when they arrived. The pieces had fallen into a very plausible and uncomfortable pattern, and she felt sure Greg wasn't downstairs looking for her. Whether or not it was him humping Sally next door, Susie realised he wouldn't be in her life for more than a few hours, even if he swore to change his behaviour. Perhaps the mild narcotic in the mince pies had helped her see the truth, that she deserved better than to be with the selfish dickhead Greg had become.

"Want to see our orgasm faces?" Emily whispered.

Susie's attention returned, and she swallowed. This is like being really nicely seduced. "Okay."

Pritti opened another folder. "We, um, well, got a bit carried away." The first image showed Pritti from the waist up, Emily behind her, one hand cupping a breast as she nuzzled Pritti's neck, and her other arm was across her tummy in a way which strongly hinted her hand was on Pritti's pussy. Pritti seemed to be totally lost in her climax, her head thrown back on Emily's shoulder, mouth open and eyes shut. Both women appeared to be naked.

Fucking hell, Susie thought. Don't think I've never felt anything that intense.

The next image showed Emily from the waist up, lying on a bed with her back arched so she took her weight on her shoulders. Susie remembered enough of the photography she'd covered in her art course to realise the image mixed the use of a flash with a long exposure, as there was a sharp and clear image with movement blur around it. Emily's arms appeared to be flailing, and she was rolling her head from side to side, her hair disarrayed, with some strands across her face. Her expression was unmistakably one of someone having the most amazing time.

"That was her third," Pritti whispered. "Just wish I'd used a video camera."

"Fourth," Emily murmured. "Number three just faded a bit, then number four hit me like a steam train and nearly blew my head off. An impressive vibrator, that one." She grinned at Pritti. "Love the video camera idea. Let's give it a try."

Susie was struck that both girls looked incredibly sexy, confident and beautiful in the pictures, and that she'd found the idea really arousing.

"Ever sorted yourself out while another girl was there?" Emily whispered. "If you really like each other, it's an awesome feeling."

Susie nodded slowly, feeling confident to share a secret. "When I was in my early teens, my best friend stayed over. We were talking about a sex education class we'd just had at school which covered masturbation. We were sharing a double bed, and when I felt it move a bit, I knew she was touching herself. I felt dead embarrassed, but excited too, so I started. It was pretty amazing. We didn't get much sleep because we were doing it over and over again. She only stayed over that once. Her family moved away soon after." And I wanted to watch her do it, maybe even touch her too.

Pritti flopped back on the bed. "Well, I'm so horny I need an orgasm. I locked the door when I came in, so no-one's going to interrupt us. Feel free to play along, girls."

Susie glanced down and saw Pritti slip a hand into her leggings and down to her pussy. She quickly turned her head away.

"You don't have to if it makes you uncomfortable," Emily whispered. "But we'd love you to feel relaxed with us."

A mixture of embarrassment, confusion and excitement filled Susie, and she didn't know what to do. The mattress shifted, and she turned to see Emily lean back on the bed and tug her dress up to her waist, revealing skimpy black panties and bare skin above her hold-up stockings.

Emily reached for her arm. "I'd love you to watch me, but not this time," she whispered. "Come with us."

Susie let herself be drawn down between the two girls. She was chilled out, a little drunk, a little high, and more turned on than she'd been in ages. She felt relaxed with these two young women and decided to give in to the temptation. She lifted her own dress, slipped a finger inside her panties and felt her pussy, hot and wet. Fuck, I'm a total tart. She rubbed her clit lightly, sure that she'd reach her climax soon.

Susie tried not to concentrate on her finger or clit, but to be aware of the bed moving, and the sounds the other two women were making; quiet sighs, increasingly heavy breathing, the sounds of movement against clothing, and of fingers in aroused, wet pussies.

Pritti tensed and let out a few quiet gasps, then relaxed and panted. "Bloody nice."

Emily came a few seconds later, silently, her whole body twitching. She lay still and let out a long, happy sigh. "Best one all week."

Susie grinned, then felt both girls roll towards her. Emily put a hand on her tummy while Pritti lightly rested her hand on Susie's right arm.

"Come when you're ready," Pritti whispered, then gave Susie a gentle kiss on the cheek. Emily lightly stroked each of Susie's breasts through her clothing with feather-light fingertips, brushing her nipples. Then her climax seemed to come from nowhere, intense and sharp. Both girls hugged her while she got her breath back.

"So, fancy posing for me?" Pritti murmured. "I'd love to capture the expressions you just made, they were lovely."

"Only if it's all three of us," Susie said. She felt confident and cheeky. "You said you needed a third person to operate the camera for some shots."

"Count me in," Emily said. "Can't wait to see you completely in the nude. There was a strawberry-blonde at school, her bush was the most lovely colour. I couldn't stop myself from staring at her when we were in the changing rooms, even though it would have been too embarrassing to be caught."

"Just had an idea I want to try," Pritti said. "Me being shaved. Close-up of my fuzzies, with white shaving foam and a cut-throat razor catching the light. Should look good in mono with my skin colour."

"Bet it'll feel lovely afterwards," Emily said.

"Ask nicely and you might find out."

Susie smiled at this teasing. "I suppose you two help each other?"

Emily stroked her hand across Susie's tummy. "That would be telling."

Pritti moved her mouth close to Susie's ear. "Can we do anything to help you? It is Christmas, after all."

I need something to keep my spirits up, got to share a taxi back to drop Greg off before I tell him he's dumped. "I want to spend Christmas with my family," she said quietly. "I want to see my brother and sister. He's got two days leave from the army and she's been working in Poland for months. Her boyfriend's a really lovely guy, too."

"Why can't you?"

Susie sat up abruptly, as tears welled in her eyes. She couldn't bottle up her frustration and anger any more, ashamed at letting Greg push her around so much, and spoil her excitement about the future. Even though she'd decided their time was up, it still had to sink in a bit before it would feel real. "Greg's a control freak, always convinced he knows best. Says we should spend more time together then move in together and settle down." She sighed and wiped her cheeks. "I've been asked to move to Bristol in the New Year, for a few months to help our branch office there which is expanding. Great experience and a major promotion. But Greg's done everything he can to make me turn it down. Said it'd split us up, even though I told him Bristol's only two hours away by train. But he thinks London's the centre of the bloody universe."

Emily hugged her. "He doesn't deserve you."

"Are you happy with him? Honestly?" Pritti asked.

"I was when we started, but not now," Susie mumbled. "He didn't even want to spend any time with me here this evening. Had to go and network, help his career, he said."

"Sad to say, Dad does approve of arse-lickers in his team," Emily said. "Loves all the boys-only banter and the egging-on. If someone's a golf fanatic too, even better. Men, of course, not women. Mum rules the roost at home, so I think Dad overcompensates at work, where he can run things his way so long as his department makes a decent profit. Not that I mind, since he bought me a flat outright, so I'm not in student digs."

Pritti squeezed her arm. "All you have to do is go downstairs and tell him he's dumped."

If only it was that simple. "Believe me, dumping him's really tempting right now. I saw him getting very friendly with a girl downstairs not long after we arrived." She felt sure Greg wouldn't back away from making an ugly public scene she'd regret once her temper had cooled.

"What?" Emily sounded horrified. "Why didn't you say? I'd have found him and kicked his arse for you."

They were distracted when the knocking on the bedroom wall

accelerated and got louder, and they could hear a woman's muffled voice calling out, "Yes, yes, yes." After a few seconds, there was only the distant, muffled music from downstairs.

"Told you Sally's noisy," Emily muttered. "Always wondered if it's for real or put on."

Pritti raised an eyebrow. "So bed one of her guys and see if he's any good."

Emily glared at Pritti. "We used to be friends, didn't we?"

Pritti turned to Susie. "A teeny theatrical falling-out means we get to make up for Christmas. That should be brilliant fun."

"Reconciliation," Susie said thoughtfully. "How do you gift wrap that?"

"In silk lingerie, of course, which you remove very slowly," Pritti said.

"Can I do the same?" Emily asked.

Pritti nodded. "Relying on it, girlfriend."

"Now that's sorted, d'you know what I'd like you to give me for Christmas?" Emily murmured, squeezing Susie's hand.

"No, what?"

"A kiss."

Susie's face heated instantly as she blushed. Um, okay, let's see. She leaned closer to Emily, who tipped her head to one side so their noses wouldn't clash. Susie closed her eyes and held her breath until Emily's lips softly brushed against hers. Then she felt Emily's hands on her cheeks, Emily's tongue against her lips, and their kiss rapidly went from friendly and platonic to slow, hot and passionate.

When they parted, Emily smiled at her. "How did you know what sort of kiss I wanted?"

Susie felt almost breathless, surprised at what she'd just done, but also feeling a thrill of finding something new and exciting. "What else would you like from me?" Oh fuck, shouldn't have said that.

Emily lay back and swung her legs up onto the bed. "I'd absolutely love you and Pritti to give me an orgasm." She pulled her dress up again. "I've done something as a nice surprise for Pritti, but I'm sure she'll be happy to share it with you." She took Susie's hand and gently guided it to the top of her thigh, almost touching her panties.

Susie stroked Emily's soft thigh, feeling nervous and unsure. Pritti moved to Emily's other side and reached down to stroke Emily's pussy through her panties, then slid a finger under the elastic.

Pritti grinned at Emily, then turned to Susie. "She's only gone and shaved herself. Look." She tugged Emily's panties down, to reveal a smooth pale tummy all the way down to a plump vulva, the inner lips puffed up with her excitement.

Susie stared, feeling transfixed. I've never seen another woman's body like this in real life. "That's beautiful," she whispered. She watched as her fingers seemed to move without her being in control, across the soft warm skin of Emily's outer lips, then the more textured protruding inner lips, which were warm and slick.

Emily reached down and spread her lips apart. Pritti gently slid a finger inside Emily, then eased it in and out. "I'll tease her G-spot," she whispered. "You work on her clit. Start off with things you enjoy, watch her reaction and figure it out from there."

Susie was still unsure and nervous but regained conscious control of her hand. She ran her index finger up Emily's pussy and found her clit, then rubbed it and moved her finger in tight circles very close to it. Feels weird from a different angle, but it's really fun.

Emily gasped quietly. "You two are right on the money," she whispered. She bit her lower lip and rolled her shoulders back, then her whole body tensed. Then she smiled at Susie. "Fancy kissing me again?"

You bet. Trying to keep her finger working steadily on Emily's clit, Susie got to her knees and took her weight on her other hand so she could lean down and kiss Emily again. Emily ran her fingers through Susie's hair as they kissed, tongues dancing together. Emily tensed, then shuddered several times, gasping into their kiss. She relaxed and pulled Susie's upper body on top of her, enfolding her in a hug.

"That was a lovely Christmas treat," she murmured into Susie's ear.

"Now it's Susie's turn," Pritti said. "But I want to kiss her first."

Susie felt another thrill. My second kiss with a woman. She got up on her knees and leaned across Emily to reach for Pritti. She put one hand behind Susie's head as their lips met. They each slowly explored the other's mouth, in no hurry to move on. Susie felt one of Pritti's hands on her breast, a light and teasing touch. Feeling a little nervous, she did the same and felt excited when she realised Pritti wasn't wearing a bra. She rubbed Pritti's nipple with her thumb, and Pritti broke their kiss.

"Keep that up and I'll get really distracted. You're an awesome kisser, every bit as good as Emily."

"I want another kiss, before I get all jealous," Emily said. "And I want it right now, Susie."

Susie leaned down over Emily again, resting on her hands and knees, and they started a long, slow kiss. Emily wrapped her arms around Susie's shoulders as Pritti clambered across and knelt behind Susie.

Susie felt intrigued when Pritti reached under her dress and slowly eased her panties down. Then she gasped into her kiss with Emily as two small, warm fingers eased into her. Surprised, but excited, she wriggled her hips around and Pritti's fingers went deeper, then slid in and out slowly.

"Pritti's got her fingers up me," she murmured.

"She's naughty like that, but cute with it." Emily wriggled an arm between their bodies and found Susie's pussy with her fingertips, then rubbed her clit. "She's just lucky to get there first," she whispered. "I'd love to see how excited you get with my fingers teasing you from inside."

Susie's climax was even more powerful than the previous one, and she flopped onto the bed beside Emily without sorting out her dress or panties. "You two are utterly evil in the nicest possible way."

Emily snuggled up to her. "Wait until we all share a bed together. You won't get much sleep, we'll want to play together all night.

"Wait until we share a shower," Pritti added. She leaned across to kiss Susie tenderly. "We'll probably use up all the hot water, and I so want to lather you all over."

You and me both, Susie thought. Being with a woman's nothing like I expected.

Pritti and Susie looked up when they heard a door opening nearby. Emily gestured to the en-suite, its door ajar. "The en-suite in this room and the one next door only have a thin partition wall." They all listened to an indistinct male voice.

"Did he say condoms?" Pritti asked.

"At least my dear sister has some sense," Emily muttered.

"Coke?" Susie said. She felt a cold wash of shock settle in her tummy. That sounded like Greg's voice.

"You okay?" Emily asked. "You think it's your chap?"

Susie took control of her anxiety. "Yeah. Not the sort of evening I expected."

Emily put an arm around her. "You think it's your chap next door, don't you?"

Susie bit her lip and nodded, suddenly on the verge of tears.

Pritti hugged her tightly from behind. "Well, if it is him and there's a scene later on, you've got two friends who'll watch your back and cheer you on."

Despite her anxiety, Susie smiled. "Be cheeky of me to accuse him of cheating, wouldn't it?"

"You don't need to justify wanting him out of your life," Emily said. "I bet they'll be going back down in a minute or two." She got up, straightened her clothing, then went over to the bedroom door. She gestured to the others, and they followed her, and they all pressed their ears to the door.

They heard a nearby door open, then a brief part of a conversation between a man and a woman, then the sound of footsteps going past the door and along the landing.

Emily opened the door just enough to stick her head through to look. "Hey, Greg, is Sally any good in bed?" she asked.

Oh my God. Susie tensed, expecting trouble.

Emily closed the door, grinning broadly. "He stopped, turned, gave me a filthy look and the finger, then walked away. Tall, overweight, short dark hair, powder-blue Pierre Cardin shirt and black trousers. And a dead chunky watch."

"That's what he's wearing," Susie whispered, her temper flaring suddenly. "But since they all copy each other, it could be a lot of the men downstairs. If it was him, I'll murder that fucking bastard for Christmas in front of all his work chums."

"Certainly sounds cathartic," Pritti murmured. "But he's probably not worth prison time."

"Hush up," Emily whispered. "I'll bump into Sally and have a dig." She went out, leaving the door ajar.

Pritti stood behind Susie and put her arms around her tummy. Susie put her hands on Pritti's arms and squeezed. That feels nice, wish some of my boyfriends had been half as affectionate.

They both froze when they heard a door open and close.

An unfamiliar woman's voice. "Oh, it's you."

"Not enjoying the party, Sally? Or pulled one, had a shag and thrown him back already? Must be a record, even for you."

"I met him a while ago," another woman said. "We've shagged a few times. Not that it's any of your business."

"Did he leave someone downstairs to screw you in your bed?"

"He did, as it happens, but he's the one cheating, not me."

"Why not charge them? You'd spend all day in bed, earn more and have a shorter working week."

Susie struggled not to laugh. Fucking priceless.

"Emily, just … just fuck off. You really do need the bitch practice but do it someplace else."

Susie was distracted when Pritti slid her hands onto Susie's breasts and squeezed them gently. She turned around in Pritti's embrace. "Stop that," she whispered. "It's distracting."

Outside, the conversation continued. "You spend too much time with your arty-farty gang", Sally said angrily. "Find some well-paid and slightly dim bloke who'll treat you to all sorts of nice stuff and just put up with the odd crap shag. Works for me. Forget romance, expensive presents last far longer. I don't care if he wants to play around, so long as he doesn't forget my treats. I've just been given a voucher for a full spa day at the Sanctuary as a Christmas treat."

Pritti snuggled into her embrace with Susie. "Lovely boobs," she murmured. "Can't wait to play with them properly. Ever snogged someone shorter than yourself?"

"Not yet," Susie replied, losing interest in the conversation on the other side of the door.

Their lips met and Susie felt her lust and passion flare as they kissed deeply.

"God, I don't know," Emily said. "Turn my back for a few seconds and you're at it without me."

"No, just keeping her ticking over," Pritti murmured.

Emily put her arms around Susie from behind. "So sorry if it was your guy with her. Whoever it was is pretty-well wrapped around her little finger."

Susie felt a mixture of resentment and anger at Greg, and excitement from being hugged affectionately by the two young women. "Makes it easier for me to dump him, less guilt." She remembered he'd cancelled quite a few dates at short notice in the last few months because of 'late nights at work', and the sharp look Craig's wife had given Greg when they arrived. He's been seeing Sally for a while.

"What d'you want to do?" Emily asked gently.

Susie took a deep breath. "I say we go downstairs, drink, chat and dance together, and ignore Greg. He's bound to end up blind drunk by the time we leave. I'll contact the taxi driver to ask him to drop Greg off then take me home." She thought for a couple of seconds. "I'll just be quiet until we arrive at his place, then tell him to fuck off out of my life and go home." She went back for her tumbler of wine and stood still, thinking, then she nodded and drained the glass. "I'll spend a lovely Christmas with my family, and Greg can fuck off."

"Where d'your family live?" Pritti asked.

"Cheshire, not that far from Manchester. Shouldn't take me long to drive up."

"Why not come up for Hogmanay? We'll be in south-west Scotland. My family would be more than happy to have another of my friends stay over."

Emily squeezed Susie's hands. "Oh yes, that'd be wonderful, please say you will."

Sugar and Spice

Susie felt excited at the idea of spending more time with Emily and Pritti, and seeing where this new friendship might lead. She liked them both, and their shared sexy play was amazing. "I'd love to, thank you."

Pritti raised her eyebrows. "The only thing is we'll all have to share my room, but I think we'll cope. King size bed." She slid under Susie's arm and put an arm around her. "We could all share it," she whispered. "Cuddling all night long, just to keep warm."

Susie imagined how it might feel to be naked with them both in the same bed, legs and arms all tangled together. She'd enjoyed their tender, fun intimacy so far and was excited to see what exploration and experimentation they might try.

"Right, it's time for the girls to go and have fun," Emily said, and ushered them out of her room.

As they walked along the landing, Pritti asked, "So, your new job?"

"I'll start early January. I'm getting relocation assistance, and the HR department promised to help me find temporary accommodation to start with."

Emily cleared her throat. "Might be able to help there. We're both at Bristol University. My flat's big enough for three, at least until you get yourself sorted out."

Susie felt a broad smile take over her face, and a delicious warm excitement filled her. She didn't know where this evening's events would lead, but she'd met two new friends, and found a fascinating new side to herself. She suspected the next few months would certainly be interesting and a lot of fun. "That's a lovely offer."

"And?"

Susie paused for a second. No harm offering. "If you want to escape for a while tomorrow, I'd love you both to visit me."

Pritti smiled. "Someone will be an ex-boyfriend by then?"

"He already is, but he doesn't know it yet." She squeezed Pritti's hand. "Bring your camera, too."

Emily nudged Pritti. "Maybe a few of our toys, too."

Susie guessed she meant sex toys. "Any samosas left over?"

Emily grinned. "We'll save at least three, for that 'sugar and spice and all things nice' vibe."

Susie high-fived them both. "You've got it, girlfriends."

"Send me a text when you wake up," Emily said. "We'll be knocking on your door as soon as we can."

"Don't wear anything tight before we arrive," Pritti said. "The marks in your skin from elastic take a while to fade."

Susie stopped and hugged both of them to her. "I know what Humphrey Bogart meant when he said this is the beginning of a beautiful friendship."

Sugar and Spice

Carlotta's Wish

by Sofia Giaconda
Twitter: @lasofiagioconda
Bluesky: @suzannalundale.bsky.social

With a satisfied hum, Carlotta examined herself in the mirror. She looked good. Great, really. Green sequined dress that was short enough to dance in and just long enough for that dancing to be at the company-sponsored holiday shindig. Red crepe de chine wrap to match the cute red boots she had borrowed from her adorably weird friend Rosalie ("Here's your something borrowed, now you need something old and–" "I'm going out with him, not marrying him!" Carlotta had objected. "Doesn't mean you don't need luuuck," Rosalie had trilled as she scooted out of the office, already answering the phone in her hand.).

Carlotta's dark curls were pinned up with a few tendrils hanging down artfully. Red and green rhinestones studded the mass of curls and helped ensure the ones that were meant to stay in place would. Yes, she looked good, and Rosalie hadn't been able to dig up anything gross about her date, which was promising.

Normally, Carlotta made a rule of not dating men from work, but Chase, the new guy on the translations team in legal, was on loan from the latest partner company. He'd be going back there full-time in the Spring. Plus, he spoke French, had a gorgeous dimpled smile, and had great hands. She was happy to make the exception.

BUZZ. And there he was.

Carlotta picked up the handset. "Chase?"

"In the flesh," he answered cheerfully. She buzzed him in and grinned for the mirror one last time before going to the door.

"Hi there," she breathed, surprised when Chase stepped forward to kiss her cheek.

"You look amazing," he responded appreciatively. "These are for you." He held out a small bouquet of red carnations in plastic wrapping.

Carlotta was very much a proponent of the thought being the important part, but a small part of her couldn't help but note that the newsstand on the corner had apparently sold one of the sad little emergency bouquets they always had on hand.

"Oh, thanks! Love the red!" she said, going to the kitchen to grab a vase. She buried her nose in a bloom and inhaled deeply. She'd say this for carnations. They might not be much to look at, but that strong spicy aroma was wonderful. As she snipped the ends, she called into the next room, "Oh, hey, so my neighbor, Tim, tends bar at Rousseau, and I told him we were going to have dinner tonight."

"Oh …"

"Anyway, when he got to work, he looked at the book and saw that somehow the reservation I made had been crossed out. Probably someone else had called to cancel theirs, and mine got crossed out instead."

"I guess we'll have to find somewhere else," Chase began.

"No, Tim fixed it up. We're back on the book."

"Oh … good."

"Crazy luck, huh?" Carlotta emerged from the kitchen with the flowers arranged in a fluted vase, looking much improved for the attention. "Don't these look lovely?" She put them on her tiny coffee table.

"We're still on for Rousseau, then?" Chase was looking at the carnations with an expression Carlotta couldn't read.

"Yes, I'm really excited for you to try it. And the servers all speak French, so we can have the total experience!"

"Oh, I wouldn't speak French in front of you and leave you out," he said gallantly, preceding her out of the door so she could lock it behind them.

"Mais, non, cher!" she smiled, turning to him with a grin. "Not at all! Didn't I tell you I speak French?"

Chase chuckled nervously, and Carlotta felt bad for putting him on the spot. She'd only said three words, but even so, it was obvious her French wasn't a spotty remnant from high school.

"I spent a few summers in Normandy with my Aunt Coco," she explained as they descended to the street.

"Aah," he said. "That explains the accent."

They decided to walk, since the restaurant was only a block away. Carlotta tucked her arm through Chase's, and they walked in silence. Carlotta resisted the urge to snuggle closer to his side this early in the date, in spite of the cold. Her mind buzzed with anticipation of the evening ahead.

As they rounded the corner, a complex array of delicious scents greeted them. Carlotta breathed in deeply. "Mmm, doesn't it smell divine?"

Chase sniffed cautiously. "Uh, yeah. Smells like food, for sure. Are you hungry?"

"Very. I've been looking forward to this for days." She reached to open the door, but the maître d' had seen their approach and was already opening it to usher them inside.

"Good evening! Good evening! You must be Mademoiselle Carlotta and her young man!" The maître d' spoke in lightly-accented English as he graciously helped Carlotta out of her coat and handed it to a waiting assistant while Chase shrugged out of his own. "We have saved for you a very special table," he said, as he led them to an intimate, candlelit table tucked partially into an alcove, effectively screening it from any curious onlookers and what little conversational noise there was.

Carlotta settled into the comfortable seat and listened attentively to the recitation of the evening's specials. She closed her eyes with a small smile and breathed in, catching the aromas of sweet-tart lemons from one of the specials, the plentiful roasted garlic from another, the rosemary crushed so fresh, it was as if it was on their table.

"It all smells delicious," she enthused. She saw that Chase was studying the menu, a small crease between his eyes. He looked up to see her watching.

"Mmhmm," he agreed absently. "Crazy how the whole menu's in French, too. They, uh, really take this French thing the whole distance."

"Oh, I think that might be for us," Carlotta said uncertainly. "I mentioned that we both spoke French when I made the reservation. Maybe they noted that down, or Tim did when he rescued our reservation."

"Yes," said Chase blandly. "Thank goodness for Tim." Suddenly, he stood. "Uh, be right back. Just need to visit the Gents'." He squeezed his confused date's shoulder as he walked swiftly from the table.

Carlotta waited, rereading the menu for the enjoyment of it, and then looking–discreetly, of course–at those diners she could see from their alcove table. An older couple caught her attention, he in a red velvet suit most men couldn't wear without looking like a discount Santa Claus, and she in a shimmering red gown. Carlotta could see their matching wedding rings when each of them took a sip of wine, but they gazed at each other like besotted teenagers. She smiled, privileged to witness their quiet joy.

Chase returned, smiling and looking more confident. The server came, and they placed their orders. Chase ordered his dish without consulting the menu, using the English words for it. Carlotta wondered if maybe his French was more focused on the written, and he'd gotten away from speaking it. Maybe that was the source of his discomfort.

"Given your selections," the server said, brandishing the wine list, "May I recommend a nice crisp white for the table?"

Carlotta started to agree, but Chase frowned. "I don't know," he said, his voice louder than it had been. "White wine is more a brunch thing, isn't it? I thought only old women drank white at dinner." He looked at the server defiantly.

"Well," said Carlotta diplomatically, "I believe there's something to be said for drinking what appeals to you, regardless of the traditional wine for the meal. I'm quite partial to a nice red, myself, so maybe we could …" She reached for the wine list in the server's hand. "Yes, how about this 2009 Chateau Nuit? It's not so heavy it will overwhelm your fish, and it's very tasty." She raised her eyebrows to Chase for his approval.

To her embarrassment, he just waved a hand, apparently not realizing she was trying to accommodate his preference and cover over his gaff. "Sure, yeah, whatever, as long as it's red," he said, his eyes following behind a young woman in a form-fitting black dress.

The server tried, and failed, to hide his sympathetic expression and nodded smartly. "An excellent choice, mademoiselle. I will be back with your wine momentarily."

Chase watched the server go. "There goes his tip," he said, reaching into his jacket pocket.

"What? Why?" Carlotta was stunned. More so when Chase pulled a small flask from his pocket, unscrewed the top, and took a long pull. He held it out to Carlotta with what he may have thought was an inviting wink.

"Put that away," she hissed. "He'll be back in a second with the wine."

"He'll be back in a second to hit on my date," Chase countered. "Who does he think is paying the bill? Not Miss Oh No They Accidentally Canceled Our Reservation But My Friend Tim Fixed It."

Carlotta sat back in shock. Chase had canceled the reservation? She watched in numb silence as the server brought the wine and presented it for her approval. She barely tasted the rich, spicy vintage and nodded mechanically. With a look of concern, he poured each of them a glass and hurried away to check on their food.

The food came, and it, at least, was perfect. Carlotta usually liked to have a conversation with her dinner companion, but this time, she was happy to make an exception. She largely ignored Chase as she tucked into the tender medallions of duck, perfectly seasoned to highlight the natural flavor of the meat. She reflected with an inward smile that the wine she had chosen was actually an ideal accompaniment to her meal.

Looking up through her lashes, she watched Chase devouring the delicate fish he had ordered as if it were a diner T-bone, taking long drafts of wine with his mouth still full. How had Rosalie not managed to dig up any dirt on this guy?

When the server came to take their plates, Carlotta made sure to praise the kitchen thoroughly before murmuring that they were ready for the separate checks, and he should put the wine on her bill.

"Mais, non, mademoiselle," he said. "The wine is compliments of the house. I will bring the checks right away."

Carlotta paid hers without a word while Chase groused about the price of his across the table. She tipped handsomely, both because she always did at Christmas, and because she thought Chase very probably would make good on his threat not to tip at all. Barbaric custom, anyway, she thought, tucking her card away.

The maître d' helped Carlotta don her coat with the air of a disapproving father. "May I call a pair of taxis to take you to your destinations?" he offered hopefully.

Carlotta smiled. "No, we'll catch one on the street, but thank you. We have a party to attend for our work."

"Eh bien," sighed the maître d'. "Ah well. I hope you enjoy the party." He glared at Chase's back, already moving unsteadily to the curb to hail a cab.

Once in the cab, Carlotta turned to look at Chase, who was busily scrolling through something on his phone. "Why did you cancel the reservation?" she asked in a small voice. "If you didn't want to come here, we could have chosen somewhere else. You could have said."

Chase's grin was closer to a sneer. "The plan was, we find out the reservation was canceled. I show you how fun and flexible I am by suggesting we get Chinese take-out from the place on the corner and eat at your place, which is right here. We snuggle up, eat Chinese food, and watch a movie. Then we decide to skip the party and have our own party, in your bed."

Carlotta looked away in disgust, looking instead out the window of the car. She tried to let the sights of the city at Christmas soothe her.

Carlotta loved the city at Christmas. She loved the big, fancy decorations in some windows. She loved the little, single-light strand decorations in other windows. She loved the Christmas trees visible through people's apartment windows. She loved watching people bundled up, hurrying through the cold on errands for festive meals and gatherings. She loved all of it. She sighed happily.

At a stoplight, she saw a vendor under an awning roasting spiced almonds in a steel drum. Without thinking, she lowered her window to inhale the spicy scent of the roasting almonds.

The driver looked at her in the rearview mirror. "You want to stop to buy some?"

Carlotta started and blushed. "Oh, no, that's okay. I just wanted to smell them." She raised her window sheepishly, shutting out the cold.

"The smell is wonderful," the driver agreed. "It is … it is spicy and warm, but carries the cold with it, too, I think."

"Yes, exactly!" said Carlotta, excitedly. "Because we only have them like that at Christmas, so the cold is attached to the scent, somehow! I've never heard it put that way before."

The driver's eyes in the rearview mirror seemed to glow as they caught the red and green lights on the street. They were crinkled with a smile. Carlotta smiled back.

Carlotta looked at the eye symbol hanging from the rearview mirror. Images of a trip she had taken with her Aunt Coco flashed in her memory. Impulsively, Carlotta asked, "Is that from Morocco, by any chance? The eye thing you have?"

His eyes looked surprised when he glanced up at her in the mirror again. "Yes, it's from my country. It is to ward off the evil eye."

"Oh, you're from Morocco!"

"Yes! You know it?"

"I went there with my aunt when I was a kid. It was wonderful."

"I am from a city called Casablanca. I think maybe you've heard of it?"

"Oh, Casablanca is my favorite m–" she broke off, embarrassed. Because, of course, what did the movie have to do with actual Casablanca and actual Moroccans?

The driver chuckled. "It's my favorite movie, too. But maybe I am biased."

"Really, my favorite thing in Morocco was the souk. Especially the spices! Those tables with piles of the most fragrant spices, so colorful and abundant. You could smell the spice market for blocks and blocks away. You can't get spices like that here. Not really. It's not the same."

Next to her, Chase snorted derisively. "Weird kink," he sneered.

Carlotta ignored him.

"My family's home," said the driver–Azhar, according to his driver ID– "is very near the spice market. It is, indeed, a magical place."

"Mmm, yes," agreed Carlotta dreamily. "Magical."

The car stopped, and Carlotta realized, with some regret, that they had arrived. Chase was already getting out of the car.

"I think your boyfriend is in a hurry to get to the party," Azhar said with a laugh.

"Oh, he is not my boyfriend," clarified Carlotta. "And he isn't going to be." She paid the fare, adding a generous tip, and watched with pleased amusement as Azhar leapt out of the car and came around to open her door like a chauffeur.

"Thank you very much, Azhar from Casablanca," Carlotta said with a warm smile.

"It has been my pleasure, Carlotta from New York," he replied with a bow. His dark eyes caught the light when he straightened to smile at her and seemed again to glow. He helped her onto the sidewalk and walked back around to get back in his taxi.

Carlotta was at the door of the building when she realized he had used her name, which she hadn't given. She turned, but the car was gone. Strange. Chase must have used it among the few words they had exchanged in the car.

With a shrug, Carlotta went in to hunt down Rosalie and fill her in on the disaster of the date.

She found Rosalie on the dance floor, right where she expected. The tiny little woman was surrounded by eager partners orbiting around her like so many moths to her irresistible flame. When she saw Carlotta, she pulled her in and refused to be drawn away to talk until there had been dancing.

"I see that face, girl," Rosalie said in her ear. "I already know it's bad. Get some dancing in you before you talk about it. Trust me."

Reluctantly, at first, Carlotta obeyed. She bumped and swayed, laughing at Rosalie's antics. Gradually, the music worked its way under the stress armor the evening had piled around her and she was able to give herself over to it. When a dance mix came on with a distinctly North African vibe, Carlotta found herself imagining a particular set of dark, flashing eyes smiling down at her. She could almost smell the piles of spices pulling her through the winding streets of the souk to them, to him.

Rosalie pulled Carlotta from her reverie when the DJ took a break at the end of that song. The two women went up to the roof terrace to cool off after the crowded heat of the dance floor.

"Okay," said Rosalie, snagging drinks from a passing tray and handing one to Carlotta. "Spill it. What happened??"

Feeling at least as amused as aggrieved, Carlotta relayed the tale, from the newsstand carnations and the "accidental" cancellation to the flask and the revelation of the plan in the taxi. By the end, they were giggling helplessly at the utter failure of yet another date.

Carlotta didn't hear Chase's approach behind her. Only Rosalie's widened eyes gave her any warning before he slurred, "Hey, Carli, there you are. Get ready to hoe-hoe-hoe under the mistletoe!"

Carlotta turned. With a sweetness whose irony was lost on Chase, she said, "Oh, gee, Chase, I don't think there's any mistletoe up here." She gestured to the open sky above them.

Chase leered. "Oh, I had something else in mind."

Carlotta followed his pointed gaze downward and saw with disgust that he had pulled down some mistletoe from somewhere and fastened it to his belt. Underneath it, his organ struggled under the weight of his alcohol consumption to achieve something close to an erection. It was sticking out of his fly and bobbing away under the mistletoe.

Rosalie laughed. "You absolute muppet," she said, her cut-glass English accent more pronounced than usual. "You know that's toxic to the touch, right? You're going to have a rash on your poor little todger for weeks." Linking arms with Carlotta, she led her away, leaving Chase frantically yanking at the mistletoe's ribbon.

In the elevator, Carlotta finally stopped giggling enough to ask her friend if what she had said was true.

"Oh, yes," Rosalie assured her. "It's very toxic. I don't know if that little bit of contact will do the trick, but one does rather hope so, doesn't one?"

"One rather does," Carlotta admitted. "And I think one has had enough excitement for tonight. I'm going to head home and get my pajamas on."

Rosalie looked like she might object.

"Seriously, Ro. I'm good. This has just been a lot. I want pajamas and cocoa and fluffy blanket and Bogart."

"Fiiine. You want me to come with you? Make it a pajama party?"

Carlotta smiled. "Nah, you've still got a lot of wiggle in you. Go dance. Greet the dawn for me. I'm good. I promise."

Rosalie pouted adorably and gave her friend a squeeze. "I will dance for both of us, then."

"My brave girl. Go, then. I'll talk to you tomorrow." Carlotta took a last look at the dance floor and made her way to the coat check.

Once outside, a small part of Carlotta wondered if maybe Azhar would happen by to pick her up. She imagined them driving around the city for hours, admiring the lights and talking about his homeland and their shared favorite movie. Maybe at sunrise, they would kiss, sitting on the hood of his car, with the sun rising over the Hudson …

A cab pulled up and Carlotta got in. Of course, it was not Azhar's cab. Carlotta gave her address and sat back.

"Is it okay with you if I have Christmas carols on?" the driver asked politely.

"Sure, that's fine with me," said Carlotta.

"I'm practicing," the driver explained. "This is my first year as Santa. You like the beard?" He fluffed the beard proudly.

"Yes, it's very nice. I didn't think most Santas did a lot of singing, though."

"Oh, this is a family gig," he explained. "My daughter and her wife have been trying to adopt for three years, and this year, they finally adopted a little boy!" They came to a stoplight, and he promptly pulled up pictures on his phone. Two exhausted and happy-looking women flanked a grinning little boy.

"They named him Teddy! Theodore, after me! After his grandpapa!" The obvious joy of the man bubbled out in laughter. "I have to make sure I know every song by heart, so I can sing to him, and teach him the words."

He demonstrated by singing a few bars along with the radio in a beautiful, rich baritone.

Carlotta smiled in admiration. "You're doing a great job already, Theodore," she said.

"Well, Theodore's my full name, and his," he explained. "But my friends call me Theo. You can call me Theo."

"Okay, Theo it is. And I'm Carlotta."

"Oh, now, that's a pretty name. I'll remember that. Carlotta. Very pretty."

They came to another stoplight, and Theo showed more pictures.

"And which one is your daughter?" Carlotta asked.

"Well, they're both my daughters, of course," answered Theo. "This one is the daughter I raised, Jasmine. She's lighter-skinned, because her mama is white. And this is her beautiful wife, Amanda. They've been together since high school. Not always an easy road, you know, but they loved each other, and we loved them, and eventually, Amanda's folks even came around." He glanced up at the light and regretfully lowered the phone to resume driving.

They pulled up to Carlotta's building singing together about eight maids milking.

"One more," said Theo, as he put away Carlotta's payment with thanks. With obvious pride, he held the phone up to show himself, in full Santa regalia, gazing adoringly at a woman dressed as Mrs. Claus. "My wife, Sasha," he beamed. "Doesn't she make a perfect Mrs. Claus?"

Sasha was standing next to Theo, her hand on his shoulder. Her head was tilted, as if she had just looked up at the camera from looking at him. And he was looking at her like she had personally invented love. Carlotta felt an overflow of joy for these loving people in her heart. At the same time, she felt a pang of longing, like homesickness for a place – or a person – you hadn't even seen yet.

"Perfect," Carlotta agreed, handing back the phone. "Thank you, Theo, for sharing those. Merry Christmas. And congratulations on that grandson. He's a lucky little boy."

Carlotta's Wish

Theo chuckled happily. "Merry Christmas to you, Carlotta. I think Santa will bring you what your heart most desires this year."

Carlotta laughed and got out of the car. She fished out her keys on the way to the door and turned back as she unlocked it. Theo was there, watching to see that she got inside. Dear man. She let the door close behind her and started up the stairs.

The carnations were there to greet her when she walked in. Poor things. It wasn't their fault. Carlotta dropped her keys and clutch on the table and went in to change.

Soon, sequins and rhinestones were traded for comfort and warmth. In honor of Theo and his Sasha, Carlotta had chosen a pajama top that showed Mr. and Mrs. Claus dozing in front of a fire. Two elves were arranging a blanket over them. The calendar on the wall showed it was Christmas Day. The matching red fleece bottoms showed sleeping elves in their beds. Her green socks were designed to look like elf boots, with buckles and bells. They had actually had bells on them when she got them, but she cut them off because it was not restful to jingle when walking around in pajamas.

Carlotta grabbed the remote and turned on the TV on her way to the kitchen. This weekend was the Bogart festival on the classic movies channel. All goodness, all the time. That was the rest of the weekend planned.

In the kitchen, she pulled down the special jar of her Aunt Coco's secret cocoa mix. She flipped open the lid and brought the jar up to her nose. Mmmm. Cocoa, cinnamon, turmeric, and at least two other ingredients Carlotta hadn't been able to identify yet. Coco had promised she'd leave her the recipe when she died, but there was also some fun in the not knowing.

She closed her eyes and sniffed again. Behind her eyelids, a pair of dark eyes glowed invitingly. Azhar. Azhar from Casablanca, with his soft-spoken purr, his ready smile, the way that slight rolling of the R in Carlotta had felt like a hand caressing her bare back. She shivered and reached for a mug. She spooned the powder into the cup and pulled the milk off the heat just before it boiled, to give it that slightly sweet flavor.

She watched the colors swirl into the milk, dissolving at different rates. Then she gave it a quick stir and added a generous dollop of honey. Cautiously, she took a tiny sip. Too hot to drink, still, but perfect. She rinsed out the pot and left it dry before padding back out to the couch.

Before she could see the screen, the familiar dialogue told her that they were playing Casablanca, and it had only started a few minutes ago. She smiled and wondered if Azhar was home yet. Did he know about the Bogart festival? Or maybe it wasn't Bogart in general for him, but only Casablanca. Maybe he didn't bother with the classic movie channel.

Carlotta snuggled into her cozy nest at the end of the couch, cocoa and remote next to her on the end table. Self cuddled into her big cozy couch blanket. Bogart on the screen looking stern about something. She settled in to watch her favorite movie, half imagining that Azhar would be coming home from work to join her before the movie ended. She sipped her cocoa and drifted into sleepy comfort, letting the ups and downs of these beloved characters unfold and resolve the way they always did.

❄ ❄ ❄

"Evening, Miss Carlotta. What are you drinking?"

Carlotta shook herself from her reverie and looked up at the bartender. "Good evening, Sascha. Just the cocoa for now, thanks. It's been a long day."

Sascha looked back at her quizzically, then looked down at her glass. "Ah, the cocoa, yes," he said finally, with a chuckle. "You can call it whatever you want to, Miss Carlotta. Rick will still cut you off if he–" he broke off mid-sentence, his face lighting up.

Carlotta turned and saw Yvonne sashaying in their direction. Funny, she thought, I never imagined they would stay black and white. Carlotta had imagined herself into this movie, and countless other silver screen favorites, more times than she could remember, but always, it was like she was there on the set with them, in living color, not in the silver hues of the film itself.

"Well?" Yvonne demanded, staring defiantly at Carlotta. "You have something to say to me?"

Did she? She didn't seem to be any existing character this time. Just herself, only– Carlotta looked down. Weird. Where her skin was visible, it was almost, sort of, well, glowing. The color of her skin, but not, somehow. By contrast, her clothes, and everything else, was fully black and white.

Carlotta looked back up at Yvonne. "N-no," she managed, finally. "I was just thinking how lovely your hair was looking tonight. I thought maybe you could give me advice."

Yvonne narrowed her eyes in suspicion. "You want advice. From me?"

Carlotta nodded. "You've, um, managed the perfect balance of curly and smooth. I can only ever manage one or the other," she tried, realizing that she didn't actually know what her hair looked like at the moment. She had just rolled it into a bun when she changed into her pajamas, but she wasn't wearing those pajamas here, so what her hair was doing right now was really anyone's guess.

Apparently, she had said the right thing. Yvonne's shoulders relaxed. She came closer and took a seat next to Carlotta. Unprompted, Sascha put a glass in front of Yvonne as she sat. She snatched it up and drank deeply. Sascha turned to Carlotta.

"Did that native man ever find you?" he asked. It was clear from his tone that he didn't entirely approve of the man, or of Carlotta, maybe, for being sought by him here.

"Native man?" Her thoughts went to Azhar. She supposed that would be how he'd have been seen here at that time. Never mind that it was, as the phrase implied, his own damn country.

"There was a native man looking for you. He said something about a tour of the souk. But you know, if you want to go there, one of us could take you. It's not safe for ..." He trailed off instinctively in response to Carlotta's icy expression.

"What was his name?" she asked, even though she knew. Of course, she had been thinking about him just before she fell asleep. Of course, he was here.

"Asram, or Azhnar, or something like that. I don't know. I really wouldn't–"

Carlotta was already standing. "Did he say where he would meet me?"

Sascha stood up straight, uncharacteristically defiant. Carlotta had to admit, she kind of loved that for him, the way Yvonne was always bossing him around. "I don't remember," he said flatly.

"That's fine," Carlotta said, putting some of the money she'd found in her clutch on the bar. "I think I know."

Almost giddy with excitement, Carlotta went out into the Moroccan night and went to look for Azhar. Glancing up at the silver moon, she steered herself away from where she thought the airfield and the military headquarters were and deeper into the winding streets of the city.

Within a few minutes, she was approached by a shy child of indeterminate gender. "You are Carlotta?" The child's English was more heavily accented than Azhar's, but with a similar lilt.

"Yes," Carlotta answered, charmed by the dream's choice to deploy a child to bring her to Azhar. "I'm Carlotta. You know Azhar?"

"Azhar," the child agreed. "Yes. You come." The boy–she thought he was a boy–slipped a small hand into hers and drew her down a narrow alley.

"Is better," he said. "More safer, this way."

Carlotta nodded and followed, dream logic leaving her safely unaffected by the child's obvious discomfort. The boy needed to think there was danger, even though the dream would protect them.

After several more turns, Carlotta began to smell the spices she remembered so well from her visit with Coco. "The spice market!" she murmured.

The boy looked at her reproachfully but said nothing. Finally, they came out in a small courtyard. There was a small fountain at the center of the courtyard, and riots of plants grew in pots and planters all over. Tiny balconies of upper floors were filled to overflowing with plants, some of which spilled over and hung down toward the courtyard.

Carlotta's senses were awash with the mingled aromas of herbs and flowers, many of which she was able to tease out from the rest to recognize, and many more she was not. "What is this place?" she breathed.

"You like it?" Azhar came out of the darkness. He handed a coin to the boy and spoke a few words. The boy bowed awkwardly to Carlotta and disappeared back down the alley they had come from. Or one just like it. She wasn't sure.

"It's amazing," she said, smiling up into Azhar's face as he took her hands. It was hard to tell, in the meager light of the moon, but she thought he, like her, was in color, though his clothes didn't seem to be.

"I hoped you would come," he purred, lowering his face toward hers.

"I hoped you would be here," she grinned, closing the distance between them.

Their lips met, lighting an urgent spark inside her. Yes, her body seemed to croon. More. Carlotta wrapped her arms around Azhar's neck and pulled him closer, kissing him again, demanding.

His chuckle when they broke apart betrayed his own shallowness of breath. "Come, my love," he purred, wrapping an arm around her. "Come inside, to your home." He led her in through one of the open doorways and up a narrow flight of stairs. He ushered her through an open door and closed it behind them.

Carlotta gasped. This room, at least, was not black and white. If anything, this room had extra colors, enough to make up for the lack everywhere else. One long wall was lined with spices and herbs of every color and consistency. Candlelight danced in reflection on the jars, showing their names, some in English, some French, others in Arabic. Some had no labels at all. The floor was lined with beautifully woven rugs of obvious quality.

On the wall to her other side, sturdy bookshelves held volumes in at least four languages that she counted, some bound in tooled leather or crisp cloth, others in humble paper covers. Carlotta thought she could spend weeks in this room happily without ever wanting to leave.

And in the center of the room, a bed on a low platform hung with colorful, diaphanous curtains, made up with fine-looking linens, and festooned with pillows of every shape and size–called to her. She walked toward, drawn by the dream and the need to touch and taste every part of

Azhar before this dream ended.

"Will you help me with my zipper?" she asked, suddenly shy in front of this dream man she was about to do every filthy thing she could think of to. He stalked closer, and she turned to let him reach the zipper. A tiny growl rumbled in his throat as the zipper went down to reveal bare skin. Carlotta smiled, glad her dream had decided against unnecessary undergarments.

As she stepped out of her dress, there was rustle of fabric behind her. She turned to see the man of her dreams, bare and in full color. He was looking at her with a low-lidded intensity that made her core throb with need.

"Carlotta," he said. "My Carlotta. You really came here to be with me?" There was wonder in his voice, and in those glowing dark eyes that had captivated her.

"Yes," she crooned, stepping forward so her breasts brushed his chest. Her nipples hardened at the contact. She shivered delightedly. "Yes, I came here to be with you, Azhar. My Azhar." She stroked a hand down his face. He nuzzled it and turned his face just enough to kiss her palm.

As her hand stroked down further, her fingertips grazing down his neck and flattening to drag down his chest, she felt him stirring against her abdomen, hard and insistent. Hungry. She cupped his hips with both hands and pressed her body against his to kiss him lingeringly.

"Come to bed," she murmured against his lips. "Come to bed with me." She backed toward the bed, pulling him after with her hands and lips. When she felt the platform against her calves, she stopped, calculating the most graceful way to lower herself.

Bending to hook an arm behind her knees, Azhar scooped Carlotta up with an ease she would not have expected from his lean form. In other circumstances, she would have made a self-deprecating joke about her not being the most petite model on the floor, but there was no mirth in the intensity of his gaze. Only hunger. Need. Possession.

Gently, he lowered her to the bed, following her body closely with his. "Carlotta," he whispered against her flesh, like an incantation. "My Carlotta." With meticulous care, he kissed her neck on one side, flicking her earlobe with his tongue. His warm breath against her dampened neck left her writhing, wanting to touch him, grab him, but he was firm. He held her hands gently, pinning them to the bed on either side of her head as his lips worked across her throat and up to the other side of her neck. Carlotta moaned.

"Yes, my love," Azhar said, encouraging. "Yes, tell me what you feel. I want to know what you like." He kissed down onto her chest, and she arched into him, waiting to feel his mouth close, hot, around one nipple. "Mmm," he hummed approvingly. "Very inviting. Do not worry. I will get there, Carlotta" Instead of taking the proffered breast, he turned and started to kiss and lick his way down her arm.

When he got to the crook of her elbow, Carlotta let out a squeak of surprise. No lover had ever stopped there before, and Carlotta hadn't known it was something worth doing. She looked down at Azhar, still impatient to get to some of the more usual star attractions but intrigued by her dream lover's versatility. He chuckled and worked his way down to her wrist.

"There are, my Carlotta," he said, his breath stirring on the damp flesh of her wrist. "Some things, I think, still to be discovered, for all of us." The hand holding her other hand released it and moved to caress her breast. Between her legs, she felt his erection pressing against her swollen clit.

"There are also," she gasped, grinding up against him, "some amazing things that have been discovered, but warrant another exploration." She flexed her hips, coming off the bed and letting her wet need guide him right down to where she needed him.

Azhar whimpered and closed his eyes. "Carlotta," he said, his voice pleading. "Carlotta …"

She answered with a triumphant growl. He was there, nudging against her entrance.

"Azhar, please." The plea proved to be his undoing. With his eyes on hers, he pushed into her with aching care, pulling back enough to give her body time to adjust before coming back to fill her more deeply, ever more deeply, until he was buried inside her to the root.

"Carlotta," he whispered– a prayer and declaration rolled into her name. "Carlotta." Together they moved, slowly at first, exploring, learning each other's bodies. Carlotta felt the pressure mounting at her core and wrapped her legs around him to open herself more fully.

"Yes. Oh, yes," she moaned, flexing her hips to meet his every stroke. "More, Azhar. More, please. Don't stop."

He bent to kiss her, long and sweetly. "Never, my Carlotta. I will not stop, until you say." Around his smiling eyes, his dark skin glowed with the exertion of their lovemaking. Carlotta ran her hands over his shoulders, down his arms and back up, across his back, marveling at his lithe perfection.

Azhar responded to her touch eagerly, his strokes coming deeper and faster, angled perfectly to give her the friction she needed, where she needed it most. "Azhar," she cried. "I'm going to–! I need to–! I'm–!" She arched her back and clenched around him, her mouth open in a silent cry of awe and ecstasy.

He smiled down at her and gentled his pace without stopping. He trailed the fingertips of one hand down her trembling flank, over her hip, and down her thigh. Tenderly, watching her face for any indication he should stop, he lifted her leg high into the air, changing his angle of entry. He brought her leg to rest against his chest, her knee resting on his shoulder.

"This is good?" he asked, bending to kiss the tip of her nose. "This is okay?"

"This is very okay," she responded, pushing aside her initial worry that this position made her tummy look bunchy. Instead, she focused on his face, and on the way he moved inside her, without any sign that he was in danger of erupting before he wanted to. His face was a picture of enjoyment and concentration. He was beautiful. Carlotta thought she could look at him forever.

"Hey," she said, unhooking her leg and stroking his face. "Let me take a turn."

"This is not your turn?" he teased, rotating his hips and drawing a long moan from her.

"Okay, this is my turn, too, but I want–That is, I like to be on top sometimes, too."

His expression of surprise sent a surge of heat through her. She grinned up at him. He was in for a treat.

With obvious regret, he withdrew from her slick depths and helped her position herself on top of him. "This is good?" she asked with a smile as she lowered herself onto him. He flexed his hips in answer, pushing up into her as she shifted her weight to take him in fully. Carlotta reached up and pulled out the clips holding her curls in their unruly pile to let them cascade down her back. She arched her back and tossed her head, letting her hair caress her back and ass, and under her, Azhar's thighs and balls. She watched his eyes flutter in ecstasy.

"Oh, Carlotta, yes. Your turn is very good, too," he said, moving his legs to feel the brush of her hair again. "It is very good."

Bracing her hands on his thighs, Carlotta leaned back and let her body undulate over his. Cowgirl had always been a favorite of hers, and now it felt as if every dude she'd ridden had been practice for this night, for this man. She was good at this, and she knew it. She was proud that she was able to blow Azhar's mind with her skill.

With effort, she kept herself at a slowish pace, watching and reveling in the sheer bliss of his expression. His hands roamed freely over her body, caressing her breasts, tracing her curves, cupping her round ass. Everywhere he touched, he left a trail of tingling heat. More than once, Carlotta was surprised to look where his hands had just been and see that the area was not, in fact, sparkling, as it felt like it should be.

She reached back to lift his balls and fondle them against her ass, drawing a sharp breath from Azhar. "How–?" he gasped, moving his hips to meet her strokes more firmly. "How does my Carlotta make this magic?" His palm pressed against her chest between her breasts burned with intensity.

"Mmm, magic," she agreed dreamily, giving herself to rising heat at her core. "Magic. So much magic, Azhar." She bore down, one hand on his chest, riding him in earnest, hard and fast, as her body demanded. He responded, holding her hips and driving up into her.

"Carlotta–I will also–I must–But I will have to stop after, for a little while. I promised I would not stop." His breath came in shallow gasps, the effort of holding back plain in his expression.

Carlotta flexed her inner muscles around him and laughed. "That kind of stopping is okay now. Come with me, Azhar. Come–" The last word became a cry of triumph in unison. Her thighs went slick against his sides, lubricated by the gush of her pleasure. Inside her, she felt the answering hot pulse of his seed flooding her.

She collapsed, perspiring on his chest with a giggle. "So that was kind of amazing," she said with a broad grin, propping herself up just enough to look at him.

"Amazing," he agreed. "My beautiful Carlotta is amazing. I want to touch you every day of my life, Carlotta. I want to see you every day and listen to you every day and hold you every day. I adore you. Is this too much to say? I love you."

Carlotta bit her lip against a giddy laugh. "It might be too much to say, but I love you too. I want to touch you and see you and do all those things with you every day." Her giddy laugh faded to a thoughtful, dreamy smile. "Maybe it's part of the magic?"

"Magic," he said thoughtfully. "Yes, it is magic." He reached under one of the many pillows and withdrew a delicate silver ring. Tenderly, he brought her hand to his lips and kissed the inside of her wrist, her palm, and each fingertip in turn. He turned it over and looked at her fingers. "I hope," he said, "Maybe this ring is magic, too, and will bring you back to me." He looked to her for approval, and at her nod, slid it onto her finger.

"Bring me back to you," she purred. "As if I'm going anywhere." She kissed him, holding the kiss and stroking his body. Half under her, half next to her, still slick with sweat and satisfaction, his body responded readily, stirring against her with flattering eagerness. She settled next to him and threw one leg over him, urging him closer, and reaching between them, guided him into her with a wanton moan.

Only when the candles had all guttered out, to be replaced by the growing light of the coming dawn, did they fall asleep, limbs and dreams tangled thoroughly in each other.

Too soon, Carlotta's sleep was broken by a persistent Zzt zzt sound her tired brain struggled to identify.

❄ ❄ ❄

"Mmm." Smiling sleepily, Carlotta nuzzled the warmth resting against her cheek. Zzt zzt. There was that sound again. Almost like–Carlotta's eyes snapped open. Almost like a notification when her phone was on vibrate on the table next to her. She looked around. She was in her living room, on her couch, cuddled into her big cozy couch blanket. Alone.

She burrowed her face into the blanket with a groan. What had started out so obviously a dreamscape had gotten so detailed, so real, she had forgotten it was a dream. Even now, her body felt pleasantly sore, not at all like it should after a night spent half-sitting, half-slumping on the couch, and she still detected the fragrant chaos of the spice market clinging to her hair and clothes.

Carlotta shook her head. Too much wine, too many emotions, and too much imagination. She chuckled ruefully. She had known it was a dream. She had known. And then she had forgotten. She swung her legs off the couch and picked up her mug to take into the kitchen. She was surprised to find one last gulp sitting cold in the bottom. "Here's lookin' at you, kid," she murmured sadly.

She took the cup into the kitchen and washed it, leaving it on the rack to dry. Time for a nice shower to wake her up, some clean pajamas, and a nice day alone on the couch watching old movies because everyone she knew would be spending Christmas Day with family.

She had picked up the carnations to move them closer to the tiny Christmas tree on the table when she saw the package. "What the—?" She glanced over at the door to make sure it was still closed and locked. She set the vase down harder than she intended and picked up the package. Rectangular, like a cereal box on its side, and wrapped in plain red paper, it was heavier than she expected. Her name was written in a neat, elegant hand across the upper left corner. A thin piece of green braid was tied in a simple bow at the center.

Carlotta pulled off the twine and opened the paper carefully. The wrapping was neat, in the way that wrapping can be really neat when a friend does it at home, and still never be mistaken for having been gift-wrapped at the store. Someone had wrapped this. For her.

The paper came away to reveal a wooden chest with intricate inlay on the lid. Fingers trembling, she flipped the latch and opened the lid to find it was a small treasure chest of spices. She closed her eyes and inhaled. It was as if she were standing again in the heart of the souk, on a narrow street lined with tables of spices warmed by the Moroccan sun.

In the center compartment, flashing silver in a bed of golden turmeric, was the ring. The ring. Carlotta looked at her bare hand and felt again Azhar's warm fingers cradling hers as he slipped this ring on her finger. A dream. It was a dream. She reminded herself harshly.

Except, her other voice whispered quietly. What is this? Hesitantly, she plucked the ring from its fragrant nest. There was resistance as she first lifted it, then a click. A drawer popped open below the main compartments and the ring came free between her fingertips. A single thread dropped away, snapped at her tugging. She rubbed away a few grains of the spice and looked at the ring. This was no plastic prop. It was real.

She opened the drawer to find a piece of creamy stationery folded into thirds. She pulled it out and opened it to find a short note, addressed to her.

Dear Carlotta,
I have learned that as fun as it is to surprise people with the fulfillment of their Christmas wishes, it is better to leave them one last chance to decide that wasn't the right wish after all.

Carlotta looked up at the spice chest and wondered when she had made a wish. She read on.

Here is how this works. You can keep the ring in the box or give it away, whatever you want to do, and you will keep your wish dream as a dream.

Carlotta's breathing grew shallow.

Or you can put the ring back where your young man put it, and keep the wish, making it real.

Carlotta sat hard on the edge of the couch. The hand holding the ring was closed around it so tightly, her nails dug into her flesh. Keep the wish, making it real, she reread, and reread again. What would making it real mean? Would she go to Casablanca to find him? But no, she had met him here last night, before she met him in her dream. All she had to do was find one North African taxi driver in Manhattan.

She groaned and sat back, holding the ring in front of her face. She saw behind it the joy that had lit Azhar's face when he slid it on her finger, felt again the burning joy in her chest when he did. She sat up, already starting to put the ring on. It didn't matter. If there was a chance to make that connection real, it didn't matter. She'd call the taxi company. She'd put an ad in the Times. If there was a chance, she would take it.

She slid the ring onto her finger and admired it, as she had the night before. She picked up the letter. Maybe there were instructions? She skimmed over it to the bottom. Real. She looked at her finger and smiled. Her eyes traveled finally to a line at the bottom she had noticed before.

Merry Christmas, Carlotta, from your friend, Santa.

Carlotta made a face. Santa? She believed in the spirit of Santa Claus and all, but–BUZZ. With a puzzled frown, she got up and went over to pick up the handset for the front door. "Yes?"

"Carlotta, I–" The voice was faint but unmistakable. Azhar.

"Azhar? Is that you?" There was a click and static, and then no more. "No, Azhar, it's me! It's Carlotta! It's–" She jammed her finger on the button repeatedly to buzz him in as she grabbed her coat and keys. She threw her door open and stumbled down the stairs, stuffing her arms into her coat as she went.

As she feared, there was no Azhar at the bottom of the stairs. She looked down at her elf socks ruefully and sighed. She had managed to grab a coat but forgot shoes. She looked longingly up the stairs and thought of the warm boots right next to the door.

Then she looked back at the closed front door. There was no time. Azhar was out there, and if he left now, she would lose this chance. Who knew if the ring would ever give her another magical assist like this? She took the last steps to the front door and opened it, peering out. Three buildings down, she spotted a retreating back that could be his.

"Azhar?" she called. "Azhar, is that you?" Carlotta stepped out and ran mincingly–touching the cold pavement with as little of her stockinged feet as possible– in his direction. "Don't leave," she called, doubt starting to build. She didn't really believe in magi–. Then he turned.

His face registered disbelief, hope, and joy, in rapid succession, mirrored by the same on Carlotta's own.

"My Carlotta?" he mouthed as she got closer. He started to run, then, rushing to her and picking her up, swinging her around easily. "Is this real?" he asked, astonished. "How?"

"I don't know how, but it's real," Carlotta stretched to kiss him, tentatively. "At least, I think–" Shyly, she lifted up her hand and showed him the ring, searching his face for a reaction.

His jaw dropped. "That ring. I put it ... but ... how?"

"Come inside. My feet are too cold. We can talk all about it in my apartment."

Azhar looked down and gave a cry of alarm. He scooped her up, one arm behind her knees and the other behind her back and walked back toward her building.

Carlotta chuckled, gazing up at him. "Is this going to be a habit, you picking me up like this?"

"I think so, yes," Azhar said, looking serious. "I like it very much." He waited for her to unlock the door and start to push it open before setting her down on the tiled entryway floor.

"Up here," Carlotta said, looking back several times on the short climb to make sure he was still there. She led him into her apartment and over to the couch, where they sat side by side.

"How did you find me?" she asked, stroking her face. He nuzzled her hand with a blissful smile and kissed her palm.

"It was a strange thing. My friend, who used to work with me … We were having a coffee because he said he wanted to celebrate."

"What was he celebrating?"

"He did not say, but his daughter adopted a baby recently. I know he was very excited about that."

A stirring of an idea sparked to life in Carlotta's mind. She traced Azhar's ear with a finger. "You were having coffee …"

"Yes, and he was showing me pictures of the mothers and their baby. He was very happy that they named the baby after him, but they don't call him the same thing. I am not sure.

"Then, he got a message on his phone, and he chuckled, and pulled a paper from his pocket. 'By the way,' he said, 'my friend Carlotta told me that she wished to see you again.'

"I dreamt of you last night. When he said your name, I thought I might still be dreaming. Then he gave me the paper and it was your address." Azhar pulled the paper from his pocket. "Then he shooed me out and told me togo at once."

Carlotta eyed the paper and made a mental note to compare the handwriting to a certain letter later on. "But then after you buzzed," she protested, "you were leaving!"

"Once I heard your voice, I thought how crazy it seemed, to just show up on your doorstep like that. I had no gift, even. And I didn't think you would wish–"

Pulling him close, she kissed him long and thoroughly. "I did wish," she murmured against his lips. "Let me show you what else I wish." She stood and took his hand, drawing him up from the couch. With a seductive grin, she led him into the bedroom to show him that wishes do come true.

Made in the USA
Las Vegas, NV
22 December 2023

83405128R00154